J. Ryan Fenzel

Descending from Duty

A NOVEL

Ironcroft Publishing

Descending from Duty

Copyright © 2005 by J. Ryan Fenzel

Cover Artist: Julie L. Brown

Printed in the United States of America

First Printing: April 2006

Library of Congress Information:

Fenzel, J. Ryan.

    LCCN: 2005931708
    Descending from Duty / J. Ryan Fenzel
    1st ed.
    Hartland, MI : Ironcroft Pub., 2006.
    p. cm.

ISBN-10: 0-9771688-0-8
ISBN-13: 978-0-9771688-0-4
1. Fiction – Thrillers
2. Fiction – War and Military

For Melynda,
Marisa, and Keira

PROLOGUE

DYLAN REESE could almost taste the Cajun spices in the air. Of all the places he imagined his new assignment would take him, a Creole dinner in downtown Detroit wasn't one of them. He scanned through the banquet hall crowd. Suits, ties, and New Orleans cooking made for an odd mix. The fact that everyone there had paid a thousand dollars for Blackened Chicken and Dirty Rice seemed odd as well.

In his dark suit and polished wingtips, pressed white shirt and burgundy tie, close-cut black hair and clean-shaven face, he blended in well with the other attendees at the political fundraiser. The only item that set him apart was the beige curly cord running from his suit coat collar to an ear jack in his right ear.

He stood at the hall entrance and looked for suspicious eyes, aggressive posture, and threatening movements. In a normal social setting he was certain this behavior would be considered paranoid, but in a Secret Service agent it was just good practice. And his proficiency in this particular practice had landed him on the security detail of a very important man: President Warren McCallum.

Dylan took note of the president's location and made eye contact with Gillespie, the agent handling close protection. Half a head taller than the surrounding people, Gillespie stood vigil down in front of the honored guests table.

Dylan turned from the party faithful and observed the lobby. Still quiet. He didn't really expect trouble. The Hilton Garden Inn was an upscale hotel, and the faces at the fundraiser all seemed friendly. Of course, when a former White House occupant with high favorables comes to town to fill your coffers, what's not to like? Still, despite the president's popularity at the end of his term two years ago, he had managed to generate his share of detractors, and one of them had recently phoned in a series of death threats. Although most threats come to nothing, Dylan knew better than to find comfort in the odds. As he'd been taught in the Service, trouble loves to come and roost on complacent shoulders.

A voice crackled through his ear piece. "Cipher is moving. Green Thumb, clear home stretch."

Green Thumb—a shot at the new guy, but he took it in stride. Being assigned to the detail was an honor in itself. Hand in jacket pocket, he hit the transmit button on his radio. "Copy."

McCallum, who in code was Cipher, had left the head table and was mingling with a group of suits near the south exit. Blue eyes clear and engaging, thick gray hair neatly cut, McCallum extended his large hand from person to person, shaking his farewells. Gillespie shadowed the president's every move.

Dylan left his position and entered the rear hallway designated Exit Alpha.

He went down the lengthy corridor, shoe heels clicking on polished marble. Cherry wood columns flanked him on either side. He felt for the service key in his pocket which would disable the elevator just ahead, but the black doors parted before he reached it. "Hold Cipher."

He unbuttoned his suit coat, clearing the Glock .40 holstered on his waist.

A man stepped from the elevator. The black dress pants and maroon vest registered. Hilton staff. The tray in his hand filled out the picture: warming dome, white napkins, arranged silverware. The man noticed Dylan's approach and startled.

"It's okay, sir." Dylan eyed him. "Wait staff?"

The man nodded, flipping over a laminated badge clipped to his vest. Official Hilton ID for a Mr. Arif Sadeed. Typical bad picture of the employee too, but Agent Reese could tell the man with the round, shaven face and black eyes on the badge matched the man standing before him. "Where are you coming from, Mr. Sadeed?"

Arif Sadeed glanced at the tray in his hand. "Room service."

Dylan heard an accent. "And you're heading back to the kitchen?"

A nod. "Yes, the kitchen." His timid eyes strayed.

"Okay, but you and your co-workers need to stay put in there for a few minutes."

Arif considered the request. "Important somebody coming?"

Dylan pointed to the scuffed and nicked white doors across the hall that led to the kitchen. "If you would, Mr. Sadeed."

Arif's eyes widened, as if he had figured out a complex calculus problem. "President?"

"The kitchen." Dylan took a step forward.

Arif motioned his hand in the air as if writing. "Autograph. Can I get autograph?"

"Not today."

The persistent bellhop pulled a tab from his back pocket. "You get for me?" He ripped the cover sheet off and waved it. "Please?"

Dylan exhaled and swiped the sheet from his hand. "I'll see what I can do."

Smiling, Arif pushed through the doors, one of which squeaked like a field mouse. Dylan followed, holding a door open and catching the aroma of sautéed onions. A dozen cooks and waiters scurried about the narrow kitchen. The sizzle of steak peppered the din of clinking dishes and shouted orders. A man with a salt-and-pepper goatee stood among the stainless steel tables. Dylan keyed in on him. "Mr. Poyer."

Dressed in a black waistcoat, Poyer carried himself like a man in authority, and with respectful demeanor gave Dylan his attention.

"Hold all traffic through these doors," Dylan said, "until I clear the area."

Poyer nodded. "Yes, Mr. Reese."

Dylan stepped back into the corridor, letting the doors swing closed. He disabled the elevator with the service key then walked the hallway's length to the red exit door. He pushed it open. Crisp night air washed over him. Three paces from the door a limousine waited. Special Agent Peter Douglas sat behind the wheel. Dylan waved and turned back into the hotel. He retraced his steps down the hall and glanced once more through the oval windows into the kitchen. Muted clinks and sizzles bled through the doors. All seemed right.

He called into his lapel mic. "Exit Alpha is clear."

"Copy."

Gillespie rounded the corner at the far end of the corridor, his stride confident. Right behind him came President McCallum with a spry step other men his age had lost. Agent LaCroix took up the rear, his expression as tight as the blond curls on his head.

Dylan glanced at the slip of paper that Sadeed had given him. Something didn't feel right. Disjointed images flashed into his thoughts. A folded napkin. Arranged silverware. Clean dishes. Why would a room service tray return in pristine condition?

He dropped a hand on the Glock and turned. Halfway through his 180 he heard the field mouse. A shadow moved in the corner of his eye.

Gillespie shouted, "Gun!"

Dylan drew his pistol and swung around.

Arif Sadeed stood just ten feet away, training a 9mm Sig Sauer square on his head. Mr. Sadeed did not smile this time.

Dylan sighted down the barrel at the gunman's chest, sucked in a breath.

Sadeed didn't back down.

Dylan squeezed the trigger. Gunfire shook the hallway. A muzzle flash mushroomed from the barrel of the Sig. Something deadly, something came at him in a blur. A terrifying shimmer touched his temple. He flinched, his head snapping left.

A red blossom burst on Sadeed's chest.

The Glock's chamber finished its stroke, springing into position for another round, but a second shot would not be necessary. Sadeed fell through the kitchen doors and into the arms of Poyer and some bellhops. Shocked, they lowered the body to the tile.

Dylan shook his head. The sheet of paper Sadeed had given him fell from his hand and fluttered to the floor. He looked at the hotel workers for signs of trouble but found none. He scanned left and right, sweeping the Glock through the hallway. The red exit door at the far end burst open and he drew down on the position.

A blond-haired man in suit and tie rushed through the door with pistol in hand, eyes excited. His boyish face clicked. It was Peter Douglas.

"We're clear in the lobby," a voice shouted from behind.

Gillespie ran up to Dylan.

McCallum was gone. LaCroix had spirited him from the area.

The hotel staff surrounded Sadeed's body.

"Get back!" Dylan shouted. "Everybody back!"

They retreated a step.

He found Poyer among them and aimed the Glock his way. "Who is he, Mr. Poyer?"

Poyer shook. "Ar...Arif Sadeed."

A bead of sweat rolled into Dylan's eye. "You two old friends?"

"I barely knew him! I hired him two weeks ago."

Dylan fought for calm. A hand fell lightly on his shoulder.

"We've got the area secured," Gillespie said.

Dylan realized he was still targeting Poyer. He lowered the pistol.

"You okay?" Gillespie asked.

Dylan nodded.

Down the hall, Peter Douglas spoke on his radio, directing Detroit Police to the area.

Remembering the blur of the bullet, Dylan rubbed a hand over his temple.

"I thought you were dead," Gillespie said. "He had you point blank."

Dylan forced a smile. "Fortune favors the bold, eh."

"I think you're just lucky"

Officers wearing the dark blue uniform of the Detroit Police Department began appearing in the hallway.

Dylan took a deep breath, as if he'd just come up for air after a long time under water. He realized he'd just faced 'the' scenario. The one Service agents keep tucked in the back of their minds. Taking a bullet. He damn near did. He didn't even have to think about it. His training, his sense of duty, it got him through. This time it was easy.

He rubbed his temple again, and then traced the trajectory of Sadeed's bullet. "You won't believe this, Special Agent Gillespie, but I swear I saw that slug coming."

"You got a freakin' bionic eye or what?"

Staring straight ahead, Dylan crossed the hallway. He stopped at a cherry wood column and ran his thumb over a pock mark in the finish. He brushed away small splinters of wood and found the tail of the slug buried deep in the column. The sight of it stirred a wave of nausea in his stomach. "I see it."

Gillespie slapped his shoulder. "You want to keep it as a memento?"

Dylan stared into the hole. "Like I need something to remember this day."

He pulled himself away from the column, but the image of the slug had burned into his mind. *This time it was easy.*

What about next time?

Book I

THINGS BEST FORGOTTEN

- ONE -

Detroit, MI.
Six years later

THE HOUSES all looked the same, like they'd been spit from a 1922 Sears catalogue, small two-stories with a narrow front porch. Unfortunately, they seemed not to have had a fresh coat of paint since they'd been spat. Close to the potholed street, the dilapidated dwellings sat on miniscule lots sprinkled with patches of crabgrass and weed. Each street of the urban grid was the same. Row after row of houses spread from the outskirts of Detroit to the suburbs beyond.

She pulled the navy blue baseball cap over her head, sliding the bill just above her eyes and centering the Old English 'D.' With the sweep of a hand she brushed shoulder-length, auburn hair from her face, tucking it behind her ear. The glasses came off next. Narrow oval lenses and a black wire frame, the high-end spectacles had cost her $400. She gently slid them into a soft leather case and tossed them through the open window of the late model Impala behind her. She fished a contact lens case from her pocket and dropped the lenses into her eyes. Peripheral vision would be important this morning.

She slid the black blazer from her shoulders and tossed it into the cranberry car with the glasses. Morning sun shone brilliantly on her white linen shirt, and a 9mm Beretta pistol rested comfortably in its holster on her waist. From the chain around her neck dangled federal credentials for Special Agent Rebecca Matthis.

Agent Matthis stood next to a young man with unkempt brown hair and a three-day beard. She turned and caught him staring, not at the gun on her hip, but up a little higher. Displeasure drew her mouth to a frown. She snapped her fingers, startling the scruffy voyeur, and pointed to his weathered, blue windbreaker. "I need to borrow your jacket, Mr. Holt."

"Sure." He stripped it off and handed it over. His gaze wandered again. "Are you really with the FBI?"

Rebecca zipped the windbreaker. "Are you really a meter reader?"

"Yeah, but I thought all FBI agents were stiff-ass, middle-age guys in bad suits."

"Hold your tongue before you get into trouble." Mr. Holt had inadvertently found Rebecca Matthis' professional tender spot. The road through Cooley Law School and into the Bureau had been grueling, but she'd made it with long days of study, a string of part-time jobs, and a lot of moral support from her mother. Still, a part of her wondered how many doors might have been opened by her appearance as opposed to her substance. It infuriated her sometimes, her insecurity. Although it drove her to try harder in her job, it also shaped a great many decisions in how she lived, dressed, and acted. Makeup light. Wardrobe conservative. Demeanor professional. Always. *This is no time for the argument.*

She caught a reflection of herself in the Impala's rear window. One thing about spending all night in a car, it certainly kept the appearance in check. She appraised the neighborhood. The house she stood in front of was just as nondescript and run down as the next, or the last. One house, however, was different, not in how it looked but because of whom was inside.

One street over, south side, six lots down. Rebecca had watched it from her car since nine-thirty the night before. An anonymous tip the previous afternoon had drawn her out there. Apparently two men had moved into the gray house in question a month before. Not venturing out very often, they seemed just two reclusive men in a small, low-rent home. One day a blanket on a bedroom window fell, and a neighbor saw the little girl.

Kara Mallory. Or so Agent Matthis hoped, perhaps in desperation. She'd been working the Mallory kidnapping for a week and thought that the girl seen in the house might be the seven-year-old who was taken from a shopping mall eight days before. The case wasn't going well. Though Karen Mallory, the girl's sole parent, owned and managed a string of retail stores, her accounts had been drained by the economic downturn and she could not meet the ransom demands. The kidnappers weren't buying it. So when the tip came Rebecca moved on it, hoping a break had come her way. At six-thirty that morning a blanket billowing in the breeze of an open second floor window provided that break.

"Mr. Holt, do you follow a consistent route each time you come through here?"

The meter reader scratched at the scruff on his chin. "I don't know; I kind of zigzag from one back yard to the next to get my readings as quick as I can."

Rebecca popped the Impala's trunk. She grabbed a pair of Reebok's and began swapping the leather pumps on her feet with the canvas cross-trainers. As she pulled the laces tight on her left shoe, a black Taurus rolled into the driveway behind her and jerked to a stop. Gerald had arrived. Stiff-assed Gerald in his bad black suit.

Maybe Holt has a future as a Bureau profiler.

Gerald stepped from the car and leaned on the open door. Sun reflecting off his receding hair line, he regarded Rebecca through dark sunglasses. "What the hell are you doing?"

Rebecca didn't look back. "She's in there, Gerald, and I'm going to get her out."

"Who's in where? Catch me up on this because all you said on the phone was that you needed me out here ASAP."

"Kara Mallory. Got a tip yesterday, checked it out, and found the kidnappers' house. Next street over."

"For sure?"

Hesitation. "Sure enough. I caught a glimpse of a girl in the house. Red hair, right age. And she's in there with a couple of knuckle-draggers. She doesn't belong there. It doesn't fit."

"Then we get a warrant and go in legally."

Rebecca dropped her foot and turned about. "It's in the works now, but I can't wait. Their ransom payment deadline is eight this morning. It's seven-thirty now. These losers are the same guys who took the Reynolds boy. You know how that case ended?"

Gerald wrinkled his brow. "They killed him."

"I might be wrong about this, but I doubt it. I'll err on the side of caution."

"Err on the side of legality, Reb. If you're right, this arrest has to stick. Don't hand them a technicality."

"That little girl's life is in danger. You going to help me or not?"

Gerald tapped his foot and studied Rebecca through tinted glass. She stared back. She could see him mulling his options. He really had only one. "Okay," he finally said. "How do we play it?"

She adjusted her cap and closed the trunk, and then held an open hand toward Holt. He gave her his digital data recorder. She reached into the Impala and retrieved a small two-way radio. "Let me get behind the house, make sure I've got a way in, then roll into the driveway. Get them thinking on the front door. Just walk up like a Jehovah

Witness or a vacuum cleaner salesman or something. You fit the part."
Gerald frowned. "Thanks. I'll go do a knock-and-talk. Give 'em
some story about the FBI sweeping the area for a guy on a terrorist
watch list. If my creds spook them, if they get squirrelly, you come in
through the back." He studied her face. "You only come in if they
spook. Right?"

"Right." Rebecca checked the Beretta, shoved it back in its holster
beneath the windbreaker, and started through the narrow alley between
houses.

"Keep your eyes open," Holt said. "Lots of dog shit out there."

"Great." Rebecca walked across spongy grass. As she rounded
the corner of the house on the left, she felt a gentle breeze on her face.
An open stretch of cluttered back yards scrolled out before her. She
moved through the obstacle course of rusted gas grills, kid toys, and
cheap lawn furniture. Stopping at a meter on a red brick home, she
held the recorder as if checking the dials, but glanced at the gray house
three lots down. Still dead quiet. She pulled the radio from the pocket
of the windbreaker and keyed the switch. "Gerald, are you rolling?"

"Heading around the block," he replied. "Be there in one minute."

She dropped the radio into her pocket and stepped away from the
meter. She walked across the grassy expanse toward the white-sided
house next to the gray. The recorder dangled loosely in her left hand,
her right hand rested atop the pistol. She felt a squish beneath her foot
and smelled the rank aroma. Holt knew his route all right. Wiping her
shoe on the grass with her next step, she kept moving, dodging toy
trucks and plastic baseball bats.

Gerald's Taurus rolled down the street.

Rebecca angled toward the gray house and the adrenaline surged.
She set the recorder on the ground and unzipped the windbreaker.
Just ahead, crooked and overturned bricks of a crumbling patio stud-
ded the ground. Two windows on the back wall of the house were
covered by brown blankets, but the rectangular pane on the rear door
was unobstructed. Rebecca reached the door and put her hand on the
doorknob. Mindful of staying out of view, she peered in through the
rectangular window.

The floor plan was open, with the kitchen and dining areas connected. Walls were bare, furniture sparse. She could see the back
cushion of a dingy, brown, couch along the far wall, but a card table set
up in the middle of the room obscured much of it. Floor space paltry,

the table seemed to fill the area. On its surface sat a laptop computer, screen flipped open. She couldn't tell if it was on or off.

A tall, thin man passed the window and her heart pounded her rib cage. Dressed in an oversized black T-shirt, he moved from the kitchen to the card table, his dark hair apparently matted from sleep. A prominent nose and a fair complexion, he sat in front of the laptop.

Recovering her calm, she inched closer.

From a darkened hallway that led deeper into the house, a short, stubby man, five-something emerged. A brush cut atop his round head and a mole on his cheek, he nodded a morning greeting to his partner and scratched at his flannel-shrouded potbelly. The tall guy with the big nose stared into the computer screen. If he looked up he'd see her. She stepped back.

Her hand was still on the doorknob, and she gently twisted. It was unlocked. She didn't see a dead bolt through the crack either. Right. These two didn't have to worry about the bad guys breaking in; they were the bad guys. She lifted the radio from her pocket and whispered. "I'm set."

"Okay, I'm heading in."

Rebecca heard the purr of the Taurus' engine as Gerald pulled into the driveway. The engine cut and a car door opened. Gravel crunched under foot. Rebecca peered through the window again. Tall Guy and Mole Face seemed unaware of their approaching visitor. The doorbell rang and turned their heads toward the hallway. They traded curt words. Mole Face waved an agitated hand at Tall Guy. Tall Guy looked back at the computer screen, quickly hitting keys and maneuvering the mouse. He was shutting down.

Mole Face disappeared down the dank hallway. After a moment light chased away the darkness. The front door was opened. Rebecca lifted the Beretta from its holster. Tall Guy stood. He closed the laptop screen and bent down to lift something from the couch. Rebecca gasped when she saw it. A pump-action shotgun. Twelve gauge. Sawed off barrel. Big trouble.

The savage bark of a dog exploded behind her. She glanced over her shoulder. A black rottweiler shrieked and roared in the yard across the way. A man in a T-shirt and sweats stood in the open sliding glass door of the opposite house, yelling at the dog. Rebecca turned her gaze back through the narrow window.

Tall Guy had the shotgun pointed right at her.

She ducked and rolled away. An explosive blast rocked the morning. The window shattered. She reached for the doorknob and pushed the door open, staying behind the wall for cover. A second blast pocked plywood as the door bounced on its hinges.

The rottweiler was going crazy, rising on its hind legs, barking at full volume.

Rebecca shouted toward the open door. "FBI! Put down your weapon and—"

Another blast roared through the doorframe. Tall Guy chambered a fourth round.

"Drop it! Drop it!" Gerald's voice thundered. Was he still at the front door with Mole Face or in the dining room facing Tall Guy? Either way, she had to get in there to back him up. She raised the Beretta, said a quick prayer, and rolled around the doorframe.

Extending the pistol, she caught sight of Tall Guy peering down the hallway. The shotgun was pointing at the floor. "Put it down!" she shouted.

He snapped his head about, lifted the twelve-gauge.

She fired. The 9mm slug tore a hole in his shoulder and put his back flat against the dining room wall. The shotgun fell, clattering on the floor. Keeping a bead on the man, she stepped into the house. She pulled the shotgun away from him with her foot. "On the floor, face down and hands behind your back!"

Faced with the 9mm, Tall Guy dropped to his knees.

She rushed over and helped him to the linoleum with a forceful push on the shoulder. Her gun at the base of his skull, she dropped her knee onto his spine and wrenched his right arm behind his back with her free hand. Holding the arm in place with her leg, she worked a set of handcuffs free from her belt and clamped them to his wrist. While Tall Guy spat a stream of profanities she secured his other hand in the cuffs. She stood, keeping an eye on him as he rocked on his stomach like a bound hog. "Gerald! Gerald, are you okay?" No response.

Leading with the Beretta, she walked across the Spartan room. Shifting footsteps and grunts sounded down the hallway. She stepped around the corner, crouched low, and aimed down the corridor.

Gerald had Mole Face plastered against the drywall, the suspected kidnapper's hands bound in cuffs behind his back.

"Unlawful arrest! Unlawful arrest!" Mole Face shouted.

"Assault with a deadly weapon," Rebecca said. "Attempted murder of a federal officer. Shut up, Flat Top." She found a stairwell leading up. "I'm going to check the rest of the house."

Before Gerald could speak she had climbed three steps. Half way up she stopped, listened. Nothing. She went on. At the top she turned right, toward a closed door smothered in decades-old lacquer. The stinking bathroom to her left was empty. She moved forward to the closed door. It locked from the outside. She unlocked it and pushed it open. Pressed against the wall for cover, she listened for signs of movement or weapons. She only heard a whimper. Slow and cautious, she peered around the doorframe.

In a barren room on a tiny cot sat a terrified, redheaded girl. Duct tape covered her mouth and bound her wrists. Rebecca stepped into the room.

The little girl flinched. Tears rolled down her cheek and onto her dirty, yellow, short-sleeved shirt.

"It's okay, honey," Rebecca said. "I'm here to take you home." Sweeping her gaze across the room, she made sure they were alone. She took another step.

The little girl saw the pistol and recoiled, tried to scramble backward on her knees.

Rebecca considered the Beretta. She set it on the floor and opened her arms. "Kara, my name is Rebecca. I'm going to take you back to your mom."

The girl seemed to understand and her trembling subsided.

Rebecca felt a rush of unsettling recognition. A dark memory long buried clawed its way to the surface. In Kara Mallory, she saw herself, twenty-six years ago, shrinking from the upraised hand of her father.

Eyes growing glassy, she came forward and gently peeled the duct tape from Kara's mouth. Like a floodgate opening the sobs gushed forth. She wrapped her arms around the traumatized girl, holding her tight as a river of salty tears drenched the shoulder of Mr. Holt's windbreaker.

- TWO -

Grand Haven, MI

BURNING LOW IN THE EAST, the sun began its long arc across a cloudless sky. A string of bright days in the high seventies had finally signaled the arrival of summer to the Grand Haven area. Behind the wheel of his black Durango, Dylan Reese followed a rickety pick-up truck down the dry, gravel road leading to the McCallum estate.

Through breaks in the maple tree clusters in the field to his right, the twelve-foot, wrought iron gate surrounding the president's property was visible. The fence had spires, and fieldstone pillars every twenty feet. Motion sensors were mounted on each pillar, and their routine functionality check was overdue. Things had been quiet in the past several months and Dylan felt his vigilance had begun to slip. With the president scheduling fewer speaking engagements, and the world in somewhat of a lull, it seemed everyone had forgotten about Warren McCallum. A perfect breeding ground for complacency.

The entry gate came up fast. Dylan tapped the brakes and turned sharp onto the asphalt drive. A cloud of dust encircled the Durango. He lifted the two-way from the passenger seat. "Tommy, I'm at the gate."

"Who's at the gate?"

Dylan smiled at the video camera pointing down from the fieldstone column to his left. "Ringleader."

A magnetic latch clinked and the gate slid open. Dylan released the brake and rolled through the opening. With 200 yards of drive ahead, he lowered his foot on the accelerator and picked up speed.

Maple and birch trees speckled the grounds inside the fence, at some points so dense their leaves arched over the drive in a cool, swaying canopy. In the north quarter of the lot the groundskeeper bounced over a rough patch of terrain on his orange riding lawn mower. The smell of cut grass blew through the Durango's open window. Dylan took it in.

The satellite phone on his belt chimed and he snatched it up.

"Reese."

"Dylan, it's me." Female voice. He knew it well.

"Sarah." His thoughts stuttered. "Is…Is everything alright? Is Danny okay?"

"Yes, he's fine."

He paused. "Then why—

"You're amazing, you know that?"

He stopped the Durango halfway through the turnaround in front of McCallum's sprawling cedar ranch home. He was missing something. "You don't mean that in a nice way."

"You're perceptive too."

He threw open the door. "What have I done, Sarah?"

She took a breath. "Damn it, Dylan, have you really forgotten about today."

He stepped down to the driveway, and then it hit him. He slapped a palm against his forehead. "Shit! I'm sorry, I had a briefing this morning with Protective Intelligence."

"Don't say sorry to me. Danny waited two hours before he realized his father was going to let him down again. He just left to go to the game with Bobby's dad." She paused. "I guess spending time with him doesn't mean a whole hell of a lot to you."

"That's not true." He made a flustered turn toward the Durango. "It's just that…My job. It demands my focus. Sometimes it blinds me."

"You weren't like this before the detail. Chasing McCallum around the country to every speaking engagement, fundraiser, and vacation he takes puts me and Danny dead last. In case you haven't noticed, it's the reason we haven't gotten married. I won't be a part-time wife, and Danny needs more than a part-time father."

"The Old Man's slowed his schedule down. I think he's finally decided to retire from public life. Haven't you noticed? I've been there for Danny, more now than ever. I've taken him to ball games. I was there for his birthday. I—"

"I, I, I. What happened to *us?*" Her voice cracked. "This is it, Dylan. You have to quit the detail or it's not going to work."

He paused an uncomfortable moment.

"You're still not willing to consider it, are you?"

"I never said that."

"Tell me Danny and I mean as much to you as Warren McCallum does."

"Don't be ridiculous. Of course you do."

"You've got a poor way of showing it." An angry tone darkened her voice. "Only one thing can fix the situation and you're determined not to do it. Good bye."

"Wait." The line went dead. Dylan cursed and slapped the phone back on his belt. Seven years with Sarah were slipping away. He closed his eyes, took a breath. How did it fall apart? How did he let it happen?

He reached into the Durango, scooped a rubber-banded stack of letters from the passenger floor and slammed the door. Good bye. It sounded final this time.

Stomach falling, he climbed the steps to the cedar deck that circled the rustic, U-shaped home. He stopped in front of an oak door laden with beveled glass and checked his watch. Eight o'clock. McCallum would be reading the morning paper around back. Dylan walked the covered deck to the rear of the house, replaying his conversation with Sarah in his mind.

The horseshoe layout of the ranch provided a center courtyard, and Mrs. McCallum had designed and installed a great circular patio of gray-and-charcoal paver stones to fill it, complete with five-foot barbecue pit. On agreeable mornings the president liked to read the Free Press there. He'd said he needed sweet birdsong and calm breezes to offset the turgid crap he typically found in the news. As Dylan rounded the corner of the east wing, he spotted the former chief executive right where he thought he'd find him.

Reclining in an ornate, cast-aluminum chair beneath a hunter green umbrella, dressed in a royal blue Polo shirt and cotton khaki pants, McCallum sat engrossed in a front page article. He looked good for seventy-eight. Though his hair was a little whiter than it had been when Dylan had first joined the detail, it remained thick. He jogged every morning and kept an athletic build. The lines in his face, however, had deepened to betray his accumulated years. Dylan had heard it said that the office of the president ages a man a decade in the span of a few short years, and McCallum was no exception. Dylan remembered how spry McCallum had been when he won that first grueling election sixteen years ago, and how tired he'd become by the end of his second term. Being the leader of the free world had its cost.

Just nineteen when McCallum first took office, Dylan recalled how he'd been wary of the smiling conservative with the tough talk and endless optimism. Over the years, however, he grew to respect the man. McCallum had led the nation out of recession, through a war to victory, and back into prosperity. After this towering figure stepped down the people, Dylan among them, missed him immensely.

The buzz of the groundskeeper's lawn mower droned in the distance as Dylan approached. McCallum heard him coming and looked up from the paper, his dark gray eyes brightening at the sight of his lead security agent. "Agent Reese, how are we this morning?"

Dylan flashed a half smile and held out the bundle of letters. "Good, Mr. President."

McCallum set the paper in his lap and took the letters. He studied Dylan a moment, and then laid the mail on the table. Picking up the paper, he concentrated on the text and spoke into the crease. "You heard from Sarah this morning, didn't you?"

"It's good to know your observational skills are still keen."

"It's not too hard to see." McCallum folded the paper. "You can't seem to get that one part of your life in order and it makes you crazy." He chuckled. "If it makes you feel any better you're not the first to face this conundrum."

"Or the last, I imagine." Dylan gestured to the Free Press. "Anything good in there?"

"As a matter of fact—" McCallum lifted the front page, unfolding it so Dylan could see. A large black-and-white photo of a woman carrying a little girl dominated the space. The headline read *FBI Rescues Kara Mallory.* "Score one for the good guys."

"There's a bunch of sick characters out there."

McCallum dropped the paper on the table. "Danny's birthday was a couple of weeks ago. What is he now, four?"

"Five. And thanks again for the gift you sent."

"We don't have little ones in the family anymore. Kate and I miss the children. Besides, in case you've forgotten, I owe you my life."

Tensing, Dylan shifted his weight from one foot to the other. The praise made him uncomfortable, and the memory knotted his stomach. "It's what they trained me to do."

Lifting the bundled letters, McCallum tapped their edges even on the glass tabletop. "Your humility is heartwarming, Agent Reese, and I might add, in short supply in the world today." He narrowed his eyes on his protector. "You do an outstanding job. So much so you were given leadership of the detail over men who were assigned before you. It impresses me. It even humbles me, your dedication to protecting my tired rear end. What drives you, Dylan? What gets you up in the morning?"

Fighting hard not to kick his toe at the ground in classic awe-shucks fashion, Dylan felt his face warming. He couldn't possibly tell the truth. He couldn't say he regarded McCallum as a precious gem in the crown of American history. He'd feel ridiculous admitting the depths to which he considered his duty; protecting king and country. Instead, he found McCallum's eyes and smiled. "In a way, Mr. President, job security rests in my own hands. And I'd hate to lose the government benefits."

With a broad smile McCallum pulled the rubber band off the letters. "I got a call from Governor Patterson yesterday." He fanned the mail across the table. "He asked me to speak at the Governors Meeting on Mackinac next week. Said he was sorry for such late notice but heard the only thing on my schedule for the next couple of months was the Tall Ships festival. He wanted to give me something to do."

"That'd be a hard one to turn down. How long has it been since you've seen him?"

"Going on two years now. Seeing we live in the same state that's sad to say."

"What'd you tell him?"

McCallum gave a look that needed no words.

"I'll get right on it."

"Please do. Patterson's a good man and a good friend. He did an outstanding job for me, especially during the Gulf Conflict. One hell of a secretary of state. Built a coalition from a bunch of quarreling Arab states in a month. Damn, can I pick 'em or what?"

"That you can, Mr. President." A cloud obscured the sun, and Dylan craned his neck to see it. "Your whole cabinet was strong. Deep bench. Have any of the others kept in touch with you?" He waited for a reply but it didn't come. Looking down from the passing cloud, he saw McCallum focused on one of the letters in the bunch. A white one addressed in handwritten print. "Sir?"

"Some," he said. "I crossed paths with Ruby on his Sunday show in New York about a year ago. Talked with Bradford on the phone awhile back. Saw Taylor in Chicago last winter; he's made a bundle with an IT company out there. We haven't connected very much. They kept busy after the administration disbanded."

"Letter from Ed McMahon grab your attention?" Dylan asked, joking but intrigued.

McCallum shuffled the mail back into a stack. "Name on a return

address looked familiar. Thought it was from my brother-in-law, except he's been dead for five years. Eyes must be starting to go."
    Dylan nodded with a smile. "I can only hope I'm in as good shape as you at seventy-eight. Enjoy the morning, sir." He turned a started to walk away, and then glanced over his shoulder. "The Governors Meeting. Next Tuesday, right?"
    "Correct."
    "We'll be ready." Dylan continued on his way.

    Bouncing the letters on the table, McCallum watched his security agent disappear around the corner. Alone on the patio beneath the shade of the umbrella, he spread the mail out in front of him. The white letter looked just like the others, a standard #10 envelope, thin, not much inside. The author had penned the address in rigid print with black ink, and assembled the words using all capital letters. The postmark showed the letter had been routed through Royal Oak, southeast Michigan's largest distribution center. McCallum's fingers shook as he started to open it. It had to be from him.
    Leaves rustled in a wind gust. McCallum ripped open the top and glanced inside. A single sheet of paper this time. White. Nondescript. Folded in thirds. He slid it from the envelope. Brushing a thumb across the paper, he considered its appearance. It felt real. It seemed harmless. But he knew a ghost from his past had sent it. He knew a phantom was calling. Mustering courage, the former President of the United States unfolded the letter.
    One word. A single word lay on the page. Centered and in large bold type, it asked a question. Something fell to the glass tabletop, but he couldn't pull his eyes from the letter. *Remember?* That's all it said. Remember what? It could have meant any one of a million things, but he knew better than to kid himself. He knew in an instant to what the ambiguous question referred.
    He finally looked for what had dropped from the letter.
    A dead yellow jacket lay on the table. Black and yellow bands striped its abdomen. Its thin, gangly legs seemed frozen.
    Panicked, he swept it off the table and stood. His chair scraped across the pavers and he nearly fell over. Seizing the letter in both hands he ripped it down the center, then again into quarters, then again.
    "Warren!"
    McCallum jerked his head toward the sound of his wife's voice.

She stood at the door in her typical morning attire, a full-length, burgundy robe. Her long, gray hair was pulled up and neatly pinned in place. At seventy-three, Kathryn McCallum's clear, blue eyes shone as bright as they had forty years before. Her steady gaze subdued him, restored his calm. After fifty-two years of marriage she remained his better half, his rational, deliberating, peaceful half. And after five decades together, he still loved her with all he had.

"Warren, is it another letter?" She came forward, out of the sun and under the shade of the umbrella. He watched her approach in silence. The graceful lines of her face had been spared the cruel erosion of time. Only light creases around her eyes and mouth hinted at her age. The years had been good to her.

"This morning's mail," he said quietly. "Another memory dredged to the surface."

"Did you tell Dylan?"

He crushed the shreds of paper in his grasp.

She came to his side and rested a hand on his shoulder. "This is why he's here, Warren. To protect us. To protect you. He has to kno—"

"He doesn't need to know this!" McCallum shook the paper in his fist. "This is just a sick prank by some political punk on the Hill, or one of Harrison's henchmen taking a jab at me." He pulled away from her and felt the heat of rage flush his face. "Hell, his administration is under fire from three separate independent councils. They're just trying to spread the misery."

"You don't believe that, do you?" She laced her tone with reason. "These letters have only been sent to you. The press doesn't know about them; nothing has shown up in the papers. Whoever is doing this is keeping it private."

He drew a deep breath, exhaled slowly, and said as calmly as he could manage, "Kate, these letters haven't done anything but raise my blood pressure. They aren't a threat to us."

"Threats have been made, and it frightens me."

He waved a hand to dismiss the notion. "I drew dozens of threats every day when I was in office. People rant to blow off steam. Anonymous letters like this are the only way frustrated cowards can make themselves feel better. And on the off chance this nut job does pay us a visit, Dylan and his detail are more than capable of handling the situation." He dropped the crumpled pieces of letter to the glass table. "I won't run to him with this."

"But doesn't it concern you? Doesn't it make you wonder?"

He turned an agitated eye towards her. "Make me wonder what?"

"Who it is and why he's doing it?"

Averting his eyes, he looked at the dead yellow jacket on the gray stones. He took a step and crushed it underfoot. "I won't go to Dylan with this, Kate. It's a sick, mischievous prank and nothing more. End of discussion."

- THREE -

Central Lake Huron
Thirty miles off Michigan's eastern coast

IN MANY RESPECTS the water of Lake Huron seemed like any of the oceans Owen Keyes had sailed during his fifteen years in the navy. With no visible coastline and the wind stirring moderate swells from the lake's surface, he could easily imagine himself steaming through the Atlantic. But there were signs that he rode the waves of a much different body of water. The smell of brine didn't permeate the air. The spray over the bow didn't taste of salt. And Huron's rolling murmur seemed a diminutive substitute for the monolithic rumble of the high seas. Having spent so much time on the waters bridging continents, he noted such contrasts as easily as some noted the difference between a vintage Chardonnay and a bottle of Boone's Farm, or a '57 Chevy and a Chrysler K-car.

He stood at the bow of the *Richard C.*, an eighty-foot tug plowing through the lake. Black hulled and low profile, the rugged steel ship kept steady on a northerly track, running parallel to the shoreline five miles away. Despite the pitch of the vessel, he maintained flawless balance. The breeze ruffled his open shirt collar. In the navy he'd have buttoned his shirt clear to the top, but with his recent departure he thought he'd loosen up.

He adjusted his USS *Hampton* baseball cap to shield his eyes from the sun, and then spat a measure of Copenhagen over the side. It wasn't all blue skies ahead. In the past few hours the western horizon had become gray and hazy, and the scent of foul weather blew in on the wind. Keyes spun about face and walked toward the bulkhead amidships. He climbed the forward ladder to the pilothouse. Choosing the port entrance, he stepped onto the tug's bridge.

Windows encircled the cabin. Discolored walls marred by scuffs and scrapes, and the dated gauges and switches across the navigation console testified to the vessel's twenty years. He breathed in the musty air and walked toward helm control, where sat a lanky man with sun colored skin, deep crow's feet, and a blonde ponytail.

A cigarette dangling between thin lips, the over-aged hippie turned his weathered face to address his visitor. "Commander Keyes, what say you?"

Keyes lifted a half-filled coffee cup from its holder beside the chart table and emptied his chew. He licked the inside of his lip and stared at the threatening horizon. "I say, Mr. Rierdon, that the storm front weather band reported moving this way had better track south or we could be in for an interesting time out here."

"That we will. *Richard C.* doesn't care for open water, much less heavy open water. She prefers huggin' the coast."

Keyes surveyed the churning lake before them. The swells were beginning to cap white. Grayness was creeping overhead. Red flags to a seaman. Invisibility to eyes along the coast had merit, but not above all else. Capsizing in a Great Lakes squall would prematurely end his ambitious endeavor. That would not be allowed to happen.

"If that front gets heavy we'll head in, make port in Oscoda, lay low 'til it passes. Keep an ear on the weather band and an eye on the horizon." Keyes glanced over his shoulder to the water beyond *Richard C's* wake. "How far back is *Wescott?*"

Rierdon puffed his cigarette and pulled it from his lips. "About three hours. Tierney radioed in a little while back. Said after we left Port Huron the harbormaster ran out of diesel. He had to wait on an afternoon delivery. Then the coast guard showed and started nosing around the docks. Did some spot checks."

"And…?"

"They were boarded but not searched, at least not very closely."

Thinking about the conspicuous crates below deck on *Wescott* and the nature of the cargo within, Keyes couldn't help but feel they'd dodged a deadly bullet. "Then why did they board?"

"Ever since 9/11 the Guard has tightened security at all ports. Tierney thinks they were looking for gentlemen of a certain ethnicity. Fortunately he and his group don't fit the profile. Things could have gotten ugly, though, if the guardsmen had looked too close or talked too long."

Keyes scoffed. "No. Tierney's got a cool head. And our cover as contractors is credible, paperwork and all. He had everything he needed to diffuse the situation"

Rierdon coughed on cigarette smoke. "Maybe Tierney's a cool one, but the other seven guys with him are question marks. They're bankrolled. We don't know them like the Circle."

"I checked them out. Those seven and the seven with us, they'll do what they're paid to do. Don't give it another thought." Keyes scowled at his subordinate.

Rierdon took a cautious breath. "How's Bowman doing ashore?" Keyes let it go. "He's accomplished a lot on his own. He's even managed to educate me on a thing or two. Right man for the job."

"It appears so." Rierdon sounded dispassionate.

"You don't seem to agree, Mr. Rierdon. What's the problem with Robert Bowman?"

"Nothing worth mentioning."

"Any comment you have is worth mentioning. I won't have this operation jeopardized by unspoken concerns."

Rierdon hesitated. "It's just that me and Bobby Bowman don't see eye-to-eye very well."

"And why is that?"

"Since he got his discharge he's changed. More volatile. Bigger asshole. We've locked horns more than once." Rierdon paused. "This operation is going to get heavy. I don't feel secure relying on Bobby."

"Bowman's an angry man but very capable. He keeps it together. Give him a chance. I'm sure he'll surprise you."

"I'd prefer it," Rierdon said, checking *Richard C.'s* heading on the console, "if he didn't surprise anyone."

"Once again, Mr. Rierdon, don't give it another thought." Keyes leaned over the chart table behind the navigation console and studied the chart of Michigan and the five surrounding lakes. He noted their current position mid-way through Lake Huron and did some quick calculations. Making twelve knots, and assuming the storm wouldn't hinder their progress, they'd crown Michigan's Lower Peninsula after nightfall and pass beneath the Mackinac Bridge around midnight. The *Wescott* would follow their route. Fifteen hours later both tugs would be in position in Lake Michigan's southern quarter. Right on schedule.

"What about the rest of the men?" Rierdon said. "How are they gonna hook up with us?"

"By land." Keyes turned from the chart and crossed his arms. He hadn't given everyone all the pieces to the puzzle. During his tenure in the navy he'd learned a number of valuable lessons, one of them being to filter information to subordinates on a need-to-know basis. And at this point, for most of his contingent anyway, the less they knew about the overall plan the better.

"The rest of the men," he continued, "are converging on Zone-1 in groups of two and three. They'll meet with Bowman before we get there, help him pave the way."

Rierdon snuffed his cigarette in an ashtray on the nav console. "This is an elaborate OP you've put together, Commander. Seems you mean to impress your point with the subtly of a sledgehammer."

Keyes considered the storm front coalescing in the west. "I'm not known for being subtle." He set his jaw. "I want them to hear my message loud and clear."

"They'll hear it all right. Question is will they get it?"

"They'll get it."

After a moment, Rierdon said, "You've put a bunch of dollars and effort into this. If you don't mind me asking, what's in it for you? I mean besides the obvious."

Bringing his gaze back inside the pilothouse, Keyes fixed on Rierdon. "There are some things the almighty dollar can't purchase. Some tenets are priceless, some codes of conduct beyond value. You understand?"

"Sure. You won't be making any money. Furthermore you're okay with it." Rierdon chuckled. "You're a better man than I, Owen Keyes. Few men would foot such a hefty bill to defend their principals. I just hope the people you plan to impress take note."

"They won't have a choice." Keyes spat a remnant of chewing tobacco onto the warped deck. He let the rumble of the tug's engines fill the pause. "Honor and duty aren't empty words," he finally said. "They have true meaning. It's time the politicians who vomit them for votes are reminded."

Rierdon cracked a smile. "Aye."

Studying burgeoning cloud formations, Keyes cocked his head. "It won't hit us hard. I feel it. We're good from now 'til morning. Carry on, Mr. Rierdon."

He left the pilothouse, and clapped the door shut behind him.

Rierdon watched him descend the forward ladder. That was that. The storm would sputter and fail to menace them. It had to be so. Commander Owen Keyes had proclaimed it.

- FOUR -

Detroit

THE HALLS AND CUBICLES of the McNamara Federal Building were nearly deserted. It was eight-thirty on Sunday morning and only a smattering of agents had filed in, Rebecca Matthis among them. The FBI's Detroit headquarters seemed to be observing the Sabbath, and Rebecca felt she should be doing the same. As a child she had attended South Haven Presbyterian with her mother, each week, without fail. She carried that compulsion with her to the east side of the state when she started with the Bureau, but found herself missing Sunday services more often than not. She really felt guilty on mornings like this when she walked through security in the marbled lobby downstairs at roughly the same time she should be sitting in a pew seat.

Curls of steam rose from her white coffee mug. She sat at her desk, reading through her report on the Mallory case. Special Agent in Charge (SAC) Kyle Bradley expected it in his hands that morning.

Fellow agents described her desktop as organized clutter, and she had to agree. Stuffed manila folders were stacked high in the corner. Stapled photo copies of newspaper clippings lined the edges of the gray, laminate surface. Coffee stained most of them. A computer monitor blanketed in Post-It notes occupied the other corner. In comparison, and not a flattering one, Agent Reager's adjacent desk was impossibly neat.

She heard the footsteps approaching from behind. Gerald had warned that SAC Bradley wanted to talk with her, in person, but the past day and a half had been so hectic she hadn't been able to make it back to the office.

A copy of the Saturday Free Press landed on her desk. A picture of her carrying Kara Mallory into St. John's hospital adorned the front page. She knew what he wanted to discuss.

"You're the talk of the town, Agent Matthis. I suppose congratulations are in order."

Kyle Bradley had mastered the art of dishing surface praise with just a hint of condemnation in his tone. This would not be an atta-girl talk.

Bradley stood there with hands in pants pockets, ruffling the flaps of his buttoned-up blue jacket. As usual his gray-streaked dark hair was combed in precise corporate fashion. His unsmiling round face didn't host a single whisker. This guy never let it go, even on Sunday.

"I got a break, sir," she said. "Anonymous tip pointed me in the right direction." She thought it best to come out of the blocks humble.

"I saw the piece FOX local did on the case last night, as well as the interviews you did for channels 4 and 7. You've been keeping busy." Again the displeased tone.

"I informed you when the media began requesting interviews. You cleared me to do them."

"I meant for you to handle the whole thing in a single press conference, not a series of profile reports on the FBI's hottest agent. Hell, Matthis, you looked like Julia Roberts with federal credentials. Not quite the professional image I expect out of my agents."

"Just following orders. Your memo last month stated we were to improve the Bureau's public image by conducting more open, amicable press conferences and projecting the 'friendly, capable face of today's FBI.' That's exactly what I've done. I've been nothing but professional."

"Have you?" Bradley bit his lower lip. "Guess you can't help you've got a face for the camera."

That tender spot took a hit and Rebecca flinched.

"Let's move to the next topic under my skin." He paused, for effect she guessed. "You handled the arrest way too close to the edge for my liking. You had the suspects in handcuffs five minutes before Judge McDonald signed the search warrant."

"We didn't go in searching for the girl. Gerald approached the house with no other intent than to ask some questions. When that guy tried to take my head off with a shotgun we had plenty of justification to enter and make the arrests. Finding Kara Mallory was a fortunate consequence of us going in, not the grounds for our being there…technically."

She felt her feet curl around the tightrope she was walking. Bradley had a point, and the distance of forty-eight hours from the arrest had her hedging the impulsiveness of her actions.

"Is that how you're going to explain it during the trial?"

She handed him the Mallory report. "That's how it's written."

He rolled the report in his palm, considered the carpet, huffed. "You've put this case ahead of every other news story in the state. Under that kind of microscope someone might decide to really dig into the details."

She tensed and her chair rattled. "I didn't do anything illegal. They'd killed before. I wasn't going to let them do it again!"

"I'm not questioning the results," he said, voice raising. "I'm sweating the possible inquisition coming our way from the ACLU, the suspects' defense attorneys, and every sleaze rights organization out there. Regardless of how it went down they'll argue you stormed the house and conducted an illegal search. Damn it, you gave them a foothold!"

"They *had* the girl! What more does the federal government need to convict them?"

He ran a hand through his hair, mussing it up. It's the first time she had seen it such. Not good. "No more high profile," he said. "You're going to let the story cool."

"Fine...sir."

"And I'm going to help you do it."

Help me? "How do you mean?"

"You're going to be unavailable to the press for the next couple of weeks."

"Fine."

"When you go home today, start packing."

Uh-oh, that doesn't sound good. "Why?"

"The RA in Grand Rapids is shorthanded. You're going to assist them for a while."

She frowned. Resident Agencies weren't exactly the hub of activity in the FBI. "What will I be doing? Except for cow tipping and gas-and-go's nothing happens on the West Coast. And those offenses aren't federal crimes."

Bradley repeatedly slapped the Mallory scroll into his palm. "An agent retired, they need an interim replacement to wrap up some things he was working on. Couple of bank robberies. A mail fraud thing. Just enough to keep you busy."

"Can't they cover it themselves?"

He smiled. "No they can't. They need you. Right now."

She sat in smoldering silence. She knew she had done the right thing in that run-down house, but she also had to admit that she had cut a corner or two. Her career just four years old, she thought better of kicking up too much a fuss. Choose your battles. That's what her mother had taught her. "I'll report in at Grand Rapids tomorrow." He wheeled about and started off. "That you will, Agent Matthis." He disappeared around a corner.

Lifting the coffee mug from her desk, she took a sip and thought about her banishment. It wouldn't be that bad. Her mother still lived in South Haven, just forty miles from Grand Rapids. At least she'd get to spend some time with her. It'd been a couple of months since they'd seen one another. She lowered the mug and let the warmth radiate in her hands. The image of Kara Mallory cowering in that barren bedroom flashed into her thoughts. Despite the hot coffee, she felt her fingers grow icy.

Mackinac Island

Aged to an ashen shade, standing one beside another, ancient trunks of timber ringed the eighteenth-century fort. Dylan Reese peered over the top of the fortification and across the Straits of Mackinac. He shielded his eyes from the late morning glare. A blue-hulled hydroplane ferry skimmed across the lake, hooking around the breakwater and heading for the tourist-busy harbor. It was the same ferry that McCallum would take tomorrow. The president had decided to stay the night at the Grand Hotel Monday night instead of rushing out early in the A.M. Tuesday to make his nine o'clock speech to the Governors Association. Keeping with his newly adopted 'schedule deceleration program,' McCallum designed this excursion to unfold at a stress-free pace.

The Old Man really looked forward to seeing Roger Patterson again. It had been a long time since Dylan had seen him so eager to make an appearance. It was a welcome change. For some reason McCallum's mood had been mired in doldrums of late. At first Dylan thought a health issue had cropped up, that maybe the president or Mrs. McCallum had been diagnosed with something. Despite being under constant surveillance, McCallum managed to keep a tight lid on private matters, so the theory seemed plausible. Dylan had hoped it was not the case. His father suffered through cancer, and he had no desire to watch another man he admired go through such brutal degeneration.

But with no supporting evidence he dropped the cancer theory.

Then Saturday, when that letter arrived, something clicked. The envelope distracted McCallum. His story of misreading the return address sounded contrived. Was he getting hate mail? Did the president identify one such letter? McCallum wasn't one to let caustic detractors penetrate his thick hide. Over the years he'd received his share of poison pen correspondence and never once flinched. Then what? Dylan didn't know.

What he did know, however, was that McCallum had brightened at the prospect of speaking at the governors meeting and anticipated catching up with his old secretary of state. Dylan looked forward to the next few days as well. Considering all the places President McCallum had traveled to in his post-presidential years, Mackinac Island promised to be a relaxing, friendly visit.

Dylan turned from the weathered timber and descended a nearby stair of gray stone. He decided to stroll around the long, narrow, two-story building that was once a military infirmary.

Fort Mackinac was in pristine condition, probably in better shape now than when in official use during the 1700s. The defensive wall stood tall and unbroken all around the perimeter. Whitewashed barracks and officers quarters sparkled in the sun, and the smell of fresh-cut grass rose from the lush, emerald parade ground. Dressed in authentic revolutionary garb, a pair of historical society volunteers crossed the manicured turf, muskets resting on their shoulders.

In light of Mackinac Island's location within the demilitarized Great Lakes, whose closest foreign neighbor was friendly Canada, it was hard to believe that it had ever possessed a strategic military value. But it had, and the French and British and Americans had all fought over it. How much the world changes with time. Back then those three nations would never have guessed that 250 years later they would find themselves allies.

Earlier in the day Dylan had explored the small island. From historical plaques he learned of the not-so-glorious military history of Mackinac. Every battle waged there had ended in defeat for the defending soldiers. Dylan supposed a theory. He imagined that the beauty of the place somehow imposed serenity on each garrison stationed there, mysteriously dissolving the soldiers will to fight. Whimsical thought, yes, but on a warm June morning with a comforting breeze blowing in off the lakes, a very plausible one.

"Done playing tourist?" A man's voice interrupted Dylan's meandering thoughts.

The towering Tom Gillespie approached, Raybans over his eyes. "Just about," Dylan said. "This island is a nice little snapshot of history."

Less than impressed, Gillespie surveyed the parade grounds and white buildings. "You've never been here?"

"No. I'm not a Michigander. Fighting Illini. Remember?"

Gillespie smiled and nodded. "Growing up in the state it was damn near a rite of passage to come to Mackinac with the family at least once. Quaint. But take it from me, when you leave here only two things will stand out in your mind: Horse shit and fudge."

Dylan chuckled. He had noticed the plethora of fudge shops along the Victorian street near the harbor. And the law prohibiting automobiles on the island certainly increased the presence of horses and their unfortunate byproduct. "Don't you appreciate how Mackinac preserves the past?"

"Sure." Gillespie pursed his lips and scanned the fort again. "I'm just appreciating it on the inside. Now can we go? It's almost eleven."

Time had gotten away from Dylan. Their scheduled meeting with the State Police and the Mackinaw City PD at the Grand Hotel was just ten minutes away. In this advance trip he and Gillespie, along with local authorities, would formulate a plan to secure Mackinac for McCallum's visit. They would define the three perimeters, name checkpoints and screening areas, and establish defensible routes through the equestrian roadways. They would locate surveillance posts and piece together a contingency plan to get the president off the island in the event of some emergency. Who would do what? Troopers and deputies all had to be placed, and they all had to agree on their roles.

This planning had become an art to Dylan, weaving an intricate web of security around McCallum. Alone, the threads of the web might seem frail, but layered properly and positioned wisely the interlacing strands fashioned an effective snare for any gadfly that might happen along. He enjoyed the challenging task. He enjoyed wresting control of unpredictable situations. Maintain a tight grip, cornerstone of the Reese philosophy. The greater control he had, the stronger the web of security he could provide. And the stronger the web the less chance of—

It hit him at once. A hot flash consumed him as if his blood was kerosene and a match had ignited his veins. He rubbed at the tickle on his temple. A thin sheen of sweat formed on his face.

Gillespie lowered his sunglasses. "You all right?"

"Yeah." Dylan shook off the spell and took another breath. He nudged Gillespie on the shoulder. "I missed breakfast. Body doesn't like that. I think I'm hypoglycemic or something. Let's go."

Gillespie stared unconvinced. "You should see a doctor. That stuff just ain't normal." They turned and started for the gate on the south wall to exit the fort. As they walked across the lush grounds, Dylan said, "Know what I learned today?"

Gillespie frowned. "If I say yes, are you going to tell me anyway?"

Dylan ignored him. "Every battle fought here was lost by the island's defenders. Each time Mackinac was attacked it changed hands. It didn't matter who held it. British. Americans. They lost."

"Suppose you've got a theory."

"As a matter of fact..." They stepped through the gate and started down the long, sloping, asphalt walkway that snaked along the face of the bluff. "Lotus Eaters."

"Say again."

"Lotus Eaters." He nodded at the surrounding green hills. "I imagine somewhere in the trees or on the cliffs there's an indigenous tribe of pacifists distributing lotus flowers."

Gillespie laughed. "What the hell are you talking about?"

"Odysseus. Remember? His crew ate the lotus and lost their desire to get home."

Gillespie gave a sarcastic nod. "Right. You know what I think?"

Dylan wiped the last remnant of sweat from his forehead. "Give it to me."

"Simple. They'd eaten so much fudge and smelled so much horse shit they just didn't want the island anymore."

- FIVE -

Muskegon, MI

ROBERT BOWMAN stepped from the cab of the pick-up truck and his boot crunched down on the parking lot gravel. He slammed the passenger door and waved to the dark man behind the wheel. The driver nodded and backed the truck away. Bowman started for the museum. He noticed a spring in his step.

On display beside the parking lot entrance was a twenty-foot long torpedo casing and he hopped onto it. Its yellow cap glowed in the noon-day sun. Nearly losing his balance, he waved his arms and walked toward the tail fin. Steady now, he read the small, wooden sign adjacent to the torpedo: *Great Lakes Naval Memorial and Museum. Home of USS Silversides.* The vessel whose name adorned the sign lay just beyond the lot, along the south wall of the channel. If he'd been wearing a hat he'd have tipped it a cordial hello.

Silversides rested low in the water. She was a vintage diesel-electric submarine six decades old. From bow to stern she sprawled 312 feet. Half a dozen mooring lines tethered her to the concrete dock. Her dull gray conning tower amidships and angular bow stood in vivid contrast against the green of the trees across the channel. Forward of the tower a 20mm machine gun pointed ominously at a small fishing boat moored downstream. Aft, her 4-inch/50 cal MK 12 deck gun was trained on an eighty-year-old U.S. Coast Guard cutter under renovation. Inoperable and empty, the weapons posed a hollow threat.

Silversides sat atop a sand bar, her ballast tanks filled with sufficient amounts of Lake Michigan to hold her in place. Bowman thought it fortunate that one month prior a motion picture company had broken the sub off the sand and towed her into the lake to film exterior shots for an upcoming film. By dislodging fifteen years of sediment the filmmakers had done him a favor.

He grinned and hopped from the torpedo onto the lawn, between two chest-high propellers on display. A treaty with Canada forbade functional warships to traverse the Great Lakes, and in accordance with this treaty the props had been removed from the submarine when she came to Muskegon. He chuckled and wrapped his knuckles on a blade.

The museum office sat at the base of a grassy hill in the far corner of the museum grounds. He walked toward the tiny building that resembled a doublewide manufactured home with cream vinyl siding. A few bulbous bushes decorated the perimeter, and a picnic table sat just outside the main entrance.

As he neared, a man limped out through the museum door. A crisp part in his red hair and a beer pouch over his belt, the man spied Bowman and nodded a greeting. "Choppy," he said. "Take the morning off?"

Lanny Stevens: museum curator. Bowman forced a smile. "Slept in. One too many at the Wayside."

Hobbling forward, Lanny laughed. "Hell, Choppy, you're getting too old for throwing 'em down with the boys all night."

"Never too old for that." Bowman shook a strand of hair from his eye.

The two men met on the lawn. "Where are you workin' today?" Lanny asked.

Bowman gestured to *Silversides*. "Conning tower. Nearly have the electrical finished. Be good as new in no time."

Lanny pointed to a yellow Hyster fork truck parked near the museum side wall. "Rental place dropped that off yesterday afternoon. Guy said you ordered it."

"I did."

"What for?"

"Welders need to hoist a load of bar stock aboard. They're replacing those corroded cross members under the forward decking. Plus Blake needs to haul away a bunch of scrap from the cutter. Thought we'd kill two birds with one stone."

Lanny put his hands on his waist. "How much for the rental?"

"On me."

"Damn, Chop, I'm sure glad you found us this spring. I get a lot of volunteers but none have worked as hard or have given as much to the museum as you. You're a godsend."

Bowman laughed. "Don't sweat it. I love the boat."

"That you do. As much as I do, seems like." Lanny took a satisfied breath. "Glad you came in today. My daughter invited me for dinner tonight and I want to make it this time. Think you can lock up at close for me?"

"Consider it done." Things couldn't get much easier.

"Consider it considered." Lanny turned about and limped toward the museum.

Bowman bit his lower lip, then spun toward the submarine and started across the parking lot. He had a hundred things on his mind. He'd gone over the details several times and felt certain he was ready, but hit the list again just the same. Commander Keyes would be coming this very night and there was no room for error.

He had completed the wiring in the conning tower as he told Lanny, but he failed to mention the modest upgrade he'd given the old boat's intercom system (ICS). Also absent in any progress report to the curator was the fact that during the Memorial Day engine start up, he had put far more diesel into the tanks than was necessary for the run. And in subsequent weeks he had managed to add quite a few additional gallons without notice. He also made sure that the compressed air valves were not secured to the engines after Memorial Day as was standard procedure.

He felt for the key in his pocket, the one he'd taken from Lanny's desk. The key unlocked a lock box in *Silversides'* aft battery compartment. The lock box housed a DC rectifier. To get the engines running tonight, he needed to reconnect the rectifier to the fuel pumps.

His biggest challenge, however, had been the submarine's numerous valves. The flood valves near the keel had undergone refurbishment prior to the movie shoot, and so didn't need repair now. That's two he owed the film company. The vent valves topside were another story. He'd checked the seals and repaired them where needed, all with Lanny's approval. He even managed to leak-test the boat's vast array of pneumatic piping, one system at a time. Yes, he had worked hard in the past five months, and soon he'd begin to reap what he'd sown.

He ambled up the gangplank and checked the time. Twelve-thirty.

Across the teakwood slats of *Silversides'* bow, a 20mm anti-aircraft gun was mounted on the cigarette deck just forward of the conning tower. He climbed to the gun mount and slipped under the handrail.

A couple and their two young boys were strolling topside, and their voices turned his head. They followed the cable handrail that encircled the deck, taking in every inch of detail on a Sunday afternoon tour. The boys were decked out in oversized Red Wings jerseys and faded jeans. They rushed over when they spotted Bowman.

One boy craned his neck to look up at him. "Does it work?" He locked his gaze on the machine gun. "Does it shoot?"

Shaking strands of hair from his eye, Bowman set a hand on the cool, black barrel. "Not today," he said, "maybe tomorrow."

The boy looked back at his brother and beamed. "Wow! They're gonna fix it!"

"Tyler, calm down." In khaki Bermudas and a Yankees T-shirt, the boy's father put a hand on his son's shoulder and thanked Bowman for the special attention. "You serve in the navy?" the father asked.

Bowman brushed his thumb on the gun barrel. "Twenty years."

The father gave a polite smile. "I'll bet you've got some stories to tell."

Bowman paused. "One or two."

Tyler's mother pressed a lens cap onto the Nikon hanging around her neck. She tugged at her husband's T-shirt near the waist. "Let's not take any more of the gentleman's time."

Tyler turned from studying the machine gun's recoil spring. "Were you in combat?"

Bowman's face fell somewhere between sneer and smile. "Once or twice."

A violent memory seized him. Thundering deck guns. Frantic reports from CIC. Inbound Harpoon. A Phalanx cannon blasting to life. He sucked in a breath, blinked.

"Thanks again." The father flashed an inexpensive smile. "Take care." He corralled the boys and herded them toward the gangplank. They descended, Tyler blasting away at an imaginary Zero with invisible anti-aircraft fire.

Hand still resting on the barrel of the 20mm, Bowman watched them go. His thoughts meandered between past and present, between today and tomorrow. He slid behind the machine gun and sighted along the barrel at the fishing boat downstream. *Why didn't they give me a command?* He set the gun sight on the fishing boat's outboard motor. *Did they think I was damaged goods?* He pulled the defunct trigger. "Their mistake."

The thought of Keyes' arrival stirred Bowman to the now. He had to be ready. He spun from the 20mm and climbed down from the rise, then walked to an opening in the deck and descended below the surface. In the divided light beneath the teakwood slats he found the forward hatch in the submarine's steel hull and clamored down. It landed him inside the forward torpedo room. In the bow, packed between gray bulkhead and white pipe, the doors to six brass tubes glowed in the dim, incandescent light. He strode beside the bunks that lined the curved inner hull and stepped through the aft hatchway into a compressed corridor. Even his narrow shoulders nearly touched the walls. He past the tiny ward room and officers' quarters and went into the control room.

He breathed in the stale air of *Silversides'* nerve center. So much mechanical machinery overlaid and intertwined inside the submarine that it sometimes made him feel as if he were standing inside a Swiss clock. But the Swiss had nothing on the engineers who designed this boat.

At the focal center of the room, periscope wells rose up through the deck and penetrated the overhead. The port side, or wet side, contained twin silver wheels about a meter across. Used for fore and aft plane control, the wheels were chained and padlocked in place. A large brass gauge, white numbers against black, hung above each and displayed depth to keel in ten-foot divisions. Several feet forward hung the Christmas Tree, a suitcase-sized gray enclosure with rows of red and green lights across its face. It currently displayed the random position of vent and flood valves.

Helmsman's Watch, where the driver of the boat sat, was on the forward bulkhead. Aft of Helmsman's Watch, the cylindrical casing of a waist-high, gyroscopic compass rose from the deck.

Starboard side, or dry side, the air and electrical controls were laid out. A sheet of Plexiglas covered the exposed contacts of the boat's main switchboard. A slew of brass pressure gauges and valve levers lay just beyond.

Bowman walked through the complexity, smiling. Swiss watch indeed.

Just aft of the control room was the radio room, where he had spent the previous couple of days installing the new ICS. A myriad of vintage communication and listening equipment filled the narrow space. Dials and switches speckled the darkness.

Bowman climbed a steel ladder that rose through the overhead and squirmed through the opening into the conning tower.

The tower housed a second Helmsman's Watch station, and the periscopes, which pierced the center of the tower's overhead. Bowman got to his feet and took two steps to the tool satchel he had left on the floor. He sat cross legged beneath the communication console and went to work, completing the wiring that would complete the new intercom system.

It was quiet aboard. Not many people had decided to take the tour this sunny afternoon, which suited him fine. Fewer interruptions. Only twice did he have to greet museum visitors and kick them off on a self-guided tour. Every so often he'd check their progress, making sure they kept their hands off certain critical pieces of equipment.

At four-thirty he went topside and strolled down the gangplank. He unwound the chain from around a timber post beside the parking lot entrance and pulled it across the drive. He latched the hook to a rusty cleat on the opposite post and padlocked it in place. He flipped the 'Closed' sign over at the chain's mid-section and surveyed the lengthening shadows of the elms lining the lot.

Back inside the submarine's control room, he removed the screws holding the Plexiglas cover over the switchboard and lowered the clear, plastic sheet to the floor. Fishing a key ring from his pocket, he went to the plane control wheels and unlocked the chains.

He then made his way aft, passing through a bulkhead hatchway and entering the crew's mess and galley. Small dining tables extended from the stainless steel wall. Stepping through yet another bulkhead, he entered the crew quarters. Stacked and packed densely on either side, metal-frame bunks lined the walls from floor to ceiling. The compartment accommodated thirty-six crewmen, but they wouldn't be bunking that many this time out.

He continued through the forward engine room, all the way to the after battery compartment, where he collected the DC rectifier. He returned to the forward engine room and stopped in the narrow aisle between two 1,600-horsepower Fairbanks-Morse diesel engine casings. He took in the scent of machine oil and diesel fuel. Clearing the hair from his eye with a shake of his head, he went to work reconnecting the rectifier to the fuel pumps.

He repeated the process in the after engine room.

One more on-board check remained.

When submerged, *Silversides* drew its power from a Gould 252-cell storage battery. Roughly half this cell complement was packed into a space below the crew quarters, and the other half far forward beneath the deck in Officer's Country. Until recently the batteries had been absent from their compartments, replaced by cinder blocks to maintain proper ballast. But with the submarine's impending move to a downtown location, they had been restored and returned to their place only weeks ago.

Bowman knelt and went to work opening the access cover in the crew compartment, then inspected each cell and cable connection. The next few days it would be crucial that these batteries take and hold a charge. It all looked good. He closed the compartment, double checked the seal. If the hydrogen gas produced by the battery during charging seeped into the interior, the explosion potential would threaten the lives of all aboard.

Bowman repeated the inspection process on the batteries in the forward compartment. He finished at nine-thirty P.M.

On the forward deck he caught a breath of fresh air in the lake breeze. Beyond the narrow channel, the horizon of water and sky burned orange. The sun sank behind a hazy veil. Pink and red hues illuminated thin layers of cloud. As the sun fell, the colors deepened. The horizon had taken on a blood red glow. He pondered the poetic implications of this, and then descended the gangplank.

Using his key, he entered the museum. T-shirts, mugs, and other *Silversides* merchandise packed the shelves in the quaint shop area. He crossed the uneven plywood floor and stepped behind the cashier counter, then into Lanny Steven's office in the back. He opened a small, white refrigerator on the floor next to a beat-up desk and pulled out a Styrofoam box containing the remnants of his lunch from the day before. Kicking the fridge closed, he exited the office. He plucked a flashlight from beneath the cashier counter in passing.

Picking a spot at the picnic table outside, he set down the flashlight and his cold burger and fries, and then bought a Pepsi from the pop machine behind him. Sitting down so he could see the sun kiss the lake, he popped the top of the can and took a bite of hamburger. He forced himself to relax and enjoy day's transition into night. It would be quite some time before he'd get the chance again.

Night descended. Stars and a crescent moon materialized in a purple sky. Bowman took the last bite of his supper and discarded the can and the empty Styrofoam box in a waste basket. He snatched the flashlight from the picnic table and walked around the side of the museum to the fork truck. He hopped aboard and laid the flashlight beside the cracked seat cushion.

He started the engine. Propane fumes swirled around him as he backed the fork truck away from museum. Because he had cut the wires to the flood light above the parking lot the previous night, the grounds were dark. He switched on the truck's single headlight, aiming the beam low at the gravel so he could navigate.

The old lighthouse south of the inlet, now a coast guard station, was dark, save for some perimeter lamps. A thin crew manned the station this quiet Sunday night. Across the water the land was even darker, with nothing but trees and field beyond the broken-concrete seawall to the north. Typical of Sunday evening, traffic through the channel was light. In the last hour Bowman had seen only one boat, a nineteen-foot Chris Craft, coming in from the lake.

He pulled the fork truck to the edge of the concrete dock amidships of *Silversides* and stopped, letting it idle a moment. The wash of the lake became audible above the engine's murmur; a beautiful night.

He hopped from the seat. As he hit the concrete, his knees buckled. Catching himself, he spun about and made for the gangplank. He climbed to the bridge atop the conning tower and opened the upper hatch. He grabbed hold of a heavy mass of dirty, gray nylon straps and pulled it out, and then scrambled back down with the tightly wrapped mass under his arm.

Near the fork truck he unbuckled a series of clasps that compressed the bundle and unrolled the nylon, allowing intertwined straps to flop onto the ground like a net. Bowman considered his custom industrial sling. He'd spent a lot of time designing it and hoped his calculations were correct. He lifted two nylon loops and slid them over the forks, draping slack lengths of strap between them into a U-shape on the ground. Mid-way down the sling he grabbed a steel carabiner and worked the spring loaded catch. It seemed in working order. When he had tugged and positioned the harness to his liking, he stood to admire his work.

A sharp whistle cut through the stillness of the dark grounds.

In the pale light of the quarter moon he saw their shadowy forms. Faces streaked, dressed in black from head to toe, four men descended the hill behind the museum. They spilled into the darkened parking lot in silence. Two men stepped forward to address Bowman while two stayed in the rear, scanning the surroundings. "We clear?" said a bulky man with an aquiline nose.

"Of course," Bowman said, noting the shoulder holsters and satchels the men carried.

"You on schedule?"

"Don't worry about my end, Dominic," Bowman snapped. "You just get your boys moving."

Dominic reached into the satchel dangling from his shoulder and pulled out a two-way radio. He tossed it to Bowman, who caught it despite the poor lighting. Dominic smirked. "Channel eleven."

Bowman palmed the radio and grumbled a response.

Imposing in presence and efficient as a soldier, Dominic had been recruited by Keyes a few years back. Bowman never understood his value to the Circle. Then again, he had never served with Dominic either. Keyes on the other hand had.

He had met Dominic on an OP in the Gulf; the Special Forces guy catching a ride with the submarine commander. That was before Bowman had become Keyes' XO. Lately, with the commander's operation in full swing, Bowman and Dominic had worked together more closely. Bowman sometimes felt the cool Italian condescended to him or questioned his decisions. And as a late addition to the Circle, Dominic shouldn't overstep his bounds in such a way.

Twisting about, Dominic sniffled and pointed at the man nearest with his nose. "Royce, you and Carson shed and get wet—Six Pack, you're with me."

Two men peeled off and ran toward the dock. A tall, blond man named Royce patted Bowman on the shoulder. "Good to see you, Chop."

Bowman returned the gesture.

Now Royce he had served with. They had a history, and a mutual admiration. They saw action in the Gulf Conflict together. Bowman thought Royce should be squad leader, not the Italian newcomer.

Shaking his head, Bowman clipped the radio to his belt and boarded the Hyster fork truck.

He waited while Dominic and Six Pack unbolted the propellers from the mounts, and then rolled in close and positioned the dangling nylon straps near the blades. Dominic came forward, seized a strap, and worked the sling around the prop. Six Pack helped from the other side. When they were done, Dominic made a fist and pumped his arm at Bowman.

Bowman fired the hydraulics and bumped the forks up. The propeller ascended a pinch and Dominic pushed it free of the mount. Bowman lifted the forks several feet above the ground and backed away. Pointing at the dock, he sped across the lot.

Using the single headlight beam to guide him, Bowman stopped the Hyster as its front wheels reached the edge of the concrete dock. Momentum swayed the propeller. He lowered the throttle and called down to the water in a low voice. "Royce, you set?"

Wrapped in neoprene farmer-john suits with BC vests, Royce and Carson floated in the channel at the submarine's stern. They checked the airflow of their pony oxygen tanks and put their facemasks in place. "We're set, Chop," Royce said. "Bring it down."

Bowman extended the forks as far as he could, and then lowered them ever so slowly, dipping the forty-eight inch, four-bladed steel propeller into the water. Royce set his regulator into his mouth and waved Bowman on. The prop submerged below the surface. Royce locked a hand around a section of the tubular framework built off the submarine's stern. Known as the turtleback, the frame's intended use had been to protect the propeller blades from damage in dock. On this night, however, it would serve another purpose.

When the carabiner came within reach, Royce grabbed hold of it and clipped it onto the turtleback. Bowman lowered the forks as far as they could go. The propeller dropped until the strap that was clipped to the turtleback pulled tight. It swung into position near level with the propeller shaft below the water's surface. Royce and Carson submerged.

Bowman held steady at the fork truck's control levers. After a moment he could see the glow of the driver's work lamp. In a few minutes, Royce broke surface and removed his mouthpiece. "Chop, pull back about six inches, and pivot counterclockwise another three." He disappeared again beneath the waves.

Bowman obliged, inching the forks as instructed, then waited. They went back and forth several more times until Royce and Carson had the propeller properly aligned. They threaded new bolts through the propeller shaft flange and secured them tight, then freed the sling from the blades and unhooked the carabiner from the turtleback. By the time they finished with the first prop they were out of air. Surfacing, they disconnected and tossed their spent cylinders onto the dock. They scavenged through their equipment pack for another pair of pony tanks.

Bowman backed away from the edge and drove back to the second propeller. On the way over he checked the time. Ten forty-five. They were making good progress.

Dominic and Six Pack harnessed the second prop with the sling as they had the first. As Bowman drove to the dock, they entered the submarine through the forward hatchway.

Royce and Carson positioned the second prop faster than they had the first. Bowman sat with the Hyster at idle, listening to the wash of the lake. The growl of an engine materialized some distance off shore. Keyes?

Straining to see through the distance and darkness, he scanned the placid water at the channel's mouth. Nothing there. Back at the lamp-lit water near *Silversides'* stern, Royce and Carson's dark forms moved beneath gentle ripples. Save for the air bubbles percolating from their regulators the channel was still.

Bowman heard the distant growl of an engine again. This time he caught sight of a pair of dark silhouettes driving across the open water, angling in toward the channel. In the moonlight he could soon see that the silhouettes were the tugboats he was expecting. He lifted the flashlight and sent a message in Morse. C-L-E-A-R.

Steady on course, the tugboats entered the channel in a staggered formation, with *Richard C.* in the lead position and *Wescott* half a length behind. From the pilothouse of *Richard C.*, a light flashed in patterned response. I-N-B-O-U-N-D.

Bouncing his knee with growing excitement, Bowman set the flashlight down and turned to check the progress with the propeller. Royce and Carson were just surfacing. They lifted their facemasks, removed their regulators, and Royce signaled with a wave.

Bowman eased the fork truck back from the edge of the dock, switched off the engine, and hopped to the ground. He hustled to a position above one of the mooring rings on the side of the concrete dock.

Royce and Carson climbed up the turtleback and onto the submarine's fantail, water streaming from their neoprene suits. Royce moved to the stern capstan and uncoiled the thick mooring line, then threw it across the water to Bowman.

Bowman caught the end, fed the rope through the steel anchor ring in the concrete, and then tossed it back to Royce.

Bowman moved to the next mooring line and, with Carson on the submarine across from him, uncoiled and cast off this line like the last. They continued down the length of the boat until *Silversides* was unbound.

The sound of engines was now very close. A tugboat drifted in next to the submarine's bow. A large man stood forward on the vessel. Owen Keyes himself.

Richard C. maneuvered about to a towing position, and Royce and Carson threw over a pair of mooring lines. Deck hands on the tugboat seized the lines and secured them to the stern capstans. Back aft of the submarine, *Wescott* crewmen did the same. In short order they had *Silversides* rigged for towing.

Bowman raced up the gangplank. He and Royce tossed the plank into the channel.

"Robert, are we on track?" Keyes called from astern of the tug twenty feet away.

Bowman walked to the cable handrail on *Silversides'* starboard side.

"Yes, sir. All done. We're ready to get underway."

Richard C.'s engines rumbled and the tug drifted away, straightening the slack tow lines in the water. Keyes spat a stream of chew over the side. "Fine work, Robert," he said above the diesels' growl. "Fine work."

Both tugboats pointed toward mid channel, and the tow lines stretched tight behind them. *Silversides* looked to be caught in a giant spider web. Bowman couldn't help grinning, and he climbed down through the submarine's forward hatch. He worked through the boat to the dry-side wall in the control room and actuated a series of valves. Compressed air hissed and pumped water from the ballast tanks to the lake. Around the sub's hull, water percolated. *Silversides* shifted. Bowman lifted the radio from his belt. "Commander, we're set to go."

In unison the tugboat engines kicked up to full throttle. *Silversides* rolled under Bowman's feet. *Richard C.* and *Wescott* dug in their heels, fighting to budge the aging submarine from her resting place. Bowman came topside to watch the effort. He whispered, "Come on, girl. Let go of the sand."

Like a lethargic serpent the old diesel-electric boat slid off the sand bar. Her keel clear, she bobbed and pitched in the channel with sluggish majesty. *Wescott's* crew unfastened the stern tow lines and maneuvered the tug around *Silversides* in a wide arc, taking a position parallel to *Richard C.* The men on deck on the two tugs redistributed the submarine's bow lines, securing half to *Wescott.* With the load behind the tugs split evenly between them, they made for the mouth of the channel.

Standing together at *Silversides'* bow, the breeze from the lake in their faces, Royce slapped Bowman's shoulder. "We're underway, Chop."

"That we are, Mr. Royce."

SIX

Grand Haven, MI

SADEED fired his pistol. The muzzle flash ballooned like a yellow blossom of fire. Dylan saw the slug leave the barrel, a 9mm hollow point. It spun on its axis so slowly he could see the grain of the lead. The bullet's trajectory lined up square with his forehead. He sensed it, saw it. He tried to turn, duck, but couldn't seem to move fast enough. As slow as the damned thing was moving, he couldn't get out of the way. In the bleary background, Sadeed smiled. Sweat dripped into Dylan's eyes. He kept trying to move, and kept failing.

A scream. Somebody was screaming. The hallway walls suddenly melted, and Dylan rolled, reaching for something. The scream.

Silence. He lay there with his cheek plastered against the pillow. The digital clock read four-thirty. He rolled onto his back and cursed. The dream had returned. It'd been about a year since the last time. Why now, and why the spell on Mackinac Island? Something had triggered that deep-buried psychological mess.

Right after the Sadeed incident the dream plagued him nightly, but over time he learned to suppress the fear that brought it on. Apparently it was resurfacing. Psychological therapy, however, was not an option. He didn't go for what he called "psycho rot-gut."

He sat up and switched on the lamp. The light blinded him. He covered his eyes until accustomed to the brightness, and then got his bearings.

He had stayed the night in the McCallum guest house, just off the main house. Kathryn McCallum had seen fit to decorate it with a Southwestern flair. It was his home away from home. Sarah would say it was his one and only home. There *were* times when he'd stayed there for long stretches of time.

In the days after September 11th for instance, he stayed a month. Or when the Shiite Brigade, an Iranian terrorist organization, bombed American and British embassies in Europe, he stayed three weeks straight. That group held a special contempt for the former president.

Dylan traced their anger to the Gulf Conflict, which played out fourteen years ago as a short-lived war with Iraq. Even though Iran and Iraq could barely stomach each other, they did share one thing in common: An unceasing hatred for the United States. My enemy's enemy is my friend and such. Regardless the reason, intelligence agencies continued to see Warren McCallum's name spring up in Brigade communication intercepts.

On the nightstand, Dylan's Secret Service shield lay open amongst a handful of change. His Glock lay beside it. The spent slug from the assassination attempt sat amongst the clutter. A memento, as Gillespie put it, of trigger man Arif Sadeed.

The FBI's investigation of the incident revealed that Arif Sadeed had entered the United States on a student visa. He never showed at the University of Michigan, and the INS failed to call him on it. He stayed beyond his visa's expiration date but authorities never sought him out. And though Sadeed was not officially on a watch list, the Bureau had linked him to the Shiite Brigade. One bureaucratic bungle after another led to that day in Detroit six years ago. The incident became one of many reasons the INS went through a major overhaul a few years back.

Lingering on Mr. Sadeed and the Brigade, Dylan had to shake his head. Their attempt to assassinate a man two years out of office led one to believe that President McCallum had truly roiled these people during his tenure. And if Sadeed was a model of what to expect from others in that organization, the U.S. would have a long, hard road ahead in dealing with them. In the words of a vaunted defense secretary, they appeared to be a gang of real dead-enders.

Wearing only his gray jockey shorts, Dylan got out of bed and picked up his sidearm from the night stand. Through sleep-swollen eyes he caught a glimpse of his disheveled self in the dresser mirror. His rigorous exercise regiment kept him lean, though at this hour he didn't feel particularly able bodied. Nonetheless, he deemed good fitness a crucial part of staying sharp. Plenty of hours on the range with the pistol in his hand didn't hurt either.

He marched into the attached bathroom, the tile almost blinding in its whiteness, and twisted on the shower. Waiting for warmth to work through the pipes, he set the Glock on the sink and thought about the trip to Mackinac Island. If the Old Man didn't want to rush in the wee hours of Tuesday morning to make his speech, why did he choose to leave in the wee hours of Monday morning? He made a mental note to hit McCallum up with that one.

After a quick shower, he dressed in a white shirt with dark slacks and suit coat. McCallum preferred business attire when traveling to speaking engagements. After cinching a burgundy tie in place, he snapped the Glock's holster to his belt and grabbed his garment bag. He collected his change and shield from the nightstand. Sadeed's bullet rolled in his palm with the change. He looked close at it as he did every morning. Nope, his name wasn't on it.

Cool morning air hit him outside the guesthouse. The sun had yet to crest, and crickets in the surrounding wood sang their pulsating song. Lights were on in the main house. He followed the stone path from his home away from home to the large wrap-around deck of the McCallum residence. His Durango was parked on the concrete turn-around in front of the house, just ahead of the president's black Towne Car. According to his plan, he'd be the lead vehicle and Gillespie would chauffeur the president.

He pushed open the front door.

Tom Gillespie stood in the foyer, wearing a suit and tie and an unsmiling pre-dawn face.

Dylan nodded a greeting. Warren McCallum stood in the vaulted great room. Dressed in blue pants and a white striped Polo shirt, he was talking with his bathrobed wife. Bantering as usual, they performed a routine perfected over a lifetime. He, running down his schedule for the last time and telling Mrs. McCallum what needed doing in his absence. She, informing him she already knew and making sure he'd not forgotten anything for the trip in his last minute rush. It struck Dylan in that moment how normal they seemed. How average they acted. No pretense or ego from their past position of power showed through in their daily lives. Even while in office President McCallum carried himself as a man of the people, devoid of pompous superiority. Of the people, for the people, it wasn't a political calculation, it was simply his character. And it was that character that endeared him to the public, and so to Dylan Reese

McCallum kissed his wife goodbye and turned to leave. Before he'd gotten too far she reached for his arm, stopping him in mid step. He turned and they talked a few moments longer, in lower voices. Dylan noticed Kathryn McCallum cross her arms. It was uncharacteristic of her. Tense body language. The president shook his head, kissed her again, and made for the front door. He entered the foyer with a crisp stride. "Morning, gentlemen."

"Ready to go, sir?" Dylan said.

"As I'll ever be."

Gillespie peered through the beveled glass then opened the door and stepped out, his head nearly touching the top of the doorframe. McCallum followed.

Dylan looked back into the great room. Kathryn McCallum stood with arms still crossed. She watched her husband go, then gave Dylan a polite wave and stepped from view into the adjoining kitchen. He got an uneasy feeling in his stomach. She didn't seem right. The letter in Saturday's mail came to mind. He had little more than fretful speculation to go on, but some grim undercurrent seemed to be swirling through the McCallum household. From past experience, when his instincts took this much notice in mundane events, they deserved closer examination. He followed the president outside.

Refusing to let anyone hold the car door open for him in his own driveway, McCallum instructed Gillespie to get in the driver's seat. He then stood between the Towne Car and the Durango, gazing at the grounds in the gray light of an imminent sunrise. Dylan compared McCallum's casual dress to his own suit and tie. They didn't quite match. "Mr. President, sir, I can't help but notice your comfortable attire."

McCallum regarded his clothes and smiled.

"This is a day of business travel, is it not?"

McCallum rolled his tongue in his mouth and turned. "In case you hadn't noticed, I've all but retired from the game. Today we're simply taking a relaxing drive to Mackinaw City and settling in on the Island. Tomorrow is business." He gestured to Dylan's suit. "You and Tom look sharp, though, and I'm proud to be in the company of such professionals."

"Uh…Thank you."

"Don't mention it." McCallum slipped his hands into his pockets.

Dylan waited for him to get into the car.

He didn't. Instead, he took a large breath and looked skyward through tree branches.

"Sir?" Dylan finally said. "Something wrong?"

McCallum caressed his chin. "Weather channel said it's going to be a beautiful day. Sunny and eighty-five. Great day for a drive."

"Yes, I saw the report." Dylan knew what was coming.

McCallum raised his hand with opened palm. "You mind?"

Dylan exhaled. "Frankly, I'd rather you not drive today. We're traveling to a specific destination within a certain timeframe, a trip the papers have been reporting for two days. The governors meeting is a high profile event and the more visible the event, the greater the incentive for surly types to disrupt it, if you catch my meaning. In short, sir, I just wouldn't be comfortable if Tom or I were not driving today."

McCallum frowned. "Your concern is duly noted. I still want the wheel."

Dylan dropped his chin. "It's more difficult for me to do my job if I don't—" He hesitated. "If I don't have control over the situation. You being behind the wheel adds an element of...uncertainty."

Indignation flashed in McCallum's eyes. "Hell, I've still got my damned driver's license and *all* my faculties."

"That's not the point. I can't protect you if—"

"If what? This isn't the first time I've driven a car, and you can be damned sure it won't be the last. I won't be so protected that I miss out on life's simple joys." McCallum stalked in a small circle then fixed Dylan with an authoritative gaze, a gaze he was certain had wilted countless senators and congressmen. "You're head of my security detail, not my warden."

Dylan faltered. He had set precedence on a number of other occasions by letting McCallum tool around behind the wheel while he rode shotgun, so to speak. But those little grains of unrest he had been feeling lately chaffed against his complacency, like sand in his shoes after a walk on the beach. The president pressed him with a stare and waved his outstretched fingers. Dylan wasn't going to win this one. He saw it in McCallum's eyes.

"Come on, if you won't let me drive I know Tom will."

Gillespie poked his head out the Towne Car. "You call me, sir?"

Damn. Tommy wouldn't have a problem with it at all. Figuring he'd rather have the president under his wing, Dylan relented. He tossed the key ring over.

McCallum snatched it from the air, then pointed and smiled at him. "Good man." He made his way around to the driver's side of the Durango.

Dylan walked over and leaned into the Towne Car. "Warren wants to drive this morning. Pull around and take the lead."

Gillespie grinned. "Chaos reigns in the world of Reese."

"Blow me, Tommy." He slapped the roof of the car and walked to the Durango, passenger side. By the time he climbed in, McCallum had the engine started. Gillespie maneuvered around the SUV and headed down the long drive. McCallum slid the gear shift into drive. "D is forward. Right?"

"That's not funny, sir."

The president laughed and hit the accelerator, jumping the Durango forward. They glided over the drive beneath the leaf canopy and brightening sky.

Agent LaCroix, who had stayed with Mrs. McCallum, opened the main gate from the surveillance command center. Gillespie turned the Towne Car left onto the dirt road in front of the estate. The president followed. The small convoy stirred a dust cloud over three miles of gravel then turned east onto state route 102. They caught the 96 junction and continued into the sunrise. Neither McCallum nor Dylan spoke for a long while. The amber horizon held their attention until they jumped onto 131 North. A few miles before Rockford, McCallum felt Dylan's stare.

"What's the matter, Agent Reese, am I speeding?"

Dylan paused. "Is everything okay with you and Mrs. McCallum?" he finally asked.

McCallum glanced across the cab. "We're fine. Why do you ask?"

Dylan read the number off a passing mile marker. "I've noticed some things lately. Could be me, but—"

"More than likely."

"But you haven't seemed yourself. At least not until Governor Patterson contacted you. Kathryn's been concerned about something too."

McCallum gripped the wheel a bit tighter and flashed the headlights, signaling Gillespie to pass a meandering red minivan ahead. "You're looking too hard at things. Too many days on the job without time off. That thing with Sarah is messing with you too."

The president cast off the inquiry so flippantly Dylan had to laugh. "So it's all me?"

McCallum accelerated around the minivan. "Don't feel bad. You're excellent at your job, but we all need time away. A break. Why don't you take Danny camping up north or something?"

Dylan turned in his seat to face the president better. "You're telling me everything is fine? That any signs of unrest I've detected in you is due to my being a workaholic and a lousy manager of personal issues?"

Sliding back into the right lane ahead of the minivan, McCallum smiled. "I worded it differently but you caught the essence of what I meant."

"How about that letter Saturday?"

The smile receded. "My personal life stays my own. You know the rules." He made eye contact to accent his next point. "Regardless of that, I received nothing in the mail that warranted your involvement. If I ever do receive a threat I deem credible you'll be the first to know. We clear?"

Dylan sat quiet a moment. "I didn't say anything about a threat."

McCallum thumped the wheel with his palm. "What the hell else would I get in the mail that would require you knowing about?"

The heat of the reaction stopped Dylan cold. He'd learned how close he could come to the line between doing his job and intruding on McCallum's privacy, and he felt he had just tripped over it. He settled back in his seat. "Sorry I brought it up. I didn't mean to pry." He sat quiet for a long while. "So how do you like the way it handles?"

McCallum raised his eyebrows. "What?"

"My ride. How does if feel on the road?"

"Great. Very responsive. And you feel the power every time you touch that accelerator."

"I feel my wallet drain with that Big Eight under the hood."

They drove past a blue sign showing food selections at the next exit. "What do you say, Dylan? Time for a Krispy Kreme stop?"

Dylan smiled and lifted a two-way radio from the seat. "Carney— Ringleader. Copy?"

Gillespie's voice squawked back. "Go for Carney."

"Cipher suggests breakfast. Two clicks and exit. The usual."

"Understood."

Dylan lowered the radio. "All set."

He sat preoccupied as the Durango swallowed up road, disturbed that he had backed down so quickly, wondering how he'd get that sand out of his shoe.

- SEVEN -

Muskegon

THE SUN had barely come over the trees when Lanny Stevens pulled his old, blue Explorer off Lakeview drive and rolled to a stop in front of the Great Lakes Naval Memorial and Museum. He didn't notice anything unusual at first. Something felt different, though, as he unwound the chain that barred the parking lot. Limping back to the Explorer, he shook his head and wondered what was making him feel so damned out of place. He climbed up with a huff and plopped behind the wheel.

Right when his rear hit the vinyl his gaze landed on the empty berth. His mouth fell open. He closed his eyes, rubbed his palms over them, hoping he wasn't seeing it right. Still gone. Anger burst like an avalanche and he gunned the accelerator, jumping the Explorer forward and spraying a shower of gravel behind. At the edge of the lot he jammed on the breaks and slid to a stop. He jumped out, but his bum knee buckled and sent him to the ground. Struggling to his feet, he hobbled to the empty concrete dock. Lanny shouted a bitter curse to the sky. A large piece of his world had disappeared. *Silversides* was gone!

Twenty minutes later, after an irate phone call to the Muskegon police department, Sergeant Jasper Cotter arrived on the grounds. He parked his white Impala cruiser next to Lanny's Explorer, kicked open his door, and rose from the seat. He rested a hand on the blue bar flashers and tilted his Smokey Bear hat low over his eyes. The spot in the channel where the submarine had been for fifteen of the seventeen years he'd been with the department was empty.

Cotter's prominent belly pushed against a beige, short-sleeved shirt. He tucked in loose tails and a smile curved his lips. He wiped it away when Lanny Stevens stormed out of the museum office.

Huffing and limping, his face as red as his hair, Lanny headed over. "They stole it!" he shouted. "Some damned thief stole my submarine."

Cotter raised his hands to slow the curator. "Hold up there, Lanny, you'll blow out your other knee. Hell, you need one good one."

Lanny ignored him. "You've got to find who did this."

Sticking a thumb under gun belt, Cotter tilted his head. "I aim to do just that, but you gotta calm yourself first." He gave Lanny a brief cooling period. "Now tell me, have you contacted the coast guard?"

"Of course," Lanny snapped. "Right before I called you."

"Was the missing submarine news to them?"

Lanny pointed an angry finger at the station at the inlet. "They've got a facility right there and what good was it?"

"Now let's just talk a little bit before we start pissing on the coast guard."

Lanny spit. "When I called there this morning the station commander told me one of his men saw something last night."

Sergeant Cotter nodded and snapped his fingers. "That's good, we're making progress already. What'd he see?"

"Around midnight a guy on watch saw *Silversides* being towed into the lake but didn't report it because, he said, I had called earlier and told them that the movie company was going to shoot more scenes. I didn't make that damned call!"

"Seems they didn't know that, Lanny. And those movie folks did take the boat out just a month ago, didn't they?"

Lanny grit his teeth. "Yes."

"Did this guardsman get an ID on the boats doing the towing?"

"No, they were too far out when he spotted them, couldn't make 'em out."

"They can't have gotten far." Cotter thought a moment. "Can she go under?"

"She can dive, but she can't come back. We disabled the surfacing systems."

Cotter scratched at his neck. "Can she move under her own power?"

"No, she has to be towed. It would take a week for qualified engineers to get her underway."

"She can't dive and she hasn't got locomotion." Cotter beamed. "Hell, the worse they can do is tow her around for a joy ride."

Lanny grumbled and kicked at the gravel. "No, the worse they can do is sink her."

"True," Cotter said, "True." He tilted his Smokey Bear up with a finger. "Do you know who might have wanted to steal her?"

Lanny threw open his arms. "I don't know." He floundered for an answer. "College kids pulling a prank comes to mind."

"When I was a young rabble rouser, the biggest thing me and my buddies made off with was the Big Boy statue from the Elias Brothers in town. Senior prank. I guess today's kids think bigger than ever."

Lanny made an off balance turn. "They weren't thinking when they did this! *Silversides* is a valuable piece of history. Why do so many people have so little regard for the past? No one cares about our fathers and what they did to defend this nation."

Cotter put a hand on his shoulder. "I care, Lanny."

"Fuck off, Jasper, I'm serious."

"So am I. That's why I'm gonna do everything I can to get your submarine back. Did the coast guard tell you they would start searching right away?"

Lanny shrugged and looked at the empty space where *Silversides* once rested. "Yes."

"Okay. I'll get my boys on it right now. We'll start questioning the early fishermen. Lawton and Wills and such. They might've seen something."

"Alright—Hey, I'm sorry I blew up. This whole thing just pisses me off."

"Don't sweat it. If someone lifted my '64 Pontiac I'd feel the same way." Cotter reached into his cruiser and snatched the mic from the radio. He raised it to his mouth then stopped.

"Lanny, do you have any coffee brewed in your office yet. This day started unraveling kind of early and I missed my morning fix."

"I'll get you some." Lanny hobbled off toward the museum.

"Appreciate it."

Sergeant Cotter let him get some distance from the police car before making the call. Sure, it seemed like an elaborate prank of some kind. And he was confident they'd have the submarine spotted and towed back by lunch. But a small part of him had begun to take the theft as seriously as Lanny had. In the days when airplanes crash into skyscrapers you just couldn't afford to let anything to chance. Neutered or not, *Silversides* was a military vessel, and some things he saw on the crime scene raised a few questions. He keyed the mic. "Dispatch, this is one-charlie-seven."

"Go ahead, Sergeant."

"That call from the naval museum turned out to be legitimate. Someone really made off with that old submarine down here. We need to mobilize the patrolmen on shore, start interviewing fishermen and charters and the like, see if we can come up with a witness to the theft." He let off the key and exhaled. For some reason he felt embarrassed over what he was about to say. Who would take it seriously? He was having a hard enough time of it himself. He keyed the mic again. "Put in a call to the Bureau office in Grand Rapids. Let the Feds know that a potentially dangerous warship has disappeared."

Outside of Grand Rapids

Driving westbound on Interstate 96 in the fresh light of a new day, Rebecca Matthis struggled to lift her eyelids. She'd been on the road since five o'clock and had finished her one cup of coffee an hour ago. For most of the drive the surrounding terrain had been open fields, but now thick patches of trees were dotting the landscape. She was nearing the outskirts of Grand Rapids. Only twenty minutes or so remained in her drive to the Resident Agency office. With the sun fully up and a cloudless sky ahead, Rebecca actually began to come alive. Sunlight burned off the grogginess that hit her while she was barreling through the Ionia corn fields. Knowing the ride was nearly over perked her up as well.

She'd been running at a hectic pace ever since leaving the McNamara building on Sunday. After Kyle Bradley banished her to the West, she had to arrange for life away from home for a few weeks. Hold the mail. Stop the paper. Ask Mrs. Clark downstairs to keep the plants in her apartment alive. Forward her calls to the new office. Let her mother know she'd be in the area soon. Everything except explain the trip to the perfect man in her life. The problem here was that there wasn't a perfect man in her life.

The expression 'perfect man' seemed an oxymoron to her. She just hadn't met one that came close. Eric, her last attempt at romance, seemed promising at first but fell apart quickly. He'd told her it was the hours she kept and her lack of commitment. Thinking back on their last conversation she had to laugh. What a reversal of stereotypes. She did find it interesting, however, that her job as an FBI agent had put off so many men. She didn't understand their problem. She knew she'd crossed a barrier when she became a field agent with the Bureau, a woman in a profession so dominated by men. It made her mother proud. But Rebecca never imagined it would sabotage her personal life. She had to come to terms with the situation. Expending so much energy and enthusiasm on her career, she just didn't have much left to nurture a relationship.

Five miles outside Grand Rapids her cell phone rang. "Agent Matthis."

The voice on the other end was chipper, with a certain nasal quality. "This is Gordon Jennings, SAC of the RA in GR."

Rebecca rolled her eyes at the alphabet soup of government acronyms. She thought she may have heard a muted chuckle from Mr. Jennings. "Yes, sir, good morning."

"Where are you right now, Agent Matthis?"

It was almost seven-thirty, but she wasn't due to check in for another half hour. "I'm ten minutes out. I hope I didn't misunderstand but I thought you were expecting me at eight this morning."

Jennings laughed. "Oh, no, I'm not hitting you for tardiness. Kyle Bradley told me about your excellent punctuality and I appreciate that. No, I just thought we'd start your tour with us right. Have you hit the ground running."

"Running?"

"We just received a call from the Muskegon police department. It seems a World War II submarine came up missing this morning."

"Missing?"

"Yes."

"A submarine?"

"Yes. USS *Silversides*. SS-236. Ever been to Muskegon to see it?"

"Afraid not." Rebecca paused. "I'm not up to speed on old war vessels. What sort of submarine is it?"

Jennings laughed again. "The big kind. A diesel-electric over three-hundred feet long. Someone towed her out of her berth last night. Real shocker when the curator came in this morning."

"How'd they manage slipping away with a whale like that?"

"Don't know yet. That's why we investigate."

It wasn't quite making sense to her yet. "Is this submarine still on the Naval Register?"

"Oh, no, it was stricken over fifty years ago. But it's still property of the U.S. Navy."

Great. West Coast criminal activity has expanded beyond gas-and-go's and cow tipping to include grand theft naval artifact. Hour-one of day-one and Rebecca could already feel her career sinking like an old, rusty anchor on an old, rusty submarine. She wasn't even sure if submarines had anchors. "Forgive me if this sounds territorial, sir, but how is this theft a Bureau concern?"

"Well, the Muskegon police feel the submarine's disappearance has the potential to become a security threat."

"Security?" She stewed for a moment. "Was the thing functional?"

"From what I understand, no, she was kept in good condition but not war ready by any means. She's a museum display, really. A big, floating museum display."

"Then what kind of security threat could it possibly pose?"

"Don't know, Agent Matthis, that's why we investigate. Closer to the point, that's why you're going to investigate."

She tapped the steering wheel with her finger. "Understood." She mouthed a curse. "I'm on 196 entering Grand Rapids right now. How do I get there from here?"

The happy nasally voice answered, "Go west." He gave her directions. She scrambled for a pen and wrote down key details.

"Glad to have you with us, Reb. Keep me up to date on what you find. I'm kind of intrigued with this one."

Reb? Nobody called her that except close and trusted friends. Having known him only three minutes, Gordon Jennings met neither requirement. "Thank you, sir. I'll keep you informed." They ended the call and Rebecca set the cell phone on the seat beside her.

A submarine?

- EIGHT -

WATER, WATER EVERYWHERE, but this stuff you could drink. Standing on *Silversides'* deck, Owen Keyes grinned at his modified version of the ancient rhyme.

A light sea gently rocked the submarine. Alongside and tethered to the long, steel boat, *Richard C.* bobbed in the water. A summer sun rose above the horizon, and a light breeze rolled across the lake. A beautiful day was unfolding, but Keyes knew he wouldn't see much of it.

From his position far forward on the bow he watched the activity on the submarine's deck. His carefully assembled contingent of men rushed about, making ready for the mission ahead. Bowman was directing a handful of hirelings to maneuver a Mark 14 torpedo, the seventh so far, down off *Richard C.'s* boom crane and onto *Silversides'* opened torpedo loading skid. The torpedoes were exact replicas of the twenty-one inch, war era model, save for the Mark-VI magnetic detonator. Knowing the Mark-VI design didn't work reliably, Keyes saw to it his version was fitted with a state of the art proximity detonator, which would allow near misses to still trigger the explosive regardless of if the contact detonator in the tip of the torpedo tripped or not. Keyes smiled at his ability to improvise. If you knew where to look and who to talk to within the navy's monolithic structure you could find nearly anything.

The 3,200-lb Mark 14 slid down into the forward torpedo room, where another group of men would guide it onto a rack. Amidships, a pair of men tossed dry goods and food stuffs through the open Potato Hatch into the galley below. One of them was Tyler Martin. Everyone called him Six Pack because of his renowned drinking binges during leave. Keyes liked the kid and thought to guide him along, perhaps in place of the son he never had.

Atop the conning tower Royce and Carson inspected the SJ radar tower and attack periscope. Despite being a bit too salty in attitude for

Keyes' liking, the Aryan-looking Royce was a good sailor. He took orders well and did his job right.

Dominic made his way to the forward hatch with a small crate on his shoulder. The burly Spec Ops man had officially signed on six months ago, though conversations about a possible partnership had taken place weeks prior to that. Dominic was a skilled soldier and a good man, and at first a bit resistant to joining. But Keyes wanted him, and that was that.

The *Wescott* was no longer with them. After her cargo of ammunition, weapons, and fuel were safely aboard *Silversides*, he'd ordered the tug away. Now two hours later she was well clear of the area. Only *Richard C.* remained. They were nearly finished, but with the sun in the sky Keyes grew restless. They wouldn't have much time before the coast guard mounted a concerted search.

Excitement welled up in his chest.

He hadn't been aboard a submarine for a year, and the moment he stepped foot on *Silversides* deck he'd been transformed. The rush that came from commanding such a vessel flooded back in an instant. He'd walked away from commanding the USS *Hampton* twelve months ago, a difficult decision. Patrolling the North Atlantic in a hunter-killer was a realized dream, but as the maxim goes, all good things must come to an end. And the end came most unexpectedly.

He felt for the papers in his breast pocket. They were there, feeling calm and cool this morning. Sometimes they seemed hot to the touch, other times cold and distant. They packed a lot of emotion, and despite the road he now traveled, he still struggled to sort through the mess in his mind.

Bowman shot orders at a few of the freelancers tinkering about with the 20mm on the cigarette deck. One man had opened a small case of machined parts and seemed to be checking them over while another studied the machine gun. Bowman gave them another curt instruction and turned about to direct the men loading the eighth torpedo onto the skid.

Not having seen him face to face in three months, Keyes noted that Bowman had changed a lot. Unkempt beard, hair long and unruly, he seemed older. His eyes, once calm and determined, now flashed with an unsettling zeal. Rierdon's observation that Bowman was emotionally unstable came to mind. Keyes wouldn't go that far, but if unpredictable tides were rising in his XO's behavior he needed to rein them in.

He pulled a can of chew from his pocket and stuck a pinch in his mouth. "Robert," he called, "come over here."

After shepherding the torpedo down the chute, Bowman walked across the teakwood to his commanding officer, the breeze blowing strands of hair from his face. "Sir?"

"How are you holding up, Robert? You've been on your own for a long time?"

Bowman smiled wide. "Never better."

"You look like you need sleep. Can't have that. When we're finished with supply I want you to bed down for first watch."

Bowman mulled the command in silence.

"I need you sharp and your judgment clear," Keyes said. "I need the solid XO I had on *Hampton*."

Puffing himself up, Bowman grinned. "You'll get better than that."

"I want the same one. Understand?"

The flash of zeal faded from his haggard first officer's eyes, and a tired stare replaced it. "You've done a hell of a job," Keyes told him, "but we've got a long way to go."

Bowman nodded.

Down the length of *Silversides,* a deep rumble spilled from open hatches. "We've been running the engines since we hit open water. Batteries taking a charge?"

"Beautifully." Bowman seemed pleased the conversation had turned back to the submarine. "We've got about half a charge in them now."

Keyes shook his head. "We'll have to surface before nightfall. That's not good if the Guard spreads a dense search net. They call in outside help and fill the sky with air recon, we just might come up right under their nose."

He spat a stream of chew over the side and estimated the coastal authority's initial response to the submarine's disappearance. "They'll go light with the search at first. No reason to believe that we'll be hard to find. Just the same, these first few hours are critical. The longer we stay out of sight, the longer we'll stay out of sight."

Bowman understood, and acknowledged with a nod.

"The statement is hitting the news stations this evening?"

"All set. Should get some mention in the six o'clock hour."

Keyes watched the men working on the 20mm machinegun. "We're cutting it close."

"Nearly finished," Bowman offered. "I'll make sure we stay on schedule."

Over Bowman's shoulder, John Tierney ascended from the forward hatch. Dressed in worn jeans and a large black T-shirt, he stepped on deck and took in a breath of air. Strapped to his waist, a Desert Eagle .357 semi-automatic pistol. Projecting confidence in his composure, Tierney looked around at the hired soldiers on deck like an overseer in a cotton field.

"Mr. Tierney," Keyes said. "How do you like my boat?"

Tierney turned and approached. He glanced at the deck as he walked, then cocked his head. Wind blew his short red hair askew. "I have to admit, Commander Keyes, that when you laid out this plan all those months ago I had my doubts."

Keyes smiled at the comment and crossed his arms. "What sort of doubts?"

Tierney set a casual stance and rested a hand atop the Desert Eagle, as he always did. "Doubts that you'd actually pull this off. My apologies."

"Accepted, but you should know by now that if I say something it will happen."

Tierney looked about the submarine. "That's evident."

"Good work back at Port Huron. You kept the Guard off our ass. That probably saved the whole operation."

"Coast guard officers are easy if you know how to talk to them. It helped that we weren't Arabs too."

Keyes gestured to a group of freelancers. "How do the men seem to you?"

"Capable and competent from what I've seen so far. Not a bad bunch considering what we had to choose from. The objective of this OP ran a lot of guys off."

"If they knew the full story I'm sure we'd have more than we knew what to do with."

Tierney squinted at the sun. "Perhaps. But don't be surprised when you find some of these guys are simple mercenaries and don't give a rat's ass about your noble pursuit. They respect money, and as long as yours is good government green they'll be happy."

Keyes simmered. *How could any soldier be ambivalent about this?* He searched Tierney's eyes. "What about you?"

Tierney feigned misunderstanding. "Me?"

"The heart of the mission," Keyes said. "The goal. How does it sit with you?"

Strumming fingers on the holster, Tierney considered his response. "Betrayal's an ugly thing and I don't much care for it. I'm in your corner."

"And what about Dominic? What's your sense there?"

"Don't fault him for this but Dom's fair minded. He sees both sides of the coin. Don't concern yourself, though, he knows where you stand and he's thrown in with you."

"That's good," Keyes said. "I need to know I can rely on him out there—on both of you."

Tierney didn't blink. "You can."

Bowman faced the red-headed soldier. "Dominic is an arrogant dago."

Keyes reprimanded him with a stern eye, and then noted the sun's position. "We don't have much longer to—"

"Commander!" Rierdon called from the tugboat. "I've got a radar contact."

Keyes whirled about. "Where?"

Rierdon leaned out the door. "Inbound from the coast. Bearing two-seven-two. Speed one-five-zero. IFF code says it's a coast guard chopper."

Keyes walked to the cable handrail. "Time to visual."

Rierdon lifted an open hand. "Five minutes."

Keyes turned. "Mr. Bowman, supply stop is over. Clear the deck."

Bowman echoed the order with a bellow. "Clear the deck! Clear the deck now!"

Every man topside stopped in mid-task. It took them a suspended instant to process the instruction, and then hands and feet broke into a flurry. Six Pack and his group threw the remaining provisions through the Potato Hatch and began dropping down themselves. Royce and Carson clamored down from the conning tower and entered the bridge hatch. The men working on the 20mm snatched up their parts and tools and made for the forward hatch. Bowman roared for help to cast off *Richard C's* mooring lines. Tierney and another man rushed to his aid.

Keyes cast an astute eye east. Adrenaline coursed through his body. It was make or break time. If Bowman had done his job right the submarine would whisk them to safety beneath the waves. If he hadn't...

"Mr. Bowman, are you certain this boat is good to go."

Bowman threw a line onto *Richard C*'s deck and turned. "Absolutely, sir. Absolutely."

Keyes considered him a long while. There was no turning back now. He gave a slight nod. "Get below."

Bowman broke for the bridge hatch on the conning tower. Tierney and his volunteer dropped through the forward hatch. Only Keyes remained standing on deck. He called to *Richard C*'s pilothouse. "Mr. Rierdon, be at the rendezvous coordinates in two days."

A fresh cigarette in his mouth, Rierdon leaned out and gave a lazy salute. "Aye, Commander."

"Do your best to look inconspicuous."

"Will do," Rierdon said. "Good luck to you."

Keyes turned without responding. Luck would have little to do with success in this matter. Preparation and skill were the primary players. He climbed to the cigarette deck, confident his plan had ample supplies of both. He squeezed through the bridge hatch, and then caught one last glimpse of the brilliant summer morning. Filing the view in memory, he slammed the hatch shut and sealed it closed. The deck had been cleared.

Standing in the conning tower, Keyes questioned the sub's seaworthiness. Sixty years was a long time between dives and, according to Bowman, the tower had been in disrepair when he arrived at the museum. He would make the first dive in a more secure area. He climbed the ladder down into the control room. As he descended he heard Royce, his diving officer, shout the command to stop the engines and switch to battery power.

Feet on the deck now, Keyes surveyed the control room compliment. Laughlin and Cory, two freelancers, manned the plane control wheels. Royce stood behind them. Carson disappeared into the radio room aft. Bowman took position near the wet-side bulkhead beside the helm control wheel, which was manned by a hired hand named Hendricks. Other freelancers manned the remaining dive control stations. All hands were in place.

The turbulent rattle of the diesels disappeared. The engine room crew had shut them down. Bowman seemed to grow more excited with each passing second.

Keyes gave his first order of the voyage. "All ahead two-thirds."

Bowman reached for the intercom box above his head and flicked the switch for the maneuvering room. "All ahead two-thirds."

Two red lights on the Christmas Tree indicated hull openings, but as Keyes watched, one of them flickered out. Just one opening remained. He padded the papers in his breast pocket. "Close main induction."

In the galley a crewman actuated the levers to close the large intake pipe that fed air to the engine room. The last red light went out. The Christmas Tree showed all green. Keyes thought about calling for range and bearing on the approaching coast guard chopper but remembered that the old submarine's SJ radar system could locate aircraft only six miles out. At that range, if they did have a contact, it would be damn near too late to slip away. "Open main vents."

Royce turned. "Sir, we haven't put pressure in the boat yet. What if our hull isn't sealed?"

Keyes smiled. "Then things are going to get real exciting real quick." The answer didn't seem to placate Royce. "Mind your station, Mr. Royce. My XO assures me this boat is ready." Keyes scrutinized Bowman, searching for any flicker of doubt on his face. The XO held firm. Keyes took a breath. "Open main vents."

Bowman nodded, and the crewman at the vent controls went to work actuating valves. Ballast tank vents along the submarine's hull opened and water rushed in, filling the space and weighing *Silversides* heavy in the lake.

Keyes considered the dive. Flooding the ballast tanks would bring the submarine to near neutral buoyancy, but sink her below the waves in a sluggish manner. Perhaps too sluggish. He wanted depth and he wanted it now. "Flood negative tank."

Royce flinched.

The crewman manning the dive manifold hesitated.

Bowman came forward and threw the lever himself.

Water rushed into the large tank in the belly of the submarine. *Silversides* became a rock, and her speed of descent increased. Keyes grinned. In comparison to the nuclear-powered *Hampton*, which he'd gradually driven below the surface dozens of times, *Silversides* felt like a roller coaster.

Royce read the large gauges in front of Laughlin and Cory. "Depth is one-five feet."

From *Richard C's* pilothouse, Rierdon watched the vintage submarine sink below the waves. Only the radar mast and periscope were still visible, and they were dropping away fast. He wondered for an instant if they'd sprung a leak, or if the antiquated air systems were functioning properly. The water here at the Mid-Lake Basin was over three-hundred feet deep. *Silversides* could be spiraling toward the bottom and he'd never know it. Keyes' order to maintain radio silence would keep him in the dark until the rendezvous. The commander had instructed him to wait at the coordinates for three hours, and if *Silversides* didn't appear, he was to assume the worst.

Rierdon took a drag off his cigarette. The radar mast disappeared from view. He shook off the eerie mental image of a submarine reaching crush depth and descended into *Richard C's* lower deck. He reappeared with a fishing pole and planted it in a downrigger on the tug's stern. He plopped into a deck chair and kicked his feet up on the side board.

Keyes noticed he had clenched his fist. He relaxed his fingers. If *Silversides* hadn't begun taking on water yet, chances were she wouldn't, at least for the time being. The old girl was seaworthy after all these years.

"Mr. Royce, rig out bow planes. Make depth one-two-five."

Royce acknowledged, and Cory actuated the controls to unfold the wings from the forward hull. They locked in place and Cory set them to full dive position. *Silversides* slid deeper into the lake. Royce called out their depth. "Three-five feet…Four-zero…Four-five."

Keyes crossed his arms. "Close all vents."

They continued their descent, Royce giving periodic depth readings. The aging hull creaked and moaned with unnerving consistency. Some men stared at the bulkheads as if expecting them to burst open and let the lake inside.

Pleased his labor had gone to good effect, Bowman just smiled.

Keyes paced to the rear of the control room then returned to his starting point.

"Depth is one-one-zero."

"Blow negative tank."

Slow and steady, the depth gauges came to 125 feet. Royce instructed Cory and Laughlin to abate the dive and adjust the trim. He slowed the boat to one-third and fussed with the trim a little more. When satisfied, he turned to Keyes. "We've leveled off at one-two-five feet, sir."

"Very good. Mr. Hendricks, set course for operation area."

Hendricks nodded. "Yes, sir."

He turned the helm wheel to steer the boat to her new heading, dead north.

Aboard *Richard C.*, Rierdon tilted his head back on the deck chair and closed his eyes. The sound of rotors approached. Taking a peek, he confirmed his thought. An HH-65A Dolphin cruised overhead, its cherry red body and white coast guard stripe brilliant in the sunlight. It circled high above the tugboat.

Rierdon sat up and waved.

After a second pass the Dolphin moved on, heading farther out over the lake.

Rierdon smiled and settled back in the chair. *Round one, Owen Keyes.*

NINE

Straits of Mackinac

HYDROPLANING across choppy water, the ferry began its long turn toward Mackinac Island. President Warren McCallum stood on the upper passenger deck with a hand on the forward rail and wind buffeting his thick, gray hair.

Dylan stood alongside, wishing the president had taken a seat on the covered deck below. They were vulnerable up top, but McCallum had made the decision to ride the straits there. Security precautions, no matter how small, should always be taken.

Very few passengers occupied the ferry on this early-morning, weekday trip to the island. A small AARP group and a family of four seemed not to pose too grave a threat. The tourists' casual attire made Dylan feel overdressed. He reached into his pocket and called, "Carney—Ringleader. How's the ride down there?"

Stationed in the wheelhouse below, Gillespie responded. "Educational. I'm learning a bunch about maritime navigation from Thaddeus, our courteous ferry pilot."

Dylan smiled and turned into the wind. "Copy."

The small, green island lay dead ahead. It was a short trip to Mackinac on a hydroplane, only ten minutes. Tomorrow morning would be a different story. It being an election year, Governor Patterson's PR people had put together an event to give his sluggish campaign a shot in the arm. Between nine and ten A.M. all ferry runs to Mackinac would be suspended to clear the way for a ceremonial flotilla to cross from Mackinaw City to the island. Twenty-two governors and their traveling staff, and of course the press pool, would crowd into a dozen vintage sailing ships and classic yachts, and then cross the straits in a convoy to celebrate fifty years of the Governors Association meeting on Mackinac.

The pomp and circumstance, Dylan surmised, was designed to cast a sense of special importance upon Patterson, he being sitting chairman of the association and all. Dylan found the degree to which politicians calculated their moves on one level amusing, on another disturbing. They could use their time and energy on more salient issues than re-election bids. Most of the political elite, however, never made the distinction between their well being and that of their constituents.

Face into the wind, the president wore a rather contemplative expression.

Having been slapped once for prying, Dylan thought better of doing so again. Instead he stood silent, waiting and wondering if the president would speak.

"Water intrigues me," McCallum said after a minute or two. "It always has. I was eighteen when I served my first tour in the navy, and the moment we put out to sea the ocean held my undivided attention." He faced Dylan. "I guess it puts a man in his place. Shows us how insignificant a piece of the creation we are."

"For being insignificant, you sure made quite a commotion in your life."

McCallum chuckled. "Don't be fooled. A man's measure is not always revealed in his public image."

"I've seen a bit of your private self too, sir. I think you're okay there as well."

McCallum received the praise with an uncomfortable smile. He seemed more a humble grandfather than former president of the free world, but then that's always how he seemed. "The world's got it backwards," he said just loud enough to be heard over the wind. "Too many people believe that celebrity status and possession of power define a man's import, but it's really the little things that reveal the measure of his character. Being a good father, a good husband, that's what counts most. That's what matters."

Dylan noted he was 0 for 2 on the 'strong character' checklist.

"It's worth the effort to patch things up with Sarah," McCallum continued. "Even if it doesn't work it's important to know you tried your best. Life's too short to carry regrets. That baggage gets heavier as the years go by."

"I haven't given up yet, but it takes more than one to make these things work."

Standing there at the handrail, silence settled between them, Dylan trying to glimpse his future, McCallum recounting his past.

The ferry had covered much of the distance to the island. Mackinac's shoreline sprawled wide on the horizon. Shining bright against the deep green of surrounding trees, the Grand Hotel's immense white colonnade stood majestic on a hill west of the crescent bay. To the north, Fort Mackinac watched over the half-filled marina from its limestone bluff.

Thaddeus throttled back the ferry's engines and slowed for a smooth approach.

As they drifted, Dylan noticed McCallum suddenly looked his age. He seemed a tired, old man. "If I may say so, sir, you sound like someone who knows a thing or two about regrets." He made a quick check on the passengers. All clear. "I can't imagine why that is. Strong marriage, successful career, you've got the bases covered."

McCallum turned sage on him. "That's the funny thing about life. Even the most considered or advised of men manage to get saddled with one regret or another. Hell, on rare occasions I even regret having been president."

"You regret—" The comment took him back. "Why?"

The ferry entered the marina, and McCallum stared at the water as if his eight years in office were flashing through his thoughts in thirty seconds. "As president," he said slowly, "each decision you make affects the lives of so many. And over the course of a term you make thousands of decisions. There are times when that responsibility becomes an obscene burden."

Dylan didn't reply.

The ferry glided past the bare masts and furrowed sails of ships in port.

"Is Governor Patterson waiting for you on the island?"

McCallum laughed. "Where's your political sense? Patterson won't show until tomorrow. And when he does, he'll be on deck of the lead vessel in that flotilla. He'll get three days worth of photo ops and sound bites out of this event."

"Right. What was I thinking?"

"Don't know. You've spent enough time around politicians to know how they operate."

"They? Are you excluding yourself or just speaking in the third person?"

Another laugh. "You tune your ear to every word. If you leave the Service you've got a future as a lawyer."

Thaddeus maneuvered the ferry into her berth at the east end of the marina. A small crowd of people had gathered there, apparently tipped off to the president's unannounced hour of arrival. State troopers had set up a rope barrier that led from the pier to the white, Victorian-style welcome center. Uniformed officers lined the path. Dylan called for Gillespie to begin disembarking the lower level passengers, and then asked the AARP group and the family on the upper level to head below. A few cameras clicked in the crowd on the pier.

McCallum looked down at the people looking at him, giving them a polite smile and accompanying wave at just the right moments.

Down near the entry arch of the welcome center stood an old man with a familiar face. Dressed in a dark blue suit and a light blue tie, hands fixed to his waist, he watched the passengers disembark. His short, white hair seemed to glow in the bright sun. An all-business expression on his face, he scanned the ferry until he found the president on the upper level.

"Hells bells," McCallum said. "My favorite senator is here to greet me."

Dylan counted troopers on the dock, made sure the full complement was there. "That sounded facetious, sir."

McCallum nodded toward the welcome center. "It was."

For twenty-five years Senator Burke had been a political thorn in McCallum's side. Opposing party, opposing personalities, it seemed they were born to butt heads. The problem with this arrangement now was that McCallum had retired from active politics while Burke kept at it hot and heavy. The senator's appearance at the president's arrival signaled that the visit to Mackinac would not be as relaxing as Dylan had hoped. "Maybe he's here to bury the hatchet."

"Good Lord, Dylan, it's your job to see that he doesn't."

"Time to go, sir."

They filed down the stairs to the lower passenger compartment and made their way forward, exiting onto the gangplank.

Towering over the crowd, Gillespie stood guard on the pier.

Dylan led the president into the dreaded rope line situation.

Straight faced and flexing their authority, the state troopers made sure the spectators didn't encroach upon the path. Dylan moved his gaze through the crowd. Public gatherings unnerved him above all else. The ever-changing dynamics and the unknown elements twisted his stomach into knots.

Most faces were smiling, just trying to catch a glimpse of their former leader. But that guy, black hair, sour expression, why wasn't he smiling? What was he thinking? Sweat formed in Dylan's palms. He kept his eyes on the unsmiling man, taking note of body language: Hands at side, intense stare at the passing procession. Sadeed's slug jostled in Dylan's pocket. He hit the transmit button. "Carney, eyes left. Second row back. Male, black hair, red T-shirt."

"Got him."

Passing by, Dylan kept focus on the suspicious man, but his peripheral vision searched wildly. *Anyone else need watching?* Movement to the left drew his gaze back. Another man, short and blond, spoke into the suspicious guy's ear. They both began laughing, and the menace he had sensed vanished. His heart settled. *I hate crowds.*

Dylan in front and Gillespie behind, McCallum strode down the roped-off path, occasionally shaking a hand or giving a pleasant greeting. Just ahead, Senator Charles Burke waited. When the president came within earshot, Burke flashed his well-worn smile, extended a hand. "Mr. President, good to see you again."

Dylan wondered how the senator could choke those words out and remain smiling.

"Likewise, Charles," McCallum said. "In the same spirit, I might add."

Falling in step side by side, the old statesmen headed inside the welcome center. Senator Burke leaned close to McCallum. "Still pandering to Michigan constituents for handing you the presidency, I see."

McCallum scoffed. "Still red-assed for loosing three recounts, I see."

"I had the votes, Warren. I won the popular vote."

"You lost the electoral vote. Those are the rules we play by."

Burked cocked his smile. "Thank God for a conservative Supreme Court. Eh?"

"Thank God for judicial common sense."

They walked beneath the green-shingled overhang and through the open set of double doors. Voices echoed inside the empty room with a concrete floor. Putting hands in pockets, McCallum shook his head. "What the hell did you come all the way out here for, to let me know a sixteen-year-old grudge is still rotting your gut? Should've saved yourself the trip."

"No," Burke said through a smile that looked like a pit bull bearing its teeth. "To let the people see that no hard feelings exist between two old antagonists."

McCallum nodded at the crowd outside. "How 'bout I go back out there and let them know you're still a sore loser."

Burke laughed. "You wouldn't, it's beneath you. Too petty."

Dylan thought it a shame Burke's comment about the president happened to be accurate. It'd be good for someone to take a shot at the sour senator. Dylan had friends in the Service assigned to the Beltway and he'd heard stories. Though Burke had somehow convinced his constituents that he was clean and fair, insider talk in DC painted him a dirty player on the Hill.

McCallum seemed tired of the discussion already. "What are you really here for, Charles? I can't believe it's simply an image-building visit."

"Of course not, I still work for the American people," he said with a rehearsed cadence slipping into his voice, "and I have a few bills coming to the floor for a vote. My proposed restructuring of the telecommunications regulatory agency and the Social Security Solvency act to be specific. Tomorrow there will be twenty-two governors here from twenty-two states. You know the game. Win the support of some of these men and their constituents just might do the same. It's a lot easier for representatives to vote 'yes' on a bill if they know it has widespread support from the people."

"True, but if a piece of legislation stinks, no measure of campaigning can save it."

Burke took offense. "Are you saying these bills are flawed?"

"That's putting it nicely."

"I authored the telecom act and co-authored the solvency act."

"Well now, I think we're getting to the root of the problem."

"You've been out of the game too long, Warren. America needs these bills to pass."

"America needs big brother out of their life and out of their check books."

"Less government and lower taxes, battle cry of the GOP." Burke let out a derisive cackle. "You Republican's talk support for the middle class, but when it comes time to legislate the wealthiest one percent reaps the rewards."

"Bullshit!" McCallum huffed. "Look, we've been having this argument for a quarter century and I've just about had it. Let's just agree to disagree, okay?"

Burke wanted to continue but the president waved him to silence.

The general public was restricted from entering the welcome center, so only a sparse collection of police, Mackinac officials, and press people milled about the open room bounded by white walls and crown molding. A group of newspaper photographers set their sights on McCallum and Burke and headed over. Dylan and Gillespie held them at bay. Before the first shutter snapped Senator Burke had an arm around McCallum and a smile on his face. Cameras flashed and McCallum leaned toward his long lost friend. "You owe me for this one," he said.

"Oh, I owe you for more than this, Warren."

The reporters initiated an impromptu press conference and Burke and McCallum rolled with it for a few minutes. Dylan noted how easily they slipped into campaign mode. It wasn't long before one of the reporters broached the only subject they were all interested in asking about.

"Senator Burke," the Detroit News guy said. "You and President McCallum ran against each other in the most controversial presidential election in American history. It was decided right here in Michigan, a state you both call home. You had the edge in the national popular vote, Senator, but President McCallum won the electoral victory. Now with sixteen years hindsight, how do you feel about the result?"

Burke paused and flashed his cocked smile before answering.

Being a rather astute interpreter of faces and body language, Dylan saw in Senator Burke a man about ready to lunge at the reporter and strangle the life out of him. But in true political fashion, Burke quickly erased any hint of discontent from his face.

"President McCallum and I played a part in a very important chapter in America's history. We proved the constitution drafted two-hundred and fifty years ago is strong enough to survive the most divisive of crises. We all came through the ordeal with our dignity and principals intact and the country, I believe, is stronger for it."

"Yes, Senator," the reporter said, "but how do you feel?"

Burke set a hand on McCallum's shoulder. "I feel the president we elected, twice, served us wonderfully. And I also feel that the course my career took after the election was...well, I wouldn't change it if I could. I chair the Senate Armed Services Committee and the Anti-Terrorist Intelligence Committee and am making contributions to this nation in ways I never thought I could. I'm very content with the outcome."

Dylan concentrated on not laughing. *As soon as this Q and A is over,* he thought, *Senator Charles Burke will be throwing down antacid tablets like a madman.*

"President McCallum," another reporter said. "In retrospect, how much did the fallout from the election controversy impact the way you progressed through your first term?"

"Not significantly," McCallum answered. "I won the office playing by the rules of the land. The founding fathers were pretty smart folks. They knew what they were doing when they designed our government and electoral process. But keep this in mind. The day we stop consulting the constitution for guidance is the day this nation will begin to crumble beneath our feet."

The questions kept coming for a little while longer, but the press soon satisfied their appetite and withdrew. Glad to be free from one another, McCallum and Burke parted ways.

"I'm looking forward to your speech tomorrow," Senator Burke said as he turned to leave the welcome center. "I imagine it will be the highlight of the day."

"I'd thank you if I thought you meant it." McCallum tried to get a read on him. "You seem happier in your misery today than when we last met. Could it be that you've finally begun to leave the past behind?"

"Perhaps," Burke said, a hint of his crooked smile appearing. "Perhaps."

Muskegon, MI
Great Lakes Naval Memorial and Museum

Rebecca Matthis parked her Impala next to the white police cruiser in the museum's lot. A rotund police officer and a red-haired man were talking on the concrete dock. A dingy, yellow fork truck sat next to them. She got out of the car, but as soon as her heel hit the ground she cursed. She hadn't planned on going into the field today and she was dressed for the office. She straightened her plum blazer, brushed bagel crumbs from her skirt, and headed toward the men.

Sergeant Jasper Cotter and Lanny Stevens heard her approach.

Cotter noted the empty Impala behind her. He put on a big, welcome grin. "Who might you be, Miss?"

Having her credentials in hand already, she flashed him her Bureau ID. "Special Agent Matthis, with the Det—" She stopped short. "With the Grand Rapids office."

Cotter's grin receded. "You out here alone?"

Rebecca stopped in front of him and threw a sharp glare over the rim of her glasses. "That's Agent Matthis to you, Sergeant, and, yes, I'm here alone. Is there a problem with that?"

"No," Cotter said after a thoughtful pause. "Just surprised they'd send a lady like you out without…a partner."

"Hell, Jasper," Lanny said. "What year are you living in? Just work with her and get my damned submarine back."

Rebecca crossed her arms. "Yes, Jasper, drop your chauvinism and let's get his damned submarine back."

Cotter shrugged, and then extended his hand. "Good to meet you, Agent Matthis." They shook. "This here is Lanny Stevens, museum curator. He came in this morning and found his baby gone."

Lanny was staring at her in deep thought.

"Mr. Stevens?"

"You look real familiar," Lanny said.

"I don't think we've ever met."

"No, no, no, I got it. You're that FBI woman who found that kidnapped girl. I saw you on the news last week."

She exhaled, checked the gravel. "Yes, that was me."

"Good job."

"Thank you, Mr. Stevens."

"Too bad you didn't put those bastards in the ground."

"Right." Rebecca bit her lip. The empty berth lay just ahead. She walked between the two men. "Is this where you kept the submarine?"

"Yes," Lanny said. "For fifteen years."

"*Silversides*, right?"

"Correct." Lanny hobbled over. "She's Gato class. Third most successful submarine in World War II. She sent over ninety-thousand tons of Japanese steel to the bottom."

Rebecca half-heard the history lesson as she surveyed the museum grounds. "Is there anything else missing? Valuables from the museum? Money?"

Lanny shielded his eyes from the sun. "Just the props, but what the hell, they go with the submarine, right?"

"The props?" She pondered that. "Of course they're gone too. Weren't they attached to the sub?"

"Naw." Lanny kicked a stone toward the empty propeller mounts across the lot. "Can't have a functioning warship on the Great Lakes, so we keep the props on display over there."

She considered the mounts. "Does having the propellers detached classify the submarine as non-functioning?"

"More or less. Her engines and diving systems are kept inoperable too. Guess the collection of things de-fangs her enough to satisfy the treaty."

Rebecca noted the fork truck on the edge of the lot. A pair of tracks in the gravel ran from the truck to the empty propeller mounts. "How heavy are those propellers, Mr. Stevens?"

"Heavy enough it'd take three men and a boy to carry each one." She smirked at the image.

Cotter considered the tracks as well. He seemed to be mulling over the crime scene in a contemplative way that only law officers do.

"This is why you put the call in to the FBI, isn't it, Sergeant?"

Cotter shifted his eyes toward her and gave a curt nod. "Why take the props unless you're gonna use 'em?"

The small town sergeant had scored some points with Rebecca. *You're not as obtuse as your social graces indicate.*

Lanny's face twisted in confusion. "What do you mean 'use 'em?' I told you we keep the diesels inoperable."

"Can you confirm, first hand, that the engines could not have run yesterday?" she asked.

"Sure." Lanny stopped to think. "Maybe...Shit, I can't say without a doubt. We fired up the engines Memorial weekend, then like every other year we broke 'em down again. But I haven't inspected them real close since then."

"Lanny," Cotter said, a bit agitated. "Is there anything else you're not sure about? Was there a magazine full of ammunition and a load of torpedoes aboard?"

Lanny limped toward Cotter in a huff. "Now what the hell would I be doing with live ammunition aboard *Silversides?*"

"Watch your knee, Lanny."

"Never had live ammo. Ever!" He wobbled to a stop. "You're starting to sound like someone's planning some serious shit, Jasper. What the hell happened to your college prank theory?"

"It's still the most likely answer," Cotter said. "But we've got to consider something else might be happening."

Lanny exploded. "Something else? *Silversides* can't dive. Mark-14 torpedoes haven't been manufactured in over fifty years. And even if someone did reattach the props, they'd need a crew of World War II veterans just to get around."

Rebecca adjusted her glasses and came forward. "Have you inspected the diving systems or any other critical equipment aboard the submarine recently, Mr. Stevens?"

"Aw, come on. There's no way *Silversides* is tooling around Lake Michigan right now."

She pressed him with a probing stare.

"I can practically guarantee it." He said it with a healthy measure of assurance.

She made eye contact with Sergeant Cotter, then Lanny. "How many people work at the museum, or more to the point, on the submarine?"

"A dozen or more," Lanny said. "I've got historical society members, coast guard officers, and navy guys, active and retired, who volunteer their time to work on her."

"Any of them quirky and capable enough to try something like this?"

"Of course not. The guys who come here do it for the love of the boat. Hell, Choppy reveres *Silversides* as much as I do. He's been coming in every day for a couple months straight now…"

Lanny's voice faded.

Rebecca raised an eyebrow. "Choppy? What about this Choppy person?"

"Nothing really. It's just that it's Monday and he hasn't showed up yet. Not like him."

She latched on. "Is Choppy his surname or a nickname or what?"

"It's a nickname…I think." Lanny scratched his chin. "Come to think of it, I never learned his real name. He's always been Choppy." His face fell as if he'd just remembered a mistake he'd made. "He locked up for me last night."

"You must have invested a fair amount of trust in him."

He nodded. "Guess I did." He stood there silent for a long while. "If I *had* to finger one guy who might think of swiping *Silversides*, it would be Chop."

"Why is that?"

"The six months he's been with us he's donated more time and money than all the other volunteers combined. Diehard dedication to the boat."

"You know anything else about him?"

"No. Chop kept the personal stuff pretty tight. He'd only talk about the submarine and where he was working on a given day, but there's one thing I do know. He's ex-navy. Told me once. Served a long time too."

"You have any photographs of him or some form of ID? Perhaps his Social Security number or maybe his driver's license number."

Lanny hedged and shifted weight off his bad knee. "Well, he

joined us pretty much on a handshake. I might have a picture of him, though. I'll check our scrapbook." He thought it over for a minute. "Now hold on. That coast guard guy said *Silversides* was being towed into the lake when he caught sight of her, so we know she didn't leave under her own power. I think you and Jasper are getting a little ahead of yourselves."

"Like Sergeant Cotter said, we have to check all possibilities." She looked to the big-bellied officer. "How long has the coast guard been on this?"

Cotter bumped his Smokey Bear hat with a fist. "They've been searching for a little over an hour now. A whole lot of nothing to report so far. I've got patrolmen working the shoreline, but they haven't come up with diddley-squat yet either."

She walked to the propeller mounts and studied the ground around them. "Whoever did this didn't do it alone. There's a bunch of imprints in the dirt here." She scrutinized the steel column that held the propellers upright. "Maybe we can lift some prints off these mounts. I'll get forensics out here."

Lanny stared at the empty berth.

"Mr. Stevens, I want to speak with all the museum volunteers. Do you have a way to contact them?"

"Most of them." He turned from the channel. "Chop was the only outsider. He didn't hang much with the rest."

"Will you go look for that photograph of Choppy, Mr. Stevens?"

"Yeah." He limped toward the museum office. "Back in a minute."

She approached Cotter. "What's your feel for this, Sergeant?"

Cotter tilted his head toward her. "You mean what's my gut say?"

She nodded.

"Yanking that sub out of here seems like a whole lot of work for pranksters."

"We're on the same page there."

"But Lanny's damned sure the thing is a dead chunk of steel. So what's the point?"

"Exactly." She brushed hair from her face. "Once we identify who, the 'why' will fall into place."

Cotter put a hand on his girth and spit on the ground. "I hope we don't find out why *before* we find out who." He kicked some dirt over the saliva. "Hell, maybe Lanny's right about us. Coast guard will likely catch sight of the sub before the day's out, drifting in the lake with a bunch of drunken Western Michigan boys on deck. That'd blow our ominous theory to shit, wouldn't it?"

"I wouldn't mind." She lifted her cell phone from her blazer pocket and dialed the Grand Rapids RA office. She connected with Gordon Jennings' phone.

"Agent Matthis," the upbeat, nasally voice said. "What's the story with the sub?"

"It is indeed gone, sir."

"Leads?"

"Few. The coast guard is searching. I'm going to interview museum workers. And I need a forensics team on site."

"What do you think; do we have cause for concern?"

Despite the lack of hard evidence, she had to quell the instinct to say "yes." According to the museum curator, the single most knowledgeable person in regards to the submarine, there was no danger. Unarmed and crippled, *Silversides* could only be classified as a big piece of flotsam. Whoever took it probably just wanted the quirky notoriety that would certainty arise when the submarine is found and towed back to port.

But Sergeant Cotter's words intruded on her rational thoughts. *Why take the props if you're not gonna use 'em?*

"Agent Matthis?"

She reminded herself to stick with the facts. No need to make a rash decision on too little evidence. That's how she ended up in Grand Rapids. She cleared her throat. "At this time I have no reason to believe the missing submarine poses a serious threat." But as a caveat she added, "There are, however, too many questions that need answering before we discount the matter completely."

"Keep at it," Jennings said, "and keep me informed." He signed off and hung up.

Standing with the phone still against her ear, she realized the submarine case had hooked her. She'd already begun to build a theory. In it, a highly skilled group had set their sights on the vintage warship. Driven by some bizarre motivation, they refurbish the submarine's primary systems and disappear into Lake Michigan. To do what? According to Lanny's vehement argument the submarine is unarmed, right?

After a moment's consideration the whole idea sounded outlandish.

She dropped the phone into her pocket. "Sergeant, you think the

Guard will find the submarine by noon?"

Cotter looped a finger under his gun belt. "If I was a gamblin' man I'd say yes."

She crossed her arms and considered the lake beyond the channel. "I don't like to gamble."

- TEN -

Aboard *Silversides*

OWEN KEYES walked the corridor between the officers' cabins and ducked through the hatchway into *Silversides* control room. He took a deep breath. Diesel fumes and decades of must hung in the air. He could already sense the early stages of oxygen depletion, heaviness in the air, his lungs not getting quite the fill they were only hours ago. He knew, of course, that their sealed sliver of steel would quickly go stale, but he cursed just the same. With her nuclear reactor and air purification systems, *Hampton* could stay under for months while maintaining a fresh, comfortable environment. Not so with a forties era vessel.

Secondary crewman stood in relief of the first watch compliment. Bowman, Royce and the others were resting in the crew compartment. Keyes needed them sharp come crunch time. This stretch of the voyage would be their only chance to sleep.

It was seven in the evening. They'd been submerged nearly twelve hours and had covered over ninety miles, farther than he thought they'd get with the incomplete battery charge that they started with.

A crisp voice emerged from Bowman's new intercom system (ICS). "Conn—Maneuvering. Batteries are near flat line."

Keyes walked to the comm. box behind Helmsman's Watch and flicked the Maneuvering Room switch. "Acknowledged. Standby."

Lying in a bunk and staring at the curved ceiling, Dominic tried to relax. He always found it difficult to get any meaningful sleep before an OP. Across from him Six Pack sat upright, stubby fingers squeezing his bunk's metal frame. Below, John Tierney stretched out on his rack, arms folded back under his head and eyes closed. He looked to be sleeping but Dominic knew he was still awake, listening to the sounds and voices around him.

Twelve other men, mercenaries in Owen Keyes' charge, lay in the crew compartment awaiting their part in the OP to arrive.

Across the narrow aisle, Robert Bowman lay propped up on his elbow, running a hand through his gnarled beard. "Hey, Dominic," he said through a mischievous smile, "you hear about the new Italian tire?"

Dominic rolled to his side, sniffled.

"Dago through rain, dago through snow, and when dago flat, dago *wop, wop, wop*."

Bemused, Dominic gave him a cold stare. "How have you stayed alive so long talking shit like that?"

"Where's your sense of humor, Dom?"

"Maybe I left it back on shore with my better judgment." Dominic sat up and swung his legs off the side of the bunk. He leaned forward on his knees and puffed his chest like a bull. "Steer clear and keep your mouth shut, or I'll shut it for you."

Bowman feigned wide-eyed fear. "Ooooh. Are we getting nervous?"

"No, we're just getting tired of you."

"Careful. That sounds like insubordination."

"Cut the bullshit," Tierney said. "Both of you." He fixed on Bowman. "Shouldn't you be in Officers Country?"

"No, I like to mingle with the enlisted rabble."

Tierney settled back on his pillow. "Keyes pulled us together to get a job done and that's what we're going to do. Biting at each others heel doesn't do a damn bit of good."

Dominic glared at Bowman. "I hear you, John; it's my friend who needs a fresh attitude."

Bowman gestured to Six Pack. "Hey, Dominic, your boy doesn't look too good." He laughed. "Better tend to his frailties."

Six Pack was sitting up, pale and sweaty, hands clamped to his bunk.

Dominic turned. "What's the matter?"

Six Pack gave a weak smile. "I guess I'm a little more claustrophobic than I thought. I did all right at first, but the longer we stay down here...I mean, every space is small, and it's like we're in a tomb."

Bowman belched a hardy laugh. "What the hell did you expect, Ice Pack, windows in a submarine?"

"Ignore him," Dominic said. "Get your mind on something else. Maybe they can use some help down in the engine room."

Six Pack agreed.

Keyes' voice came through the ICS. "Primary crew report to Conn."

Bowman hopped to his feet. "Finally, back to work."

Dominic eyed him. "What's going on?"

"We've been down a while. I'd say we're headed to the surface for a few hours."

The news relieved Six Pack. "I can really use a few minutes out of this can."

"Sit tight," Dominic told him, "just sit tight."

Bowman arrived in the control room. Carson was in the radio room, monitoring the ancient hydrophones and sonar equipment. Dive Officer Royce nodded a greeting. Keyes and his command crew had already ascended the ladder into the conning tower.

Bowman joined them in the cramped compartment. He approached Keyes.

"Batteries?"

Keyes nodded. "We need some surface time."

"There's a lot of daylight left up there."

"We won't be staying up long. We need to bank just enough juice to give us a short dive, one that will carry us into nightfall. Once it's dark, we'll make way on the surface."

Bowman acknowledged and called through the ICS. "Sonar—Conn, any traffic above?"

"No, sir," Carson replied. "It's quiet up there, as far as I can tell with this antique equipment."

Keyes said, "Periscope depth."

Royce barked an order, and Laughlin and Cory worked the plane control wheels. *Silversides* climbed from the depths on a gradual angle of ascent. At sixty-five feet she leveled out. "At PD," Royce announced.

Keyes raised the search periscope, watched the shaft rise through the lifting collar, then settled behind the eyepiece. Grabbing the control handles, he peered into the scope. He selected a fitting filter for the waning daylight and began scanning the area. His initial view to the north looked clear, nothing but water and sky for as far as he could see. He rotated the periscope counter-clockwise, walking in a small circle. "Give me a radar sweep."

Bowman relayed the order.

"Sky looks clear," Carson said. "Nothing up there for six whole miles. Jeez, how did we ever win the war with this suck-ass scope?

"No one else had anything better, Mr. Carson." Keyes continued his circular arc. When he reached dead east a small white vessel came into view. "We've got company." He studied the image. "Looks like a fishing boat, drifting with lines in the water." He hit the range finder button on the periscope's control handle. "A thousand yards to starboard, bearing zero-six-zero. Could be a thirty-footer." He lowered the periscope.

"Did they make us?" Bowman said.

"Can't tell." Keyes stood silent, calculating.

"Why don't we find a shallow section of lake bed and rest on the bottom 'til dark?"

"Can't afford it. We don't have the juice to search for a shallow, and we don't have the time. We'll lose three—four hours waiting on darkness. We won't make it to the OP area in time."

Bowman tucked his hair behind his ear. "Right. Plus we don't know if that fishing boat spotted the periscope—They've probably heard about *Silversides* disappearance. Somebody might put two and two together."

"Can't take that chance," Keyes said. "Slow to one-third. Mr. Hendricks, bring us about, course zero-six-zero. Come up on his starboard." Keyes turned from the periscope, a frown on his face. "Can't take the chance, Robert."

Bowman nodded. "Understood, Commander."

Uneasiness simmered in the crew quarters. Collectively the men had concluded that the authorities were surely hunting for the submarine by now, and most of them were sitting or standing instead of resting on their backs any longer. Conversation floated in waves of whispers.

Dominic sat on his rack, facing Six Pack. The imposing Italian knew the frustration hours of waiting could breed better than most aboard. Foot soldiers in the belly of a submarine grow anxious quickly. He'd played this part before, during the Gulf Conflict, and again in the Mediterranean. *Lord, get my boots on dry land where I can determine my own fate.*

Yes, he knew this feeling, but he had to concede that John Tierney knew it just as well. Tierney, however, seemed the only one disinterested in the buzz around the quarters. He still lay peaceful on his bunk.

Dominic, on the other hand, had a difficult time psyching himself for combat. Combat? Keyes' mission, his crusade, didn't resemble any combat situation he had ever known. It was all in one's perception, he had decided. Nevertheless, he had his orders and would follow them like a good soldier. Funny thing was, ever since joining with Keyes, he had been feeling less and less like a soldier and more and more like...

"Mr. Tierney." Keyes voice through the ICS again. "We've come across some company. Prepare your squad to go topside and welcome them to the neighborhood."

Tierney rolled from his bunk and stood beside the intercom box. He keyed the switch. "You want a clean sweep, Commander?"

A long stretch of silence elapsed. "Yes, Mr. Tierney, a clean sweep."

Tierney turned from the box. "Team-A, get your gear prepped. Topside in five."

A handful of men in the forward section of the crew quarters reached for their gear bags and pulled out Heckler and Kotch submachine guns and ammunition clips. They loaded their weapons and checked them for firing. Tierney eyed Six Pack. "You should come along, Mr. Martin. It'll get your head in the game." He flashed a devious smile then walked to his men.

Six Pack picked up his head and brightened somewhat. He moved to hop off his bunk but Dominic placed a powerful hand on his shoulder. His mentor wore a grim expression.

"You don't want any part in this," Dominic warned. "Stay put."

They'd left the Charlevoix docks at seven in the morning in the old twenty-eight foot cabin cruiser. Captain Rodney Boggs had run his charter boat service for eleven years and had the chart numbers to all his choice hot spots etched in his mind. Sometimes trolling, sometimes drifting, Boggs nearly always had his clients' lines in the water. And when they weren't fishing they'd be talking tackle, women, and sports. Rodney Boggs knew his trade well. He'd noticed over the years that his clientele consisted primarily of lawyers, engineers and autoworkers, not necessarily in that order. On this outing he had one of each, a Mr. Simmons, a Mr. Kelly, and a Mr. Furst, respectively.

They'd had a successful day and Boggs was five minutes from heading in. He stood in the cabin, taking a short break from his duties as host. Kelly, the young IT man from Southfield, came in looking for a first aid kit to treat a knife cut sustained while cutting free a tangled line. Scratching at his long, bushy sideburns, Boggs directed him to a cabinet below the navigation console.

Bending over to open the cabinet, Kelly glanced at the fish-finder scope at eye level. The entire display suddenly blurred with an immense contact. It took a few moments for the screen to clear. "Jeez," he said. "A freaking whale just swam by."

Boggs lit a cigarette, scrutinized the display. "Never seen that before."

Kelly kept watching the scope. "This thing on the fritz?"

Boggs checked the dial settings and indicator lights. "Looks alright."

Someone astern shouted, sounded like Simmons. "Check this out!"

Boggs and Kelly piled out of the cabin. They stood next to Simmons and Furst.

Thirty yards off their starboard bow, a large gray structure rose out of the lake, long and sleek and menacing. Water rolled off its skin and the object took shape. The unmistakable profile of a submarine loomed before them.

"What the hell is this, Boggs?" Furst said.

"A submarine, Furst. Use your eyes."

Before the water had fully run off the deck, the submarine's forward hatch flew open and a tall man with short red hair climbed out. Dressed in a black shirt and jeans, he had what looked to be a holster on his waist. Four men clad in dark clothing followed him out, each carrying…no. Automatic weapons? Boggs' eye twitched.

"Didn't know the navy had vessels on the Great Lakes," Simmons said absently.

"They don't." Boggs watched the four men line up beside the red-haired man.

Kelly rocked on his heels. "This a movie shoot or a reserve exercise or something?"

"No." Boggs instincts went afire.

The red-haired man shouted across the water, "Any luck?"

He drew a pistol from the holster.

What's going on? Boggs looked to the radio inside the cabin.

A loud report, a gunshot, rolled across the waves.

Simmons fell backwards, landing against the sideboard, a splatter pattern of blood on his chest. Kelly and Furst stood stunned, terrified.

Cover! Cover! Damn it, get to cover! Boggs dropped. The four dark-clad men aboard the submarine cut loose with their automatic weapons. Bullets pounded the fishing boat. Fiberglass popped and cracked

and split. Glass around the cabin shattered. Someone screamed.
Boggs didn't look back. He crawled on his stomach, frantic to reach
the cabin. A round drilled through the hull and razed his back. He
kept on, reaching for the radio. He touched the console and switched
to the emergency channel. A bullet tore through his forearm. He
screamed and pulled the mic down with his other hand. Gunfire was
tearing the boat apart.

Three bloody bodies lay astern.

This can't be happening. He called for help, cried for help.

And then the unrelenting barrage found him.

John Tierney raised a hand to quiet the gunfire. His men let off
their triggers and the air turned deathly silent. The bullet-riddled fishing boat turned slowly about in the swells. Nothing moved aboard her.
Tierney surveyed the scene, appraising their work with the concerned
eye of a professional. He reached for the mic draped over his shoulder
and keyed the switch. "Neighborhood secured."

Bowman and two crewmen emerged from below and swarmed
over the anti-aircraft gun on the cigarette deck. They completed the
rebuild they'd started earlier that day in quick fashion and loaded a
drum of 20mm ammunition. Bowman stood behind the weapon and
turned it about, angling it down at the lifeless fishing boat. He fired a
long burst. Amid the heavy rattle of gunfire, he swept the 20mm
across the fishing boat's broadside. Large sections of fiberglass hull
disintegrated. She listed hard to starboard, eventually rolled keel up,
then disappeared beneath the surface.

Commander Keyes stood on the submarine's bridge, watching debris bob on the water. A cooler, a tackle box, life jackets, symbols of a
relaxing day on the lake. Keyes spat a stream of chew over the side,
closed his eyes, opened them on the scene again. A part of him wished
the aftermath would have vanished. He thought about his father, and
how he'd said that the men who provide liberty and justice were the
only ones who knew their true cost. He galvanized himself on that
thought. Those unfortunate men on that fishing boat were simply collateral damage in the war he waged. There would be more to come. A
lot more.

Muskegon

Rebecca Matthis sat at the picnic table outside the maritime museum, rolling a bottle of water on its edge and staring at the photograph of Choppy that Lanny Stevens had found. Restlessness descended with the falling sun. The coast guard had searched the entire day for *Silversides* and had come up empty handed.

She had just spoken with the last museum volunteer. After a full day of interviews no new information had come to light. From everyone's perspective the submarine could not possibly be functioning as a submarine, and Choppy was a single-minded loner.

The forensics team fared a little better. Though the propeller mounts came up clean, the techs did manage to lift a print off the fork truck's steering wheel. And Rebecca digitized the photograph of Choppy with her laptop scanner and gave the investigators a copy to take back for analysis. If Lanny was right, Chop had a navy record. Perhaps they'd get lucky and find a match with the print, or the photo, in a military database and get a real name.

She set the photograph on the picnic table and cracked open the water bottle. In the picture Bowman had shoulder-length hair and a scruffy beard. He certainly didn't look navy. As she took a sip of water, the museum door opened behind her.

Lanny Stevens hobbled out, distraught, and took a seat across from her. He glanced at the empty submarine berth as he had a hundred times that day. "They sank her, didn't they." He looked back to Rebecca. "Whoever these bastards are, they sank my submarine."

She swished a mouthful of water around then swallowed it. "Now why would anyone go through the effort of taking her out of port just to sink her?"

"Why do people steal cars and crash them into trees?" He waved a dismissive hand. "There're a sorry lot of people out there. No respect for others property, or the past, or even their future." He exhaled his disgust. "Bastards."

"We don't know that she's been scuttled. I wouldn't lose hope yet."

He considered Choppy's photo. "This is the first day in over a month that Chop hasn't shown up. He just might have something to do with this. That'd really disappoint me."

"You like him?"

"Sure. We seemed to understand each other. You know, old navy men, common bond, that kind of horse shit." He strummed his fingertips on the picnic table. "Has Jasper checked back with you yet?"

She shook her head. "He's touching base with the first shift patrolmen as they come off duty at the station house. No word yet."

The last of the crime scene techs had left and the museum grounds were deserted, quiet. There wasn't much more she could do there, and she really needed something to eat. She stood. "I'm heading back to Grand Rapids. You have my card with my cell on it. If you think of anything that may help the investigation, or if Choppy calls or shows up, call me immediately."

Lanny agreed.

She left him sitting at the picnic table and climbed in her car. After a short stop at a drive-through, she headed for the RA office.

It bothered her. Like Sergeant Cotter had supposed, the coast guard should have spotted a three-hundred foot, cigar-shaped barge without a problem. Perhaps Lanny's fear that *Silversides* had been sunk was true. That theory, however, didn't fit her thoughts on the matter. They took the props. Choppy, dedicated volunteer and long-time navy man, had vanished. And even though everyone said the submarine's dive and propulsion systems were inoperable, no one would go out on a limb and personally guarantee it. Lanny came close, but even he waffled. Without that confirmation it remained a possibility that *Silversides* was staying out of sight not because she'd been sunk, but because she was submerged.

Then that stumbling block tripped her up again. Why? Motive. Are the thieves really just taking the sub for a joyride to crash it into a tree, so to speak, later? What else could they do with it?

She nearly missed her exit and turned off at the last second, squealing the tires on the curved ramp. The time from Muskegon to Grand Rapids had breezed by, much like the day had. She stopped at the traffic light at the bottom of the off ramp.

She hadn't been to Grand Rapids in three years and tried to reacquaint herself with the downtown district, which was somewhat cozy in size. She turned onto Michigan Street.

After working in Detroit for so long, Grand Rapids seemed smaller than she remembered. In comparison, the office buildings were fewer in number and not quite as tall, but the streets connecting them were cleaner and better maintained. She came upon Federal Square and turned right onto Ottawa. The underground parking garage entrance came up fast, next to the ugly, orange abstract sculpture sitting in Delaney Plaza. She pulled into the parking garage at quarter past seven. The garage was nearly deserted, as was the lobby of the Federal building at 110 Michigan. Lugging her laptop over a shoulder, she flashed her creds to the night security guard and identified herself as the new agent on the block. He gave her directions on how to get to her section. She rode the elevator up.

When the doors opened she came face to face with a short man plagued by severe pattern baldness. He smiled, and the lines on his thin face deepened. "Agent Matthis, I presume," he said in a nasally voice. "You're showing yourself quite the workhorse."

"Gordon Jennings?"

"Correct." He extended his hand and they shook. "I just about gave up on seeing you in here today, especially after the news report."

Rebecca adjusted the laptop on her shoulder and stepped from the elevator. "News report?"

"Yes, at six o'clock. It made radio as well as television. You didn't hear?"

"No. I had the radio off on the way back from Muskegon."

"Someone has claimed responsibility for the theft of *Silversides.*"

She stopped and stared at him. "Who?"

SAC Jennings gestured for her to walk on toward a row of cubicles. "Humanitarians Organized for Peace and Environment. Call themselves the League of HOPE. They claim to be pacifists and they say they took the submarine, a symbol of war, and scuttled it in Lake Michigan in protest."

She mulled over the story as she walked. "Did they put out a spokesman to make the statement?"

He stopped next to a cubicle in the middle of the aisle. "No, the major news outlets in town all received sealed letters prior to their evening broadcasts." He nodded to the desk inside. "This will be your office for the next few weeks. Good to have you aboard."

The office looked spotless, unused. A file cabinet stood in the corner, clean, with drawers closed. The desktop was clear, except for a single manila folder. She walked in and set her laptop next to the folder.

"IT people will be in tomorrow to set you up on the network," Jennings said.

She lifted the manila folder.

"That's the information we dug up on that museum volunteer you wanted checked out." He considered her long face. "You look dejected, Agent Matthis."

She sat on the corner of the desk. "I just didn't expect the investigation to head in this direction." She thought a moment. "A pacifist protest?"

"Which direction did you expect?"

Short on evidence, explanation, and confirmation, she decided her undeveloped theory of a skillful submarine heist might remain just that. "I guess I'm not entirely sure. But this HOPE league certainly wasn't on the table."

"It does make sense though," he said. "It's late in the day. We'll convene on this first thing tomorrow. Pacifists or patriots, regardless of how these people see themselves, they need to be apprehended. You just can't go around destroying government property." He pointed at the folder. "Maybe your friend there will lead us to them."

"Did we get a name?"

Jennings smiled. "A name and a little bit more. We found a match for the print in a military database." He turned and started toward the elevator. "See you bright and early, Reb. Good effort today."

Later Gordo.

He disappeared into the elevator. She stepped behind the desk, sat down, and opened the manila folder. A LaserJet copy of Choppy's picture from the museum had been paper clipped to a black-and-white photo. She pulled the copy from the clip. A clean-shaven man with a military haircut stared up from the photo at her, that serious soldier expression on his face. He wore a navy dress uniform. It was Bowman but he looked entirely different. The eyes though, they were the same, a deep intensity. There seemed to be intent behind them. She compared the haggard Choppy to the fresh navy man. Same guy, different mileage.

Beneath the black-and-white photo she found a dossier.

Lieutenant Commander Robert Bowman, age forty-one, twenty years service, retired. Honorable discharge eleven months ago. Served aboard the aircraft carrier USS *Stennis* in the Gulf Conflict as Lieutenant JG. Decorated for courage under fire during a suicide attack by Iraqi jet fighters. Promoted to full Lieutenant. After the war he transferred to a nuclear submarine, the USS *California*. Served two tours, then transferred again to another submarine, the *Hampton*. Based on a recommendation by *Hampton's* CO, Commander Owen Keyes, Bowman received promotion to Lieutenant Commander. He served three more tours on *Hampton*, his last two as the boat's XO. Then he retired.

Two letters of reprimand marred his record. On the *Stennis* after the Gulf Conflict, he ordered a radar officer to paint a civilian Saudi airliner that had entered the fringe of the carrier's airspace. While on patrol aboard the *California* he did much the same thing, ordering the sonar officer to ping an Iraqi oil freighter that the submarine had come across while the captain was off the deck. Both incidents showed provocative tendencies to ambiguous threat situations. In short, they indicated that Bowman was a loose cannon.

Rebecca leaned back in the chair, perusing the file. From his record, Lieutenant Commander Bowman didn't appear to be a pacifist, quite the contrary. So how did he end up tied to the League of Faith, or Hope, or whatever they called themselves? Or was he even involved in the sub's disappearance? Too many questions flooded her tired thoughts.

She tossed the folder on the desktop and closed her eyes. She felt the urge to keep going, but exhaustion had crept up on her. The prospect of *Silversides* already having gone to the bottom of Lake Michigan at the hands of anti-war protestors reduced her drive. Time to go. She needed to check in at the hotel and get situated there anyway. The particulars of the case rifling through her mind, she stood, lifted the laptop bag, and left the building.

Mackinac Island

The Milliken Suite at the Grand Hotel was plush, classical, and, well, presidential. It was not, however, the actual Presidential Suite. Much to Dylan's chagrin, McCallum politely declined to take that room when offered, his humility surfacing once again. Having inspected the Presidential Suite on his advance visit, Dylan had to quickly do the same for the Milliken, appraising its location and layout in regards to security concerns and such. He found the alternative to actually be better than the Presidential, at least in his estimate. The parlor seemed more spacious, with a curved wall of full-length windows overlooking the straits. It was furnished with turn-of-the-century furniture: cream couch, mahogany dining chairs around a heavily lathed table, a crystal chandelier, and deep garnet drapery. The suite managed to strike a balance between opulence and warmth, something Dylan perceived to be tricky.

After having been on the go for fifteen hours, he felt thankful to stretch out on the bed in the west bedroom. McCallum had already retired to the main bedroom across the parlor. It amazed him how much energy the Old Man had.

After checking with the troopers and Service agents on night watch around the hotel, he allowed himself to relax. He propped pillows under his head and clicked on the television, which was tucked neatly inside an antique cabinet.

The ten o'clock news had just begun and Dave Bellamy, standard handsome news anchor, opened with a local bank robbery story. Dylan loosened his tie and kicked off his shoes.

After giving a quick rundown of the facts, Dave handed off to Muriel Blair, his equally attractive co-anchor, and she delivered a story about a World War II submarine that had disappeared from a maritime museum. The news station ran file footage of the vessel in port.

Dylan sat upright to empty his pockets but kept his eyes on the television screen. Muriel rambled on in reporter-school cadence how a group of peace activists called the League of HOPE claimed to have scuttled the vessel in protest to projection of U.S. military power overseas.

Dylan spilled his change onto the nightstand. He remembered an incident several years prior in California. An unbalanced man had made off with an Abrams tank from a National Guard base and ran amok in the streets. The police had to let him run out of gas before they could move in and force the hatch open. They shot him dead. Dylan decided that making off with military hardware must be an attractive prospect for kooks.

He set his Glock next to the change and lay back down. Muriel threw a cue to Dave, who ran down the latest news concerning the independent counsel investigating illegal fundraising by the current President of the United States. And so it goes. Theft, protest, corruption, grease for the gears of prime time news. Only thing missing was murder. *Not to worry,* Dylan thought, *I'm sure it will turn up sooner or later.*

He stayed with the news long enough to catch a preview of the Governors Meeting on the island. McCallum garnered a small mention as guest speaker for friend and political ally Roger Patterson. They did a close-up feature on the traditionally rigged sail ships that would be used in the flotilla. And Senator Charles Burke managed to get a ten-second sound bite, pushing his bills, expressing bygones, all in fewer than thirty words.

Dylan undressed and turned off the television. He crawled beneath the covers. There in the dark, something visceral made him uneasy. The Machine was at work.

The Machine.

He had had it all his life, a restless thought process that simmered below the surface and never shut down. A part of his mind that forgot nothing, filed everything, took bits and pieces of information, twisted them, turned them, wove them in search of a picture, or an answer, or a pattern. It had latched onto something, but he couldn't put his finger on what it might be. Despite this mental foray, exhaustion settled in and he drifted off to sleep. The Machine, however, worked on through the night.

- ELEVEN -

DYLAN JUMPED and slapped his hand down on the alarm clock. A sharp burn ran from shoulder to skull. A kink had settled in his neck. He massaged it and sat up.

Early sun filtered in through the small window beside the bed. The weather looked fair, but he cursed anyway. Once his neck knotted it tended to stay that way for a while.

He listened to the silence in the suite. The period furniture, the décor, it reminded him of a trip he had taken with Sarah some years back, before Danny was born. They'd gone to Chicago for the weekend and stayed at a bed and breakfast, which had furnishings similar to those in the Milliken suite. Those days were the best for them. That rush of a new relationship, Saturday morning lovemaking on a down comforter. Sundays at the coffee house with no plans other than to spend time together. Somewhere along the line it had all changed.

He reached for his suit coat hanging over a chair in the corner. Pain pulsed in his neck. He grunted and dug into the coat pocket for his satellite phone. Hitting Sarah's speed dial button, he tapped his foot and waited. It rang once. He took a breath. Twice. The line clicked.

"Hello." A man's voice.

Dylan's jaw fell and his stomach knotted. He punched the disconnect button on the phone. "Shit!"

His curse bounced off the walls, died away. His neck burned. He tossed the phone on the bed and stood, paced back and forth, started to curse again but managed to hold his tongue. Storming into the attached bathroom he tripped on his overnight bag. He barely caught his balance on the ceramic basin. *Crappy start to the day.*

He showered, shaved, and dressed in appropriate business attire, another black suit coat with white shirt and purple tie. Collecting his sidearm and change from the nightstand, he stopped and glared at the near-death memento before throwing it into his pocket.

McCallum was already in the parlor, dressed in a charcoal gray suit and gazing out the windows to the straits. He turned and smiled in that genteel way that warmed so many. "How is she this morning, Agent Reese?"

Dylan swallowed a caustic remark. Not good form to jab the former Commander-in-Chief with a snide comment. "Breakfast starts in five minutes," he said instead. "Ready to go?"

Hands in pockets, McCallum chuckled. "She pushes your buttons, doesn't she."

Dylan bit his lip. "That she does." He spoke into his collar mic. "Carney, we're coming down. Clear?"

Stationed outside the Main Dining Room, Gillespie responded. "Good to go, Ringleader. All posts report clear." It sounded like he had something in his mouth.

"Salt bagel with sour cream and strawberry jam. Right?"

"Ringleader," Gillespie said, "your deductive powers are astounding."

"Your stomach is predictable." Dylan opened the door and stepped into the hall.

McCallum followed. "Western Omelet sounds good. Why don't you join me at my table? Don't want to have to entertain a bunch of politicians this morning. I'm here to see Roger and do him a favor, not hobnob with self-serving statesmen."

They took the elevator down and walked past Gillespie in the hallway. Dylan motioned for him to wipe a bit of jam from the corner of his mouth. Gillespie did and licked his finger. "Sorry, sir."

"Was it good, Tommy?" the president said.

"Yes, sir."

In the dining room white linen lay on every tabletop. Waiters in white waistcoats darted here and there, some balancing trays with plates of food, others taking orders with polite nods and courteous smiles. The aroma of butter, sausage, and scrambled eggs wafted through the air. State congressmen and honored guests filled the tables set with fine china and crystal water glasses.

A man with frosted hair and a black suit approached McCallum. Dylan recognized him as the maitre d'. "Good morning, Mr. President," the maitre d' said with an eager smile. "My name is Philip. I'm glad you've chosen to breakfast with us. Please walk this way."

Several diners took note of the president's arrival.

Philip led them to a table draped in white near a window, far away from the main traffic area. Dylan sat with his back to the glass,

McCallum across from him.

After their coffee cups were filled, McCallum said, "I look around this room at some of these young up-and-comers and I see myself forty years ago." He shook his head. "Frightening."

"If you could, would you go back and do it over again?"

"Hardly. Knowing what I know now, having run the gamut of campaign after campaign, I can honestly say once was enough." He appraised the room full of politicians. "It never stops though, does it? Nothing new under the sun." He brought his gaze back to Dylan. "Ecclesiastes. Read the Book, it's a good guidepost."

"I'll try to fit it in." Dylan realized he was 0-for-3 on the "good character" hat trick of being a good husband, a good father, and reading The Book. *Got to get going on this.* "Generally speaking though, Mr. President, are you satisfied with what you've accomplished? I mean, you've stacked up some impressive achievements."

McCallum pondered the question. "Most of it, yes. I could have done more though—In some cases, I should have done less."

"What do you mea—"

Dylan caught sight of Senator Burke approaching. "Here comes your buddy."

The president glanced over his shoulder and frowned. He lifted his coffee. "Shoot him."

"Sir?"

McCallum sipped his coffee, set the cup down. "Nothing."

"Good morning, Warren," Senator Burke said, stopping at their table.

"Charles. I was just talking to Dylan about the political machine and in you walk. Strange."

Burke seemed to take the comment as a compliment. "Mind if I join you?"

McCallum considered the request. "Don't know. There is a table of Democrats right over there who'd welcome you. What do you think, Dylan, should we invite him to sit? Let's take a vote."

Burke pulled out a chair and sat down. "Hollow victories are frail foundations for such pride."

"Landslide. Second term," McCallum said curtly.

Burke flashed a restrained smile. "Let's not go down this road again."

"Agreed."

An awkward moment of silence passed. Burke set his square jaw.

His crown of white hair matched the color of the razor-thin pin stripes in his dark blue suit. He crossed his legs and folded his hands in his lap. He seemed to be contemplating something.

Dylan glanced at McCallum's charcoal gray attire and didn't miss the subtle irony. The blue and the gray, the North and the South, McCallum and Burke, these men had been fighting a civil war with each other for most of their professional lives.

"You angling for another photo op?" McCallum finally said.

"Of course not. I'm just here to wish you well in your speech. I'll be leaving the island this evening and doubt we'll see one another again today." He paused. "We may never see each other again. You're not getting any younger, Mr. President."

McCallum took umbrage. "Speak for yourself, Senator."

Burke laughed. "Are you certain I can't get you to mention my bills in your speech?"

"Not the way you want me to." McCallum's turn to chuckle.

"Look at us, talking like old friends." Burke's smile betrayed a hint of insincerity.

"Sometimes looks are deceiving, aren't they?"

"Indeed." Burke uncrossed his legs, slapped his knees, and then stood. "Hope your day goes well, Mr. President." He turned to leave then stopped, something else coming to mind no doubt. He faced the table again. "Even though you've been a royal pain in my ass all these years, I'd be lying if I said I didn't enjoy the fight. You're a worthy opponent, Warren McCallum." He added, "Sometimes too worthy."

McCallum seemed at a loss for words, but only for a moment. "Good Lord, Charles, you sound human."

Flashing his cocked smile, Burke regarded the president. "You don't understand me, Warren. Never did." He turned and walked off, stopping a few tables away and talking with some congressmen eating breakfast.

Burke and McCallum had been going at it forever, and now a friendly encounter? To everything there is a season, a time for war and a time for peace. Dylan was certain that bit of wisdom came from Ecclesiastes too. Or was it the Yard Birds? "Think he's trying to mend fences?"

McCallum shrugged. "Political calculation of some sort. A zebra can't change its stripes, especially the Burke variety." He thought it over. "Probably just wants me to give some tacit approval of his bills. Can't do it. They're bad legislation."

"He has to know you'd never support him."

"You'd think."

The waiter returned and set an omelet and sausage in front of McCallum. "Cholesterol and grease, all the things Kate rations at home. Sometimes being on the road isn't so bad."

Dylan thought back on his fractured relationship with Sarah, and then on the encounter with Sadeed. *And other times, Mr. President, it's not so good.*

Grand Rapids

Although small and nondescript, the hotel room was clean; not to mention competitively priced. Rebecca Matthis had to keep cost in mind when traveling. The federal government loved to spend money, just not on its agents' travel expenses.

She'd been in dozens of rooms like this one. Starving artist watercolor paintings on the walls blended into a pastel color scheme. A nineteen-inch television sat in a dark varnished cabinet across from the queen bed. Tasteful but cheap, MO of the Bureau.

She had slept hard and morning came quickly. Monday's flurry of activity seemed long ago. She clicked on the television to a local news channel and walked into the small bathroom. She grabbed the damp towel hanging over the shower curtain rod. A mud splatter had dried on her shoe. She closed the toilet lid and sat down to wipe the caked mud. "Jeez, when did this happen." Her voice ricocheted off cream tile.

The cell phone in her pocket rang and she jumped. Who would be calling so early in the morning? She surmised Gordon Jennings, imagined his nasal voice. "Morning, Reb. Where are you? Been waiting an hour. Got to get going on this sub investigation."

On my way, Gordo. She answered on the second ring. "Matthis."

"Good Morning, Agent Matthis. Hope I didn't wake you."

It wasn't Jennings but she recognized the voice. "Sergeant Cotter?"

"Yes, Ma'am, hot on the trail of our submarine thieves."

"What have you found out?"

"Sounds like you're in the can. You want me to call back in five?"

She stood and walked from the bathroom. "No, Sergeant, just fill me in."

"Well, I think I know what direction they're heading."

"Heading? Sergeant, haven't you heard? The League of HOPE claimed responsibility for sinking *Silversides* last night. It can't be heading anywhere."

"Awe, now I was startin' to think you were a clever lady. You bought that story?"

She stayed silent a second or two. "It makes sense, doesn't it?"

"When someone comes up from behind and taps you on the shoulder, which way do you look?"

She sat on the bed. "Depends, Sergeant. Talk to me."

"Okay. Seven forty-five last night. Coast guard picks up a broken transmission on emergency band. Some guy screaming for help. Says he's being shot."

"Shot?"

"Yeah, but the transmission drops out after ten, fifteen seconds. Folks listening from shore scratch their heads. They've got no coordinates, no ID on the caller, nothing. So they check with marinas up and down the coast, see if anyone has radioed in with trouble or if any boats are overdue into port. Nothing."

Rebecca scrambled for the pen on the nightstand and began scribbling notes on a pad of Comfort Inn paper. "So we're talking about eight o'clock by then?"

"There about."

"Why didn't we hear about this last night?"

"They had nothing but ten seconds of anonymous panic."

The weatherman was giving the three-day forecast. "There's more I hope."

"Stay with me, Hon—Agent Matthis. Three hours later Charlevoix contacts the Guard, says they've got a fishing boat overdue. Guy named Rodney Boggs runs a charter out of there. Harbormaster knows him, says you can set a watch by his departure and arrival times. Boggs had an all-day charter with a scheduled return time of nine-thirty. By ten o'clock the harbormaster knows something isn't right. He gets on his radio and tries to contact Boggs. He tries for forty minutes. Nothing. Next call he makes is to the Guard."

She glanced at the sheen on her wet shoe. "Well after nightfall by then. Did they try to launch a search?"

"After talking with some fellas who knew Boggs' route, yeah, but they didn't have any luck 'til sunrise. A little after seven this morning they spotted debris floating in the vicinity of Boggs' favorite hole."

"Where?"

"About ninety-three miles north of Muskegon, twenty-seven miles out."

She stood. "You think Boggs came across *Silversides* and they sank his boat?"

"It's a wild-ass guess but yeah."

"Is the submarine capable of covering the distance between the museum and this debris site given the timeframe we're working with?"

"Talked with Lanny right before I called you. He says it's well within *Silversides'* specs while running on the surface. She'll make seventeen knots. Hell, I even got him to admit they could have gotten that far if they were running submerged, all ahead full at eight knots."

Bouncing on her heels, her heart quickened. "Lanny conceded that they could have submerged?"

"Not entirely. He was just playin' hypothetical with me."

"It would explain the coast guard not locating *Silversides* after a full day of searching."

"So would the League of HOPE scuttling her."

She smirked. "You said not to put much stock in that report."

"I did. But that doesn't mean we should shit-can the idea altogether."

"I haven't seen any video of the sub going down." She caressed her chin. "You'd think the League of HOPE would have a video recording of their handiwork as proof. You see any video, Sergeant?"

"Not a single frame."

"So let's keep going. The thieves manage to submerge *Silversides* and elude the all-day aerial search. For some reason they surface and Boggs spots them. They don't like the attention and decide to shut him up." She paused. "If they were running submerged and eluding the search, why did they surface?"

"Now here's where I'm comin' up with more questions than answers. Didn't hit Lanny with 'em yet, I was too fired up to get your take on my theory."

"I like it, Jasper. Thanks for making the connection. I'll call Lanny and dig deeper. Keep me informed if anything else comes to mind." She disconnected and reached for the Palm Pilot in her shoulder bag. She pulled up the museum's phone number and dialed. While it rang, she watched the weatherman. The next few days were going to be partly sunny, hot and humid. The line clicked.

"Great Lakes Naval Memorial and Museum."

"Mr. Stevens, this is Agent Matthis. I have a few questions regarding *Silversides* for you."

"Have you talked to Jasper this morning?"

"Yes, just a moment ago."

"He thinks these bastards are submerged."

"It's a possibility, isn't it, Mr. Stevens?"

A pause. "Well, I don't think so. Those HOPE radicals said they sank her."

"That's also a possibility. We're gathering a lot of information and need to separate the wheat from the chaff."

"I hope she's still afloat. It'd be a damned miserable shame if I lost her like that."

She didn't agree. She'd rather the submarine was sitting on the bottom of Lake Michigan than on the loose. If the thieves were gliding through the Great Lakes somewhere, their intentions remained a gloomy, gray void. "For the sake of argument, let's say *Silversides* is indeed submerged. Why would the thieves surface in daylight and risk detection?"

"A bunch of reasons," Lanny said. "Low battery charge, air going stale, the boat sprung a leak, take your pick."

"What is the most limiting factor for staying submerged?"

"Air. With a full crew compliment, maximum down time is nearly twenty hours. After that, carbon dioxide makes the air toxic."

"I doubt they have a full crew, and based on information we've received, they may have surfaced just twelve hours after diving. What's factor number-two?"

"Batteries. We just re-installed the cells for the move to the downtown port facility a month ago, but they were completely dead. If the thieves didn't have enough topside time with the diesels running to get a full charge, it would force them to the surface earlier."

"How long do the batteries hold a full charge?"

"Max time is about twenty-two hours. But that was back when they were new. These cells are sixty years old. They may not be operating at peak performance." Lanny grumbled. "I don't believe it, but if the thieves did get *Silversides'* systems operational and they submerged, what would they do with her? Her guns are disabled and they don't have ammunition."

"Think about it. If these people have the knowledge and skill to steal the submarine and repair her drive and diving systems, how much more of a stretch is it for them to fix the weapons as well, and then come up with ammunition?"

Lanny exhaled. "Not too much if you put it like that."

Rebecca thanked him for the answers and hung up. A television reporter was doing a live report amongst a throng of people on a wooden pier. The caption at the bottom of the screen placed him in Mackinaw City, covering the arrival of twenty-two governors attending the annual meeting on Mackinac Island. She turned up the sound and listened to the reporter comment on the gathering crowd of politicians, and the majestic collection of ships that would carry them across the straits in Governor Patterson's celebratory flotilla.

The cameraman panned away from the reporter and focused on a line of ships sitting in port at the Mackinaw City marina. Varying in size from seventy-five to two-hundred feet, graceful vessels of teakwood, oak, traditional rigging, and polished brass lay moored end to end at the docks. Others were anchored out in the harbor. Governors and staffers climbed gangplanks. Some were riding skiffs out to their designated ships.

Panic hit her so hard the breath left her chest.

Silversides was heading north through Lake Michigan. If she ran through the night on the surface at seventeen knots she could easily make the straits. And running on the surface that long would give the batteries a full charge by sunrise. The sub could be submerged again, this time for at least eighteen hours. It made sense, it fit, and the hairs stood up on her neck.

The flotilla is the objective.

Grabbing her bag, she sprang from the bed and raced to the door. She threw it open and bounded into the hall. Forget the elevator. She burst into the stairwell and started down. On the ground floor she grabbed her cell. The RA office number eluded her, and she realized that dialing while running would be rather difficult, so she palmed the phone and broke out through the east exit.

Parked across the small lot, her Impala waited with dew-covered windows. She hit the keyless entry button with the keys still in her pocket. The taillights flashed. She hopped in and threw on her glasses. The keys got tangled on a thread in her pocket. She yanked them free and started the car. The motor roared.

She slammed the Impala into reverse, squawking the tires over the blacktop. The car was in drive before it stopped rolling backwards. She flicked on the wipers to clear the dew and stepped on the accelerator. The car flew out of the lot and onto the main drag.

It popped into her head, the RA office phone number. She dialed with her thumb, waited for the ring, dodged a white Grand Am pulling onto the road. She pushed through the receptionist who answered and Jenning's secretary with curt instructions. He finally came on the line himself.

"Jennings here."

She tried to level her voice enough to sound coherent. "Sir, this is Agent Matthis. There's trouble heading for the Governors Flotilla."

"What sort of trouble?" His nasally voice didn't sound as upbeat as it normally did.

"The big, bad kind. I believe the thieves who stole *Silversides* are planning to use it to attack the ships carrying the governors to Mackinac Island this morning."

"Hold on, now. The League of HOPE claimed responsibility for sinking the submarine."

"It was a feint to buy time. Think about it, sir. There's no video of the sinking, no identifying piece of the boat presented as proof, no proof at all that she went down, just a rambling letter quirky enough to sound legit. She's out there, fully operational and dangerous."

"What evidence do you have to support this claim?"

She blew through a stoplight. A rusty pick-up truck just missed her broadside and laid on the horn.

"Where are you, Agent Matthis?"

"Heading for the expressway. I'm going to Mackinaw City."

"Hold on!" Jennings actually sounded angry. "You better explain yourself before running off half-cocked."

"Last night a fishing charter was attacked and sunk by unknown assailants ninety miles north of Muskegon. Coast guard's got recordings of the captain calling for help while his boat is being shot up, only they didn't know it at the time. They found debris from his boat this morning on the lake."

"That's mighty circumstantial."

"I don't believe it's a coincidence."

"Everyone you've talked to said that submarine is incapable of functioning."

She merged onto I-31, accelerating north. "Robert Bowman has twenty years naval experience, three tours on a nuclear submarine. I believe he's behind this, or is one of the key players. He'd have connections; know people who could help get *Silversides* up and running."

"Speculation at best."

"Damned good speculation, I think."

"How do you conclude the flotilla is in danger? The sub is un-armed."

"If they can fix it they can arm it. The flotilla leaves at nine this morning. We've got to stop it."

"We have plenty of assets on site. You don't need to be there. I want you back in the office. Kyle Bradley warned me you had a ten-dency to overreact."

She burned to the core. "I'm losing this cell," she lied, "you're breaking up." She disconnected. "Bradley you bastard, you're next." She dialed the Detroit office and found out that Special Agent in Charge Kyle Bradley was in the field. Pressing, she learned he was scheduled to be in Mackinaw City for the governor's big event. She finagled several minutes on the phone until she reached Bradley on a field agent's cell.

"Agent Matthis." His voice had a hint of aggravation. "How do you like Grand Rapids?"

"The Governors Flotilla is in danger."

"Gordon Jennings just called me. He was very flustered. It takes a special kind of irritant to rattle that cheery guy. Congratulations."

She stifled a curse. "Did you hear what I said?"

"Yes, and I heard what you told Jennings, a submarine attack." Bradley chuckled, more annoyed than amused. "You've been there one day, one fucking day, and you're already stirring the pot…What do you propose we do?"

"Stop the ships from leaving. Cancel the flotilla."

"Just like that, call Governor Patterson and inform him his big-deal campaign event that he's been planning for six months is canceled due to irresponsible speculation. I need a hell of a lot more than that, Agent Matthis."

"It's not irresponsible. A navy vet with extensive submarine ex-perience has disappeared right along with *Silversides*. This isn't the work of a prankster—"

"Make your case."

"A fishing charter was attacked, the captain radioed he was being shot to pieces—"

"Will the U.S. Coast Guard substantiate that the message they re-ceived came from this charter captain?"

Rebecca hedged. "I haven't confirmed that with them yet."

"Are you absolutely certain the boat sunk due to gunfire?"

She pounded the steering wheel. "That charter went down ninety miles north of the museum. I'm sure it was the submarine thieves who did it. And I'm sure they stayed on a northerly course up to the Straits of Mackinac, right to the flotilla. It's the only target worthy of stealing a sub. Twenty-two United States governors are crossing the water this morning. Twenty-two. We can't afford to take a chance."

"I'll decide what we can and can't afford." Bradley took a long breath. "That submarine is at the bottom of the lake. Burn your energy finding the protestors who did it, not coming up here on a wild goose chase."

"*Silversides* is—"

Bradley exploded. "That submarine is not going to show up in the straits! Turn around and head back to Grand Rapids or I'll have the State Police put an All Points out on your car and have you arrested on site. You clear on that?"

She bit her lip so hard she thought it would bleed. "Yes, sir, I understand you."

They listened to silence a long while.

Bradley spoke in a much calmer tone. "We're already on site watching the flotilla. The coast guard has cutters patrolling the area. We've got the situation under control."

"Yes, sir." Rebecca disconnected and tossed the cell into the passenger seat. She gripped the steering wheel, kicked off her shoes, and kept right on going toward Mackinaw City.

Inside the white surveillance van parked at the edge of the marina lot, Kyle Bradley handed the cell phone back to Agent McGlinen. He sat on a stool with hands on knees, still riled from the conversation. He glanced through the van's dim interior lighting at the radio and listening equipment, thinking rather fervently. He pursed his lips, exhaled, and turned to the sandy-haired McGlinen. "Contact the coast guard. Tell Lieutenant Commander Jacob to put his cutters patrolling the straits on high alert."

McGlinen waited for details. "Anything more specific, sir?"

Bradley glanced crosswise at him. "Just have them keep their damned eyes wide open."

"Yes, sir." McGlinen reached for the radio.

Bradley stepped out of the van onto the parking lot. Morning sun made him squint. He lowered his eyes and scanned the marina where the ships in the flotilla were moored. Most of the governors and their staff had boarded already.

Flagship of the fleet was the *Commodore,* a replica of a nineteenth-century American warship. One hundred and ninety-eight feet from the tip of her spar to her stern, the two-masted brig ranked largest in the flotilla. She looked majestic with dark rigging set against blue sky, furrowed sail, cannon ports ready to unleash a full broadside, and plenty of decorative brass.

Governor Patterson strolled about at the bow, talking with the state attorney general and some staffers. *Commodore* would spearhead the convoy, and Patterson would be right there, leading the visiting governors. Leading the leaders, as it were. Bradley was certain the symbolism had been thoughtfully calculated.

The last of the press pool was heading out on a skiff to the eighty-four foot gaff schooner *Rio Grande.* Dual mast with dark oak plank hull, *Rio Grande* shared *Commodore's* era of origination. The press schooner would bring up the rear of the flotilla. That symbolism wasn't lost on Bradley either.

The ships would head out in forty-five minutes.

"Damn it, Matthis. Leave it to you to screw up a beautiful morning like this."

"We've got a pretty good view from here."

President Warren McCallum stood with Dylan on the large, circular balcony extending from the Grand Hotel's third story. They and a handful of state senators had moved to the balcony after breakfast to catch the parade of ships.

Civilian boats lined the procession route through the straits. Spread thin and stretching back to the Lower Peninsula, the crafts defined a several-hundred yard wide corridor. Two coast guard cutters patrolled the water, making sure the spectators didn't interfere with the ships. To the west the Mackinac Bridge arched across five miles of waterway.

"This will be good for Patterson," McCallum said to Dylan. "He's a rising star in the GOP. Some think he'll be the presidential candidate in four years."

"You going to mentor him?" Dylan said. "Show him the ropes of the campaign trail?"

"If I'm still here, I'll be glad to give a word or two of advice."

Two senators, Bingham and Scalia, approached from the far side of the balcony and initiated a round of political small talk with McCallum. They touched on poll numbers, the coming election, who was a shoe-in, and who was an also-ran; all the things that made their world go around. The president slipped into the conversation with ease. Interest or instinct, Dylan wondered which allowed McCallum to converse so naturally.

The Machine.

It still hummed below his subconscious. Every now and then it disturbed his thoughts. Here it comes again. *Stay alert,* it said, *something is wrong.* A sixth sense some would call it. He preferred more mechanical terminology, because that's how it felt. The Machine. What was it trying to tell him?

Beyond the western tip of the island, in the rippling waters of the corridor, a ship appeared. Two masts with sails billowing, the size and beauty of the vessel identified her as the *Commodore*. Behind her followed a hundred-foot brigantine. The flotilla had left Mackinaw City.

McCallum let his conversation with the senators fade.

All eyes turned toward the approaching nautical parade.

Mindful of the kink in his neck, Dylan scrutinized the people on the balcony. Representatives and hotel wait staff gazed down on the approaching ships. He leaned over the edge of the handrail. People had filled the great colonnade that stretched the length of the hotel's ground level. They all were focused on the flotilla too.

The flotilla. It reminded him of the ten o'clock news, the special segment on the Governors Meeting, the stolen World War II submarine story. He stepped closer to McCallum. "You hear the news report about that old submarine, Mr. President?"

"Nah. I haven't tuned in to the outside world since we got here."

"A group of peace activists towed USS *Silversides* from a museum in Muskegon and claimed to have scuttled her in protest of U.S. military policy. Group calls themselves the League of HOPE. You know of them?"

McCallum whirled his head about. "Don't know the group, but I know the boat."

"Yeah, it's been berthed in Muskegon for…what, fifteen years or something."

"No." McCallum looked perturbed. "I know that boat intimately. I served on her in my first tour of duty."

Dylan just stared at him a suspended moment. The Machine was making an awful lot of racket in his brain. "You served on *Silversides*?"

"Yes." An angry frown turned his face down. "Damned peace-niks just destroyed a piece of my past." He scoffed. "I don't understand pacifists. There isn't a single instance in recorded history when a nation has successfully appeased its way to peace and security. Just ask Neville Chamberlain." He turned back to watch the ships.

Dylan did the same, thinking about the submarine, and McCallum, and...

The *Commodore* had reached the halfway point. Eleven ships strung out behind. Blue sky and brilliant sun bestowed luster to the water. Dylan focused on *Commodore*. Tiny figures were barely visible on deck through the sail and rigging. One of them was Governor Patterson.

McCallum shielded his eyes as if trying to make out the faces so far away.

An odd shimmer in the water drew Dylan's attention. West of the *Commodore*, off her port side. Closing. Something was moving below the surface, and fast.

He lost it in the sun and waves.

One second, maybe two, he tried to pick it out again. Gone.

A ball of fire suddenly erupted from *Commodore's* port bow, right at the water line. Her hull bulged and broke, shattering to pieces. The forward deck heaved, came apart, fire and smoke rushing between ruptured planks.

The explosion hurled flailing bodies high into the air. Seeming to last forever, the brilliance of the blast finally receded. Black smoke poured from the devastating hole. Fire consumed *Commodore's* bow and the remains of her forward deck.

Four seconds after the first, a second explosion blew a hole amidships. The wooden broadside disintegrated. *Commodore's* rear mast buckled. It toppled backward, ripping the main sail like newspaper. Water rushed in through her hull breaches. She began listing hard to port.

Trying to avoid a collision, the two-masted brigantine that followed her broke hard to starboard. A staysail schooner third in the procession steered to port. The flotilla broke apart. Fleeing ships drove headlong into the spectator boats along the procession route.

The senators on the balcony stood in stunned disbelief. Bingham gasped. Scalia cursed. Someone down on the colonnade screamed.

At the sight of the burning ship, McCallum had frozen, then he slumped forward and caught himself on the white handrail.

Gathering his wits, Dylan came forward and put a hand on the president's shoulder, the other he shoved into his pocket. "Carney— Ringleader. Report."

Gillespie's reply was abrupt. "Morbidly quiet."

Dylan pulled McCallum from the edge of the balcony, back toward the hotel, toward cover. "All positions report."

One by one they checked back: east post, west post, courtyard. All clear.

"East marina, chaos down here. They're scrambling an emergency response ship. What the hell happened?"

"West marina, same story. People rushing all over the place."

"Fort Mac clear."

Dylan steered McCallum into the hotel.

Pale and bewildered, the president stumbled inside. "Damned Brigade."

"We don't know what happened," Dylan said. "Could have been an accident."

He didn't believe it for a moment.

McCallum didn't buy it either. "This was no God damned accident! You saw what happened. You know it wasn't an accident."

Framed by French doors, a column of black smoke rose over the straits.

"Oh God, Roger. All those people."

Dylan put a calming hand on his shoulder. "We'll find out what happened, sir."

Their eyes connected. They both already knew what had happened.

Dylan revised his statement. "We'll find out who did this."

McCallum nodded and turned from the window, dragging a shaking hand through his hair.

Dylan called through his collar microphone. "Carney-Ringleader. Double the troopers on the hotel's perimeter and lock down all entry points except for the main lobby. Restrict access to guests only. Verify ID and reservations of each person crossing the threshold. I'm taking Cipher to the Bullpen." He turned to McCallum. "I think we'd be more secure back in the room."

He waved off the suggestion. "Hell, they didn't come after me! The victims are down there on the water. I'm staying here."

Dylan measured his resolve. "Carney, cancel trip to Bullpen. We're staying in the Loft."

- TWELVE –

Silversides Conning Tower

OWEN KEYES pulled away from the periscope, a slug of chaw in his cheek. "Two hits. *Commodore* is going down."

Bowman cackled with delight.

Keyes settled behind the eyepiece again. "Convoy is breaking up." He watched quietly for a few seconds, rotating the periscope a fraction. "Second target moving off, circling west." He stepped back and lowered the periscope. "Make depth zero-eight-five. Heading zero-nine-zero, all ahead full. Mr. Royce, keep close watch on our depth. The straits are shallow." Finding his empty coffee cup on the floor, he lifted it and spat a stream of chew inside. "Load forward tubes three and four."

Laughlin and Cory finessed the plane control wheels, driving *Silversides* deeper. Hendricks set their heading dead east with the helm control wheel. The submarine slipped through the cool water, free and clear of the chaos it had caused on the surface.

Keyes crossed his arms, waiting. He gave Bowman a glance.

Silversides creaked and moaned with the increasing depth.

The forward torpedo room reported tubes three and four loaded.

Royce perspired behind the plane control men. Keyes understood his concern. Running a fleet submarine just twenty feet off the bottom was nerve-wracking. Fouling the keel on the lake bed would be all too easy if the dive officer didn't stay on top of the instrumentation. But Royce was there, eyes fixed on the gauges, holding Laughlin and Cory on a very short leash.

Keyes checked his watch. "Mr. Bowman, flood tubes and open outer doors. Reduce speed to one-third. Mr. Royce, periscope depth. Mr. Hendricks, give me a wide, easy turn to port. Bring us to heading two-nine-zero."

Silversides climbed and came about.

Keyes pulled the well-creased papers from his breast pocket. He studied the worn documents. They felt warm, like they knew what was happening. Like they knew justice was at hand. He tapped the edge of the papers against his chin and waited.

Bowman announced their arrival at sixty-five feet and heading of two-nine-zero.

Keyes spat a measure of chew into the cup, set it down. He raised the search periscope and grabbed the control handles.

Breaking surface, the periscope cleared the wave crests and showed him where he stood. Several hundred yards out a knotted collection of ships tossed in the swells. A thinning column of smoke remained in the air but the *Commodore* had disappeared. Drifting near to where she had gone down, a coast guard cutter bobbed. Its crew pulled survivors from the water. Spectators who had come to see the flotilla now watched the rescue with rapt attention. A few of the larger craft, however, came in close to assist in fishing out bodies, living and dead.

Making a lazy circle around the epicenter of activity, her diesel engine engaged, the gaff schooner *Rio Grande* ferried the press pool passengers in for a close look.

Keyes rotated the periscope, moving its crosshairs over *Rio Grande's* starboard broadside. "Bearing," he said. The crosshairs sat dead center amidships. "Mark."

Holding back hair from his eyes, Bowman read a number off the bearing ring around the periscope shaft. "Bearing—three-three-seven." He moved to the large, square faceplate of the Torpedo Data Computer (TDC) and entered the target information on its series of input dials.

Keyes hit the range-finder button on the control handle and called for his XO to take the reading. Bowman spun to the periscope shaft and checked the small, black dial. "Range—nine hundred yards." He returned to the TDC and dialed in the numbers.

Scrutinizing *Rio Grande*, Keyes calculated. "Angle on the bow—one-zero-five."

A speedboat crossed his field of vision just fifty yards out. It cleared and he refocused on the schooner. *Rio Grande* moved across the degree divisions in the periscope's optics. He remembered the range Bowman called and did a quick computation. "Target speed—4 knots."

Bowman rotated dials on the TDC. The targeting information was complete.

"Firing solution plotted. Gyro angles programmed." Bowman

patted the side of the complex electro-mechanical device. "Not bad for a sixty-year old computer."

Keyes thought back on *Rio Grande's* specs, recalled her draft. "Set run depth at seven feet. Fire three."

A steam-driven torpedo launched from forward tube three, accelerating to forty-six knots. It climbed to its shallow run depth and closed the distance to *Rio Grande*. Three seconds after the first launch, a second Mark 14 reproduction fired from tube four.

A crew member aboard a twenty-foot catamaran spotted the first torpedo's exhaust wake as it streaked past the starboard pontoon. "What the hell is that?" he shouted.

The second torpedo followed close behind.

Gary Perez, owner of the catamaran and former naval reservist, stood forward on the deck and shielded his eyes from the sun. He tracked the exhaust trails. They were heading right for the schooner a hundred yards out. "Oh my God."

In less than five seconds the lead torpedo reached *Rio Grande* and detonated under her keel. The schooner lifted out of the water on a fountain of fire and spray, splitting in two and sliding back down. Her uneven halves wallowed in the water, fire and smoke eating her decks and roasting the passengers.

Running along its programmed trajectory, the second torpedo found *Rio Grande's* half-sunken stern. The fractured hull blasted into countless fragments of planking and brass. Flaming debris fell on deck of a nearby yacht, setting fire to the wheelhouse.

Panic swept through the disbanded flotilla. Crews tried to run from the chaos. They dropped sail and started their engines. Some made for Mackinac Island, others to Mackinaw City. Two ships collided in the disorganized rush to safety. They sideswiped one another, tangled their rigging. Other ships tried to help with the *Rio Grande*, but the frantic exodus made a rescue effort nearly impossible.

"Scratch two," Keyes said, dropping the periscope through its casing. He drank in his success, but only for a moment. The coast guard and authorities might be quick in discerning what had just happened. They might already be looking for the submarine. The longer *Silversides* remained in the straits, the greater the chance of detection. And he had other objectives that needed tending.

He lifted the cup at his feet and emptied the remaining chew from his mouth. "Go deep and run. All ahead full. Clear the straits and lay in a course for the rendezvous coordinates."

Bowman balked. "They haven't got a clue we're down here. We've got four more torpedoes. Pick another target. The cutter. Send it to the bottom."

Royce hesitated increasing their depth.

Laughlin, Cory, and Hendricks remained silent at their stations.

Keyes expanded his barrel chest. "Our objectives here are met. We stick to the plan."

"Blood for blood. Make them think about what they've done."

"We've done that." Keyes glared at Bowman and stepped forward. "We're not out here for sport."

Bowman weighed the comment.

"Do you understand, Mr. Bowman?"

The haggard XO paused; disappointment on his face like a boy refused a favorite game. "Yes, sir," he said at last.

Keyes whirled about. "Get this boat down, Mr. Royce. Now!"

"Aye, sir." He directed the plane operators to take *Silversides* deeper.

Keyes stepped close to Bowman, a taut, angry, whisper on his lips. "Never oppose my orders again, Robert."

"That's not what I meant," Bowman said quietly. "I just—"

Keyes raised a reprimanding finger. "Never—Again."

He stormed away and climbed down the ladder to the control room. Ignoring the crewman at their stations, he started for the officers' quarters.

John Tierney waited for him in the narrow corridor. "Dissention in the ranks?"

Keyes cocked his brow at the question.

Tierney pointed back into the control room. "I heard."

Keyes brushed him back with a gesture and walked into the tiny captain's cabin. "I don't think dissention is the right word."

Tierney stepped into the doorway.

Keyes faced him. "I'm afraid it's worse than that."

"Now what could be worse than insubordination?"

"Mr. Bowman's operating on the ragged edge." He sat on his bunk. "He looks like hell and doesn't care, and his behavior is becoming erratic."

"Erratic enough to put the OP in danger?"

Keyes studied the green floor plates. "Hard to say. Bowman and

I have a good history together, I know he can be solid...Still, he's not giving me reasons to invest full faith and confidence."

"Then remove the element of uncertainty." Tierney placed a palm on his large holstered pistol.

Keyes eyed his movement. "Bowman hasn't gone that far over the edge," he said, "but I'll keep a close watch on him."

"You're in charge, Commander, and I respect that. But if Robert Bowman does something to put this submarine and, by association, my ass in undue danger, I'll put a bullet in his head myself."

"Secure that talk. Bowman knows more about this boat than anyone aboard, including me. He's too valuable at the moment. Besides, his zeal may assist us in reaching our next set of objectives. Before we're finished, Robert Bowman is going to get a taste of what he wants most in life. It will be up to him what he does with it."

Mackinaw City

The first radio reports began popping on the airwaves as Rebecca Matthis drove into town. Information was sketchy, but she gleaned that there had been an explosion on a boat in the Governors Flotilla. There were several casualties on the scene, with unconfirmed reports that Governor Patterson himself may be among the dead. As she barreled toward the marina, two ambulances raced around her. They seemed to be heading toward the marina too. Her heart sputtered and her stomach dropped. She hoped that some innocent accident had prompted the news bulletins, but her intuition screamed otherwise.

Silversides had struck. It had to be. But how bad? She soon got her answer.

Yellow EMS units, white ambulances, blue police cars, and brick-red fire engines jammed the marina parking lot near the docks. Catastrophe's rainbow. Someone on a bullhorn ordered onlookers back. Medical response personnel rushed from their vehicles with stretchers and trauma gear, disappearing into a throng of people surrounding the docks. Another group of paramedics rushed out of the crowd carrying stretchers with wounded.

Burned, bleeding, writhing in pain, they were an appalling collection of victims. Police officers stood post throughout the grounds, holding gawkers at bay, trying to marshal order among chaos. A breeze blew in from the lake, carrying the scent of burning wood.

She spotted several Bureau agents in the mess, some on the perimeter with submachine guns in hand, others in with the crowd, taking note of every person, every detail. She could see they were shaken, unsure of the situation. They didn't know exactly what had happened and were afraid that whoever had struck might not be finished with their to-do list for the day.

Jerking the Impala to a stop, she cut the engine and jumped from the car. Police had taped off a corridor to allow emergency services people access to and from the docks, and she headed for it. A uniformed officer saw her approach, held up a hand to ward her off. She flashed him her creds. He scrutinized the badge a second or two then waved her through.

Excited voices buzzed on either side of her. A few references to terrorists reached her ear. She sidestepped once, clearing the way for a paramedic team to hurry another stretcher through. The man on it had burns over half his body, scorched black, blistered. He moaned in agony. She'd never before heard such a sound. The anger started in her chest. Her heart beat faster, then her skin heated up and her hands shook.

She marched on. Two flotilla ships were moored at the end of the dock. Firemen and EMS crews were all over their decks treating the wounded. Near a gangplank that led to a single-mast yacht, Special Agent Kyle Bradley stood with two men in suits. He had his hands in his pockets, and a livid expression twisted his face. He saw her coming. His glare nearly singed her hair. He clenched his jaw. "I told you to stay in Grand Rapids."

"I told you the flotilla was in danger."

"Don't start with me, Matthis. We don't know what happened out there."

"I do. A World War II submarine just attacked twenty-two United States governors."

"It's a hell of a lot more likely that bombs detonated on those ships."

"Ships? How many were hit?"

Bradley looked skyward. "Two. The *Commodore,* Patterson's ship, and the press pool vessel, the *Rio Grande.* Both of them sank after explosions tore them apart—A lot of casualties."

"Patterson?"

"Dead."

She crossed her arms and fought the urge to strike Bradley square in the throat. *I warned you, you idiot. This could have been avoided.*

His nondescript government-issue brown-nosers gave him their moral support.

"Bombs on board." She played along. "How did they get planted? Didn't we sweep the ships prior to the passengers boarding?"

"Change that tone, Agent Matthis. Of course we swept the ships, but the nut jobs that did this might have gone aboard posing as legitimate passengers, and had themselves wired with TNT vests. Hell, the Palestinians have been performing that trick for years."

"So you're thinking Mid-Eastern terrorists?"

"It's not a bad place to start. They've got a history of doing this kind of thing."

She truly hated the condescending tone of Bradley's voice. "I want to talk to survivors."

"I've got plenty of assets handling that area of the investigation."

"Then let me interview witnesses from other vessels."

Bradley considered her request. "Why do you believe that submarine did this? You don't have a shred of concrete evidence supporting you."

"Why do you think a suicide bomber did it? I've got more backing my theory than you do."

He began to respond but stopped short.

She saw the chink in his armor. "Let me talk to witnesses," she said. "Regardless of how this happened we've got to find out who did it."

"You're damned right we need to find out, and quick. Media's going to get hold of this story and tell everyone from coast to coast that the FBI didn't learn a damn thing from 9/11."

"Did we?"

Bradley's lackeys didn't much like that one.

A tall, thin man wearing a U.S. Coast Guard uniform picked that moment to walk up to the group. Bradley faced the dark-haired officer in lieu of answering her question. "Lieutenant Commander Jacob, what's our progress?"

Jacob scratched the side of his small, pointy nose. "We've searched through four flotilla vessels and haven't found anything resembling a bomb. We're moving to the fifth now."

For the first time Rebecca took note of the ships anchored seventy-five yards beyond the dock. She surmised they were being kept at a safe distance in case any of them had explosives on board. "How many ships took part in the flotilla?"

Jacob hesitated answering. She didn't have her creds on display. It took him a few seconds to deduce that she must be with the Bureau. That was a few seconds too long.

"I'm not his secretary, Lieutenant Commander Jacob, I'm Special Agent Matthis, so it's okay to answer my question."

Bradley slapped her with a cross look. "Agent Matthis just arrived on the scene," he said to Jacob. "She's a bit on edge from all that's happened, like the rest of us."

Jacob retained a polite demeanor. "Sorry, Agent Matthis. There were twelve vessels in the flotilla. We have six more to search."

"What if you had to search for a submarine?" she asked. "Is the coast guard prepared for that kind of undertaking?"

Bradley frowned at her.

"You're not the first one to raise that specter," Jacob said. "Some of the guys linked *Silversides'* disappearance to this attack right away."

The comment seemed to irritate Bradley. His suited cohorts harrumphed to themselves. Rebecca swore one of them coughed "bullshit" into his fist.

"How likely is it," Bradley said, "that *Silversides* played a part in this?"

Jacob mulled through his thoughts. "Not very. She's an old boat. It'd take a lot of work to get her seaworthy again. The thieves would need a great deal of skill and know-how to pull it off. Why would anyone even attempt such a thing? Planting a bomb would be much easier."

Bradley quelled a grin. "My thoughts exactly."

"Easier in some ways," Rebecca said. "But the risk of getting caught planting a bomb is pretty high. It would be difficult to breach our security measures. Using the submarine bypasses all that. Just look at what's happened. They've struck and are gone, and we haven't got the slightest idea to where."

"Thing is," Jacob said, "that peace group said they sank *Silversides*."

She shook her head. "No video tape, no spokesman, no evidence, I've seen nothing to convince me that it happened." She glanced at Kyle Bradley. "Have you seen anything, sir?" She pointed at his pals. "How about those two?" Back to Jacob. "And you, Lieutenant Commander, see any evidence to support the theory that the submarine was scuttled?"

Jacob shrugged. "Just the fact that she's gone and someone claimed responsibility."

"Your theft theory is every bit as lacking in proof," Bradley said.

"No, sir. I have a suspect, and an excellent one at that. He has all the right knowledge and skills. And based on his naval record, he doesn't strike me as much of a pacifist."

Silence fell over the group in conference. "So the question still stands. Is the coast guard capable of searching for a submarine?"

"Hardly," Jacob said. "Our cutters are not fitted to hunt submarines. Some of them, however, do have echo sounders aboard that would detect *Silversides*, given they're lucky enough to stumble across her. But this type of search requires far greater resources than we have available to do a good job of it. There's over fifty-thousand square miles of lake out there."

"Our starting point is right here." She pointed to the straits. "They can't have gotten that far yet."

"Right," Jacob said. "And the longer we delay, the wider the search radius becomes."

Bradley rubbed his closed eyes. "In your professional opinion is this submarine theory tangible enough to jump into with both feet?"

Jacob chose his words carefully. "It's possible. But if we're going to jump in, both feet is the only way." He considered the wounded being tended to on the nearby ships. "You said you had a suspect, Agent Matthis. Is it a terrorist?"

"I don't know yet. Too little information to point in that direction."

"How certain are you that *Silversides* is out there?"

"Very, just ask Special Agent Bradley."

Bradley didn't say anything, but his eyes groaned a confirmation.

Jacob pondered the situation. Rebecca figured he was weighing the facts, trying to decide whether to invest millions of dollars of coast guard assets into a potential wild goose chase.

Another FBI agent in a dark suit joined them. He seemed anxious. Bradley acknowledged him. "What have you got, Agent McGlinen?"

"Sir, I just talked with a guy who had his boat anchored alongside the flotilla during the incident. Name is Gary Perez. Get this. He swears he saw two wake trails dead end into the *Rio Grande* right before the explosions."

"Wake trails?" Bradley grimaced.

"He thinks they were torpedoes," McGlinen said. "He says he's ex-navy and knows what he's talking about."

Bradley clenched his teeth behind tightly closed lips.

Jacob digested the news for a full three seconds. "I'm mobilizing right now."

Rebecca grabbed her cell. "I'll contact the Great Lakes Naval Museum and tell Lanny Stevens what's going on. If anyone can help us find *Silversides,* he's the guy."

"Supposing this submarine is out there," Bradley said to Jacob. "What are the odds you'll be able to find it in all that water?"

Jacob exhaled. "When she's submerged our chances are slim, but she has to come to the surface sooner or later. And since she's not a nuclear boat, it'll be sooner."

"Twenty hours max," Rebecca said. "According to Lanny Stevens, after twenty they'll need to surface for air. If they've managed to extend their air supply, then the batteries will force them up after twenty-two hours. Either way, they're going to be on the surface again soon."

Jacob smiled at her assessment. "Not bad, Agent Matthis."

"You mean not bad for a woman?"

Bradley grumbled. "Not bad for anyone. Accept the compliment and move on."

She fumed but kept her mouth shut and dialed the museum.

Lanny Stevens answered. "Hello."

"Mr. Stevens, this is Agent Matthis. I've got some news for you."

Book II

STRIKING AN ARC

- THIRTEEN -

Mackinac Island

WARREN McCALLUM sat in the big Victorian chair, slumped forward with his head in his hands. He'd been in that position for twenty minutes. Dylan hated to see the Old Man so grieved. An hour ago they'd received official word from the authorities, namely the FBI, that Roger Patterson was among the dead.

In the morning, after watching the *Commodore* and *Rio Grande* go down in flames and the tangle of ships scatter for shore, McCallum had seen enough. He and some of the senators went into the Woodfill Conference Center Theater, where McCallum had been slated to give his speech, and huddled around a television that the staff had pulled from a vacant room. Apart from a growing list of casualties, news from Mackinaw City was sparse. It became apparent that the perpetrators were not going to be apprehended with any immediacy. After three hours of monitoring news coverage, Dylan succeeded in talking the president into returning to the suite for quiet repose. So there he was, reposing in grief.

Dylan sat at a round tea table across the parlor from McCallum. The air in the Milliken Suite tasted stale, something he hadn't noticed before. His neck ached incessantly. It seemed the somber mood that had settled in the wake of the tragedy amplified even minor irritations.

Tom Gillespie sat across from Dylan, tapping his foot on the carpet and staring out the windows toward the Lower Peninsula. He strummed his fingertips on the tabletop, glanced at the president, let out a breath.

Nobody knew what to say.

McCallum lifted his head. A portion of strength seemed to return to his tired frame. A hint of defiance flashed in his eye. "Dylan, Tommy, I want to go home. I want to be there with Kate. She'll be a mess watching the news coverage. She liked Roger, and she knew other people on board that ship. This won't be easy for her."

Dylan snapped to. "Yes, sir." He called one of the contingency numbers he had set up after his advance visit. Connecting to the Air National Guard base in Alpena, he called in the helicopter that had been waiting on standby all day. Reese's Golden Rule: Always leave yourself another way out.

He hung up. "We'll be flying out shortly, Mr. President."

McCallum raised a puzzled eyebrow. "Flying?"

"I'm certainly not taking you across the water today."

McCallum grumbled, and then lifted himself out of the chair. "I'm going to pack my things. Where's the pick up?"

"On the grounds south of the hotel," Dylan said. "It'll be here within the hour."

The president disappeared into his room.

Gillespie stood and spoke in a low voice. "What do you think?"

Dylan made sure the president's door was closed. "You want conventional thought or something more creative?"

"Both."

He returned to the tea table. "Conventional thought: Bomb on board."

Gillespie flashed a disingenuous smile. "Those astounding deductive powers again. Okay, now give me creative."

He hesitated. "I saw something in the water before the first explosion…something closing fast on the *Commodore*."

Gillespie waited for him to continue.

"Did you hear about the disappearance of that old submarine in Muskegon?"

Gillespie nodded slowly.

"She's USS *Silversides*. McCallum served on her back in the day. His day."

"Uh-huh."

"Think shark in a school of fish."

"You mean—"

"That's exactly what I mean. Hey, no one would expect it."

"That's real creative, my friend." Gillespie sank into deep thought. "Okay, for the sake of argument, let's go with your screwball idea. Who did it?"

"Don't know."

"Motive?"

"Don't know."

"You're not very good at this, Reese. I see now why you're in protection instead of investigation."

Dylan frowned. "Look, I know it's out there, but you asked to hear it. The only thing I know for sure is that this was no accident."

He actually had figured a bit more than that, but he wasn't prepared to share those thoughts. The Machine hadn't refined them enough. In his mind pieces of information were forming a crude Picasso. A clear, high resolution image hadn't materialized yet. He sensed a connection between the president and the attack, albeit by a thread so thin he'd need a micrometer to gauge it, he sensed it just the same.

Former President of the United States Warren McCallum once served aboard *Silversides*.

Silversides is used to attack Governor Roger Patterson's ship in the flotilla.

Nine years ago Patterson served in McCallum's cabinet.

Yeah, that's thin. And what did it mean? And what about the press pool ship? News reports said that the *Rio Grande* had been ferrying reporters covering the Governors Meeting. Why was it attacked? And what about the letter that shook McCallum? Did it have something to do with all this? He bet that it did. It all fit together. Somehow.

Gillespie snapped his fingers. "Ringleader—Carney. You copy?"

"Yeah, I'm just thinking it through. Tell the detail we're leaving."

After fifty minutes Dylan received a call from the ANG base in Alpena. The helicopter would arrive in five minutes. He and Gillespie ushered McCallum out the door and down the elevator, their bags right behind them in the hands of two bellhops. They reached a southern exit door and Dylan stepped out into the warm afternoon. He walked to the edge of an open field bordered by a seven-foot hedgerow.

The *thump, thump, thump* of the UH-1 Huey's rotor became audible from above. The black chopper approached from the southeast. It came in fast, setting down with a modest bounce on the lawn. The side door slid open and an ANG reservist in fatigues and flight helmet waved to Dylan.

Suit and hair buffeting in the rotor wash, he signaled back and returned to the hotel. McCallum and Gillespie waited at the door. "Our ride is here, Mr. President," he said above the noise of the helicopter engine.

They started across the field. McCallum followed Dylan's lead, like he had a thousand times before. Gillespie brought up the rear.

"The last time I rode in a helicopter," McCallum said in a raised voice, "was a week before I left office. Marine One set me down on the White House grounds for the last time."

Dylan called over his shoulder. "You miss it after you left?"

"No. I don't trust helicopters."

Dylan smiled. "Sorry, sir."

McCallum looked back. "Make sure you duck your head, Tommy."

They climbed aboard the Huey and sat in the bench seats. The airman who had waved to Dylan assisted with strapping them in. "I'm Corporal Woodring," he said to McCallum. "Glad we could help you out today, Mr. President."

"Thanks for the lift, Corporal."

After checking Dylan and Gillespie, Corporal Woodring slid the side door closed. He called through his helmet radio that the passengers were secure and started for the cockpit. Before disappearing forward, he stopped and turned to McCallum. "I voted for you, sir. Both times."

That genuine smile creased McCallum's face. "Hope I didn't disappoint you."

"No, sir. We in the service supported your whole tenure in office."

McCallum took a few seconds to digest that. His smile fell a few degrees. "I appreciate that, Corporal." He considered the airman a moment. "You seem kind of young to have cast a ballot sixteen years ago."

"I was just eighteen, sir. You were my first vote." Corporal Woodring saluted his former Commander-in-Chief and moved toward the cockpit.

Gillespie leaned in to Dylan's ear. "That was a sweet moment, wasn't it?"

Dylan jabbed his ribs.

The helicopter lifted from the ground, increased speed, and banked into a wide turn. It crossed over the southeastern coast of Mackinac Island and headed out over the water. McCallum stared out the small window near his seat, gazing down at the straits. Dylan watched him. Sorrow painted the president's face a pale hue. Patterson's death, and the others, it affected him deeply. When the president had learned of *Silversides* disappearance he lost a piece of his past. When Roger Patterson died he lost a friend. Warren McCallum was losing a lot of things today.

Dylan unbuckled and walked forward, giving the president a reassuring pat on the shoulder as he left. He leaned into the cockpit and got Corporal Woodring's attention, then asked to be dropped off near the Mackinaw City marina. The corporal acknowledged with a nod and Dylan returned to his seat. "Mr. President," he said. "I'm getting off in Mackinaw City. I'm going to drive back, and arrange to have a trooper drive your car. The pilot will take you back home. Tommy's going to stay with you."

McCallum gestured his understanding.

The helicopter arrived over the marina. Activity there had died down considerably since the incident. News reports had made it look like a war zone, which in a way it was, but enough people had now left to allow Corporal Woodring to touch down in an empty section of parking lot.

Dylan threw back the door. He jumped down, cringing at the windstorm above his head. His suit collar turned up in the gust as he jogged from the helicopter.

Fixing his collar and brushing his hair back in place, he started for the marina. A cluster of FBI agents and uniformed officers remained on site. He headed for a small group of suits near a moored sloop and produced his Secret Service credentials. "I'm Special Agent Reese with President Warren McCallum's security detail."

"Agent McGlinen," one of the suits said. "What brings you here, Agent Reese?"

"What do you think?"

McGlinen nodded. "I read that McCallum was going to give a speech on the island. Everything okay with him?"

"As well as can be expected. He and Patterson were good friends." Dylan gazed at the ships anchored away from the docks, then brought his eyes back to McGlinen. "I saw something out there today. Not sure what it was, but I want to tell somebody about it. Is there someone in particular I should talk to?"

Footsteps clicked on the dock to the right. McGlinen pointed his thumb. "Right there."

Dylan turned his head and the kink throbbed. He cursed in a whisper.

A woman walked toward him. She nearly matched his height. Shoulder-length auburn hair in a professional cut framed an attractive face with full lips. She wore narrow, wire frame glasses. Determined blue eyes gazed through the lenses. A tailored dark blue blazer wrapped around her just right. She smiled briefly but he could see that it was a forced professional courtesy. "I'm Agent Rebecca Matthis." She extended her hand.

Dylan took it in his. A firm, crisp shake and it was gone. "Agent Reese with Secret Service," he said. "President McCallum's protection detail."

"I heard. I also heard that you saw something you want to talk about."

"Yes. This morning during the—" He studied Rebecca's face. "I think I've seen you someplace before."

"I get that a lot."

He snapped his fingers. "The Mallory kidnapping. That was you, right?"

"Yes...Now the issue at hand."

"Very modest of you, Agent Matthis."

She adjusted her glasses. "Thank you."

"I have a son. He's five."

For the first time their eyes met.

"When you see something like that," he said, "you imagine the worst happening to your own. It's good to know there're people out there doing something to stop it."

"We do all we can. I'll convey your thanks to the team I worked with in Detroit." She paused a moment to break from the subject. "This morning," she said. "What is it that you saw?"

"Right." He realigned his thoughts. "We were watching the flotilla from the Grand Hotel. Just before the first explosion..." The closer he came to voicing what he thought he had seen, the less sure he became of the incident. Standing in front of a real live federal investigator gave him pause. "I saw something in the water."

She gave him a second to continue. He didn't. "Something like what?"

"It moved fast. Came from the west. Looked like it was on a beeline for the *Commodore*." He took a few steps back in thought. "That submarine that disappeared from Muskegon, I don't believe the League of HOPE sank it. I've never even heard of the League of HOPE."

"Do you think the submarine is involved with what happened here today?"

He hedged. "I think it's a good possibility."

"What do you think you saw in the water?"

He paused five seconds. "A torpedo."

To his surprise, the revelation didn't faze her. More professional courtesy?

"You took that well."

"I've been—" She glanced at McGlinen. "We've been thinking along those lines most of the day."

"You have? I thought it might seem a bit off-the-wall to you."

"We're one step ahead of you today."

The comment got under his skin. How much did the Bureau know before the incident? "Apparently someone else was one step ahead of you."

She glared through her glasses.

"*Silversides* disappeared yesterday," he said. "Did anyone think to consider the flotilla in danger?"

She stared calmly at him for a long while. It looked like she might be counting to ten.

"Until this morning," she said, "we had nothing solid to go on."

"A lot of people died today. Anything you had could have saved lives."

She leaned forward, keeping him in her sights. "You work for the government, Agent Reese. You know the kind of roadblocks we run into."

He studied the planks of the dock beneath his feet. "One day we're going to have to learn how to stop this kind of shit from happening."

McGlinen cleared his throat. "Actually, Agent Matthis suggested holding back the flotilla. Unfortunately the idea didn't gather a consensus with the people above our heads."

Rebecca's eyes darted to McGlinen, thanking him without saying thank you.

Dylan bit his lip. He did know about the lethargic nature of federal bureaucracy. He also knew about politics. Decisions to move or not move often depended on potential political fallout and who it would fall on. Prevailing winds this morning would have favored carrying on with the Governors Flotilla. A bit awkward, he felt for an olive branch. "I didn't mean to comment on you personally."

"Do you have anything else to tell me concerning the incident, Agent Reese?" Her pleasant tone sounded strained.

He shook his head. "I'm short on facts. A lot of that going around."

She procured one of her business cards from her shoulder bag and handed it to him. "If anything comes to mind call me on my cell. Is there a good way to contact you?"

He felt around his suit pockets and put on a half-smile. "Don't have a card on me. Not much occasion to hand them out in my line. Give me another of yours."

She did, and he scribbled down his sat-phone number with a pen from his breast pocket. "I would appreciate being kept up to date on the investigation."

"Why is that?" she asked. "Make sure we're doing our job?"

"Not quite." He turned; a prelude to walking back toward the parking lot. "President McCallum isn't taking this well. He and Patterson had a long history together."

"That's right." Rebecca searched her memory. "Patterson served in McCallum's cabinet. He was the..."

"Secretary of State. But they weren't just political allies, they were friends. The Old Man doesn't take personal relationships lightly. It hit him hard."

He started for the parking lot.

She kept with him. "As you pointed out, a lot of people were hit hard today. Believe me, more than anyone else, I want to see the people who did this dealt with accordingly."

He processed that a second or two. "Don't you mean brought to justice?"

She crossed her arms and stood her ground. "I think I meant what I said."

- FOURTEEN -

Aboard *Silversides*

HEAD PROPPED on an under-stuffed pillow and feet hanging over the edge of the bunk, Owen Keyes stared at the white-washed overhead. Even though the captain's stateroom was the only private space aboard, it left a lot to be desired in the way of comfort. The width of the bunk barely accommodated his wide back, and the narrow path between the bed frame and port bulkhead was difficult to navigate through. A stainless steel wash basin hung on the forward bulkhead near the foot of the bunk. Having shaved an hour before, he had it folded down.

He'd come with the intent of getting some sleep but hadn't been able to surrender to it yet.

He checked his watch. Only five minutes had elapsed since his last look.

In twelve hours *Silversides* had put 104 miles between it and the site of the morning attack.

He sat up and took readings off two alarm-clock sized gauges above his head. The black gauge indicated they were gliding 130 feet below the surface. The gray gauge showed *Silversides'* heading to be one-eight-five degrees, a general southerly course.

He lay back down.

They would stay submerged another hour, then surface and drive through the night with the diesels. Chances of coast guard search craft spotting them in the dead of night were slim. They'd gone the whole first day after the attack without a single incident, without a single hint of being detected. Things were going smoothly.

The closeness of the cabin drove his thoughts to the past. His quarters aboard *Hampton* were luxurious in comparison. Hell, the whole boat dwarfed *Silversides* in every way. Size, depth capability, firepower, stealth, *Hampton's* package of Los Angeles-class goodies represented the best the United States or any other nation had put in the water previously. But all that high-tech equipment had been built on the humble foundation of the common fleet submarine of World War II. In her time, *Silversides* was state of the art, and needed a highly skilled crew to man her. In that respect submarines hadn't changed much in sixty years.

Still, when Keyes walked the cramped warship he had to admire the men who piloted similar vessels during the war. Submariners of that day possessed an impressive grade of mettle to go out on patrol in such an intricate boat in such a dangerous time. They put their lives on the line for their country in a way very few had before.

It wasn't just those men he thought on now, but the countless others from each branch of the service. The men who had fought in every American war, the ones who offered the supreme sacrifice for their nation, the common man fighting with uncommon valor. They were the ones that drove him to undertake this mission. It was his duty to champion them. He would not fail.

If his father were alive he'd be proud. But that was the irony of the situation, wasn't it?

He pulled the documents from his shirt pocket and opened them. He read through the historical record of wrongdoing like he had so many times in the past year. The names of the traitors were all there, as well as their contribution to the crime. He returned them to his pocket.

With a weary breath, he switched off the wall lamp and tried for sleep.

A knock on the cabin door startled him.

"Commander," a voice called. "I have a report."

He sat up and pressed the nightglow button on his watch. He'd been asleep a little over an hour. "Come in, Robert."

The narrow door opened and the bearded XO stepped inside. "We've been down for seventeen hours, sir. We're preparing to blow ballast and run on the surface."

Keyes wiped a hand over his face. "Good. We'll get seven hours topside to charge and circulate fresh air before sunrise." He looked up to Bowman. "How close are we to the rendezvous coordinates?"

"About two hours. Did you get some rest, sir?"

"Some." Keyes stood.

"McCallum was there this morning," Bowman said.

"I know."

"You think he saw it happen?"

"I'd be surprised if he didn't."

"You think he knows why?"

"Of course he knows why. And he knows what's next." Keyes let the thought hang out there.

Bowman stared in silence.

"Out with it, Robert."

It took him a moment to find his tongue. "We have an opportunity. We need to take it." He paused. "I think we need to turn your mission into a full-fledged campaign."

Keyes searched the tiny desktop near his bunk for his can of chew. It wasn't there. "If you were king, exactly how would you do that?" He faced Bowman. "Or should I say, if you were CO, how would you wage this campaign?"

Bowman's eyes came alive. "I would be relentless. Each day I'd pick a new target. Each day I'd press the point. A freighter. A cutter. I would bloody the Great Lakes until I had ruined marine commerce and shattered public security. And with each kill I would let the world know why it was happening. I'd tell them about corrupted leadership, about incompetent fools pulling the strings. The people will listen, they'll understand. They'll force a change."

Keyes saw the passion of a zealot animate his XO. "How would you keep this campaign going? We've got four fish left. That wouldn't sustain a revolution for very long."

Bowman cracked a smile. "Once the news of what we were doing got out, sympathy among the ranks would snowball. They would help. Hell, we might inspire others to rise up and fight too. We'd receive more arms, ammunition, and recruits than we'd know what to do with."

Keyes couldn't quite believe what he was hearing. "Listen to yourself. What the hell has happened to you?"

"We have an opportunity to reverse years of erosion. Don't you see?"

"I see a man with twenty years of missed opportunities on his shoulders. I see a man searching for someone to blame."

Bowman shook a strand of hair from his eye. "You said you launched this operation to cut out a cancer, but it won't work. The patient is terminal. We need to pull the plug."

"I know what I'm doing." Keyes felt his face flush. "We take what needs to be taken. No more."

"It all has to change. We have to go further."

"No!" Keyes jabbed a finger into Bowman's chest. "You have to go further! You want to hurt them for keeping you on a leash. Ever stop to think that maybe, just maybe, you screwed yourself along the way?"

Bowman slammed a fist against the bulkhead. "I deserved a command! After twenty years I deserved it!"

"Naval officers don't deserve a command just because they've put in their time, they earn it." Keyes seized him with a powerful glare. "I know your record. I've watched you in action. You're a damn fine XO, but that's all you're capable of being. The brass saw it. I saw it."

Bowman stood silent, wounded.

"You're unpredictable. And it's getting worse."

"You kept me on *Hampton*. You got me my last promotion. You made me part of the Circle and we laid out this OP together." Bowman's forehead wrinkled in question. "And all that time you saw me as an incompetent?"

"That's not what I said."

"Right. I'm a damn fine XO."

"You were, until you started losing your grip." Keyes shook his head. "I've stood behind you every time somebody questioned your actions, but lately I'm running out of excuses. Rierdon and Dominic want to kick your ass. John Tierney wants to put a bullet in your head. I've defended you. Now do something for me. Get your head out of your ass and put it on straight for the rest of this OP. Do that, or you're going to find yourself in a world of hurt."

Bowman gazed right through him.

"I'm counting on you to be solid. Show me you can handle it."

He gave a curt nod. "Aye, sir." His voice reeked of dispassion.

"Let's get to the Conn. We need to surface."

Keyes slapped his shoulder and they exited the cabin. They went to the control room and brought *Silversides* to periscope depth. The surface sounded quiet and the skies looked clear, and SS-236 rose from the lake. Her diesels engaged and fed a rush of power into the electric motors. The props bit into the lake and the submarine increased speed from eight to twenty knots. For two hours they sailed through light seas, Robert Bowman being every bit the professional officer Keyes knew him to be, not once revealing to the others the conversation that took place in the captain's cabin. When they neared the rendezvous coordinates, Keyes called Tierney and Dominic to meet him topside. He left the Conn to Bowman, a modest show of confidence.

A warm breeze and the light of a crescent moon made the evening on Lake Michigan perfectly placid. Keyes, Tierney, and Dominic gathered on the cigarette deck. Apropos of their location, Tierney lit a Marlboro. Dominic brooded with arms crossed and stared at the dark water.

Keyes had found his chew and had since loaded a slug into his mouth. He spat over the side. "There's been a change in plans."

Tierney took a calm drag off his cigarette.

Dominic turned. "What sort of change?"

"I'd planned on taking just John and two of his men with me to Chicago, but I've decided otherwise." He gestured to the large Italian. "You're coming along with us now, you and two from your squad."

Dominic sniffled. "If I may ask, sir, why is that?"

Keyes spat again. "The dynamics aboard this boat have shifted, let's leave it at that."

Tierney grinned. "Bowman's off his rocker."

"Don't spread caustic rumors, John."

"Did the coast guard catch our scent?" Dominic asked.

"I'm just being prudent, Dom. Back in '41 when the Japanese attacked Pearl, the aircraft carriers weren't caught in port with the rest of the Pacific fleet. It saved our ass. There's a valuable lesson in that."

"You sense disaster coming?"

"With Bowman involved, bet on it," Tierney said.

Keyes rebuked him with a glare. "There's nothing to be concerned about. I'm just dividing my eggs between two strategic baskets." He paused. "When we leave the boat, take all your gear and provisions, both of you."

Tierney and Dominic exchanged a glance.

Dead ahead on the black horizon, a flicker caught Keyes' attention. A small white light played out a staccato pattern. He watched and read the message. "It's Rierdon. Grab your gear and get your men."

They descended through the bridge hatch. In the conning tower Keyes ordered *Silversides* to come to a full stop. He told Bowman to prepare for *Richard C.* to come along side. Tierney and Dominic continued down through the boat to the crew quarters. They rousted the men. Dominic went to Six Pack's bunk and slapped him on the chest. The kid jumped.

"What happened?" he said. "We taking on water?"

Dominic turned to his own bunk and reached for his equipment pack hanging off the side. "No. Get your weapon and all your gear.

We're heading out with Keyes."

"We are?" He hopped down from his bunk.

"Change of plans." Dominic threw the pack on his rack. He reached over to the groggy man coming to life on the bunk behind his. "Griffin, snap to. We're heading out."

The dark-haired man rolled off his back and set his feet on the deck. He wrinkled his pocked and scarred face. "What's going on? Our part in this deal isn't for two more days."

Checking the content of his pack, Dominic eyed the unsmiling man. "We live in a fluid environment, Griffin, and its ebb and flow is dictated by Keyes."

"Where's he dictating we flow to now?"

Dominic hoisted the pack to his shoulder. "For now, we're going for a ride on the tug."

Six Pack pulled a black shirt over his head. "Sounds good. Just get me out of this steel coffin and I'll be happy."

Dominic pondered Six Pack's comment a little longer than he would have an hour ago.

Tierney nearly had his men ready to go. He had picked Wilke and Roth to take along, two surly mercs known in the group to be slow with a thought but quick on the trigger. They followed orders well enough though, so for Tierney's purposes they fit the bill just right.

Dominic mumbled his disapproval. Those men, including Tierney, enjoyed their trade far too much. He surmised that if in the end that trio didn't receive the balance due them they wouldn't care, just as long as they had gotten to kill a few people. Regular chips off the old executioner's block. The feeling that he had made a mistake joining with Keyes began to grow. He shook the thought and took hold of Six Pack by the back of his neck. "Topside, nubie."

Keyes stood with Bowman alone in the conning tower. He had meant to give final instructions to his XO in this private meeting, but it felt more like a stand off. Since their last discussion he figured Bowman would have thought over a lot of things. None of it, he concluded, would be favorable to him. "Phase two of the OP," he said, "is where I need you at your best, Robert."

"I'm well aware of that, Commander."

Even though they stood eye to eye, Bowman's tone carved a great distance between them.

"What I told you earlier," Keyes said, "was meant to get you back on track."

Bowman nodded with disinterest. "I'm there, sir."

"This is your shot. *Silversides* is yours for the next forty-eight hours."

A hint of defiance flashed in Bowman's eyes. "That she is, sir."

"Stay deep, away from the coast. There's not a snowball's chance in hell that the coast guard is going to find you if you're careful. Be sure to make the next set of rendezvous coordinates on time. We'll be in the home stretch by then."

"It's a shame it has to end so soon."

"All good things," Keyes said.

"Good luck finding your justice." Bowman extended a hand.

In that instant Lieutenant Commander Robert Bowman seemed very much the man Keyes knew him to be. In contrast to the past few days, his eyes were clear and his bearing remarkably lucid. Keyes took his hand. They shook and stared at one another. Peering into the man's soul, Keyes got the feeling he would never see Bowman again. "Good luck to you, Robert."

Keyes let go and headed for the hatchway that led outside. He stopped. "If we miss each other at the rendezvous, get yourself to Thunder Bay. We'll meet there per our plan of withdrawal."

Bowman laughed. "If we miss at the rendezvous, we won't be meeting in Thunder Bay either."

"Understood." Keyes pushed through the hatchway door.

Richard C. had arrived, and when Keyes climbed down to *Silversides* forward deck he found Tierney, Dominic, and their men loading packs and provisions aboard the tug. He had instructed a crewman to load his gear earlier, so he climbed over to *Richard C.* with only a can of chew in his pocket. Acknowledging Tierney and Dominic in passing, he climbed the starboard ladder and entered the pilothouse.

Rierdon studied a chart on the chart table in the dim cabin light. His blond-gray ponytail draped over his shoulder, and a cigarette burned in his lips. "Congratulations, Commander. It's all over the airwaves. I take it things went well."

"Clockwork, Mr. Rierdon, as planned." He breathed in the musty pilothouse air layered with cigarette smoke. "How have things progressed on your end?"

"Much the same. I've got a slip reserved for us in Belmont Harbor, right close to downtown. I'll get us refueled there while you're out and about." Rierdon stabbed his cigarette in the ashtray bolted to the chart table. Through the pilothouse windows he saw Dominic and his men. "We've got more passengers than I thought we'd have coming along on this leg. Any particular reason for that?"

"Precautionary change of plans, nothing more."

"Any other precautionary changes on the horizon?"

Keyes glanced at *Silversides* lying in the water beside the tug. The shard of moon gave her a ghostly appearance. "I'll let you know."

All hands aboard and their gear stowed, *Richard C.* was ready to depart. Crewman on the submarine cast off her mooring lines. Rierdon fired the engines, throttled up, and guided *Richard C.* into a southwesterly heading.

Owen Keyes watched *Silversides'* long, dark silhouette become smaller with the distance. After several minutes he turned about, walked to the chart table, and inspected the course Rierdon had plotted for them. He never looked back again.

- FIFTEEN -

Coast Guard Station, Grand Haven

DUE TO ITS CENTRAL LOCATION on Michigan's west coast, Lieutenant Commander Jacob chose the Grand Haven Coast Guard Station to headquarter the submarine search effort. He initiated morning briefings for the agencies involved in the investigation, and picked a room with windows overlooking Lake Michigan to hold them.

Rebecca Matthis sat at the long, wooden table in the center of the room, chin resting on clasped hands. She gazed through large glass panes to the vast expanse of choppy water beyond shore. She couldn't see the horizon; it just blended into a fuzzy gray hue. The new day had begun with an overcast sky and moderate winds off the lake. She thought back to the weather report she had heard the previous morning. Apparently partly sunny had given way to mostly cloudy. Figures. Her cynical self fully expected an onslaught of foul weather to move in and impede the search for *Silversides*.

But it wasn't a search anymore. No, after the attack on the flotilla it had become a hunt. Unfortunately, the information divulged in the briefing thus far made the great hunt sound more anemic than avenging. Not for lack of effort, she noted, but rather for inadequate resources in insufficient numbers.

A wide array of familiar faces had joined her in the brick-walled room with a drop ceiling. Lieutenant Commander Jacob and an aide, 1st Lt. Wesley, stood at the head of the table and shared what little progress they had made since launching the search just twenty hours ago. Lanny Stevens sat to her left, present in an advisory capacity, and to make damn sure his baby would get returned to him intact.

Gordon Jennings was there also. He sat across from her, behind a box of doughnuts he'd carried in. She wondered if he was still angry with her. Despite the disastrous day behind them he still wore a cheery expression.

Sergeant Jasper Cotter had sauntered in just after the briefing had gotten underway. He claimed a spot next to Jennings. According to the rotund sergeant, since *Silversides* had been boosted within the jurisdiction of the Muskegon Police Department, the Chief of Police had decided to keep tabs on the progress of the investigation and search.

They were all listening to Jacob rattle off a list of reasons why the coast guard chose the search pattern that the cutters and smaller craft were using to sweep the lake with their sounding equipment. In the end it all came down to numbers and probability. With only three true sonar-capable craft to work with and just over three dozen Motor Life Boats (MLB) equipped with Fathometers, they had to concentrate on areas the submarine would most likely be hiding, namely deep sections far from shore. Unfortunately, those criteria described an awful lot of water.

"Let me boil this down for you," 1st Lt. Wesley said. "The haystack is monstrous. The needle is moving. And we're blindfolded and wearing gloves."

"Don't sugarcoat it, Wesley," Cotter said.

Jacob cleared his throat. "We've contacted the Canadian Coast Guard and they've agreed to assist us with every vessel at their disposal. There's a lot of Canadian commerce on the Great Lakes too, so this renegade submarine is as much their problem as it is ours." He glanced at some notes and then at the large nautical chart lying on the table. "Since we initiated the search yesterday the cutter *Woodbrush* has been combing the water from the Straits of Mackinac east into Lake Huron. She's equipped with side-scan sonar, making her one of our best bets at finding the sub. Two Canadian cutters, the *Chinook* and the *Baybridge,* are also towing sonar fish and are heading south into Lake Michigan. The balance of our search craft consist of MLBs, which are not equipped for this type of operation. We've instructed them to use their Fathometers to try and detect *Silversides.* Although those echo sounders are only designed to provide crude profiles of the lake bottom they can pick up large objects suspended in the water, like a fleet submarine."

Rebecca leaned forward. "Forgive me if this question sounds naive, Lieutenant Jacob, but what about privately owned craft? Don't a large number of fishing boats and the like have fish finders aboard, which are basically little sonar scanners?"

"That's actually a good question."

She wondered if he was placating her after she had cut him off at the knees yesterday.

"We've put out a dispatch to all civilian craft to report any anomalous readings they may pick up. We've also contacted a number of research and salvage companies who may be able to assist with their sonar capabilities. Problem is a lot of private craft have fled the lakes. After yesterday's attack and the sinking of the Boggs charter, not too many people want to be out there."

"Why didn't the coast guard issue a warning for all craft to stay off the lakes in the wake of the attack?" Jennings asked. "The submarine thieves have proven themselves a dangerous bunch."

Jacob scratched his neck. "We gave that serious consideration, but we came to the conclusion that it would do more harm than good. It might incite panic. We don't need that. It's analogous to a serial killer at large in a city. Do the police tell the citizens to stay at home and not go outside? No, they recommend extreme caution instead, and that's what we've done."

"Tell that to Rodney Boggs," Cotter said.

Rebecca strummed her fingers on the table. "Special Agent Bradley and I conferred with Lieutenant Jacob on the matter yesterday." She paused. Jennings gave her a blank stare that told her he knew nothing about it. She continued. "We formed a consensus that the men who attacked the flotilla would not likely target John Q. Public in a Chris Craft. The attack itself was complex and deliberate, not at all fitting the profile of a random act of violence."

Jacob added, "We have, however, issued a more grave warning to commercial shipping. We believe that a freighter or tanker would make an attractive target for the perpetrators, so we've instructed the shipping lines to hold off running Great Lakes routes until the issue is resolved. Some of the companies told us they couldn't afford to delay their runs."

No one in the room responded verbally, but all seemed to understand the ripple effect the submarine attack was having on the region.

"In addition to contacting the Canadians," Jacob continued, "we've requested assistance from the navy. They're sending several side-scan sonar units that we can mount to our cutters. We're also discussing other possible assistance."

"What's your plan if you find the submarine submerged?" Jennings asked. "I don't believe depth charges are in the coast guard's arsenal."

Jacob thought a moment. "Our action will depend in large part on the circumstances of the detection, which of our vessels located her, where she is, and so forth."

"It will also depend on the equipment and resources that the navy provides," 1st Lieutenant Wesley added.

Lanny had opened the meeting with a dissertation on *Silversides,* but hadn't said much since. He piped up now. "The plan should be to hunt *Silversides* to exhaustion."

Cotter grimaced. "Hunt her to what?"

"Exhaustion, Jasper. It means we locate her with our dragnet, track her, and wait for her to come to the surface. She'll have to when her batteries drain. We then pursue and surround with surface vessels. Those bastards who took her will know the game is up and will have to surrender."

Sergeant Cotter leaned back and wedged a finger under his gun belt. "Commander Jacob, if you find *Silversides,* and you exhaust her to the surface, do your boys carry enough firepower on them cutters to put a hole in her?"

"Hold on!" Lanny came out of his chair. "Nobody will fire on *Silversides.*"

"We may have no choice, Mr. Stevens," Jacob said. "Given what the thieves have done already, I can't believe they'll give up without resisting."

"But she's valuable historical property. We can't destroy her"

"We'll make every effort to disable rather than destroy."

Lanny sank back in his chair. "Like hell."

"What if they launch a torpedo at one of your ships?" Jennings said.

"Then we run like hell," Wesley replied.

Jacob cleared his throat again. "We hope it doesn't come to that, but if *Silversides* does attack with torpedo the order will be to evade. Fleet submarines of that era used Mark 14s, not a highly sophisticated piece of ordinance. We hope to detect a running torpedo with enough advance notice for the cutter to successfully evade. Mark 14s run on a pre-programmed course, they can't home in with active sonar like today's models."

"What if they ain't shootin' old Mark 14s?" Cotter pressed. "What if they're using something a little more up to date?"

"For the sake of our men out on the lakes let's hope they're not." It seemed he wanted to change the subject. "Agent Matthis," he said. "Has the FBI come up with any thoughts on who is behind this mess?"

She shook her head. "At this point we believe a retired naval officer is either behind it or is deeply involved with the theft. Apart from that we really don't know much more."

Lanny turned toward her in his chair. "Why was the flotilla attacked?"

Rebecca hesitated. She disliked not having all the answers. "Again, any theory we have at this point is speculative. That being said, based on the targets chosen it could be someone who hates the government and the press, like the Anthrax mailer after 9/11."

Lanny frowned. "People used to drink to handle their problems, and then they started bringing guns to work, now this. The world's going to hell in a bucket."

"People are getting angrier," she said.

Jacob collected his notes from the table. "That's all we have this morning. Next briefing is seven tomorrow, unless of course some startling development unfolds today." He addressed Jennings. "I'm briefing the press in two hours. Does the FBI have someone assigned to field questions?"

Rebecca settled back in her chair, silent. Since the Mallory case she and press conferences mixed like baking soda and vinegar.

Gordon Jennings sat upright. "I'm handling that, Lieutenant." He stood and approached the coast guard officers, giving them his thoughts on how they should face the cameras.

Rebecca made eye contact with Cotter. "Will the coast guard get them, Jasper?"

Cotter cocked his head. "If they can exhaust 'em like Lanny says."

"I'll say one thing." Lanny nodded toward Jacob and Jennings in conversation. "If Chop is at the Conn and he's as good as I think he is they're going to have a hell of a time of it."

McCallum Estate, Grand Haven

"We just ran the perimeter systems through a check two days ago. You really want it done again?" Special Agent Paul LaCroix sat in the surveillance room at the McCallum estate, his tight blond curls growing tighter with Dylan's request. Behind his chair, the control board for the security equipment glowed with lights and video monitors.

The room sat at the heart of the large ranch house, so there were no windows. And the overhead lights were dimmed to enhance the pictures from the video cameras keeping watch on the gates and grounds.

"It doesn't hurt to be prepared," Dylan said. "Things are a little crazy out there right now. You know how I get when the world's not at peace."

"The world is never at peace. How do you live at such a high level of anality?"

"I don't think that's a word."

LaCroix spun his chair toward the control board. "It should be, just for you."

Dylan smiled. "Get on it as soon as you can, Paul."

A red light blinked and a beep sounded from the console. LaCroix startled and called up a screen on an imbedded monitor. A grid appeared, atop a diagram of the estate grounds. A red icon blinked on the south wall. "Hold on a minute," LaCroix said. "Motion sensors just detected something. It could be the bogeymen you're concerned about."

Dylan looked at the screen, anxiety growing. The video monitor swept the south grounds. With a series of keyboard commands LaCroix instructed the camera to point at the wrought-iron fence where the sensor had picked up movement.

It wasn't a squad of bogeymen. Trotting toward the house was Simon, the McCallum's smoke-gray tabby cat. Dylan frowned. Kathryn McCallum had saved the scraggly kitten three years ago from the shelter in town and had brought it home, much to the Old Man's bemusement. The cat had taken to venturing into the woods on a regular basis. Simon must have tripped the southern motion sensors at least a dozen times.

Dylan couldn't decide whether to be angry at himself for forgetting about the cat's security breaches, or at LaCroix for playing it up.

"Should I alert Gillespie?" LaCroix said. "Send him out there with his assault rifle? He's a good shot."

"I don't think so. Kathryn would be very upset."

"Looks like the perimeter systems are working just fine." LaCroix leaned back and smiled.

"Check them anyway."

Dylan huffed and left surveillance. He walked into the short hallway that connected garage, laundry, pantry, and kitchen. The monotone delivery of a news reporter flowed from somewhere inside the house. In the kitchen he found Mrs. McCallum standing near the corner of the white ceramic countertop.

Cradling a mug of coffee, she watched a television that she had set on the island beneath an overhead rack filled with silver pans and kettles. The cable news channels were still going wall-to-wall with the attack on the flotilla. Half of them had already crafted catchy logos to plaster in the corner of the screen. The channel Mrs. McCallum watched displayed a graphic of Michigan with the caption 'Terror on the Great Lakes' imposed over the top in a fire-red military font. Slick packaging of tragedy repulsed Dylan, and he wondered if the news agencies realized how blurred the line between entertainment and journalism had become.

Despite his misgivings over the coverage, he had tuned in to one of the less sensational networks to track the story. Someone had leaked the speculative information that the assault may have been carried out using a vintage World War II submarine. He had seen a few military 'experts' and naval consultants interviewed, giving their opinions about the theory's validity. They made a convincing argument that although the idea seemed fanciful, it could quite possibly be true. The current reporter announced an upcoming interview with the curator of the museum from which the submarine in question had been taken.

"Good Morning, Mrs. McCallum." Dylan used a calm voice so as not to startle her.

She lowered the mug and gave him a slight smile. "Morning, Dylan."

He pointed to the television. "They're overdoing it again, aren't they?"

Her face saddened. "It's terrible, all those innocent people." She sighed. "Roger was a good man. Who could have done this?"

"I don't know, but the FBI and coast guard are being aggressive in their search for the guilty party. I spoke with one of the Bureau's investigating agents yesterday. She's very determined in the matter."

Mrs. McCallum looked back at the television. "They're saying that *Silversides* may have been involved. Did you know that Warren served on her?"

"I didn't until yesterday. Ironically, we discussed it minutes before the attack. It's the first I'd heard of it."

She began to speak but stopped herself. She sipped her coffee instead.

He noticed. "Is there something you want to say?"

The lines around her eyes deepened. Something was there ready to come out, but she stared into her coffee mug. "Warren is in the study. He's been there since sunrise, watching the coverage. This has shaken him. Could you please go and talk to him? I'm concerned...He likes you a great deal. Practically thinks of you as a son after these years with us. Please go and see him."

They stared at one another. He nodded. "Okay, I'll check on him." He turned to go but a scrolling list of confirmed dead from the *Rio Grande* drew his attention to the television. He read the names off in his mind, growing angry inside. Agent Matthis had the right take on it. Whoever had done this needed to be dealt with accordingly.

One of the names on the list suddenly stood out. He watched it slide down the screen until it disappeared. Stepping back, he let his jaw go slack and dug into his memory.

"What is it, Dylan?"

He paused. "Have you seen the victims' names from the press pool ship?"

"No. I mean I've seen the list but I haven't read each name."

The scroll had stopped and a reporter was now on the screen. Still thinking about the name, Dylan left the kitchen.

Warren McCallum's study lay in the east wing of the house. It looked pretty much like any other study of a well-to-do statesman. Plush leather chairs were positioned around a dark-stained colonial desk. A globe of the earth with textured terrain stood in the corner near the desk. A wall-length bookshelf stretched across the far wall, filled with legal tomes, historical titles, and a healthy collection of De-Mille, Clancy, and Coonts novels. To the left was a mahogany side bar. A television had been built into the wall above it.

The bar hadn't been in use much these past several years. That is until this morning.

The scent of whisky hovered in the air. Warren McCallum stood at the bar with glass in hand and a decanter of bronze liquid before him. He stared at the television. It was tuned to a news channel. He seemed mesmerized by the glowing pictures. The station was re-running footage of the attack. First the *Commodore* blew apart amid two fiery explosions, and then *Rio Grande* met her violent demise in excruciating slow motion.

Dylan stepped into the room. "Watching it over and over again won't help, sir."

McCallum ignored his entrance. "I'm saying goodbye to a friend. To an idea. To my past." He didn't slur his words, but the alcohol had given him a slight drawl.

"A little early for that isn't it?" Dylan gestured to the decanter.

"Mrs. McCallum is going to be upset."

The president emptied the last ounce of whisky and set the glass down. "We've been married fifty years; she'll understand."

"What will she understand? The grief that made you pick up that bottle? She's seen you grieve before, and so have I, when your brother died, and Kathryn's sister. You never once took to drinking. What's different about this loss?"

McCallum slewed his head around and glared. "With all due respect, Agent Reese, you've known me six years, and I'm damn near eighty. There's a lot about me you don't know."

"You're right about that." Dylan came closer. "And it's not all due to my limited number of years at your side."

McCallum plopped into one of the leather chairs. "What are you talking about?"

"That letter last week—"

"We've had this discussion." McCallum snapped. "End of story."

"What was in it?"

"Fan mail."

"Did it have something to do with what happened yesterday?"

"Trust me; it didn't say a damn thing about that mass murder we witnessed."

Dylan glanced at the television. "I just saw the list of casualties from the *Rio Grande*. Do you know whose name was on it?"

McCallum rubbed a hand over his eyes.

"James Ruby." Dylan watched for some acknowledgment.

McCallum didn't react.

Dylan sat in the chair across from him. "James Ruby, former defense secretary for the McCallum administration."

Still no reaction.

"You knew about this already, didn't you?" Dylan exhaled. "When did you find out?"

The president lifted his head. "Got the call an hour ago, the confirmation."

"Why was Ruby going to the Governors Meeting?"

"He's a freelance political analyst for FOX News. You tell me why he was headed to Mackinac Island."

Dylan noticed he had clenched his fingers around the armrests.

McCallum resumed watching the news coverage.

"Sir, doesn't it strike you as odd that both Roger Patterson and James Ruby were killed on the same day in the same attack?"

McCallum flared to life. "No, Agent Reese, it strikes me as tragic."

"You know what I mean. Is that why you're drinking?"

Rising out of the chair, McCallum stood over his protector like an angry old giant. "Patterson and Ruby weren't the only ones killed. Not everyone who died was part of my administration. You're fishing for a conspiracy."

Dylan matched him. "I'm exploring the possibility that some sort of plot is unfolding."

Flustered, McCallum turned and walked to the bar.

"I think you're entertaining that same possibility."

The president lifted his empty glass. "The only thing I'm doing is mourning two lost friends."

"And an idea," Dylan said.

McCallum looked at him funny.

"You said it earlier."

Annoyed, McCallum shook his head and reached for the decanter. "It doesn't help. When my dad died of cancer my mother went to the bottle. It didn't work for her either."

McCallum bowed his head and rested a hand on the container of whisky.

In an odd way it looked like he was blessing it.

"Right after the attack you blamed the Shiite Brigade. Why do you think this is their work?"

The fire returned. "Those bastards are always first on my lips when innocent people are bombed or gunned down."

Dylan searched his thoughts. "I had a briefing with Protective Intelligence last week. There wasn't anything on the Brigade. They've been pretty quiet this past year."

"It doesn't matter how quiet they are, they're always looking for newer, more sensational ways to strike." McCallum's face fell, and the fire seemed to exhaust what little energy had kindled it. He stared at the mahogany bar a long while. "I'm an old man, my time has past. It doesn't matter what I think or do anymore. Hell, why should the world give a rat's ass about Warren McCallum?" He gazed into his glass. "Why do they assign a talented security detail to protect a man not worth protecting anymore?"

"I think that's the Tennessee whisky talking."

"I see the dedication you have, Dylan. It's why things are so messed up between you and Sarah." McCallum spread his arms as if presenting himself. "You're putting your personal life in the shiter for this, a one-time GOP shining star, now a worn statesman with little tread left."

"We tend to respect our leaders in this country. You are not an exception."

McCallum dropped his arms. "Perhaps some of us should be excluded from such reverence."

"There are cases I might agree with you. Not this time."

Leaning against the bar with one hand, McCallum pointed at Dylan. "Ever been to a sausage factory? You may love Polish sausage, but if you ever saw how it was made you might swear off it forever. The American public only sees the glossy surface of American government. They make their decision on who to follow based on who has the best PR going for them. I had some good PR."

"No, Mr. President, you led the nation through tough times. Any good PR you received was well-earned."

"There's that glossy surface." McCallum snapped his fingers. "Being among the select group of men who have held the office of president, I believe I speak for myself and the forty-one gentlemen before me when I say that we tend not to publicize our poor decisions. You think Roosevelt trumpeted his internment of the Japanese-Americans? How about Nixon and Watergate, he went a long way to keep that under wraps and it cost him his presidency. We don't like our dark little secrets getting out."

Dylan stared at him. "What's your secret?"

McCallum lifted the lid off the decanter. "Go away and leave me be, Dylan. Like you said, the whisky is talking."

"If this secret has something to do with yesterday I need to know what it is."

McCallum poured another drink. "It doesn't have a damn thing to do with yesterday." He lifted his glass and spoke quietly. "It couldn't have."

Dylan stepped toward him. "You have to help me—"

McCallum warded him back with an outstretched hand. "Enough! There are lines you don't cross. This is one of them."

"I'm here to protect you. You have to talk to me."

The president turned a weary gaze on him. "Can you protect me from myself?"

"I'll give it a hell of a shot, sir."

McCallum chuckled and turned away. "I've no doubt you would." His eyes became glassy.

The news channel began running the flotilla footage again and, like a junky, McCallum focused on it. "Leave me alone... Just leave."

For a full minute Dylan watched him. Neither one spoke. Giving up on the conversation, Dylan left the study. He returned to the kitchen. Mrs. McCallum was sitting on a stool near the island watching an interview with a man named Lanny Stevens.

Dylan approached. "Anything new to report?"

"No, but this gentleman knows a great deal about *Silversides* and he thinks it will be nearly impossible to find her with the resources the coast guard is working with."

"Let's hope he's wrong."

Mrs. McCallum turned from the television. "How is he?"

"Not good right now. I think he needs more time alone."

She nodded. He could tell she was drawing strength for her husband's sake.

"I have a question," Dylan said. "Do you know if the president has received any letters recently that were of a threatening or disturbing nature?"

She had apparently anticipated the question. She took a deep breath and reached into a drawer in the island. A tear rolled down her cheek. She lifted a white envelope from the drawer and held it out to him. "Yes. He has."

- SIXTEEN -

Off the Chicago coast

MAJESTIC, triumphant in a way, the Sears Tower lorded over the high-rise monuments of Chicago's sprawling skyline. An overcast sky oppressed the city. The tug boat *Richard C.* approached Belmont Harbor like she was swimming into the maw of a great fish. Keyes stood in the pilothouse, watching the long shadows of the skyscrapers consume the inbound tug.

The dense cluster of buildings that stretch along Lake Michigan's coast stirred in him images of some great ancient city on a distant shore. Medieval imagery perhaps, but that was the state of his mind this warm June afternoon.

Back in the age of armor and honor, as he liked to think of it, good and evil and right and wrong were simple equations to understand. In that reality, knights of the realm embodied chivalry and justice. They ruled by the sword with noble blood in their veins, keeping royal decrees with strength and integrity. Their lives they dedicated to king and country. Simple times, simple solutions; if only it were so clear today.

Sliding the 9mm into his shoulder holster, Owen Keyes pondered those knights and their creed. Duty to king and country, he believed it once. His father believed it. Every Keyes dating back to the Civil War believed it. Regardless the glorious history, the grand illusion had been shattered with a single phone call just twelve months ago.

But Keyes believed he could restore the faith, if not for him, for those who would follow.

He had a charge to keep, and with strength and integrity he was determined to do it.

He pulled a blue shirt over his shoulders and concealed the pistol with the shirttails. He grabbed a .38 snub-nose revolver and ankle holster from the nav console and strapped the weapon in place.

Rierdon guided the tug into the harbor's southern water.

"It's two-thirty Eastern Standard," Keyes said. "I'll be in position downtown within the hour, but from then on it's a guessing game as to when we pull out. Hopefully by nightfall."

"And if not?"

"If I'm not back by eight, contact our friends and tell them our meeting has been postponed, but make it clear to them they are to wait until I set a new time. Understood?"

"I understand, but they may get jumpy with such a last minute change."

"They'll go along. As unappealing as it is, they've got a vested interest in dealing with us." Keyes' face soured. "This OP has made damn strange bedfellows."

Rierdon spun the wheel, hooking *Richard C.* toward her assigned stall.

Belmont Harbor could accommodate well over 400 boats with its array of stalls, star docks, buoy mooring, and dry mooring facilities. The place was big enough for *Richard C.* to come and go without drawing attention.

Several boats were packed into the harbor this afternoon. Apparently the threatening weather kept many safely in dock. Rierdon slid *Richard C.* into her slip between a thirty-foot sail boat and a sixty-foot yacht.

Dominic, Griffin, and Six Pack climbed onto the dock with lines in hand and tied them off.

Tierney came up from below with Wilke and Roth in his shadow. All three were dressed casually in jeans and loose fitting button shirts. The warm weather made it difficult to conceal their pistols, but they had done a passable job of situating Glocks in holsters at the small of their backs.

They gathered on deck and conferred with Keyes on the task at hand. They set a common channel on their tiny Motorola two-ways. Each man clipped a radio to his belt, and then stepped up to the dock. Keyes and his selected three made their way toward shore.

They walked Belmont Harbor Drive, which snaked along the harbor's northern contour, and met up with Lake Shore Drive. Keyes and Wilke hailed a cab and slipped in the back. They instructed the driver to take them to the corner of Addison and Southport, several blocks inside the city.

Tierney and Roth grabbed a cab as well, but headed south to Belmont Avenue, ultimately stopping at the Southport intersection.

Trendy and upscale, the Southport Corridor exudes charm and reeks of money. Amongst a healthy collection of fine restaurants and chic bars, some very expensive housing stands. Keyes and his men converged at one such dwelling, a brick-faced duplex fronted by trees.

Keyes and Wilke walked down Southport Avenue from the north. Tierney and Roth did likewise from the south. They met across the street from the brick duplex, satisfied all was quiet along the avenue.

Late afternoon traffic was picking up, and Keyes grew anxious to move inside. He sent Tierney, Wilke, and Roth to stand post at points along the avenue and behind the duplex, and then walked across the street. He strolled through the entry in the waist-high, wrought-iron fence and up to the front door like he belonged there. He produced a ring of lock pick tools from his pocket, handling them like a set of keys. He worked the lock with little effort and stepped inside. He closed the door behind him and re-locked it, then drew his pistol and chambered a round.

Sweeping the weapon through the foyer, he kept alert for any sounds. The man who lived there shouldn't be home. Not yet. Keyes figured he had at least a two hour wait ahead of him, but checked out each room just to make sure it was clear.

The place was immaculate, he noted with distain. Hardwood flooring covered every square foot. The glossy natural finish shined even in the muted afternoon lighting. The great room boasted a twenty-foot cathedral ceiling, a brick fireplace, tasteful furniture, and three full-length windows that provided a southern exposure. The open floor plan gave access to the kitchen, which contained a central-ized island with tall bar stools, recessed lights, white appliances, and granite counters.

He stood in the center of the great room, taking in the beautiful home, catching the peach scent from a candle on the fireplace mantle. Betraying one's countrymen must be a lucrative business. He checked his watch, walked into the kitchen, and took a seat on one of the bar stools. He set the pistol on the island. Drawing the small can of chewing tobacco from his back pocket, he took a pinch into his mouth. His first spit went straight onto the hardwood floor.

Two-and-a-half hours slipped by before Keyes' radio squawked. Tierney's voice emerged. "Commander, he's coming down Southport. Should pull into the garage in about a minute."

"Copy."

He rose off the stool and walked to the sink to spit out the remains of his chew. He came back and lifted the pistol from the island, then sat back on the stool and clicked the safety off.

A door opened. The sound rolled down the short hallway beside the kitchen. Keyes sat up straight and clenched the 9mm tighter.

The man who rounded the corner wore a tailored black suit and carried a small leather briefcase. He jumped at the sight of the stranger in his house. Keyes noticed his hair had turned silver and his face had aged since last seeing him.

The man tried to regain composure. "Who are you?"

"My name is Owen Keyes. We've never officially met, Mr. Taylor, but you did speak with my father on one occasion. He was very proud of that day."

Taylor saw the gun in Keyes' hand. "What do you want?"

"Something I can't have. Something you took but can't give back."

"I don't...I don't understand what you mean."

Keyes stood, and Taylor fell back a step. "Let's start at the beginning."

Taylor dropped his briefcase. "You want money? Take my wallet and whatever valuables you see."

"Don't mistake me for a common thief. Not every man is governed by gold." Keyes waved the pistol about the lavish home. "But then again, some men are."

"If you don't want money, then—"

"Then what could I possibly want? Is that what you're thinking?" Puzzled, Taylor searched the room, perhaps for a way out.

Keyes flashed an insincere smile. "Do you think yourself a wise man?"

"What do you mean?" Taylor loosened his tie.

"You once made a living giving advice to a very important man. I imagine that would require you to possess a certain amount of wisdom."

Taylor stared blankly.

Keyes walked in a slow circle around his captive, pistol at his side. "Do you have fond memories of your days as National Security Advisor?"

Taylor wiped the corner of his mouth. "What does that have to do with you breaking into my house with a gun?"

Keyes stopped, glared at him. "It has everything to do with it." He resumed his circle.

Taylor tracked him. "If you must know, I am proud of my stint as NSA."

Keyes extended the 9mm. "Think hard, Mr. Taylor. You'll find yourself in error."

Taylor began to protest but stopped short. He seemed to remember something.

Keyes looked hard at him. "Ever been stung by a yellow jacket?" The question melted the old NSA.

"It hurts like hell and the pain lingers a long time. Some people have even died."

Taylor stammered, tried to find his voice. "How—how do you know about that?"

"It couldn't stay hidden forever. The dead want their justice."

A sparkle of recognition flashed in Taylor's eyes. "Keyes?"

"Is it me or my father you remember?" Keyes kept the pistol pointed at Taylor's chest and reached down to the ankle holster for the revolver. "Doesn't matter I suppose."

Fear suddenly overtook Taylor. "What are you doing?"

"I'm giving you an opportunity those men never had." Keyes set the .38 on the kitchen island. "I'm giving you an honorable way out." He nodded to the revolver. "Pick it up."

Taylor shook his head and stepped back. "No. You'll shoot me."

"I'll only shoot you if you don't put the barrel to your temple."

"We did what we had to do."

"Pick it up." A little louder this time.

"We had no other choice."

"Pick it up!"

"You don't understand. It could have meant war. Another war in a region where we'd already claimed victory."

"No, Taylor, you don't understand. You betrayed the very men sworn to defend this country. Why does their blood mean so little to politicians?" Keyes spat on the floor. "To hell with you all."

Taylor raised his hands as if trying to calm the situation. "I wasn't alone in this. It takes more than a national security advisor to make that kind of decision. It takes—"

"I know damn well what it takes. Haven't you been keeping up on the news?"

Taylor's mouth fell open. "Patterson." He searched Keyes face. "That was you?"

"James Ruby too. I know who was involved, and I'm balancing the scales." He glanced at the revolver. "Pick it up."

Taylor rolled his eyes from Keyes to the .38, back and forth.

Sweat glistened on his face.

Keyes lowered the 9mm to his side. "Go ahead, Phil. You just might make it."

Leaping for the island, Taylor grabbed the revolver and swung it around. He never had a chance. Before he had touched the trigger, Keyes drew a bead with the 9mm and fired. The bullet struck Taylor square in the chest, knocking him against the island. He slid to the floor, eyes fading, a gurgle in his throat

Keyes stepped forward and aimed the pistol at Taylor's head. He considered his suffering and lowered the weapon. It seemed more fitting to let him struggle those last few minutes.

He retrieved the .38 from Taylor's limp hand and holstered it on his ankle, then returned the 9mm to its place beneath his shirt. He walked into the kitchen and picked up a cordless phone from the counter. He dialed 9-1-1, put the phone to his ear, and waited for the operator to answer. When she did, he threw it into Taylor's lap. He lifted the two-way radio from his belt and keyed the call switch. "Objective complete."

It was six forty-five EST.

"We head out in one hour."

- SEVENTEEN -

Somewhere in central Lake Michigan

THE RIDE aboard United States Coast Guard Cutter *Wolverine* was choppy. With twenty mile winds capping the swells, she pitched just enough to keep her crew on their toes. She belonged to the Marine Protector Class, and was the newest addition to the coast guard's Ninth District fleet. The eighty-seven foot vessel represented the next generation of cutter. For years the aging Point Class Patrol boats had been the workhorse of the fleet, but they were nearing the end of their run and needed to be replaced. The Marine Protectors were designed for just this purpose.

Longer by five feet than the Point Class cutter, the Marine Protector boasted a nearly unsinkable hull design, twin turbo-charged diesel MTUs for power, state-of-the-art communication gear, and an electronic chart display and information system (ECDIS).

Skippered by Lieutenant Junior Grade Alan Delgadillo, *Wolverine* had left port that morning in search of the renegade submarine. To assist in the effort, she'd been fitted with a military side-scan sonar unit on loan from the navy. The *Wolverine* crew had the dual frequency device functioning on the low 100K mode. At the lower frequency setting it lost some image resolution, but gained in range and area scanned. Operating such, the sonar beam reached 600 meters out from each side of the boat; a 1200 meter swath.

LTJG Delgadillo strolled through *Wolverine's* pilothouse. His crewmen manned their stations all along the command and control console that stretched the full width of the forward bulkhead. He loved the added space in the design of the Marine Protectors. At over 200 square feet, the pilothouse outsized the old Point Class version fourfold.

He approached the makeshift sonar station and gazed at the seventeen-inch color monitor that was hooked up to the sonar data processing module. The blue-gray images of the lake bed passing beneath the keel looked ghostly.

Coxswain Jason Sharp sat at the station, monitoring the images and double-checking them against the hard copy print-out scrolling off to the side.

"Anything interesting, Mr. Sharp?"

The young, blond-haired crewman shook his head. "Nothing but rocks and sand down there. Looks more like death valley than Lake Michigan."

"The ocean is a desert with its life underground and the perfect disguise above," Delgadillo said.

Coxswain Sharp glanced back at him. "Sir?"

"It's a line from an old song by America. *A Horse with No Name.*"

Sharp smiled. "Never heard it, sir." He turned back to the monitor. "About an hour ago I saw debris from an old wreck. Wasn't much left of it. I noted its location with the GPS input. This sonar unit is pretty cool."

Delgadillo patted his shoulder and returned to the commanding officer's chair at room's center. He checked the ECDIS display on the forward console. The display showed him *Wolverine's* position on the lake via digital nautical chart. The boat's surface radar sweep overlaid the chart image. It was a clever set up, and it provided the command crew a true sense of what was out there in proximity to their vessel.

Delgadillo addressed his 1st lieutenant at the helmsman's station. "How's traffic this evening, Mr. Richey?"

Tall, dark, and stocky, 1st Lieutenant Richey replied, "Light, skipper. That submarine has got everybody rattled. We've only had a handful of radar contacts all afternoon, just some fishing boats. Those guys are diehards."

"That they are." Delgadillo settled back in his chair and looked out through one of the seventeen windows that encircled the pilot-house. The sun hovered well above the horizon but a thick overcast masked most of its light, so it appeared like a large full moon.

Delgadillo had just relieved his Executive Petty Officer from bridge duty. He preferred evening watch, and had spent the later part of the afternoon resting in his cabin. Search operations fatigued him faster than did search and rescue operations. The urgency, the adrenalin, it wasn't there.

Operating the side-scan sonar system only compounded his doldrums. *Wolverine* had to tow a torpedo-shaped "fish" through the water at slow speed to allow the unit optimal performance. Making only five knots, they had covered precious little area in several hours of searching.

In reality, Delgadillo had doubts about finding *Silversides,* even with military equipment aboard and every MLB from Detroit to Chicago pounding the lakebeds with echo sounders. In the navy he had served aboard a destroyer that took part in a search for a downed airliner. It had taken them thirty days to locate the wreckage. If it took that long to find a 757 lying static on the ocean floor, how long would it take to find a submarine on the move, actively trying to evade. In this sort of cat-and-mouse game, he believed the coast guard to be outmatched.

Still, he'd give it his best shot. They had to try. *Silversides* had to be stopped. A part of him, though, didn't want to come across the submarine. If they found her surfaced, then they might have some chance to puncture her pressure hull with the two .50 caliber machine guns on deck. If they encountered her while submerged, well, he'd rather not dwell on that possibility.

Delgadillo sat upright and stared across the pilothouse at the spectral images on the sonar monitor, wondering what a 300 hundred foot submarine might look like rendered by the reflection of 100K sound waves.

Aboard Silversides

Hands clasped over the headset, Carson closed his eyes and strained to hear the faint buzz coming through the submarine's hydrophones. He concentrated on the sound until becoming certain. Yes, definitely mechanical, definitely engines, and definitely getting closer. He reached for the intercom dial on the wall and turned it to the setting labeled 'Control Room.'

"Control—Radio Room. I hear screws turning, bearing two-eight-zero."

On watch in the control room, Robert Bowman whirled on his heel and keyed the lever switch on the intercom box above his head. "Range, Mr. Carson?"

"Best I can guess, about 1500 yards. But I can tell you without knowing her pitch that she's moving slow. I'd say less than seven knots."

Bowman checked the large depth gauges above the plane control wheels. *Silversides* was 100 feet down. He stood there, considering the pipe runs through the control room.

Royce stepped forward. "Should we go deeper, Commander?"

Bowman turned, a smile curving his lips. "We should, Mr. Royce, but I think I'd like to have a look at who's up there."

Their eyes met in a devious moment of connection, and Royce smiled too. "Aye."

Bowman ordered the command crew into the tower. He called up the secondary crew to stand ready in the control room. With Hendricks at the helm, Laughlin and Cory at the plane wheels, and Royce in position as dive officer, Bowman stood on his piece of floor plate as captain of the boat. "Mr. Royce," he said. "Take us to periscope depth."

Silversides climbed to sixty-five feet. Bowman raised the search periscope. He tucked his hair behind his ears and peered through the eyepiece. Turning counterclockwise twenty degrees, he spotted a white-hulled boat with a red diagonal stripe in the waning light of a cloudy day. The craft was nearly a mile away. He adjusted the scope's optical power from 1.5 to 4. "It's a cutter," he announced. "They're trolling."

"Have they detected us?" Royce said.

Bowman observed a moment longer. "Not that I can tell. I'm sure they're not equipped to find us this far out."

A long stretch of time ticked by in which nobody spoke.

"Orders, sir?"

Bowman lowered the periscope. "Commander Keyes wants us to stay clear of the Guard, stay hidden. If we do that we can't make our voice heard."

"Agreed."

He thought hard for five more seconds. "Load forward torpedo tube one." He spun to the helm station. "Mr. Hendricks, make our heading two-three-zero."

Aboard *Wolverine*

1st Lieutenant Richey stared at the ECDIS display. Some errant pixel of light had caught his attention. Forty degrees off starboard bow, a mile or so out. He rubbed his eyes, blinked, and then focused on the screen again. It had vanished. No, there it was again. Then gone.

"Lieutenant Delgadillo, surface radar is picking something up."

Delgadillo rose from his chair and approached, gazing at the digital chart. "Where?"

Richey pointed at the suspect section of screen. "Here." The display didn't show a contact blip. "For about a minute a little anomaly has been fading in and out."

"Sure you're not seeing clutter from the water? It's a bit choppy out there."

"Maybe." Richey watched the screen a little longer, waiting for the flicker to appear again. It didn't. "I thought I had something."

Delgadillo rested a hand on the control console and watched the ECDIS display. "Do you have any guess as to what it was?"

"If it was a real contact, it had to be small. It barely registered. Probably just a gull or some other wonder of nature." He leaned back. "Or just an anomalous refraction."

Awakened by the first bit of anything to have happened all day, LTJG Delgadillo grew interested in the flicker. "Let's see if there's anything worthwhile out there. Alter course toward your anomaly, Mr. Richey. Increase speed to ten knots."

Coxswain Jason Sharp turned from the sonar station. "Sir, we'll lose some resolution at that speed. We might miss something."

"We'll throttle back again when we get to the area, Mr. Sharp." Delgadillo nodded to Richey. "Let's go, 1st Lieutenant."

Richey nodded. "Aye, sir."

Aboard *Silversides*

The pitch and sound level of the screw noises changed in Carson's headphones. Barely audible, he had to really listen, but it was there. He rotated the dial on the intercom box to the Conning Tower setting and called. "Cutter has changed course and increased speed. She's closing."

Bowman's eyes darted left and right. Could they have caught the sub on sonar? Doubtful. Were they responding to a dispatch? Possible, but he didn't put much stock in coincidences. Did they see the search periscope? Perhaps. That made the most sense. "Mr. Royce, make depth one-zero-zero. Mr. Hendricks, alter heading to zero-four-five. Give me a wide berth around the target."

"What could they do if they did spot us?" Royce asked. "The coast guard is not equipped with ASW weaponry."

"I'm not concerned for our hides," Bowman said. "I just don't want them to make a run for it. Those cutters move at a pretty good clip. I'd hate to see her slip from my grasp." He gestured to

Hendricks. "Come slowly to two-five-zero. Set up another line of intercept."

Hendricks turned the silver wheel in front of him.

Bowman set a combative stance. "Flood forward tube number one and open outer door. When we come to PD we're going to make at least two target observations. I only want to expend one fish here. Mr. Royce, double as approach officer."

"With pleasure, sir."

For three full minutes the conning tower remained quiet, and then Carson's voice came through the ICS. "Target has throttled down her engines. She's back to trolling."

Bowman smiled. "Take us up, Mr. Royce."

Aboard Wolverine

"Nothing here, sir."

Alex Richey checked the ECDIS display again, and then peered out through the pilothouse windows. "So much for our diversion."

Delgadillo stood over his shoulder, eyes scanning the water. "Maybe so, but if we didn't check it out it'd bother me the rest of the night. Mr. Sharp, anything to report with sonar?"

Sharp shook his head. "Just that desert, sir."

Delgadillo returned to his chair. "Resume previous course."

Wolverine angled back to her original heading, towing the sonar fish at five knots. Ten minutes elapsed. LTJG Delgadillo had almost put the radar anomaly out of his mind. Almost.

"Sir, I just saw another fleck on the display." Richey's voice sounded excited.

Delgadillo leaned forward. "Where, Mr. Richey?"

"One-five-zero degrees off starboard bow, just under a mile out."

"Is it still there?"

Richey scrutinized the ECDIS screen. "No, sir, it's gone again."

Delgadillo stood. "Once is an anomaly, twice is peculiar."

"Maybe our surface radar needs calibrating."

"Perhaps…"

Delgadillo pondered the contact. If that insignificant radar return wasn't clutter or a gull, than what could it be? The first answer that came to mind sent a shiver to his fingertips. Perhaps the hunter is being hunted. Perhaps that contact is the head of a periscope. Maybe that submarine is marking their position. If *Silversides* stayed over 600 yards from the towfish, the sonar beam would never touch her.

"There it is again," Richey said. "Just about the same location, maybe a little closer."

"Watch it, Mr. Richey. How long can you track it?"

He exhaled. "Gone."

Stepping up to the command console, Delgadillo's heartbeat accelerated. *How many bearing marks would they need to acquire their target?* He wasn't about to wait any longer to find out. "Mr. Richey, all ahead—"

"Sir, sir, sonar contact, bearing two-five-zero, 600 meters and closing fast!"

Delgadillo leapt to the sonar station.

A blurry object moved towards *Wolverine* on the screen.

He fixed on the image: a torpedo.

Thoughts scattered. He tried to collect them, prioritize them. Time to impact. He made a hasty calculation, figured they had less than twenty seconds to act. But what should he do?

The torpedo had to have been fired ahead of *Wolverine's* path, but how far ahead? If the lead was short enough, he could throttle up and run past it. If they gave the torpedo a long lead, throttling back and reversing course might elude it. Maybe he could simply turn out of its path.

No, the firing solution was plotted while *Wolverine* lumbered along at five knots. The lead had to be short. He should try to run. *Damn it, Alan. You're wasting time.*

"All ahead full! All ahead full!"

Richey slammed the throttle levers forward.

Wolverine responded. Her props bit into the lake and her bow rose.

Delgadillo scanned the water to starboard. He saw it, the torpedo's exhaust wake, racing toward the cutter's broadside. "Come on, *Wolverine*," he whispered. "Move."

He locked his hands onto the console. "Brace for—"

An explosion thundered through the bulkheads. *Wolverine* buckled. The pilothouse windows shattered. Blast concussion knocked Delgadillo and his crew off their feet.

The world went dark.

The next time he opened his eyes Delgadillo found himself lying prone, bobbing atop the waves in an inflatable life raft. Tiny scrapes on his face trickled blood. A laceration seared his neck and his head throbbed and ached.

At his feet sat Richey, expressionless, silent. A deep cut bled down his cheek.

Burning fuel oil and fiberglass scented the air.

Delgadillo lifted his head.

Cloud cover stole color from the world and bestowed drab shades of gray on the water, the sky, Richey's face. A thin haze of black smoke dissolved in a light breeze. Its scarce residue carried toward shore.

USCGC *Wolverine* was gone.

A massive shape rose from the water just fifty yards away. Like a leviathan from the abyss, *Silversides* came to the surface. Her propellers churned the swells white, and she headed due north, giving no acknowledgment to the survivors in her wake.

Delgadillo watched her go; the gray monster on a gray lake under a dull sun.

EIGHTEEN

Grand Rapids

BEHIND HER DESK in her cubicle at the RA office in Grand Rapids, Rebecca Matthis balanced the phone on her shoulder with her chin and reached for the manila folder in the left corner. She'd just gotten back after a long day of getting nowhere. The speed with which unproductiveness burned hours amazed her. After the morning briefing she had gone back to Mackinaw City to interview witnesses with Agent McGlinen, hoping someone had seen something that might indicate the direction the submarine had gone, or whether or not the perpetrators had accomplices in the flotilla or on shore. Nothing turned up.

She'd talked with the Bureau crime lab and discovered that they'd examined charred pieces of debris from *Commodore* and *Rio Grande*. Through residue samples they managed to determine the explosive used was a mix of TNT and RDX, the components found in Torpex, the same material packed into the head of war-era Mark 14 torpedoes. Such authentic detail at such a deep level, the intricate planning required to successfully execute the submarine heist, and the apparent selective nature in which the targets were hit told Rebecca that the architect of the scheme was a perfectionist. And as such, this person would likely be extremely confident. The two personality traits just went hand-in-hand, which is the reason she now reached for the manila folder on the desk.

Before opening it she paused. She realized that she'd been on the west side of the state for two days and hadn't called her mother yet. Of course she did have a good reason for this and figured Anne, her mother, would understand. She felt that quiver of guilt just the same, so she decided to push the world away for five minutes and make the call.

Anne expressed her relief that Rebecca was all right, even though her daughter had been nowhere near the scene of the attack.

"Is it the terrorists? Do you think there will be more attacks?" She sounded concerned.

"We don't have any evidence that points to terrorists," Rebecca said. "More attacks? We don't know."

"Well, I'm sure you and your friends are working hard to catch these people. By the way, I saw you on television last week. You looked very nice, and you sounded very professional."

"Thanks, mom, but that was last week. We have a whole new problem this week."

"You sound frustrated, dear. Remember; take the day as it comes. Handle the things in front of you one at a time. You'll do fine."

"I'm doing my best. Hey, I'll try and stop by this weekend, if I can get away. Okay?"

"Sounds wonderful." Anne paused. "I'm so proud of you. You've done so well for yourself, but I'm not surprised. Even when you were a child I saw it in you, Reb. You put your mind to something, you make it happen."

"Let's see if I can catch the guys who carried out this attack. Love you, mom, see you Saturday."

She hung up and balanced the manila folder in her hands, thinking how she could not have asked for a better mother. From her twelfth birthday Anne had raised her alone. Affection and love had always been in ample supply, and she could not remember a time when food on the table or having a comfortable place to live had ever concerned her. Anne had struggled to provide these things, working her fingers to arthritis at an electrical assembly factory during the week and herself to exhaustion on the wait staff at Antonio's on the weekends. If Rebecca had a strong work ethic, there was no question as to who it came from.

But dark memories came to her too.

Before she and her mother had left her father, life was different. When dad came home drunk, home wasn't so sweet. When dad came home strung out on coke, Rebecca tried to become invisible. Nights spent hiding in a closet make quite an impression on an eight-year-old. Dodging the fists of a man reeking of whisky make a little girl grow up fast. She learned early that she needed to become as big and as strong and as smart as she could to deal with life.

She marveled with a sarcastic smirk. *How could I have been given so wonderful a mother and so horrible a father all in one lifetime?*

She opened the folder and took out the pictures of Bowman. She laid them side by side on the desk. To the left, ratty-haired, bearded, intense loner Choppy stared up at her. To the right, clean-cut, spit-

and-polish Lieutenant Commander Robert Bowman stared up at her. They looked like two different men. No, they *were* two different men. Bowman had somehow transformed into Choppy.

Based on his military record, his appearance, and what Lanny and the other museum volunteers had said about him, Choppy was not the confident perfectionist Rebecca had theorized on a moment ago. Something didn't fit there. She stared at Choppy's frozen image. *Why are you doing this, Robert Bowman?*

Tapping her fingernail on the desktop, she glanced from one Bowman to the other. Her throat felt dry and she rubbed her eyelids. It had been a long day. She left her cubicle and walked through the office maze into the meeting room across the floor. Two agents were sitting at the long table, gazing into laptop screens, engrossed in some information search. Tuned to CNN, a wall-mounted television hung in the far corner. Coverage of the submarine attack continued unabated.

She reached for a water carafe on the table and tried to ignore the television. She'd seen all the footage the networks had to offer fifty times already, heard dubious "experts" interviewed on every subject from terrorism to submarine warfare, and had decided that enough was enough for one day. So while pouring a glass of water, it surprised her to hear an unrelated story being reported.

She put on her glasses and watched the reporter as she drank the water.

"Police responding to a 9-1-1 call found prominent Chicago businessman Phillip Taylor shot to death in his downtown home. Taylor was chairman of LAN-Global, the Midwest's fastest growing IT services company. He was heralded as a business genius when he turned LAN into a multi-million dollar corporation. Twenty years ago Taylor had a successful career in government, which culminated in his appointment as National Security Advisor in the McCallum administration."

Rebecca swirled a mouthful of water. Phil Taylor had been NSA to McCallum? Her thoughts turned immediately to Roger Patterson, former Secretary of State.

Taylor and Patterson had been murdered within twenty-four hours of one another.

She remembered McCallum's security agent, Dylan Meece or something, and how he wanted to be kept informed on the investigation. She considered McCallum too, and his tenure in office. He presided over the Gulf Conflict, a war in which Robert Bowman had fought. A bunch of threads were pulling together. She got the warm, fuzzy feeling that she was on to something. She set down the water glass and headed back to her cubicle.

At her desk, she found the business card with the number of the Secret Service agent. Reese, that's it. She picked up the phone and dialed.

McCallum Estate, Grand Haven

Standing beneath the brass light fixture that hung over the kitchen table in the guest house, Dylan Reese and Tom Gillespie laid out their arsenal. Atop a cream tablecloth lay an Uzi submachine gun, four ammunition clips, a Remington 870 shotgun with shortened barrel and pistol grip, a box of shells, a disassembled Remington 40X tactical rifle, and a 10x night scope. Including the Glock .40s holstered on their waist, the security agents had quite a variety of ways to throw lead.

Gillespie had just cleaned the rifle and was now reassembling the weapon. "So tell me, why are we doing this?"

Dylan surveyed the guns. "We've been a little complacent lately. McCallum has slowed down and so have we. A couple of times I found myself wishing we had a little more firepower at our fingertips, just in case."

Gillespie continued piecing the rifle together. "Come on, we have plenty of assets in place when we take the Old Man out and about."

"I'm talking about us personally. I want these weapons within reach from now on."

Gillespie worked a while in silence. "You heard from Protective Intelligence, didn't you? They told you the Shiite Brigade has got something in the works. They don't know what, but there's definitely something cooking. Is that what's going on?"

Dylan walked around the table. "I would have told you if that were the case."

"Then what is it?" Gillespie motioned to the arsenal with the rifle barrel. "Pulling this stuff together is a little paranoid, even for you."

"It's my nature to be paranoid."

"Then why don't you wear a vest 24/7?"

"Vests don't stop head shots. I'm pragmatic too."

Gillespie laughed. "Sometimes I think that Sadeed incident screwed you up, my friend."

Dylan cocked his head. "The who incident?"

"Right. You don't fool me, not for a minute. That bullet you said you saw coming, it's got some kind of Lord of the Rings hold on you. You carry it around all the time. You have these, like, panic attacks. Like the one at Fort Mackinac."

"That wasn't a damn panic attack."

"Hey, I'm not slamming you for it. It probably keeps you on your toes."

You got that right. "Drop the Sadeed thing, would you, Tommy?"

"Sure." Gillespie screwed the barrel in place. He smiled. "You think those guys who stole that submarine are going to take a crack at McCallum?" He laughed.

Dylan didn't say a word.

Gillespie noticed his silence. "I don't like what you're not saying."

"What should I be saying?" Dylan walked to the kitchen counter and lifted the letter Mrs. McCallum had given him that morning. He handed it over. "I just want to be especially vigilant until this *Silversides* deal is over."

Gillespie took the envelope. "What's this?"

"A letter McCallum received three weeks ago."

Gillespie opened the envelope and took out the letter. He skimmed through it. "Betrayed the nation, blah, blah, blah, traitorous partners, blah, blah, blah, sentence of death."

He peered over the paper. "Warren didn't tell you about this?"

"No, and when I first suspected a threat he denied receiving any."

Gillespie read it through again. "I like the part about the past coming to judge the present."

"*Silversides.* McCallum served on her. She also symbolizes the military power he wielded as Commander-in-Chief. And as far as the president's partners, that could easily mean Patterson and Ruby, two members of his administration."

"Uh-Huh. But to play devil's advocate, this letter doesn't actually spell out any names. And the judgment stuff is so vague it's easy to twist current events to conform to the threat."

"That isn't the only letter he received. Others referenced some incident during his presidency, but Mrs. McCallum didn't know what that event could have been."

"Why don't you just ask him about it?"

"I tried this morning, but he wasn't forthcoming."

Gillespie snapped his fingers. "Hey, I've got it. Let's just keep

McCallum off the water. That submarine can't get him here at the house."

"Do you work hard at being an asshole, or were you born that way?"

Gillespie rested the stock of the tactical rifle on the table. "It's all natural."

Dylan's satellite phone chimed. He answered, listened a few seconds. "Yes, Agent Matthis, I remember. What can I do for you?" He listened some more. "I've been thinking along the same lines." He glanced at Gillespie. "Why don't we meet someplace to discuss this in more depth?" Dylan checked his watch. "I know it's a little late, but I haven't eaten yet. How about meeting in South Haven in an hour? It's a little out of the way but there's a great steak house there. Good." He rattled off the restaurant's name and directions to it. "See you there. Thanks for the call."

Dylan hung up. "Apparently the FBI is considering a McCallum connection to the *Silversides* incident too."

Gillespie pointed at the sat phone. "Who was that?"

"Special Agent Rebecca Matthis. She's investigating the submarine theft and wants to discuss some things she's discovered that may involve the Old Man."

"Things like what?"

"Don't know yet, that's what we're going to talk about."

"Matthis. I know the name. Have I ever met her?"

"No, but she got some press from the Mallory kidnapping."

"That's right; I've seen some interviews with her." Gillespie grinned. "She's hot."

"We're meeting for work, Tommy. Her looks are irrelevant."

He shrugged his shoulders.

Dylan lifted his suit jacket off the back of a kitchen chair and threaded his arm through a sleeve. "I'll be back in a few hours." He grabbed the Remington short-barrel from the table and headed for the door.

"Uh, Dylan, are you expecting trouble from her?"

He opened the door and lifted the shotgun by the pistol grip. "From now on this weapon rides with me."

South Haven

Rebecca got out of her car in the restaurant's parking lot and buttoned her blazer. The place Agent Reese had chosen sat just off Main Street in South Haven, two blocks from Lake Michigan. With the summer season well under way, tourists filled the sidewalks, drifting in and out of craft shops, bars, and outdoor cafés.

Daylight had all but disappeared, and the clouds that had blanketed the coast throughout the afternoon had begun to break. The temperature had fallen about ten degrees.

She hit the "lock" button on her remote and walked toward the split-log building with the blue neon sign that read, PRIME QUARTER. As a child she had spent a lot of time at South Haven Beach, but this quaint establishment had not been there then. Cars filled the lot and she figured the warm, friendly-looking restaurant had become a favorite gathering place for townie and tourist alike.

She had nearly reached the well-lit awning over the front door when a man stepped down from a black Durango to her left. She recognized him right away. She also remembered his biting remarks from the previous day. "Agent Meece," she said.

"That's Reese," Dylan politely corrected her.

"Sorry, sometimes I'm not good with names." *White lie.*

"Call me Dylan." They met in the center of the asphalt and shook hands. "Any trouble getting here?"

"No, I know this town pretty well from when I was a kid."

"Oh, you're a local?"

"Yeah, I grew up here on the west coast of the mitten."

They walked to the restaurant entrance. Dylan reached for the big brass door handle but she beat him to it and held the door for him. His chivalry stymied, he walked inside first.

The place was crowded. Rebecca noted the unique layout. The floor plan was set up in a theater-like manner with three levels. Patrons sat at rustic tables and booths on the outer two levels, while the lower level, where the stage would be in a theatre, contained two large grills roughly the size of pool tables. They were built with fieldstone. Cleverly concealed exhaust fans hung above them among an arrangement of milled timbers. Artificially aged copper light fixtures threw down dim cones of light.

Patrons stood around the grills with drinks in hand. Steaks and garlic toast sizzled away. A mesquite aroma permeated the place, and the drone of 500 conversations pulsated from wall to wall.

"It's kind of busy," Rebecca said. "There's probably an hour wait to get a table."

"I phoned ahead," Dylan said. "I'm kind of a regular here."

At that moment, a dapper host in black vest and white shirt greeted them. Dylan knew him, and he escorted them to a table on the upper level. Rebecca moved for the chair that would face her into the restaurant. Dylan took a step toward it also. "You mind if I sit there?"

She stopped short of the chair. "No. Go right ahead."

He claimed the seat. "I'm in protection, remember? I don't feel comfortable in a room unless I can see everything going on, and have a clear line of sight to the door."

She sat across from him. "Your protectee is not here tonight."

"I can't switch it off." He smiled. "It's comical when a bunch of us from the Service go out to dinner. Everyone tries to keep their back to the wall and their eyes on the door."

They sat quietly for a few seconds.

She removed her glasses and leaned forward. "I've got some thoughts concerning the *Silversides* investigation and I need to ask you some questions."

Dylan leaned forward a bit too. "That's why I'm here."

She set her palms on the table. "I think we're seeing a well-organized plan play out, one that goes beyond the attack on the flotilla yesterday, and I think McCallum is tied into it somehow."

"I'm with you on that, Agent Matthis, but I'd like to know how you came up with it."

"Rebecca, please. I prefer a little informality when I'm working a case with someone."

He thought about that a bit. "Didn't know we were working together. I thought you were just interviewing me."

"You're about to get more involved. Yesterday Roger Patterson was killed. Tonight the Chicago police found Philip Taylor shot to death in his home." She waited for him to put it together.

His jaw dropped.

"That makes two cabinet officials in twenty-four hours," she added.

He looked her in the eye. "Three."

"Three? What do you mean three?"

"Secretary of Defense James Ruby was aboard the *Rio Grande*. The media hasn't picked up on it yet. I guess they lost so many of their colleagues that the Ruby angle got buried."

"What's McCallum saying about it?"

"Not a word. Something's got him spooked but he's not talking." Dylan shook his head. "He hit the bottle this morning after hearing about Ruby. He's hiding something."

"You have any idea why someone might be targeting McCallum's cabinet?"

He sat back and exhaled. "Nothing I can point to. McCallum alluded to some unfortunate decision he had made but refused to elaborate."

"I want to talk to him. Maybe he'll divulge more speaking to a federal investigator."

Dylan put on an insincere smirk. "Rebecca, I've been at this man's side for six years, nearly got killed saving his life. If he won't open up to me, I seriously doubt he'd do so for you. Besides, he's sleeping off a morning of Tennessee whisky right now."

"You believed a McCallum connection existed before I called," she said with a bit of ice in her voice. "What got you thinking about it, just the Patterson-Ruby angle?"

"I've noticed the president acting a bit off lately. I suspected he'd been receiving disturbing letters, hate mail or threats or something. McCallum prefers to keep his private affairs private and, out of respect, I honor that, but on our way up to the Governors Meeting I questioned him on a suspect letter. He denied any reason for concern on my part and shut the conversation down."

"You let it go at that?"

"My job is to protect him, not intrude on every facet of his life. If he tells me things are okay I have to believe him."

She studied his expression. "But you didn't believe him, did you?"

Dylan shook his head. "This morning Mrs. McCallum confirmed my suspicions. She confessed that the president has been receiving threatening letters. She even showed me one. Someone out there knows about McCallum's dark secret, and they're angry about it. The letter I saw was vague on details but communicates pretty clearly that certain associates of the president were in the crosshairs."

"I want to see it, let the crime lab guys have a crack at it."

"You'll have it in the morning." He paused. "On more thing, and I don't think this is just a bizarre coincidence. Back when McCallum was in the navy he served on *Silversides*. I believe there's a psychological game being played here as well."

"This just gets deeper and more complex as I go. The guy behind this has thrown together one hell of a sophisticated plan."

"Could be a woman," Dylan said. "I've learned you can't underestimate them."

"That's a good bit of advice, Agent Reese."

The waiter came to the table with water glasses and menus. They both declined to order drinks, sticking instead with the water. She opened a menu and scanned through the small selection of steak, seafood, and poultry. "What's good?"

"They have great cuts of sirloin, but their swordfish is excellent too." He perused the menu a few seconds then put it down. "You think they sailed *Silversides* to the Illinois shore and sent a hit team in to snuff Taylor?"

"Based on everything we've discussed that seems plausible. Wouldn't you agree?"

"Yes. I guess I'm just surprised to hear someone else voice such a wild theory besides me." He gave her a brief smile. "Any leads on who the perpetrators might be?"

"My prime suspect is a retired naval officer, Robert Bowman. He disappeared with the submarine. He fought in McCallum's Gulf Conflict, had an admirable career for the most part. I'm sure he's involved, I'm just not certain if he's the one pulling the strings."

"Don't forget the usual suspects," Dylan said. "The Shiite Brigade has tried to assassinate McCallum before. They've got short fuses and long memories."

"Is that how you nearly got killed, during this assassination attempt?"

His expression turned uncomfortable. "Yes, that would be the one."

"What happened?"

He hesitated. "I was point man leading McCallum out of a hotel. Gunman confronted me in the hallway. We exchanged shots at point blank range. I'm here, he's not. I got lucky that day."

"So McCallum owes you one."

Dylan crossed his arms on the table. "That's not how I look at it."

She probed his face. "How do you look at it?"

"Warren McCallum is part of a very small and distinguished group of men who have led the United States of America. He wasn't chairman of the PTA or president of the Elks Club; he was leader of the free world, the only remaining superpower. I take my duty to protect his life very seriously. He owes me nothing. I did my job, was proud to do it, and will do it again if required."

Raising her eyebrows slightly, she lifted her glass of water. "No offense intended. I respect your sense of duty. We could use a few more men who actually believe in something."

He relaxed his shoulders. "Pardon me while I step off my soap box."

She held out her water. "A toast to duty."

Their glasses clinked just as the waiter returned. He took down their order, Dylan's sirloin and Rebecca's swordfish, confirmed their side dishes, and then said, "You may step down to the grill whenever you're ready."

The waiter left and Rebecca tilted her head. "What did he mean by that?"

Dylan stood. "This is the Prime Quarter. Follow me."

He led her down to the grills on the main floor and weaved through the crowd to a large, glass-faced refrigerator door. Large cuts of raw steak and seafood lay on shelves behind the glass. He opened the door and searched the selections. "Here you go." He pulled out a plate with a swordfish fillet and handed it to her.

She eyed the cold fish. "This isn't cooked."

"Of course it isn't." He grabbed a ten-ounce sirloin and closed the door. "Let's go stake a claim at the grill."

She stared at her raw dinner. "Are you serious? We have to cook our own food?"

"That's the charm of this place. You'll always get your dinner cooked the way you like it. Come on, there's seasoning racks alongside the fieldstone." He melded into the crowd and found an open section of grill between an attractive couple and three college boys watching an NBA playoff game on the overhead television.

He waved for her to come over. She came with a reluctant step.

He lifted his steak and placed it on the grill. Juice from the sirloin flared and he yanked his arm back.

She grinned and stabbed her swordfish with a fork. "Come here often, Chef Tel?"

He swiped a bottle of cracked pepper from the rack and shook it over his steak. "Laugh it up, Matthis."

She did, and set her swordfish on the grill. Her eyes drifted to Dylan's hand. "Yesterday you mentioned you had a son. Are you divorced, separated, or one of 'those.'"

He thought a bit. "What's one of 'those'?"

She padded the top of her swordfish. "Married but playing the field."

"Why isn't happily married an option for me?"

"I'm in investigation, remember?" She gestured to his hand. "No wedding band."

"Hmm." He poked at his steak. "None of the above."

She tried to decipher his answer.

"Sarah and I had Danny, uh, out of wedlock. We planned on getting married but it's looking like it isn't going to happen. She's apparently found someone to spend more than a weekend a month with her."

Rebecca dashed her fillet with seasoning salt. "Hazards of the job, I suppose."

"How about yourself?"

"No comment."

"Now wait, you started this personal inquiry."

"You didn't have to answer."

"What, and risk being labeled a hostile witness."

She faced him. "I could only do that if I were cross-examining you on the stand, which I am not. You came here on the pretext of an interview, correct?"

He pointed his fork at her. "Are you a lawyer?"

"I got my law degree at Cooley. A lot of Bureau people are attorneys."

He was about to say something, then shook it off and tended to his sirloin. "So how do we proceed on this *Silversides* thing?"

"Contact McCallum's surviving cabinet members and warn them that they may be in danger. I'll check if Robert Bowman ever received special orders originating from a presidential directive, see if he had been on any special mission or something. We need to ascertain motive. I'd like to know what's driving the man to attack a retired administration."

"Good luck. Orders like that are typically classified, and when the military starts throwing in national security concerns, you can just about forget getting a peek at them."

"Maybe, but I'm definitely going to try. As for you, I recommend stepping up security measures for McCallum. If his cabinet members are targets it's a logical assumption that he'll be at the top of the hit list."

"I'm one step ahead of you on that one. We've got a nice tight perimeter around the estate, and I've alerted my team to the increased threat." He stabbed the sirloin. "Of course this theory of ours is speculative, and supporting evidence is circumstantial."

"Hey, transfer to the Bureau and apply for Bradley's job. With an attitude like that you'd be a shoe-in."

Dylan frowned. "I'm just playing the other side of the record."

"Like you reminded me the other day, Agent Reese, any information we have may save lives. We have to move forward on it."

He nodded. "We need to contact the coast guard. If *Silversides* dropped a hit team near Chicago, we should throw more resources into the southwestern portion of Lake Michigan to find her."

"Good point." She grabbed the cell phone from her pocket. "Watch my dinner for me. I'm going to find a quieter place to make a call to Lieutenant Commander Jacob."

Before she took a step away, the phone rang in her hand. She put it to her ear and tried to block out the restaurant noise with her free hand. "Matthis."

"Agent Matthis, this is Sergeant Cotter."

She could barely make out his voice. "Jasper?"

"They did it again."

"Speak up, Jasper, there's too much noise in here." She moved toward the restrooms for quiet.

"*Silversides,*" Cotter said louder. "She attacked a cutter an hour ago."

She slowed her steps in the dim hallway. "Attacked?"

"She torpedoed it. Sent it right to the bottom."

"Any word on survivors?"

"Not yet. Coast guard has choppers in the air to fish out anyone they find."

"Where did it happen?"

"Smack dab in the middle of Lake Michigan. We're gettin' together in an hour or so in Grand Haven to sort through the mess."

"Thanks, Jasper. I'll see you there." She dropped the phone in her pocket and marched out through the crowd to the grills. She put a hand on Dylan's shoulder and leaned into his ear. "*Silversides* sank a cutter an hour ago. I'm going back to Grand Haven for a briefing."

"Keep me up to date. I'll try to dig more information out of McCallum."

"Right." She started off, but then stopped and turned around.

"The next time we do this," she said rather seriously, "I don't want to cook my own dinner."

- NINETEEN -

Coast Guard Station, Grand Haven

REBECCA sat in the same chair she had started the day in. She took inventory of the faces gathered for briefing number two: Lieutenant Commander Jacob, 1st Lieutenant Wesley, Lanny Stevens, Sergeant Cotter, even Gordon Jennings had driven in from his Grand Rapids home. A new face was among them too, and Jacob wasted no time introducing him.

"This is Nelson Finch, Deputy Director of Homeland Security." He gestured to the middle-aged, African-American with the broad shoulders and gray tinged hair. "He is here to assist in our efforts, and to report our progress to Washington."

Nelson Finch stepped forward, standing tall and looking every bit the man in control. His presence filled the room and he reeked of authority. With dark eyes he appraised the group. He cleared his throat.

"I'd say good evening but if it were good we wouldn't all be here." He clasped his hands behind his back and considered the CD player on the table for a second.

"You have President Harrison's undivided attention here in the Great Lakes," he continued. "He's asked me to help in any way I can with the search and capture of *Silversides*."

Lanny raised a hand. "You do mean capture, right? Not destroy."

Finch assessed him with a critical eye. "Mr.?"

"Stevens, sir. Lanny Stevens, caretaker of *Silversides* for fifteen years."

"Mr. Stevens, forgive me for not speaking with complete clarity. What I should have said was that the president has instructed me to put an end to this situation, and I am prepared to do whatever is necessary to make that happen."

"Shoot," Cotter said. "I hope you packed a fleet of attack submarines in your briefcase, 'cause these old Guard boys, bless their hearts, they just ain't equipped to deal with what's going on."

Jacob shot a cross look at him.

Finch unclasped his hands and leaned forward on the table. "The president is quite serious about this matter. He has no intention of letting the anxiety of the people escalate as it did following that certain day in September."

"He's already loosing ground on that count," Rebecca said. "The media's stoking the terrorism fire with rampant speculation."

"All the more reason to end this story as quickly as possible."

"And how will that come about?" Jennings asked.

Nelson Finch straightened himself. "I bring you good tidings of great joy."

"The last time someone said that a savior appeared."

Finch smiled at Rebecca. "Not a savior in the sense of our Lord Jesus Christ, but one from the United States naval arsenal." He addressed the group again. "Six P-3 Orions are in flight as we speak, on their way to Selfridge Air National Guard Base. Concentric from the point of the attack on *Wolverine*, they will initiate an intensive search of the Great Lakes to locate the renegade submarine and, if we're lucky, blow it to pieces."

Lanny sank in his chair.

Some cheer returned to Gordon Jennings face.

"I've already expressed the coast guard's appreciation," Jacob said. "The *Wolverine* incident made it apparent we need additional help." He nodded to the CD player. "Especially now."

Rebecca raised an eyebrow. "What do you mean?"

"After the attack we received a radio transmission from the son-of-a-bitch skippering *Silversides*."

"Did he give his name?"

Jacob reached for the play button. "We have his message recorded here on disc. I'll let you listen for yourself."

The room fell silent.

An excited voice shattered the quiet. "This is Commander Robert Bowman, captain of USS *Silversides*. There's blood in the lakes, blood that will bring about change, blood that signals the beginning of the revolution. America is dying under inept leadership. National security is disintegrating behind foolish White House policy and incompetent Pentagon directives. I will not stand idle any longer. Their reign must end. Tonight I bend their ear. Tomorrow I bring them down. The wheel turns."

Silence.

Lanny rubbed his eyes. "Oh, Chop, you sorry bastard."

Cotter crossed his arms. "This Bowman fella sounds like a loon."

"An intelligent loon with a calculating mind," Jennings added. "Just look at what he's accomplished, how far he's gotten."

"I lost friends on *Wolverine* tonight," 1st Lieutenant Wesley said. "All he's accomplished is murder."

"At least this message confirms that Robert Bowman is the guy we're after." Small comfort, but Rebecca had to pull something positive out of the evening.

Nelson Finch's voice boomed. "I don't give a damn who he is or why he's doing this. He has declared war on the government and has threatened the President of the United States. His days are numbered."

"He never mentioned the president by name," she said.

Finch cocked his head. "He mentioned the White House, and as far as I'm concerned that's synonymous with the man in the Oval."

"He could have been referring to a previous president, McCallum for instance."

Finch seemed annoyed. "It sounded to me like the current leadership crop is what displeases him."

She thought about Bowman's wording. "He did phrase it that way, but I think McCallum is part of his problem."

Gordon Jennings sat forward. "And why is that?"

She took a breath and went through the conversation she had had with Dylan an hour before. She became a bit discouraged when the faces staring at her didn't look entirely convinced of the plot.

"If McCallum and his cabinet are the targets," Finch said, "then why didn't Bowman state that in his pronouncement?"

"He's not finished yet," she answered. "He doesn't want to make his job any harder than it already is."

Jennings shrugged. "Bowman is on the run. How is he supposed to get to McCallum? The president certainly isn't going to be caught in a boat now."

"Taylor wasn't in a boat. I think their plan is to maneuver close to the coast with *Silversides* and send the killers ashore. When they've hit their target they board the sub and disappear again. No roadblocks, no check points."

Jacob shook his head. "*Silversides* can't move around so easily anymore. The whole Ninth District is searching for her."

She pushed away from the table. "Don't take this wrong but Bowman hasn't been given much reason for concern yet."

"That's going to change," said Finch.

She glanced at him. "Let's hope so."

"Still," Jennings said thoughtfully. "Something doesn't square with what you've said and what Bowman announced. He sounds angry more with the people making decisions now than the ones who made them ten years ago. I mean, why fix today's problem by attacking the past?"

"There may be some connection between Bowman and McCallum, but we haven't been able to find it yet. Dylan Reese also believes there is a link. McCallum has been receiving threatening letters alluding to as much."

"Bottom line is," Finch said, "we nail Bowman and the matter is closed."

Rebecca wanted to pound her fist on the table and say, "Absolutely", but something held her tongue in check. Jennings was right, something didn't square. She tried to sort it through. Bowman didn't fit the profile she had assumed, but his attack on *Wolverine* and his declared revolution shifted all the pieces on the game board. Perhaps her first impression was skewed by incomplete information. Who else but a lunatic would steal a submarine and go on a rampage? Still...

"We don't know what the bottom line is," she finally said. "But one thing's for sure, *Silversides* needs to be taken out of the equation."

Aboard *Richard C.,* off the Illinois shore

The pilothouse lights were extinguished, and the only illumination came from the gauges on the instrument console. Keyes stood in darkness near the chart table, recounting in thought his visit to Phil Taylor's house and the attack on the flotilla. Unconsciously he reached for his breast pocket and felt the edges of the documents. They were warm this evening, warm with satisfaction at what had been done, but there was more to do.

A large, brown paper envelope lay stuffed on the chart table.

The next phase of the OP made Keyes cringe, because to make it work he had to shake hands with the devil. His recent successes, however, fueled his drive. He could see the end of the odyssey approaching, the final objectives drawing nearer, and his profound sense of duty carried him forward. Very soon the justice he sought would be met out in full.

At the tugboat's nav console, Rierdon read the position of the radar contact he'd been watching. "Small craft dead ahead," he said, "should be our friends."

"Friends my ass." Tierney scowled in the shadows next to Rierdon. He put an unlit cigarette between his lips and gestured for a light. "It'll be a cold day in hell when I consider a sandnigger my friend."

Rierdon lit the cigarette with a Zippo. The yellow flicker highlighted their faces in a nefarious way.

"A means to an end," Keyes said. "That's all they are."

Rierdon snapped the lighter closed. "I doubt they enjoy dealing with us either."

"To hell with their enjoyment." Tierney drew off the cigarette.

Keyes approached them. "We share a bitter common thread, and that makes them useful. Don't be concerned though, this is a one-time arrangement. When we're finished with this OP I just might have something special in store for them too."

Coming out of the shadows, Dominic shook his head. "That's why the Arabs are pissed at us. We're always using them for something. Oil, political checkers, we just keep pulling their strings. After all these years they're getting tired of it."

Tierney scoffed. "Don't cry too hard for the Arabs. They may hate America, but they love American dollars, and a lot of the cash they rake in selling us oil goes right into their second biggest export: Global fucking terrorism. Bastards teach their kids from toddlers to hate the West, that the United States is the Great Satan, all the while turning the screws on their own people, keeping them in the dark ages. You got a problem with somebody, Dom, make sure it's with them"

Dominic sniffed. "Some people would call us terrorists for doing what we're doing."

Keyes snapped his head around. "There's a difference, Dom, a damn big difference."

He studied the body language of the Italian in the dim lighting. "You do see it, don't you?" The remark amazed him. There was a fundamental understanding of the operation that every participant had to understand. Dom seemed to be missing it.

"What I mean," Dominic said, "is that terrorists carry out their deeds to further a cause not everybody understands. I'm sure our cause is not understood by everybody either."

Tierney blew out a stream of smoke. "You seem to be wondering if we're a posse or a lynch mob."

Dominic flashed a sarcastic smile. "Which one do you think we are?"

"You know the answer," Keyes said. "If you think about it, you'll
see it."

"The boat is dead ahead," Rierdon said.

Keyes considered Dominic a bit longer. "We have to do this. If
we believe the things we were told all our lives, and take seriously the
oath we swore to, we have to do this."

In the faint moonlight through broken cloud, a thirty-foot Mercruiser appeared ahead of the tug. Windows around the cabin were
tinted dark and nobody appeared to be on deck. The boat looked
abandoned.

Instinctively Keyes' hand twitched and he touched the butt of the
9mm in his shoulder holster. "Mr. Rierdon, take us around them,
make sure they don't have any surprises in store. Then bring us alongside with our starboard facing east. John and Dom, call your men
from below. Let the Iranians know our trust goes only so far."

Tierney and Dominic acknowledged the order and exited the pilothouse.

Drawing his pistol, Keyes walked to Rierdon and chambered a
round. "This won't take long," he said. "On my signal get us out of
here."

Rierdon nodded. "Aye."

Richard C. rounded the bow of the Mercruiser on a thirty-yard perimeter. A man stepped from the boat's forward cabin and stood in
the open stern. Lack of fair lighting cast him as a tall, dark, featureless
form.

Rierdon guided the tug in closer.

A second man emerged from the Mercruiser cabin. Standing beside one another, the men watched *Richard C.* maneuver alongside.

Rierdon throttled back the engines to idle. Keyes flicked a switch
on the control console. A pair of flood lights mounted on the pilothouse exterior ignited. Harsh white illuminated the boat and the two
men standing astern.

Dark hair and dark skin, the tall man wore a full beard and had a
pronounced nose. The shorter man was clean shaven, and his dark
eyes surveyed the tugboat. They seemed perturbed at the lights, and
when they caught sight of the six men armed with submachine guns
lining *Richard C.*'s deck, they squabbled and waved their hands with
angry gestures.

Keyes swiped the large, brown paper envelope from the chart table, left the cabin, and climbed down to main deck.

Dominic, Six Pack, and Griffin had taken positions far astern and had their MP-5s leveled at the two Iranians. Tierney, Roth, and Wilke had lined up amidships and had also brought their weapons to bear on the two. Satisfied, Keyes strolled to starboard and stood next to Tierney.

He regarded the bearded Iranian. "Omar Abdullah, how the hell are you?"

"Not so good." Omar's words came out rapid and his tone was angry. "Are you going to shoot me? This is what I expect from Americans. Are you going to shoot me?"

"Only if I have to. Look, I'm just being cautious. You are what intelligence reports call a dangerous man."

Omar smiled, his teeth shining through his beard. "This is true, dangerous and cautious as well." He pointed toward his boat's dark cabin windows. "Behind all those windows I have rifles pointing right back at you. You like?"

Dominic ordered Six Pack and Griffin to swing their weapons toward the cabin.

The short man standing next to Omar laughed.

"Think he's telling the truth, Dom?" Six Pack whispered.

"Eyes forward, mouth closed."

Omar relaxed his stance and wagged a finger at Keyes. "One more thing. I have explosives aboard. A lot. Enough to incinerate you and all your men, should you decide to attack us. You like this too?"

Keyes eyed him, thoughtful, and grinned. "You expect me to believe a bullshit story like that? There's a whole lot of coast guard activity on this lake these days. You're too smart to risk being boarded while carrying such illicit material. But all that is beside the point. We're here to finalize a deal, so let's do it and be on our way."

Omar pointed to the submachine guns trained on him. "I do not like the way you do business but, yes, let's get on with it."

Locked in a firing posture, Roth trained his MP-5 square on Omar's chest. "What do you think about these towelheads?" he said quietly to Wilke. "I'll bet they're buddies with those bastards who took the towers down."

"Could be," Wilke replied.

"I think we should burn 'em right here and now."

Tierney cut in. "Keep your mouths shut and your fingers off the trigger unless I say."

Keyes lifted the brown envelope to shoulder height. "Here're the details, Omar. Just how we discussed. There's a timetable, addresses, and a good faith down payment." He threw the bulging envelope across the water. It landed at Omar's feet. "Look it over, but I suggest you do so quickly. Americans have a nasty tendency toward individual thought, and some of my boys might get it in their mind to even some scores."

Omar stopped short of picking up the envelope and wagged his finger at Keyes again. "I told you what will happen. You will die. You will all die!"

Keyes waved his hands, absolving himself from any wrongdoing. "I'm just letting you know the sooner we part company the better."

Six Pack clenched his MP-5. "What about the explosives, Dom? True?"

"Zip it, nubie."

Omar retrieved the envelope and ripped it open. He rifled through the material.

Keyes faced the pilothouse to give Rierdon the departure signal.

"Commander Keyes."

Owen Keyes froze.

That wasn't Tierney or Dominic who called him. It was Omar. And he'd never given the Iranian his name.

He exchanged glances with Tierney. A rogue element in the plan doing his homework wasn't good. Keyes weighed the option of opening fire.

"I see intelligence reports too," Omar said. "We are not as stupid as you think us."

"No one said you were stupid, at least not until now."

Omar scanned *Richard C.* and the men pointing their weapons at him. "As you can see, I need to know who I am dealing with, and why they are dealing with me."

"Can't say I blame you."

The Iranian stood silent a moment. "I know your name, Commander Keyes; I understand why you are doing these things."

Keyes sneered. "Don't bet on it."

"You are doing a service for my people too. You may find favor with them."

He fought the temptation to draw his pistol and give the order to shoot. "I have reasons for everything I've done and, believe me, making friends with Iranians isn't one of them."

Omar smiled. "I know why you sought us out."

"Whatever you think you know doesn't matter," Keyes said. "Do your part and that's the end of our relationship." He stabbed a finger at Omar. "And I'd better never hear another word from you after this. I suggest you and your friends leave the country. If you stay and stir the pot, we'll meet again, and our next get-together won't be nearly as cordial as this one."

Keyes signaled Rierdon. *Richard C's* engines revved. The floodlights outside the pilothouse went dark and the tugboat pulled away from the Iranian boat.

Keyes and Omar stared at one another as the distance increased.

Roth kept his MP-5 pointed at the boat. "That's two Arabs we'll have to kill another day."

Wilke agreed.

Keyes moved toward the forward ladder but stopped near Dominic. "If we were a lynch mob," he said. "Those Iranians would be dead."

Dominic didn't reply.

Keyes continued up to the pilothouse and stood next to Rierdon in the semi-darkness.

"That went well," Rierdon said.

"As well as could be expected. Set course for the rendezvous."

Rierdon raised a finger. "One minute." He reached down and turned up the volume on the cabin radio. It was tuned to an AM news channel out of Chicago. "Listen to this."

A news announcer gave a report on how the hostile submarine that was loose on the lakes had attacked and sunk a coast guard cutter.

"Bowman wasn't supposed to do that," Rierdon said. "Think he'll meet us at the rendezvous coordinates now?"

"Not likely." Keyes paused. "It'd be foolish for us to even try."

Rierdon shook his head. "What the hell is he doing?"

"He's trying to prove some people wrong, but he's only proving their point."

"Did you know he might do something like this when we left him?"

"It was a possibility."

"Then why did you leave *Silversides* in his hands?"

Keyes didn't answer.

Rierdon grinned. "Did you set Bobby Bowman up for a fall?"

"Lay in a course for Grand Haven," Keyes said stoned faced. "I'm heading below for some shut eye." He turned and left the pilothouse. Standing on the port wing, he gave one last look behind *Richard C.* to where the Iranian boat had been, and then descended the ladder.

At the McCallum Estate

Dawn arrived and Dylan hadn't slept much. He sat up in bed in the guest house and ran a hand through his hair. The thought that had plagued his fitful dreams now filled his conscious mind. *Someone is going to try and kill Warren McCallum, and I have to stop them.* In and of itself that thought is not what troubled him. Protecting McCallum was his job. He'd done it for years. But one particular possibility, one scenario, frightened him beyond anything else.

As if drawn by a magnet his eyes went to the nightstand and fixed on the slug from Sadeed's pistol. The scene in the hotel hallway played out in his memory. He'd nearly taken a bullet for the president that day. He felt it touch his temple. It had happened so fast he didn't have time to think. He just stood his ground and did his duty. But a long time had past since then, and he'd done a lot of thinking on the matter, perhaps too much.

He could handle the prospects of a chaotic firefight where random chance might get him, but knowingly standing in the line of fire while some sleaze took aim and fired unnerved him. He searched his soul for the answer to the question he'd asked himself a thousand times in the past six years. If he had to put himself between McCallum and a bullet again, could he do it? If he had no other choice would he carry out his duty? He couldn't answer yes, but he didn't say no. A hot flash consumed his skin and his palms broke into a sweat.

He cursed and stood and grabbed his Glock from the nightstand. He stared at the spent slug for a whole minute.

In the shower he put his mind to work on the reality of the situation that faced him. People were coming for McCallum. He had to work on that assumption. When he'd returned from his meeting with Rebecca Matthis, the president was deep in sleep, or more likely, passed out. He hadn't had a chance to speak with him. That would be the first order of the day. After the shower he dressed in khaki pants and a blue Polo shirt, and strapped the Glock to his waist.

Sun shimmered on dew-covered grass across the estate grounds. It was a fair weather morning. Dylan knew he would find the president around the house in the rear courtyard.

McCallum sat beneath the green umbrella on the patio. Dressed in a wrinkled, burgundy robe, he read the morning Free Press.

Dylan noticed the large headline. *Cutter Torpedoed.*

"Why is this happening, Mr. President?"

McCallum didn't look back. "How should I know?"

"I'm convinced this involves you. Three from your cabinet are dead now."

McCallum swatted the newspaper down. "I know they're dead! Hells bells, do you think I'm blind?"

"What happened in your administration to get these people going?"

McCallum cocked his chair sideways, grinding the aluminum legs over the stone. His eyes were fierce and bloodshot. "Nothing happened to make these sons of bitches go on a killing spree."

"But something did occur, something you're not proud of. You said it yesterday."

"Alcohol does that to a man; it makes you blather on with incoherence."

"With all due respect, sir, I don't believe that."

McCallum dismissed him with a wave. "You're entitled."

Dylan stepped closer and raised his voice. "No. I'm entrusted to protect you."

"I'm not stopping you."

"You sure as hell aren't helping me."

McCallum stood and glared at him. "Watch your mouth, Agent Reese. When it comes right down to it you work for me, not the other way around. If you keep this up I'll bounce you off my detail. Do we understand each other?"

Dylan simmered. In a low voice he said, "No, I don't understand. I don't understand a great leader falling apart before my eyes. I don't understand a man ignoring the danger when his friends and colleagues are being murdered. I don't understand a man who lies to the people protecting him."

McCallum froze. "Lie?"

"Kathryn showed me a letter. Betrayal, judgment, death, it had a lot of bad stuff in there."

McCallum opened his hand. "Show it to me."

"I don't have it here. It's going to the FBI this morning."

He huffed and dropped back in his chair.

"How many letters have your received?"

The president grumbled. "A handful."

"All threatening?"

"Some threatening, some cryptic, all put together by a deranged mind."

Dylan circled the table and sat across from him. "Who's sending them?"

"I haven't the slightest idea."

"Does the name Robert Bowman ring a bell?"

"No."

"The FBI believes he's the one who stole the submarine."

"Good for them. I've never heard of the man. There's a hole in you theory right there."

"The letter I saw mentioned betrayal. What does that mean?"

McCallum fidgeted. "It means some irresponsible bastard got his hands on information he didn't understand."

Dylan leaned closer. "What information?"

"It's classified, and that's where this conversation ends."

"People are dying—"

"Not because of my administration! I won't believe it!"

"The victims, *Silversides*, the letters, they're all linked to you."

McCallum slammed his fist and rattled the glass table. "I'm not responsible for the actions of a sick mind. Now I said it once, Dylan, you keep pushing and you're gone."

He meant it, that threatening glare said it all. Dylan slid his chair back. He wasn't about to let himself get booted from the detail, especially during such a volatile time. He considered the president a long while in silence. McCallum didn't blink. "Sir, I recommend you stay here at the estate until the authorities resolve the *Silversides* issue."

"Recommendation noted. I'm still going to speak at the Tall Ships festival in two days."

Dylan's jaw fell in disbelief. "But those ships are still anchored in Traverse Bay; they're not taking the chance to sail down to Muskegon with the submarine at large."

"The ships may not be there but the festival still is, and I have a commitment to be there."

Dylan scratched his chin. "Have you heard a single word I've said?"

"Have you heard me?"

"There must be a death wish floating around inside your head, if I may say."

"Don't think so little of your abilities. You're good. Now a little peace, Dylan. You've gotten the day off to a rocky start and I want to get it back on track."

Dylan rose. "Think about what I've said. You shouldn't go out there."

"I haven't stopped thinking about it since you arrived." McCallum brushed him away.

The door had been closed again.

Dylan left him alone beneath the umbrella.

McCallum sat there until the sound of Dylan's footsteps had vanished. "Death wish," he said quietly, part jest, part contemplation. He reached between the pages of the newspaper and pulled out the envelope he had hidden there. It was another letter from the nut-job with a chip on his shoulder. It had come in the mail the day prior, but he hadn't had the gumption to open it yet. He thought about tearing it up right then, destroying it without so much as a peek. But a dark part of him wanted to read it, wanted to see what grim message had been sent this time.

He grabbed the corner of the envelope and ripped it open.

TWENTY

Aboard *Silversides*

"TARGETS," Bowman said. "Find me some targets. They haven't heard from us in over thirty-six hours. It's time we make some noise."

He and Royce stood face to face in the mechanical complexity of *Silversides'* control room. The air smelled of sweat and diesel. Condensation dripped off pipe runs along the close bulkheads. Pressure from running deep coaxed a steady stream of creaks from the aging hull. Tired and wearing thin, the primary crew members manned their stations. They'd been piloting the submarine for the better part of eleven hours with little if any reprieve and were starting to show signs of fatigue. Being shorthanded for crewmen, they weren't going to get relief anytime soon.

Standing with his back to plane control men Laughlin and Cory, Royce listened to Bowman's desire for action. "What did you have in mind, Chop? Another cutter?"

Bowman shook his head. He brushed away the hair that had fallen into his eyes. "It's got to be something bigger. We only have three fish left, and I want each one to make a bold statement."

Royce glanced around at the tired crew. "We can't afford to search too long. The men need a break."

"This is revolution, Mr. Royce. Washington's men didn't get a break."

"Washington's men weren't manning a submarine. Besides, we've got to start thinking about making a trip to the surface. We only ran four hours with the diesels last night before the coast guard search forced us to dive. That wasn't enough to give the batteries a full charge. I'd say we've got five, maybe six more hours of down time left."

Bowman checked his watch. "It's 1400 hours, broad daylight."

"I know we can't surface yet, but there are more hours of light in the sky than juice in the cells. Let's do what you suggested to Keyes earlier; find a quiet section of lakebed to settle down on until nightfall, and then come up in darkness."

"Don't be hasty. We can't let them forget we're out here." Bowman spent a moment in thought. "We'll head north for a few hours, keep our ears open for a worthwhile target. I'd love to come across a commercial freighter." His eyes widened. "No, wait. The *Badger*. We're close to where she crosses to Wisconsin. Sinking a passenger ferry would definitely cause a stir." He brightened at the dark prospect.

"I doubt the ferry is still making the run, not while we're on the prowl."

Bowman growled at the logic. "It's worth a shot. If we don't find the ferry or some other high profile target by 1700 hours we drop to the bottom and wait for dark."

Royce nodded. "Aye, Captain."

Captain. After so many years of waiting it felt good to be addressed as commanding officer. It felt right. How could Fleet Command have failed to see his worth? Well, they'd see it now, and realize their mistake. He clapped his hands and rubbed his palms together, then leaned forward on the gyroscopic compass. "Mr. Hendricks, make our heading zero-one-zero. Dive Officer, stay steady at one-five-zero feet."

Two hundred feet above Lake Michigan a pair of turboprop engines droned. An Orion P-3 maritime surveillance aircraft broke from its search pattern and banked into a wide turn that brought her over a particular tract of water for a second time. In the pilot's seat, Lieutenant Michael Kirby finessed the controls, completing the turn and leveling the plane.

He had been coasting along with just two of the aircraft's four engines running to conserve fuel, but if this detour got interesting he'd re-start the others. He and the rest of Combat Crew 11 from squadron VP-47 had lifted off Selfridge's tarmac at 0600 and had been cruising over the water ever since. They'd searched for that old fleet submarine the whole day, but all they found was a pair of coast guard cutters a few miles back.

They were only in the second day of the search and Lieutenant Kirby didn't fret. With six Orion P-3s in the air, all loaded with Jezebel sonobuoys, directional radar, infrared cameras and magnetic anomaly gear, the odds were good they'd locate that diesel-electric before too long. Kirby just didn't have the feeling it would be his flight.

Earlier they had dropped a handful of sonobuoys, but the small frequency ranging sensors failed to pick up a trace of *Silversides*.

The whole operation made Kirby uneasy. "I can't believe we're prosecuting a hostile submarine in our own back yard," he said to his co-pilot.

"This ain't our back yard," the co-pilot said. "This is inside our house."

Just two minutes before, Kirby's Tactical Coordinator (TACCO), Matthew Bodden, had called forward from the main cabin. "Lieutenant," he'd said. "Youngblood reports a possible MAD contact. Come around for another pass."

The magnetic anomaly detector, MAD, identifies abnormalities in the Earth's magnetic field, which are typically caused by large ferrous objects such as submarine hulls. But sunken shipwrecks could produce the same effect, and Kirby knew the Great Lakes were strewn with them. He doubted they had found the submarine. He thought rather his TACCO and his electronics operator had been monitoring silent equipment for too long and wanted something to break the monotony. He had to admit, a possible bit of something was a welcome change from a whole lot of nothing, so he brought the plane about while Bodden (TACCO) planned a search pattern and programmed the sonobuoy panel.

Bodden called forward from the main cabin. "Come five degrees to heading two-seven-two."

Kirby altered the P-3's course as instructed and flew in silence for a few minutes. "TACCO, maybe your MAD gear picked up a shipwreck down there."

"Maybe," Bodden said. "It was a weak read…Here's another bearing."

"This is beginning to feel like work. Starting one and four." Kirby fired the dormant engines. When they had come to speed and achieved proper temperature, he guided the plane into a hard turn, aligning the aircraft to Bodden's requested course.

"Yank and bank," the co-pilot said. "Love it."

Kirby spent another minute listening to engine buzz and scanning the lake surface. "Ten bucks says it's a wreck."

The co-pilot smiled. "You're on."

Kirby thought on it a bit. "Just the same, I'm going to alert those cutters back there that we may be on to something."

Seated in *Silversides'* radio room and listening to the sounds of Lake Michigan coming in through the hydrophones for several hours had nearly put Carson to sleep. He snapped to attention when the acoustical pattern of a machine emerged from the clutter. He tuned his ear to the noise, became certain, and keyed the ICS switch to the Conning Tower. "Conn—Radio Room."

Bowman had manned the tower in hopes of locating a worthy target. He stood on station there when Carson's hail came through. He whirled to the intercom, an expectant smile beneath his beard. "Go ahead, Mr. Carson."

"Screws turning, more than one set. They're two miles out, bearing zero-zero-six."

Bowman rolled his eyes. "What else can you tell me about them?"

"Small craft moving slow. I'd say they're cutters, Point Class."

Dejected, Bowman glanced at Royce. "Not quite what I had in mind."

"It's something. If we're going to strike today, this has to be it."

Bowman opened his arms and threw his head back. "Is it too much to ask for you to send me tonnage to shoot at?" He dropped his chin and strands of hair fell over his eyes. Annoyed, he grabbed the strands and fished a jackknife from his pocket. He bared the blade and cut the hair with a swift slice. His eyes were clear now. "That was a long time coming."

Hendricks looked over his shoulder at him.

"You okay, Chop?" Royce asked.

"Absolutely—Mr. Hendricks, plot an intercept course to those cutters." He selected the Forward Torpedo switch on the intercom box. "Load tubes one and two." He whirled about to give another order but stopped cold. "You know, Mr. Royce, you would have made a good U-boat officer."

Not knowing how to reply to that, Royce kept silent.

Bowman laughed and slapped his back. "Take us to periscope depth."

"MAD, MAD, MAD!"

Bodden's sudden shout through the headphones startled Kirby. TACCO had a contact. For a split second he didn't believe the report. It wasn't likely they'd nail the sub magnetically before buoys were in play. "Are you shitting me, TACCO?"

"Negative. MAD just made a strong contact. Pegged the needle.

Must have flown right over that damn sub. I'm putting sonobouys in the water to figure course and speed."

Bodden's dropping Jezebels. This is getting exciting. Kirby ordered his co-pilot to contact the command post at Selfridge and inform them of the action.

He heard the shotgun-like slam of the first sonobuoy launching from its chute.

Adrenalin pumped like water from a hydrant. "Talk to me, TACCO."

"Bring us about, Lieutenant, back over the contact coordinates."

The sledgehammer thump and bang of the second sonobuoy launch rang in the flight deck.

Kirby began to think that maybe they would be the crew to snag the sub after all.

The third buoy hit the water and Bodden called out a new heading.

Kirby pulled the P-3 through another tight turn. "Yank and bank."

Leaning forward with head hanging and hands outstretched on the periscope column, Bowman waited out the approach to the cutters. "Distance to target."

"Two thousand yards and closing," Carson reported.

"Prepare to go active with sonar."

Royce turned. "If those cutters are equipped with sonar they'll get our location."

Bowman rested his chin on his outstretched arm. "And then what will they do? We can get them before they run, we've proven that already." He dropped his hands and stood straight. "Sonar will give me a good solid fix, eliminate the guesswork. Remember, every shot has to count."

He read the depth gauges above plane control. Ninety feet and rising.

Pride welled up inside. The things he will accomplish with a sixty-year-old boat will make the navy brass rue their decision to keep him down. He thought about Owen Keyes and their last conversation. That was a blow. After having served under the man aboard *Hampton* for four tours, he wondered how Keyes could have misjudged his abilities and character with such severity. Well, he'd have to reevaluate his opinion of Lieutenant Commander Robert Bowman in the days to come, and the next event to spur this change lie dead ahead.

"Conn—Radio Room. Targets are changing course and increasing speed. They're heading toward our position."

Bowman's brow furrowed. "Did they catch us with a side-scan towfish?"

"Doubt it at this distance," Royce said, "but if so, why are they coming at us instead of running?"

"Maybe the coasties got their hands on some ASW equipment."

"We're being pinged!" Carson again, but this time he sounded very excited.

"Pinged?" Bowman thought maybe he'd heard it wrong.

"Source bearing one-eight-zero. Range one mile."

"It's not a ship, we'd have heard it," Royce said.

It came to Bowman in an instant, the source of the sonar trying to echo range them. "We've got company up there."

"Another source just went active, bearing one-one-three, range 1.5 miles."

Bowman faced Royce. "They're sonobuoys."

"Shit, there's a Seahawk or a P-3 dogging us. This isn't good."

"On the contrary, we finally have a worthy challenge to contend with." Bowman considered the situation. "Stop our ascent. Dive to two hundred feet, ten-degree down bubble. Mr. Hendricks, turn us away from those buoys, left standard rudder to course two-seven-zero. Maneuvering Room, ahead two thirds."

Newly commissioned CO Robert Bowman couldn't help the smile that curved his lips.

"Third buoy in the water," Carson reported. "Bearing zero-nine-zero, range two miles."

"Adjust course ten degrees to starboard. Let's see how well they lay down their net."

Silversides drove through the water, diving deeper, changing course as new sonobuoys entered the game. Bowman's initial joy receded as the chase wore on. The pattern of the drops and the coverage of the acoustic dragnet attested to the skill of the P-3 crew in pursuit. Eluding the dogged search became a more ethereal goal than he had thought.

Sweat rolled down Kirby's face. Flying low and aggressive worked him hard, and the afternoon sun through the cockpit windows didn't help matters much. Gun smoke from the shells used to launch the sonobuoys had drifted into the flight deck, and the acrid smell filled his nostrils. Part and parcel of sub hunting, he let none of it bother him. He barely noticed it. The exhilaration of the chase pervaded any and all negatives.

Back in the main cabin the TACCO and acoustic operators were sorting through data coming in from the buoys, getting a fix on *Silversides.* Kirby figured that between the MAD contact and the echo ranging they'd get a handle on the target before too long.

He was right.

"We're on top of them," Bodden called forward, "tracking solid."

The proclamation sounded sweet in Kirby's ears. Aboard a P-3 prosecuting a submarine it was perhaps the sweetest thing one would hear. "Stay on top," he said. "I'm informing Selfridge." He radioed their situation to VP-47's commanding officer at the airbase, and received the order he had expected to hear. Switching back to ICS, he called the main cabin. "TACCO, we have orders to strap onto *Silversides* with a 48. We are not, repeat, not to let that submarine slip away."

"Understood," Bodden said. "Torpedo is programmed with target coordinates."

Tension squeezed the crew in the conning tower. Laughlin, Cory, Hendricks, anxiety showed on their faces, their nervous eyes, the sweat soaking their clothes. They knew their chances going up against a state-of-the-art antisubmarine aircraft in an ancient fleet submarine were poor.

Royce managed to mask his concerns better than the others, but even he had to wipe perspiration from his brow at regular intervals. They'd been trying to evade the relentless pings from the sonobuoys for thirty minutes but it just wasn't happening. "They have us," he said, "right by the balls."

Bowman turned on his heel and cast a fierce glare. "Hold your tongue, Mr. Royce. Your clothes are dry and there's air in your lungs, you're doing just fine."

"Until they fire," Hendricks said. "Keyes isn't paying me enough for this."

"You signed up like the rest of us," Laughlin chimed in. "You knew the risks."

Cory's hands were shaking. "Surface and surrender. Prison is better than drowning."

"Everybody quiet and mind your stations!" Bowman shouted. "I'm in command and I decide our actions."

Hendricks scoffed from Helmsman's Watch. "A lot of good you've done so far."

Bowman came forward and brought a savage fist down on Hendricks nose. Blood splattered. In a flash he had the jackknife in his hand. "One more word and I'll gut you where you sit and drive this boat myself."

Holding his bleeding nose, Hendricks stared at the gleaming blade. He slowly turned back to his station.

"Commander Bowman is captain of the boat," Royce said. "Everybody had better respect that."

Bowman gave him a slight nod.

Suffocating silence settled in. The groans of the hull carried through the submarine like the cry of a tortured ghost. Bowman felt his confidence erode a little more with each second. He couldn't get out from under the sonar umbrella.

Frustrated, he scanned the bulkhead, desperately trying to see what was happening in the water beyond the steel. He expected an attack soon, depth charge, torpedo, he didn't know which. He just wished they'd get on with it. *What the hell are they doing up there?*

He didn't have long to wonder.

Carson shouted through the ICS. "Torpedo in the water! Torpedo in the water!"

Finally! Bowman stood straight.

Carson sang out the bearing and range of the incoming fish.

It was most likely a standard Mark 48. Bowman calculated they had about a minute and a half before impact. "Right full rudder. All ahead full."

Silversides laid over in a hard turn.

He had to pull that torpedo into a wide arc. Wide enough to run past them.

It was all he could do.

Twenty seconds elapsed. Carson reported. "Torpedo on track and closing."

Royce let slip a nervous chuckle. "Anyone have a countermeasure in their back pocket?"

Countermeasure? Something clicked. *Forward tubes one and two are loaded and flooded.* Fingers of desperation closed around Bowman's throat. He turned to the Torpedo Data Computer. "Mr. Carson, read off the bearing of that torpedo. Mr. Hendricks, make our heading match that bearing line. Understand?"

A shaky acknowledgement.

Carson reported the numbers on the inbound fish.

Hendricks swung *Silversides* about to meet it nose to nose.

Hands unsteady, Bowman adjusted the dials on the TDC. Bearing: dead on straight. Range: He tried to calculate the distance to intercept. It would be damn close. Speed: It didn't matter. Run depth: 200. Zero gyro angle. "Fire tubes one and two!"

He backed away from the dials.

Carson called, "Torpedo 1 away." Three seconds later. "Torpedo 2 away."

Royce forced a smile. "That's a million to one shot, Chop."

Bowman kept silent. He knew the odds. Hell, those outbound torpedoes might not even have enough run time to arm themselves before reaching the intercept coordinates. But he hung his hopes on the fact that maybe, just maybe, he didn't have to score a dead-on hit. When Keyes had ordered these Mark 14 reproductions, he stipulated that they have a proximity trigger in addition to the contact trigger.

Proximity. That's what Bowman hoped for. One of his shots had to get close enough to trip the proximity mechanism.

"Torpedo 1 nearing inbound fish." Five long seconds ticked by. "Clean miss."

Someone cursed. Cory crossed himself.

Bowman realized he was holding his breath.

"Torpedo 2 nearing inbound fish." Three seconds of silence. Four. Five. "I hear an explosion! Torpedo 2 has detonated!"

They all shouted. From one end of the submarine to the other they howled. All except for Bowman. He held back, he wanted to be sure.

Carson's next report cut the celebration short.

"I'm still tracking inbound torpedo. We didn't get it."

But Bowman still hoped. He hoped the explosion had skewed the 48's trajectory just enough to…

A sickening screech echoed through *Silversides'* interior.

The Mark 48 skittered along the submarine's pressure plate.

Bowman watched a drop of condensation fall from an air pipe.

The torpedo struck dead on the propeller guard at the stern and exploded on impact. *Silversides* shook, a violent shudder, and power dropped away. Darkness enveloped Bowman and the crew, and they stood in their dark, steel tomb, waiting for the water.

Emergency power kicked in. Red globes flickered on throughout the boat and bathed the spaces in ghastly crimson.

Bowman tired to get his bearings. The lake had not rushed in to claim her victims. It amazed him. "Report," he yelled. "Damage report."

Royce snatched up the air phone and shouted for information on *Silversides'* status. A chaotic exchanged played out for several seconds between the maneuvering room, the engine room, and the conn.

"The explosion tore up our driveshafts," Royce said, breathless. "Starboard is frozen. Port turns but it's making a hell of a racket. We're taking in water through a hull fracture in the aft torpedo room. They can't stop the leak. They're sealing off the compartment. Still don't know why the primary power buss went down."

At the plane control station, Laughlin struggled to turn his wheel. "Stern plane controls are seized."

Grim thoughts clouded Bowman's mind. He shouted a curse at the overhead.

No propulsion, no control, taking on water, that Mark 48 packed a lot of hurt in its punch. The deck was tilting in response to the aft section sinking. The bow seemed to be up plus five already, and the lake depth below them reached beyond the submarine's 300-foot crush tolerance.

It hit him all at once. It was over. His revolution had ended. His self-vindicating mission had failed. He slumped against the periscope column.

"Orders, sir?"

Bowman didn't notice Royce's urgency. "I failed."

Royce realized his CO had cashed out. "Blow the tanks!" he shouted. "Blow the tanks!"

A gurgling sound materialized as compressed air displaced water in the ballast tanks. *Silversides* began to rise, but the water from the hull breach aft slowed her ascent. "Hope like hell we get to the top," Royce said.

Bowman stared at him through the red lighting, confused. "How could it have ended so soon? What did I do wrong?"

"You kept us alive, Choppy. You didn't fail completely."

Bowman gave him a defeated smile. "You know, we'll be captured as enemy combatants and tried in a military tribunal."

"Right now, that sounds like a fair deal if we don't drown."

"I won't let them sit in judgment of me." Bowman stared into a dark corner. "They've done it my whole career and I won't let them do it again now."

Royce saw defiance in his friend's face. "What are you going to do, Chop?"

"When you're taken into custody," Bowman said, "make sure they know that Robert Bowman commanded this boat, that I caused them all this heartache. Tell the crew not to mention Owen Keyes. We owe the commander that much."

"What are you going to do, Chop?"

Bowman stood straight. "There's an ASW flight crew up there who've taken something very valuable away from me. I need to explain to them how much that hurt."

Like a beast from the depths coming up for air, *Silversides* broke the surface of Lake Michigan. She bobbed heavy in the water.

Five hundred yards away, United States Coast Guard cutter *Buckeye* and Canadian cutter *Chinook* spotted the wallowing submarine and throttled up to intercept her.

Before *Silversides* had settled, the bridge hatch flew open and Bowman climbed on to the cigarette deck, an ammunition drum in his hand. He slapped the drum in place on the 20mm and tilted the weapon skyward. He ignored the approaching cutters.

From the east Lieutenant Kirby's P-3 approached at 200 feet off the water.

Bowman swung the 20mm around and opened up, spitting cannon fire into the air.

Crewmen aboard *Buckeye* and *Chinook* manned the deck-mounted .50 caliber machine guns. The telltale puffs of smoke and the *thunk, thunk, thunk* of the 20mm was all the guardsmen needed to determine that the pirates weren't giving up without a fight.

The cutters attacked, blanketing *Silversides* with machine gun fire. Armor piercing .50 caliber rounds tore into the submarine's hull, shredding and pocking the aged warship. Caught in the deadly hail, Robert Bowman took four rounds in his body and dropped. He fell from the gun mount and splayed out on the forward deck, his riddled body staining the teakwood with blood.

The lone man topside of the submarine had gone down, and the gunner aboard *Buckeye* decided he'd done enough damage. He let off the trigger but kept the barrel pointing at *Silversides* deck. Nothing moved. Feeling the sting of the laceration on his neck, Lieutenant

Alan Delgadillo let go of the machine gun and reached for the bandage. He thought about *Wolverine's* lost crewmen, grieving that his small act of vengeance wouldn't bring them back.

TWENTY-ONE

McCallum Estate

DYLAN had assembled the security team in the surveillance room where they could watch the grounds via the video monitors during their pre-event briefing. Despite the fact that the schooners and frigates of the Tall Ships armada remained anchored in Traverse Bay, the festival in Muskegon went on as planned and, in turn, McCallum would still make his appearance there.

The Old Man had really roiled Dylan this time, totally disregarding his advice to stay put at the estate. He couldn't help but picture a big red target on the president's chest whenever he saw the man around the house. The unfortunate thing about that being that if there was a target on McCallum, there was a matching bull's eye painted on him.

Leaning back on the surveillance room door, he checked each video monitor one last time before beginning. The team already knew the details of the outing, but he liked to recap the plan before striking out.

Seated at the control console, Paul LaCroix sipped from a glass of cola. Peter Douglas, boyish face stretched in a yawn, stood in the far corner of the dark-paneled room. Hovering over the others, Tom Gillespie crossed his arms and tapped his foot, anxious to get moving.

In code they were known as Freak, Sideshow, and Carney, respectively. Their codenames didn't really reflect their personalities so much, except for Tommy who in some aspects fit all three. They were a good group and they'd developed an instinctual rhythm working together over the years. Dylan was glad he had them.

"President McCallum has decided to have dinner with Mayor Cooper, so we're moving out early, at 1700 hours. I've informed the State Police and the Muskegon Police Department. They're moving their assets around accordingly."

"What about Enigma, has she decided to go along now too?" LaCroix asked.

Enigma was Kathryn McCallum's codename, which is how Paul

LaCroix referred to her even in secure conversations.

"No, Paul, she's staying here," Dylan said. "And so are you. Tommy, Pete, and I are escorting McCallum to the festival. Hopefully he'll stick with his plan and leave right after his dusk speech at the docks." He pointed to Gillespie. "Tommy is handling close protection. Pete is working with the locals on securing the middle perimeter around the marina. I'm coordinating with the State Police protection unit working the crowd at the landing. We'll have two rifles watching the festival grounds from the roof of the industrial complex across the expressway."

"Any new info from Protective Intelligence?" Douglas asked.

"No, all is quiet."

Sure, it seemed quiet, but he sensed unease in the team. He'd told them about the assassination plot two days ago. They received the news rather coolly. Knowing there may be crosshairs on your forehead has a way of putting one on edge. Dylan had put out feelers to beef up manpower around the estate but had yet to receive a positive response from anyone. With half the governors of the United States in Michigan during the *Silversides* scare, the Secret Service, the FBI, and the State Police were all working around the clock on security measures to keep them safe.

Dylan's satellite phone rang. "Reese."

"Dylan, this is Rebecca Matthis. I've got news."

She sounded wired. "What's going on?"

"We got them."

Her words didn't register at first. "What do you mean?"

"Forty five minutes ago a P-3 forced *Silversides* to the surface. The coast guard boarded and took the crew prisoner. Gordon Jennings and Lieutenant Commander Jacob are going in front of the cameras in two minutes to make a statement."

Dylan felt buoyant. "They put up much resistance?"

"Not much. Only one guy decided to go down in a blaze of glory."

"Don't tell me, let me guess. Robert Bowman."

"Correct. It must have been him all along."

"Isn't that what you thought?"

"Yes. And no. Hold on…" Her voice trailed off and she talked with someone at her end of the line. She came back. "I've got to take care of some things. Just thought you'd like to know. Where are you right now?"

"At the estate, but we're moving out soon to the Tall Ships Festival."

"Maybe I'll catch up with you there, fill you in on the details."

"Sounds good. Thank you, Agent Matthis." They ended the call. Freak, Sideshow, and Carney stared at him.

"Was that that hot FBI agent?" Gillespie asked.

Dylan snapped his fingers and pointed at a small television in the corner of the console. "Turn that thing on. There's going to be a press conference."

Peter Douglas fired up the television. "They get the submarine?"

"That's what Agent Matthis just told me."

Deadpan Paul LaCroix actually smiled.

The television hummed and the screen lit up. Jennings and Jacob stood behind a podium buried in microphones. Behind them a group of supporting players shared the stage, most likely participants in the *Silversides* investigation and search. Among them he spotted Rebecca Matthis. The caption at the bottom of the screen read *Live—Grand Haven Coast Guard Station.*

Cheery as ever, Jennings stepped forward and made some opening remarks about how well the Guard and the FBI worked together to apprehend the submarine thieves, blah, blah, blah.

Dylan found himself staring at Rebecca. *Gillespie has a point about her.*

Some action at the podium drew his attention. Jennings stepped aside and Jacob came forward. The lieutenant commander launched into a summary of how the submarine had been located and forced to the surface in a brief encounter with an Orion P-3 aircraft. A video flashed on screen showing *Silversides* floating in Lake Michigan. It looked to have been taken from a helicopter circling above. The crawl at the bottom of the screen trumpeted the footage as being exclusive to the station. In it, a handful of coast guard vessels had surrounded the submarine. On *Silversides'* deck, a group of men knelt with hands behind their back. Uniformed guardsmen armed with M-16 rifles stood post, keeping watch on the prisoners.

LaCroix, Douglas, and Gillespie fixated on the footage. Dylan felt the tension dropping in the small surveillance room.

Gillespie turned about. "I don't know about you guys, but my puckered ass is starting to relax. It looks like they got these pricks cold."

"Right there in living color," Douglas said.

Dylan breathed a sigh of relief, but caught himself. "No need to let our guard down, gentlemen. We still have a job to do today."

They did, but, if the president hadn't seen the news already, he wanted to be the first to tell him about the capture. He left the surveillance room and found McCallum in the kitchen sharing a quiet moment with Kathryn. The words they'd exchanged the previous day made his approach awkward. "Sorry to interrupt, sir, but I have good news. They've captured *Silversides*."

McCallum maintained his composure, but Dylan saw a weight lift off the man's shoulders. "Have they released any names of the men who did it?"

"Nothing yet, it all went down just an hour ago. I'm sure more information is coming. I do have one name, though. An FBI agent I've been talking with told me that Robert Bowman was with them, most likely the leader of the operation."

The president cocked his head. "Is Bowman talking, telling why he did it?"

"No, sir. He's dead. Went down fighting."

"Just as well I suppose."

The comment hit Dylan's ears funny. "Sir?"

"A murderer like that can't possibly have anything of value to say."

"Perhaps not."

At 1700 hours McCallum and his security contingent rolled down the long estate drive and out the main gate, a bit lighter in their hearts. Dylan spearheaded the two-car convoy in his Durango. The president's Towne Car followed with Gillespie at the wheel and Peter Douglas in the passenger seat. They entered Muskegon at six o'clock, just in time for Mayor Cooper's chicken barbecue.

Muskegon had hosted the Tall Ships once before, and had enough success with the venture to improve and expand its waterfront facilities, building Heritage Landing and the largest deep-water berths in the state. Boasting the artsy Johson Pavilion, expansive festival grounds, and docking facilities to accommodate nearly twenty Tall Ships, Muskegon had put itself on the maritime map. The recent trouble on the lakes, however, had blunted this season's landmark event.

Since the main attractions of the festival were not on hand, a light crowd had gathered at Heritage Landing. All the better for containment and surveillance. Mayor Cooper's dinner had been set up in a large white canvas tent south of Johson Pavilion. While the public and invited guests entered through the metal detectors at the west entrance, Dylan, Gillespie, and McCallum entered through the security entrance to the south. With Gillespie his shadow, the president found his place at the honored guests table and began hobnobbing with Cooper and his political ilk.

The mayor was short and stout with Julius Caesar pattern baldness but an effervescent personality that had lifted him to victory in many an election. Dylan noted that McCallum seemed to genuinely like the man, which probably explained his agreeing to come to the festival in the first place.

After making his rounds between the picnic tables under the dinner tent and speaking with the State Troopers present, Dylan positioned himself at the west entrance, getting a good view of everybody there. It also happened to put him in line with a cool breeze, which in his suit he really appreciated. Across the aisle stood something like an easel, with a large cardboard-backed nautical chart of Lake Michigan resting on display. The route the Tall Ships were to follow down from Traverse Bay had been drawn in with red arrows. They hadn't quite made it yet.

Mayor Cooper stood and did his thing, welcoming everyone, thanking the president for coming, and generally ingratiating himself to his constituents. He asked McCallum to say grace before the cooks pulled the chicken off the grill. The president obliged and started into a prayer of thanks. *If he hadn't gone into politics,* Dylan thought, *he'd have made a decent preacher.*

Feeling a pinch guilty, he took the occasion of bowed heads to scan the crowd for suspicious types. People with bad intent on their mind typically don't respect reverence.

As the president brought grace to a close, Dylan caught a glimpse of a woman in a dark suit and skirt approaching his position from the screening area outside.

"...So for the abundant blessings we've been given," McCallum said, "we now give thanks to God. In Jesus' name we pray..."

"Amen," said the female voice to Dylan's left.

"How did you get through our security screeners, Miss?"

"I work for the government."

"Not good enough, I'm afraid." He glanced at Rebecca. "You carrying?"

She didn't reply.

"No iron in the tent. I'll have to have a word with my boys outside. They shouldn't have allowed you in, let alone armed."

"It's all right" she said. "I've got contacts in the Muskegon Police Department. Sergeant Cotter got me through."

"Sergeant who?"

"Cotter. He's a good man."

Dylan smirked. "That sounded like it was hard to say."

"Normally it is. Men can't seem to drop their superiority complex with me."

He glanced at her. "Perhaps it's not their complex that's the problem."

"Are you going to make me sorry I came, Agent Reese?"

"Aren't you sorry already?" He noticed she didn't smile. "I'm sorry. I'm just giving you a hard time."

"Glad you found a moment for frivolous banter. Feel better?"

"You have issues accepting apologies from people, don't you?"

"Not all people, just some of them."

Glancing around the tent for suspicious folk, he reached over and extended his hand to her. "Peace."

She accepted. "Peace."

"I'm surprised you're here. I thought you'd be crawling all over that submarine with fifty other agents by now."

"The coast guard is towing *Silversides* to Grand Haven. They should have it in port by nightfall."

"Is any of the pirate crew talking?"

"Not from what I've heard." She found an empty picnic table bench near him and sat. She crossed her legs and straightened the skirt over her knees. "The ones making statements are backing Bowman's revolution."

"Revolution?"

"After sinking *Wolverine* Bowman transmitted a short manifesto of sorts, said he was fighting against a corrupt, incompetent hierarchy of power." She laughed. "Aren't we all."

"That doesn't quite fit with our assassination theory, does it."

She set her leather shoulder bag on the picnic table. "No, it doesn't."

"Does that bother you as much as it does me?"

"More." She pulled Bowman's file folder from the bag and thumbed through the pages. "For the most part Robert Bowman had an admirable twenty-year career in the navy. Two minor incidents marred his record and brought into question his judgment. If he believed he deserved a higher rank or perhaps a command then his revolution against the power structure makes sense."

"And at one time Patterson, Ruby, and Taylor held high positions in a very powerful structure. Maybe it does all fit into a nice tidy box."

"They held those positions sixteen years ago. Why go after them now?"

"Don't know yet, but I alerted the rest of McCallum's cabinet of the possible threat after we spoke the other night. Your cronies in the Bureau assigned them some protection." Dylan bounced on his heels. "McCallum admitted to some dark incident during his term, but I doubt Bowman's ascension in the ranks had anything to do with it."

"What did it have to do with?"

"That information is classified. The president informed me of this in no uncertain terms."

Across the tent, Gillespie spied them in conversation. He gave his partner an approving wink. Rebecca saw it. "Is that tall guy in a suit a friend of yours?"

Dylan smiled. "That's Tom Gillespie. He's part of my detail."

"Juvenile behavior is another pet peeve of mine. Call me old fashioned."

"Tommy can be…pig-like at times, but he doesn't know any better. It's part of his charm."

"And what's your charm, being apologetic and sensitive?"

"That sounded sarcastic." He checked on McCallum. "My charm comes from my protective and caring nature, hence my profession."

She considered him standing vigilant in defense of President Warren McCallum. It suited him well; she saw it in his posture, his alertness. "You know, Dylan, I think you believe that."

A bit uncomfortable with her assessment, he studied the nautical chart on the easel. "One of the troopers told me the Tall Ships left Traverse City this afternoon, after the announcement of the submarine capture. They're on their way."

Turning her attention to the folder in her hands, she seemed not to hear him. "Something still doesn't feel right about this. It's hard to believe Bowman led the effort. He sounded unbalanced on that recording. How could he get a group of skilled crewmen to follow him on a revolution doomed from the beginning?"

"Maybe deranged minds think alike." He stared at the chart. The Machine started making noise. Rebecca was saying something but his thoughts forced her voice to become vague background chatter. Chicago, Lake Michigan, something was ringing a bell.

"Are you listening, Dylan?"

He raised a hand to silence her. "What time do the police think Phil Taylor was killed in Chicago?"

She thought back. "Somewhere between six forty-five and seven P.M."

He faced her. "And when did *Silversides* attack *Wolverine?*"

"About nine that same night." She caught on. "How did *Silversides* get from the Chicago shore to central Lake Michigan in two hours?"

His mind raced. "What's her best speed?"

"According to Lanny Stevens, top speed is twenty knots on the surface with diesels running."

He studied the chart again. "She couldn't have covered a 130 miles in two hours. We assumed a hit team had been dispatched from the submarine. Maybe we're wrong. Maybe there's another element at work here we're not aware of."

"Or maybe the hit team did originate from the sub, but was never extracted."

"Then where are they now?"

"Illinois?"

"Hmmm." He scanned the people in the tent eating grilled chicken, wondering if one of them might be a professional assassin. "Maybe Taylor's death is just coincidence." He shook his head. "I don't like it. We're missing something."

"Agreed." She stood and shoved the folder back in her shoulder bag. She reached for her cell phone. "I'm going to check with Jacob, see if everything's on schedule with getting *Silversides* back to the coast. Touch base with Agent McGlinen too; see if we've learned anything new from the prisoners." She headed out of the tent.

At the head table, McCallum talked with Mayor Cooper.

The sense of danger that had temporarily disappeared reasserted itself.

Dinner past quickly, and Dylan dreaded the moment when he would have to move the president from the tent to the pavilion for his speech. Rebecca had disappeared after making her calls, saying she wanted to update Jasper Cotter on the investigation. Dylan spent a good deal of time thinking about her too, and not entirely in a professional sense. She came on bold and brash but once in a while he sensed a subtle allure. Finally, he realized where his thoughts were taking him, and switched back to the business at hand, namely, protecting the president from unknown assailants. But the diversion surprised him. Usually the job completely commanded his thoughts. Not good. As a matter of fact, it was rather unsettling.

Before he knew it the dinner crowd was breaking, and McCallum and Cooper were on their feet. Dylan made for the security exit where the politicians were heading and caught up with Gillespie. They took positions in front and behind, and called their departure to Douglas. "Sideshow—Ringleader. Cipher is moving."

"Copy," Douglas replied. "Perimeter clear and corridor is open."

They exited the tent, Dylan and some troopers leading, McCallum and Cooper following, Gillespie bringing up the rear. The tent and the pavilion were close together, alleviating some of Dylan's concerns. Even though the crowd at Heritage Landing had been light all afternoon, it was still a crowd.

Peter Douglas and the local police had roped off a path to the pavilion, and the politicians followed their security men right down the center of it. They entered another white tent, smaller than the dinner tent, erected to screen off the rear of the pavilion. Once inside with McCallum, Dylan took a breath. He realized his palms were sweating. *This just doesn't get any easier for me.*

Black speaker cabinets and amplifiers filled half the space under the canopy. Cables ran along the ground and out of the tent to the pavilion platform. The equipment was for a swing band and a couple of local rock groups scheduled to come on after McCallum's address.

A pair of lanky technicians with long, black hair worked in the tent, unrolling cables and setting up the sound system. They looked like brothers and seemed in a hurry. They didn't give McCallum or Cooper so much as a glance. Dylan recalled having them screened for access a few days before. They checked out fine.

A portable television was tuned to a news channel covering the *Silversides* capture. The same footage of the prisoners on deck broadcast earlier was running again. Dylan wondered if there were other men in that group, men who were not accounted for.

McCallum and Cooper talked near a small picnic table in the far corner of the tent.

Gillespie approached. "You've got that look. What's wrong?"

"Nothing—for sure."

The technicians lifted a cabinet onto the stage.

A trooper near the tent entrance coughed into his hand.

"Keep on your toes, Tommy."

"Always," Gillespie said. "Where's Matthis?"

"Off doing her job."

"Looked like you two were hitting it off."

"We were discussing the submarine capture."

"Maybe you should give me her number."

"Why don't you take a walk around the pavilion? McCallum goes on stage in thirty and people are starting to fill the grounds."

"Dog." Gillespie took the three steps to the stage floor.

Paranoia crept up. Dylan scanned every corner of the tent, the amplifiers, the cables in the grass, the picnic table.

McCallum looked his way and their eyes met, but only briefly.

Dylan reached into his pocket and hit his transmit button. "All units, report."

They called back, one by one, telling Ringleader the grounds were clear.

Counterintuitive as it was, the lack of trouble made him uneasy.

He became cognizant of his breathing, and that damned bullet weighed heavy in his pocket. *Who killed Phil Taylor?*

Beyond the pavilion people continued to fill the field.

The technicians completed their cable patchwork and the sun fell a few degrees.

Warren McCallum stepped on stage to address the crowd gathered on Heritage Landing. Gillespie stood near him, one step away. The president opened with a quip about running for a third term, which garnered a round of cheers.

"I have it on good authority that the Tall Ships left Traverse Bay on the heels of the news that the submarine had been captured." Another roar of approval rose from the people. "I expect them here rather soon."

As if on queue, the spars and sails of a two-mast schooner appeared out on the lake from behind the trees north of the harbor.

Despite his concerns, Dylan smiled and shook his head. Timing is everything.

The crowd became aware of the ship and burst into applause.

The portable television drew his attention. A burning building surrounded by fire trucks was on screen. It struck him as odd. Ever since *Commodore* went down, the news stations had saturated the airwaves with pictures, experts, and commentary on the submarine story. The recent capture only intensified their coverage. Why did this building fire bump the lead?

The crowd settled down and McCallum stepped in. "I think it appropriate now to observe a moment of silence for those lost these past few days."

Quiet came, and the calm felt eerie.

The television drew Dylan's eyes back. He read the crawl at the bottom of the screen and every fear he'd had that afternoon rushed at him full on. "Son of a—"

He jammed his hand into his coat pocket and hit the button. "All units evacuate Cipher!"

Leaping onto the stage, he sprinted to McCallum. Gillespie was already there. Shielding the president, they took hold of his arms and forced him away from the crowd.

McCallum stumbled, but Dylan and Gillespie kept him on his feet, kept him moving. "What's going on? What's happening?"

Dylan didn't answer.

They ushered him down the steps and burst from the rear of the tent. A unit of State Troopers encircled them. Douglas joined the human shield. The group of officers and agents moved as one, keeping McCallum protected in the center.

The Towne Car lay thirty yards ahead.

Dylan's sole focus was to get the president inside.

Whisking McCallum offstage during a moment of silence electrified the crowd, and many spilled around the sides of the pavilion to see what was happening. A line of Muskegon police officers had formed a chain and held the public back.

Rebecca pushed through the crush of people to the police line. She shoved her creds out in front of her. "I'm with the FBI. I need to get through."

"Sorry," a uniformed officer said. "Nobody gets through."

Two steps behind, Sergeant Cotter bowled through the crowd. He anchored his girth in front of the officer speaking to her and adjusted his Smokey Bear cap. "Step aside, Officer Baker."

Baker caved to his superior and opened the line for them. Rebecca rushed through. She headed for the troopers moving McCallum to the Towne Car. "Dylan."

The rear passenger door swung open. Dylan shoved the president's head down and into the big, black car. He heard his name and whirled about.

Rebecca jogged toward him.

Their eyes locked for an instant. He couldn't wait.

He slapped a key ring into Gillespie's hand. "Lead back to the estate."

"What the hell did you see?"

"I'll explain later. Let's get out of here first."

Gillespie broke from the troopers and sprinted for the Durango parked just ahead. He threw open the door and plopped behind the wheel.

The passenger door opened.

He drew his Glock and swung it toward whoever was trying to get inside the cab.

Rebecca stared up at the barrel. "Don't shoot, Agent Gillespie. I'm on your side."

He holstered the sidearm. "What do you think you're doing?"

She climbed in. "The Bureau has a vested interest in what's going on here. I'm coming along."

Dylan's voice spilled through his ear jack. "Carney, get moving."

Gillespie started the engine. "You want to come, fine. Sit your pretty ass down and be quiet."

She slammed the door and glared at him. "A little more professionalism if you would, Agent Gillespie."

He threw the Durango into gear. "Absolutely, sweetheart."

He hit the gas and roared off the festival grounds. The president's car followed close behind.

Rebecca settled in her seat. "Why did you pull McCallum from the stage?"

He shook his head. "I thought you'd have that answer."

"I don't." She looked back through the rear window. "You don't know why you're racing away from the festival at sixty miles an hour?"

He jabbed his thumb at the Towne Car. "Dylan called for the pull-out. You want answers start with him."

"Pete, get us back to the estate fast."

Dylan sat in the black leather seat in the rear of the president's car. He stared out the side window at the passing small town scenery. Beside him, Warren McCallum fumed. He hadn't said anything to the president yet; he'd been too fixed on getting clear of Heritage Landing. His heart was racing and he tried to get it under control.

McCallum pressed him with a heavy stare.

Douglas made a sharp turn and they struggled to right themselves.

The president kept his protector under scrutiny. "What the Sam Hell is going on?"

Dylan met his gaze. "I saw a breaking news report back there. A car bomb exploded in Los Angeles, right outside the law office of Joseph Bradford."

McCallum went pale.

Dylan leaned forward. "Joseph Bradford, First Council to President Warren McCallum."

Sinking in the seat, McCallum covered his face with his hands.

"This thing isn't over. You have to come clean with me."

Book III

CODE OF A SOLDIER

- TWENTY-TWO -

NEITHER MAN SPOKE for a long while; they sat there surrounded by black interior, not connecting at all. Dylan bounced his knee, waiting for the president to talk. McCallum slumped in his seat and stared through his window. They past the Muskegon city limit sign in a blur.

The sun hovered near the horizon.

Grief had turned McCallum's skin ashen. Dylan had never seen him so distressed. Even his day of binge drinking was better than this. Regardless of his condition, Dylan needed answers. "What happened while you were in office that triggered this?"

Staring blankly through the glass, McCallum's voice was very low. "I never intended for it to happen."

"You're not talking the recent murders, are you? You're talking about the past."

McCallum seemed not to hear him. "We all thought it the right thing to do, the most viable solution." He looked over at Dylan. "I still have nightmares about it."

"About what? Tell me what happened."

Anger surged from despair and McCallum slammed his fist against the car door. "Yellow Jacket!" he shouted. "God damned Operation Yellow Jacket!"

Dylan searched his memory, rifling through intelligence reports, news stories, history, anything he could think to make a connection. "What is Yellow Jacket?"

The click of the tires over concrete expansion seams peppered the quiet. "As president," McCallum said finally, "I made hundreds of decisions that affected millions of people. One of those decisions concerned just a handful of men, but it has imprinted my life more than all the others." He drew a solemn breath. "You ever wonder why the Shiite Brigade hates me so much?"

"You're the Great Satan who defeated Iraq."

"It goes beyond Iraq, far beyond." He laid his head back on the seat. "After the Gulf Conflict we predicted political stability would take root in the Middle East, but Muslim fundamentalists vowed to not let it happen. Remember the terrorist attacks of that time?"

Dylan nodded. "Right after the war a string of embassies and military bases were hit by suicide bombers and gunmen. But those attacks ended about six months later."

"You don't know the whole story. Those attacks didn't just end. We ended them."

"I don't remember another military campaign after the Gulf Conflict. How did you end the attacks?"

"Covert Ops aren't advertised on CNN. Believe me; if we want to keep something a secret, we do a pretty good job of it."

"Why did you go covert? You had public support. You could have waged another open campaign without issue."

"We couldn't afford to go public. Central Intelligence had made a series of sobering discoveries. Nabil Masood led the Shiite Brigade back then, and we had tapped the cell phone he used to coordinate his chaotic little empire. We monitored Masood's conversations for months and realized he had to be taken seriously. We managed to place assets inside the Brigade who provided a gold mine of information concerning the organization's structure, active cell locations, strength in numbers and arms, and, most frightening of all, future plans. My God, Dylan, those evil bastards had planned a reign of terror inside our borders that would put Los Angeles on par with Tel Aviv. I mean, they had blueprints for operations that would make the World Trade Center attack look second rate."

"But if you had all that, the public would support anything you did."

"Don't be so sure about that. The Shiite Brigade was a rogue confederacy. They were not a country to invade. They had no capital to capture, no conventional army to obliterate. They existed as a loose affiliation of individual terror cells, active in several nations across the globe. Some governments harbored them. Others didn't even know they were there. The scope of the operation to eliminate the Brigade required military action in dozens of hot spots. If we announced our intentions with a proper declaration of war, they would scatter from the camps and bases we knew about and disappear from sight. And remember, pre-9/11 America would not have gone for it. We're a benevolent country in case you've forgotten."

McCallum shifted his weight in the seat. "Don't think we didn't debate whether or not to try and gain world support for the campaign.

Our stumbling block was that we had uncovered plans for future attacks. The Brigade hadn't acted on a large scale yet. They were still trying to organize a coordinated global offensive. Without a smoking gun, which would most likely have been a city reduced to rubble, we'd never have gotten the nod from the UN, or NATO, or anyone else to go military globe trotting." McCallum paused and took a breath. "We were convinced the Brigade was going to act. We knew they were capable of causing a lot of damage. So we decided to bypass diplomatic channels and move against them in complete secrecy. They couldn't know we were coming, and they couldn't discover how much we had learned about them."

Dylan mulled it over. "And that's what Yellow Jacket was all about? Taking out the Brigade?"

McCallum sat silent a full minute. "There's a proverb in the Bible that reads, *For lack of guidance a nation falls, but many advisers make victory sure.* Dylan, I went to my advisors on this. We conferred and thought it through and came to the conclusion that it was the only way to go. But we had to be ready for any contingency that might come up, any fly in the ointment."

"Contingencies like what?"

McCallum dropped his chin and picked up his account at a point Dylan judged to be a little farther down the line. "We'd lost a hundred-and-thirty seven soldiers and eleven diplomats to Brigade terrorist attacks. That was proof enough for me that they meant business. I wasn't about to let their next target be on American soil." He raised his head, defiant. "I gave the order to launch Operation Yellow Jacket."

"We went after those sons-of-bitches with a vengeance. We hit camps and mountain hideouts in Afghanistan. We hit cells in the Philippine jungle. We wiped out network bases in Nicaragua, El Salvador, and Panama. Somalia, Chechnya, Pakistan. The Brigade had spread across the globe like a disease, and we were hunting the parasites to extinction."

Dylan fixated on the tale. "How did you manage to keep an operation that large secret?"

"Very carefully. Friendly nations were embarrassed when we told them the Brigade had set up shop inside their borders. They helped us root out the cell with a promise of secrecy. Unfriendly nations, well, they weren't about to kick up a fuss when elements of the most reviled terrorist organization in the world turned up dead in their back yard.

It'd paint them willing accomplices to the kind of indiscriminant murder the Brigade carried out wholesale."

Dylan heard the other shoe falling. "It sounds like the operation started out successfully. When did the trouble start?"

"When we got to Iran." McCallum's voice left him. He took a moment to find it. "Nabil Masood had set up a training camp inside Iran, in the northeast near the Afghan border. We dropped a Spec Ops unit on the ground to scratch the camp, but the raid went sour. Most of the team was killed, some were captured. Word of the raid reached the Iranian government and they immediately suspected the soldiers were Americans. But we had sent them in without telltale U.S. equipment in their hands or uniforms on their backs. No dog tags, no standard issue weapons, they were as generic in appearance as we could make them…for just such an occasion."

"Is this the contingency you had planned for?"

"We planned for it, but I prayed the day wouldn't come. The Iranians contacted us through back channels, trying to get us to admit the men were American soldiers. Lord, they had taken pictures of them, the dead, and the survivors." McCallum covered his face.

Dylan sat quiet as the president's grief unfolded.

McCallum lowered his hands. "If the Iranians could prove the team was American they would have gone public in a big way, and the whole Arab world would have coalesced around the illegal intrusion of United States military forces. The shaky stability we had achieved in the region would have collapsed, our allies would have denounced us, and we could have found ourselves in another war, this time against a united Middle East and on the wrong side of global opinion. The stakes were too high."

"How did you handle it?"

"It was horribly simple…We disavowed the team."

Dylan sat silent.

"Everybody knew it could happen. Hell, my trusted advisors and I were the architects of Yellow Jacket. But it didn't make that damned decision any easier."

"What about the soldiers? Did they know what could happen?"

McCallum flared up. "My God, don't think me a heartless bastard. Each soldier taking part in Yellow Jacket had volunteered, and each one knew what could happen in the event of capture. They knew, but they also understood the importance of the mission." He paused for breath. "I knew men on that team, damn it. I lost friends in Iran that night, and I was the one who let them die by turning my back on them. That horrible truth gives me nightmares, the pictures of those men haunt my waking hours, and my decision to disavow them has sickened my soul. I've asked God to forgive me every day since. I've prayed for the forgiveness of their families too."

"Sir," Dylan said. "I asked only to try and determine if a man like Robert Bowman could have found reason in the operation to lash out as he has."

"Anything is possible. But my guess is that the Shiite Brigade is behind this, some surviving faction."

"Nabil Masood?"

McCallum cast a knowing glance. "Not likely."

"Is he dead?"

A nod. "I made sure he was the last casualty of Operation Yellow Jacket. Took us two years to track him down, but we did."

"What about the letters? You told me they alluded to classified information. Was that information Yellow Jacket?"

"It's the only thing they could be referencing."

"Then how did the Brigade get their hands on classified files?"

McCallum pounded the door again. "How the hell did anyone access those files?" He grabbed the seat back in front of him, calmed himself down. "The letters," he said. "I'm sorry about lying to you. I didn't want to believe the connection." He closed his eyes and frowned. "I might have been able to save Joe Bradford."

Dylan sat up straight. "What do you mean?"

McCallum reached into the breast pocket of his suit and produced an envelope that had been torn open. He handed it to Dylan with shaking hands. "It came in the mail yesterday. I didn't let you know about it." He dropped his hand. "I was going to show you this morning, but the news about the capture stopped me. I thought it was over."

Dylan pulled glossy paper from the envelope and unfolded it. It was the cover of an issue of Newsweek Magazine from ten years back. McCallum was on the cover, surrounded by Roger Patterson, James Ruby, and Phil Taylor. Joseph Bradford smiled over their shoulders. The caption beneath the men in suits and power ties read, *Round Table of the West Wing*. A type-written note had been taped to the bottom of the page. *How long until all of these traitors are dead?*

"These are the men who put Yellow Jacket together," McCallum said. "And I'm the only one left. How long until we're all dead? Not long now."

Dylan tossed the picture down. "Old age might get you, but this maniac won't."

McCallum offered a weak smile. "Confidence and optimism, hallmarks of youth." He searched Dylan's expression. "What kind of man do you see before you now?"

"I see the same man I've always seen. I see a man who led through his convictions, who believed that what he did, he did in the country's best interest."

McCallum stared with sullen eyes. "I don't feel that way, not now."

Years of regret had been eating away at him, and it all seemed to catch up with him right then. Dylan felt thankful he didn't carry the burdens that the president did. Then again, he was only thirty five; there was still plenty of time to screw things up. He had made a good start with Sarah.

"Ringleader—Carney."

Gillespie's voice brought a welcome break to the silence. "Go, Carney."

"The FBI and I would like to know why we evacuated Cipher."

"The FBI?" Dylan said.

"Yeah. Agent Matthis saw fit to join me."

Something about that encouraged him. "Another of the president's men was killed today. Tell Agent Matthis our suspicions were right. There's still trouble out there."

"Copy that."

Twenty seconds went by before another voice came through. "Who was killed?"

Rebecca had apparently usurped Gillespie's radio.

"Joseph Bradford," Dylan said, "McCallum's First Council."

"He's not a cabinet member." She sounded thrown.

"No, but something links them all together."

"Something like what?"

"Can't get into it right now, but I'm very concerned that President McCallum is next on the list."

"Okay, you're the security professional. What's our next step?"

Our? Sounded like she'd just joined the team. "We're heading to the Nest, but I'm having second thoughts." He'd never explained to her that the Nest was the code name for the estate. He figured Gillespie would tell her.

After a few seconds she said, "What's wrong with the Nest? Poor security there?"

"Hey." Gillespie piped up in the background. "Watch your—" The transmission cut out.

Her little jab got right to the point of Dylan's concern. The man who had put this assassination scheme together had proven himself an intelligent, meticulous planner. Orchestrating the *Silversides* theft, the attack on the flotilla, Taylor's murder in Chicago, and then Bradford's in L.A., he really had his marbles together. One would have to assume that he also drew up detailed designs on McCallum's estate and its security measures. The president's big ranch house with its high-tech surveillance system suddenly didn't seem all that safe.

"Carney," Dylan said. "Scratch playbook. I'm calling an audible. We hit the Nest, collect Enigma, then make for the Igloo."

"Copy that," Gillespie said.

"I haven't kept up with the codes," McCallum said. "What's Igloo?"

"A safe house." Dylan grabbed his sat-phone and hit a speed dial key. "In the Upper Peninsula."

Paul LaCroix spun his chair and checked the main gate video monitor. It was nearly dark, and the light posts on either side of the drive blinked on. Noting nothing of interest there, he moved to the north grounds monitor, and then to the courtyard, and on he went from one feed to the other.

After hours of sitting in the small surveillance room, the low lighting and solitude had quite a sedating effect. To keep himself alert he'd designed a system check routine. The mug of coffee that Kathryn McCallum had brought in to him didn't hurt either.

He held the coffee under his nose while inspecting the video images. Something about that aroma really pleased his senses.

Movement on the south grounds got his attention. Setting the mug down, he studied the monitor. Simon the cat trotted through the center of the screen on his way back to the house from a foray into the woods beyond the gate. LaCroix leaned back in his chair. "Damn cat nearly got me—"

Wait. That couldn't be right.

How did Simon get through the perimeter without tripping a motion sensor?

He called up a sonic grid of the estate grounds on a recessed computer monitor. No red icon flashed on the south wall. He rolled his chair to the keyboard and typed in a command to pan the camera up to the fence. Nothing seemed out of the ordinary. He opened a diagnostic program and sent a trigger signal to the south wall motion sensor.

It didn't respond.

He sent to trigger the next sensor in the chain. Nothing.

"Shit."

He slammed his hand down on the switch to activate the perimeter flood lights. He nearly jumped out of his seat when the console phone chimed. He picked up the secure line. "LaCroix."

"Paul, it's Dylan. Listen to me. The assassins are still out there and McCallum's on the hit list. Get Enigma ready. We're moving to the safe house."

LaCroix panned the video monitors. "Tell me this is one of your exercises."

"Exercise? What are you talking about?"

"South wall motion sensors are off line."

LaCroix heard a suspended moment of silence that frightened him. "Get Kathryn out of there now!"

He didn't hang on for more conversation. He dropped the phone and bolted from the surveillance room. Cutting right in the hallway, he ran into the kitchen and found Kathryn McCallum reading a book on a stool near the island. She dropped the book when she saw his panicked face. "What's the matter, Pau—"

LaCroix took hold of her arm. "We have to leave right now, Mrs. McCallum! Right now!" He lifted her off the stool and pulled her to her feet.

Dressed only in a bathrobe, she objected. "Paul, my clothes."

"No time." He led her from the kitchen and down the hall.

In the cool darkness of the woods several yards beyond the south gate, Owen Keyes stood very still behind the thick trunk of a large oak tree. Tierney, Roth, and Wilke had dispersed among the trees to his left. Dominic, Six Pack, and Griffin had taken positions to his right. They all had submachine guns in their hands, MP-5s, except for Dominic. The big Italian held a small black box, and he stared at a bank of dim, green indicator lights.

"Motion sensors orphaned," he whispered.

Technology is a wonderful thing, especially the kind you buy on the sly. Months ago Keyes had learned that McCallum's security team had installed RF controlled motion sensors to watch the perimeter. Digging deeper, he discovered that the manufacturer of the system, Secure Technologies, tethered the sensors to the central system with a modulating frequency schedule. They had designed a very difficult system to disrupt without triggering. Difficult, that is, if you didn't know the modulating schedule.

The right combination of dollars and connections could uncover just about anything you wanted to know, including design specifications for a state-of-the-art alarm system. As a result, Keyes had the black box in Dominic's hands built.

In passive mode it identified the pattern of the frequency rotation, and in active mode it sent clone signals to the central system, thereby isolating the sensors from the network.

Yes, the black box purchase was well worth the money. Getting inside the grounds undetected would be a whole lot easier now. And when McCallum returned from the Tall Ships festival, Keyes intended to be waiting for him in his own living room.

President Warren McCallum, the last name on his list.

How sweet it would be to condemn him to hell and pull the trigger.

As Keyes prepared to give the word to go, he thought about Robert Bowman. Radio reports had informed him of the submarine capture, and of the one casualty among the pirates. Though no names had been released, he knew it was Bowman who had been gunned down. The news troubled him, but he could not pity Bowman's last hours. In the end Bowman realized his dream of command and chose the means and time of his death. Not every man is given those precious gifts. No, some of them are treated far worse.

Flood lights suddenly ignited on the estate perimeter. The inner grounds lit up like mid day. Keyes cursed. "Somebody's paying attention in there. Dom, you and Six Pack get over to the junction box feeding those floods. Cut the line. John, you and Wilke move down and breach the gate at the main entrance. Make sure nobody leaves. I'm taking Roth and Griffin with me to the main house."

The men acknowledged their orders and broke from the woods.

LaCroix burst into the garage. He pulled Kathryn McCallum along. He threw open the rear door of the black Crown Victoria and shoved the former First Lady inside. "Sorry, Mrs. McCallum, but lay down and stay down."

He slammed the door, swiped a shovel from a wall rack, and smashed the light bulb in the garage door opener. Dropping the shovel, he ran around the hood and jumped into the car. He reached beneath the passenger seat and pulled an Uzi from a hidden compartment, then laid the weapon down where he could easily reach it.

He fumbled with the key ring.

The ignition key. Where the hell was it? There.

He started the engine and hit the button on the garage door opener. Large wooden panels rose in front of the car. The rumble of casters through steel tracks filled the garage.

As the door cleared his line of sight, the long, twisting asphalt drive appeared. The flood lights lit it up nice and bright. LaCroix gripped the steering wheel. The door was almost clear. "Come on, come on."

The floods blinked off. Darkness.

He dropped his foot on the accelerator. The front tires squealed on the concrete floor and the Crown Vic leapt forward, but the door hadn't cleared yet. The car slammed into the lower cross member. Cracking on impact, an oak panel split. A twisted piece of steel scraped across the car roof.

LaCroix felt acceleration, heard the tires howling on asphalt, and from the corner of his eye saw a muzzle flash.

Peter Douglas turned the steering wheel hard, sliding the Towne Car through a dirt road intersection a quarter mile from the McCallum estate. Twenty yards behind, Gillespie stayed glued to his bumper, the Durango's headlights piercing the Towne Car's dusty wake.

Ahead the glow of flood lights lit the tree tops on the estate grounds.

As they approached the trees went dark.

Dylan drew his Glock. "Hurry up, Pete."

McCallum clenched his fists and fixed his eyes on the dark plot of land.

Dylan called Gillespie through his collar mic. "We've got action in the Nest. Prepare to go in hot."

"Copy."

In the Durango's cab, Gillespie gripped the wheel and shook his head. "They better not hurt Mrs. McCallum. She's like a mother, you know. Stick around her long enough she sort of takes you into her family. Bastards just better not touch her."

Beretta in hand, Rebecca clicked the safety off. "Mama's boy, huh. You're starting to make sense, Tommy."

"Stick it, Reba. I'm close to capping someone. I can't think straight to come up with a snappy retort."

He stayed tight on the Towne Car's tail lights.

"How far?" she said.

"About thirty seconds. Stay close and you'll be all right."

"Close to you? Why don't I feel safer?"

"Suit yourself." Gillespie glanced down at the driver's door. Dylan had affixed the Remington short-barrel in its holster to the side panel. Good old Mr. Paranoid. Gillespie sure appreciated it now.

Brake lights ahead. The Towne Car decelerated and slid sideways. Its headlights pointed through the gate left of the main entrance.

Gillespie turned and jammed his brakes as well, skidding parallel to the president's car but to the right of the main entrance. The instant the gearshift clicked into park, he had his hand on the Remington. Rebecca threw her door open.

The Crown Vic screamed up the drive toward the main gate. The gate was opening slowly. Headlight beams from the Towne Car and Durango caught two human shapes crouched in a firing position to the left. Ammunition spit from their weapons. Red tracer rounds assaulted the Crown Vic's broadside.

Dylan drew down on one of the gunmen. They were nearly out of his pistol's range but he fired a cluster of shots just the same.

To his right more gunfire erupted. Rebecca had entered the fray with her Beretta.

Left flank, Peter Douglas opened up with an Uzi.

Racing around the drive's final curve, the Crown Vic surged forward. The tires were blown out and the rims screeched on the asphalt. Its body was bullet-riddled and the bulletproof windows pocked, but the car was still moving, and that was all that mattered. The main gate was half way open. Dylan calculated LaCroix's chances of getting through without a collision. It didn't look promising.

The fleeing Crown Vic crossed in front of Dylan's field of fire and he let off the trigger. He took the precious seconds to reload. He ejected a spent magazine. "Agent Matthis, are you okay?"

"So far."

He slapped in a new magazine. "Where's Gillespie?"

"Looking for better ground."

The Crown Vic cleared his line of sight.

A fresh barrage of gunfire suddenly struck at the Towne Car. But it didn't come from the two men south of the drive. Red tracer rounds were blazing in from an oak cluster to the north. And there were four separate muzzles.

McCallum called from inside the car. "My God, where's Kathryn?"

Dylan barely heard him above the pops and pings of bullets striking the armored car.

"LaCroix is getting her out. Stay put."

The maelstrom subsided, and he spun around to assess the situation.

Four men were advancing through the big oaks on the north grounds. He drew a bead on the man leading the new arrivals, a barrel-chested man, and fired. The shot missed, but the man knew he'd been targeted and signaled the three following to slow their advance. They used the oaks for cover. Dylan took aim again. "Come on, LaCroix."

Gillespie hadn't run like this since his War College days. He rounded the southwest corner of the gate and barreled through a stand of maples. He wanted to be on the gunmen's flank, and this was the route to get there.

He found his quarry safe behind thick tree trunks, protected by hundred-year-old timber and distance too great for Dylan or the others handguns to be truly effective. Gillespie, however, had gotten a whole lot closer to them.

Clenching the Remington's pistol grip, he sprang from the maples and up to the gate. He shoved the shortened barrel between the fence's wrought iron bars. At thirty yards out he hoped the shotgun would still be effective. He blasted a round at the nearest gunman.

Pieces of bark splintered from the oak near Wilke's leg. He shouted and spun, swinging his submachine gun and opening up. His aim was off base. Gillespie pumped a new shell into the chamber and fired again. Wilke took the spread of 12 gauge shot in the neck, the shoulder, the face, and died there at the base of the tree.

Tierney threw his body against the bark, rolling away from where the shotgun blast had come. He reached around with his MP-5, sprayed the area. Gillespie answered with the 12-gauge. The spread of shot tore out a chunk of tree.

Gillespie sidestepped toward a fieldstone column. His target, now completely behind the tree, did not return fire this time. After a few seconds of silence the MP-5 was tossed to the ground in the open. Gillespie lifted the Remington, tried to aim between the bars of the fence.

Tierney called from behind the tree. "Alright, you have me."

"Come out where I can see you," Gillespie said, "hands on your head."

"Please don't shoot," Tierney said. "I'm coming out."

Gillespie inched closer to the column.

Tierney stepped around the tree, left hand raised, right hand clenching something. Darkness concealed what it was. His movement was so smooth, so calm, it threw Gillespie off. A split second too late he read the threat. This was no surrender. He dove for cover.

Like a thunderclap the Desert Eagle fired. A .357 caliber slug drilled the fence column, blowing off a slab of stonework. Tierney advanced and fired a second time. Stone shards and mortar dust exploded into the air. Gillespie winced at the debris. He stuck the Remington around the pillar and fired.

In deference to the scattergun's bark, Tierney jumped behind an oak ten yards closer to the gate than he had been positioned, ten yards closer to Gillespie.

At the Towne Car they were taking so much fire that Dylan couldn't look over the car door. Images of Sadeed popped into his head, clouding his thoughts. For years he'd been worried about that one bullet with his name on it, but now there were dozens coming at him. He felt himself shutting down, but his voice of survival screamed at him. *Get up! Get up, damn it!*

The Crown Vic's quarter panels smashed into the gate.

Dylan snapped back to reality.

LaCroix had managed to breach the main entrance, but the car had sustained so much point blank gunfire damage that it rattled to a stop before its tireless rims touched the dirt road. The Crown Vic came to rest just ten feet askew from the Towne Car.

Staying low, Rebecca rounded the Durango, trying to get to the bullet-riddled hulk.

Peter Douglas crouched behind his car door, a bullet graze bleeding on his head.

"LaCroix made it out," Dylan said. "Let's get Enigma and get the hell out of here."

Douglas nodded.

"On three we stand and throw back. Let them know they're not getting any closer. We hold them off first. Then I'll go for Kathryn. You stay with Cipher."

"What if we don't hold them off?"

"On three."

Dylan raised a finger. One. Two. Three. They stood and opened fire at the four men advancing. The assassins had covered twenty yards since he last saw them, and that put them in a far more open section of land. Less trees, less cover, closer targets. He concentrated his fire on the man to the right. After four shots his target went down, grabbing at his shoulder. The others dispersed. Their charge momentarily faltered.

Dylan moved fast. He kept his pistol trained on the men to the north and sprinted to the Crown Vic. He pulled open the rear passenger door. It swung on its hinges like metallic Swiss cheese.

Rebecca hovered over Kathryn McCallum in the back seat. La-Croix was trying to kick open the driver's door but it had been jammed shut in the collision. Dylan reached in and grabbed Mrs. McCallum's arm. He made eye contact with Rebecca. "Is she okay?"

"I think so. Just scared."

LaCroix kicked the door again.

Dylan slapped his shoulder. "Forget it, Paul. Come this way."

LaCroix cursed and twisted about, grabbing the Uzi from the passenger seat.

Dylan heaved Enigma from the Crown Vic. An arm around her and huddling close, he guided her to the Towne Car. Rebecca moved with them, one hand on Kathryn's back, the other firing the Beretta over Dylan's shoulder. They piled into the armored luxury car, Rebecca in front, Dylan and Kathryn in back. Peter Douglas drained his clip and dropped behind the steering wheel.

Outside LaCroix stood firing his Uzi through the gate. "Go! Go!"

Douglas went, spinning the tires over the gravel, backing away from the estate perimeter.

Back against the fieldstone pillar, Gillespie chambered a round in the Remington. He had three shells left in the shotgun and a full clip in the Glock. He'd need them all. This character trading shots with him was tenacious. Most baddies who come under this kind of fire crumble, especially after one of their own has gone down, but not this guy. He played it cool. And that surrender rouse. It took a lot of balls to come out like he had and go on the offensive. Cool and confident, that kind of criminal just pissed Gillespie off. Of course, the guy might be cool and cocky, a slight difference but one that would play better for him in a shoot out. Cocky makes mistakes, confident usually doesn't.

At that moment, though, Gillespie had to come up with a smart play. The Remington gave him a better chance to score a hit, but he'd only get one shot off before Cool Hand Luke hit him with a .357 slug-fest.

He switched the short-barreled shotgun to his left hand and drew the Glock with his right. Two-fisted gun fighting worked well in the movies, but in actual combat situations it had a rather dubious history. He wasn't qualifying for marksman here though; he just needed to put more lead in the air faster than his opponent. Hopefully the Remington's pattern density or the Glock's speed would do the rest. He decided to step off to the left of the column. The angle through the gate might give him some protection.

"Gillespie, we got her," a voice said in his ear piece. "Get back here. We're pulling out."

He stalled. That cocky paramilitary reject needed to be shot. But he didn't like the idea of thumbing a ride out of there either. Right. A fighting withdrawal.

He steeled himself, took a breath, and broke from his fieldstone concealment.

The Remington swung about easy, and he blasted a round toward the tree where his nemesis held up. Pellets tinged off the wrought iron gate. Just as he thought, that damned big handgun opened up at him. Feet moving fast toward the stand of maples, he reached around with the Glock and responded in kind. Slugs bounced and ricocheted off the fence.

He made it through the stand with a few rounds left in the Glock. Breaking from the trees, he saw the Durango waiting with passenger door open. He dove inside. Acceleration threw him back. He scrambled to close the door.

Paul LaCroix sat behind the wheel. Pain twisted his face and blood stained his leg.

He spun the SUV in a tight circle and headed down the dirt road after the Towne Car.

Four gunmen ran up to the gate and fired submachine guns at them. The hail of bullets peppered the Durango's side panels and snapped on the protective glass surrounding the cab.

Gillespie slapped his middle finger against the window at them.

"Can you believe that puss Dylan had bulletproof glass installed in his private vehicle?"

"Yeah." LaCroix pressed down on the wound in his leg. "Thank God for that, eh?"

"You, bet."

TWENTY-THREE

HER HANDS WERE SHAKING. Rebecca tried to steady them but she couldn't seem to manage it. *Good thing it's dark in here.* She sat in the front seat of the Towne Car next to Peter Douglas. The fire fight had affected her more than she realized, at least her body told her that.

In the dashboard display's soft lighting she read their speed at eighty. They'd turned onto pavement a few minutes before and the tires bit into the asphalt. Blackness surrounded them. They drove along a narrow road through rural flat land, nothing but tree and field on either side for miles.

She still held the Beretta in an iron grip.

Kathryn McCallum sobbed in her husband's arms in the back seat. The president hugged her, burying his face in her long hair. Dylan sat beside them, twisting around to watch the road disappear behind the car. The taillights made the white lines pulse red as they faded into darkness. A single pair of headlights followed half a mile behind; Gillespie and LaCroix.

Rebecca fixated on the McCallums, how they held each other. It must be remarkable to feel strongly about someone. They'd lived over fifty years of their lives together and still shared a very deep, genuine love. She'd decided long ago that such a relationship couldn't exist. No man she'd met seemed capable or willing. But why did she really feel that way? Because her father's abuse instilled fear and mistrust in her? Because her mother encouraged her to compete with men rather than relate? What a strange time to be thinking these thoughts. Lives had nearly been lost, including hers. She had to pull it together, get her focus back. She had to be that perfect Bureau agent. Some very dangerous men were out there with assassination on their minds. *Come on, Matthis, compartmentalize.*

"Dylan," she said, "What's the common thread?"

He faced her, taking his time to respond. "Thanks for your help back there."

She balked. "It's part of the job."

"It's part of my job, not yours. You come out of it okay?"

"I'm fine. Why do you ask?"

"I don't know? We just traded shots with a squad of assassins. Maybe I'm concerned that you took a hit or something."

"I didn't."

He watched her through the darkness a few seconds longer. "What was the question?"

She let out a frustrated breath.

"I'm jerking your chain. It's how I cope with stress. What do you do to cope?"

"I try to get to the heart of the matter."

He faced McCallum. "Sir, this is Agent Matthis with the Bureau. She's been working the *Silversides* investigation."

The president greeted her as cordially as he could under the circumstances.

Dylan paused. "We need to discuss the situation."

McCallum gave a nod.

"Ten years ago," Dylan said, "President McCallum and members of his administration put together a covert military operation named Yellow Jacket. The objective of Yellow Jacket was the elimination of the Shiite Brigade terrorist organization. The primary designers of that plan have all been killed in the past four days. The president is the only one left."

"You think Shiite Brigade terrorists have a hand in this too?"

"We don't know yet."

"Who else could it be?"

Dylan glanced through the rear window. "The operation ran into trouble in Iran. A Spec Ops team was captured."

Rebecca sifted through ten-year-old memories. "None of this sounds familiar. It seems to me this would have been quite a news story."

"I said covert operation," Dylan reminded her. "News media didn't know about it."

"Why didn't the Iranian's make a public stink about American soldiers on their soil?"

"Because," McCallum said, "I denied they were Americans."

She stared at him five long seconds. "What happened to the captured soldiers?"

His silence answered her.

Kathryn sat up and looked into her husbands eyes. It seemed the First Lady hadn't known about this either.

Rebecca fumbled for a follow-up question.

"I know what you're thinking," McCallum said somberly. "I've lived with this brutal secret for a decade. Not a day goes by that isn't tarnished by the memory."

She had her follow-up. "Could members of that Spec Ops team have survived?"

McCallum shook his head. "Not to my knowledge."

"But is it possible?"

Dylan understood. "You think a survivor of the failed Yellow Jacket raid feels betrayed and is out for revenge?"

"No," McCallum said. "What happened was tragic, and I wish I could change the past, but Lord Almighty it wasn't betrayal!"

Rebecca softened her voice. "Maybe some of the soldiers saw it otherwise."

"They volunteered," Dylan explained. "Each man taking part in Yellow Jacket volunteered knowing what would happen in the event of capture."

"Don't be so certain of their understanding. How many decisions do you regret only after the consequences land on your doorstep?"

McCallum pulled his arm from around Kathryn. "I knew the man who led that team, Agent Matthis. He went in with eyes wide open, proud to serve his country, and I know he picked men to go with him that felt the same way. Hell, as far as I'm concerned those men rank among the greatest patriots this country has ever seen. The heart-wrenching fact of the matter is nobody will ever know about their sacrifice."

"Somebody does know," Rebecca said. "And they're not very pleased about it."

McCallum huffed. "Damned Brigade. It has to be."

"But the letters point to someone with more information than the Brigade could possibly have." Dylan wagged his finger. "How could the Brigade know exactly who designed Yellow Jacket? And the submarine angle, it seems too sophisticated a scheme for them."

"The car bomb in L.A. is right up their alley," McCallum countered.

"But the rest of it just doesn't fit." Dylan pondered it a bit longer. "A U.S. soldier out for revenge just might make sense here, sir."

"We already know one U.S. serviceman was involved," Rebecca added. "Robert Bowman put in twenty years with the navy, and he announced his battle was with governing authorities from the Pentagon to the White House."

McCallum wrung his hands. "But the navy played a small part in Yellow Jacket. If vengeance is the motive, I wouldn't expect it to come from someone in that branch."

Rebecca finally holstered the Beretta. "I still think the man most likely to concoct this plot, the one with the greatest motivation, is the one who somehow survived Iran."

"Damn it, nobody survived! God rest their souls I wish it weren't true but I know in my gut that the Brigade would not have let any of those men live. And if any of them did somehow survive, I know none of them would come back and do this. They understood what they were doing and why it had to be done in that way. I personally pinned the Medal of Honor on Lieutenant Commander Keyes a month before he left. I looked him in the eye and saw a man willing to put his life on the line for his country and ask nothing in return, and that sort of man doesn't come home and commit mass murder."

Rebecca's ears perked. "I know that name."

"What name?" Dylan said.

"Keyes. It's ringing a bell." She rifled through the particulars of the *Silversides* investigation.

"Michael Keyes is dead; he can't be involved," McCallum said. "And even if he were alive he'd be incapable of doing the things these bastards have done. You're barking up the wrong tree, and you won't convince me otherwise."

She eyed the curly cord running into Dylan's ear jack. "Call Gillespie."

A bit puzzled, he transmitted. "Carney—Ringleader."

She motioned for him to lean toward her.

He did, tilting his head. "Our newest team member wants a word with you."

She yanked the cord from his ear and held the ear piece so she could listen. She met his eyes and nodded for him to hit the transmit button in his pocket. "Tommy, it's Agent Matthis."

"Agent Matthis," Gillespie said with a rather dry inflection. "Only coded communications are permitted on unsecured channels."

She signaled Dylan to transmit. "Fine. Freakshow, find my shoulder bag in the cab. I need some information from it."

"You confuse me with my partners, Red Dragon."

"Just get the damn bag, Tommy." *How did McCallum survive so long with this guy?*

"Don't get your skirt in a bunch, sweetheart, I have it right here...What do you need in this mess?"

She set her jaw. "A file folder, one labeled R. Bowman."

"One second."

Leaning close to one another, Dylan and Rebecca waited. She realized she hadn't been this close to a man in quite a while. The thought distracted her. "Come on, Carney, there's not that much stuff in there."

"I got it. Now what?"

"Skim through Bowman's military record. Keep your eye open for the name Keyes."

"Skimming in progress."

She caught Dylan studying her face. He looked away.

"Okay," Gillespie said. "Bowman served as XO on USS *Hampton* under Commander Owen Keyes. It says here Keyes helped Bowman get his last promotion."

She slapped the car seat. "That's it." She signaled Dylan to transmit. "Thanks, Carney. You can go back to sleep."

"Copy, Red Dragon. And by the way, thanks for waiting for me back at the estate."

"You're a big boy. You didn't need my help."

Gillespie chuckled. "No dirty talk on unsecured channels."

She pulled away from Dylan and handed him the curly cord. "Your friend is a piece of work." She faced the president. "Do you know if Michael Keyes had a son?"

McCallum sat and thought. "I believe he did."

"I'll bet his name is Owen and that he served in the navy."

His eyes searched the empty space before him. "I think you're right. But..."

"It's not Michael Keyes murdering your administration, it's his son."

"Now wait," McCallum said. "How did you get there?"

"Owen Keyes and Robert Bowman served together on a submarine, USS *Hampton*, for four tours of duty. They had a good relationship and appreciable knowledge of submarine technology. Add in the fact that Owen Keyes is the son of Michael Keyes. If Owen discovered an alternative truth as to how his father died, something at odds with what he was told ten years ago, he may not have taken it well."

"That's heavy on the circumstantial side," McCallum said. "All you really know is that Keyes and Bowman served together. The rest is conjecture. Bowman still might have initiated the plan on his own."

"Then who shot up your car ten minutes ago?" Dylan said. "If Bowman was the leader, why didn't the operation die with him?"

Rebecca watched the road disappearing behind. "It's been bugging me for a while now. I didn't think Bowman was capable of swiping *Silversides* on his own, or putting together a skilled crew who would follow him and all that. Owen Keyes is the brains of the plot. Think about it. He discovered the government lied about how his father was killed. Imagine if he philosophically disagrees with the Yellow Jacket directive to disavow in the event of capture? He'd perceive a great injustice had been perpetrated on his father by the very people he swore his trust and loyalty to."

"I didn't betray those men!" McCallum roared.

"That may not be how Keyes sees it."

Rebecca settled in her seat. "The question remains; How did Keyes find out about Yellow Jacket?"

No one had an answer.

Dylan leaned forward. "Pete, how close are we to Linder's Airfield?"

"About five minutes."

He lifted the phone from his pocket and dialed a secure line into the Secret Service Field Office in Grand Rapids. He was patched through to Special Agent in Charge Trevor Novak, which surprised him a bit. Ordinarily, SAC Novak couldn't be found in the office this late in the evening. "Impeccable timing, Agent Reese."

Something was up. Novak wore his stress on his sleeve, and Dylan could tell he was talking with a Swisher Sweet in his mouth. He never lit them. Heaven forbid that cigarette smoke ever pollute the air in a federal building. But when things got buzzing in the office he'd always gnaw on a Sweet, like a forty-year-old with a pacifier. "What's on your plate?"

"Someone made an attempt on the McCallums at their home ten minutes ago."

"Jeez, the Grand Haven police just called here. They've received reports of gunfire in the area and wanted to know if we knew anything about it. I told them we were clean."

"This was an impressive attempt. At least half a dozen men armed with automatic weapons assaulted us outside the estate."

"My God, was anybody hurt?"

"The McCallums are okay." Dylan checked Douglas' bleeding graze. "The team took some scrapes."

"Where are you now?"

"Crossing into Bauer on the way to Linder's Airfield. We're heading for the Igloo."

"You think these guys are going to take another whack at McCallum?"

"It's likely. You hear about that L.A. car bomb?"

Novak laughed, but not out of humor. "Hear about it? Hell, this office is a bee hive because of it. The submarine attacks got everyone jittery, but the car bomb sent them ballistic. Homeland Security thinks the Middle East bunch is to blame, and Director Simon elevated the threat level to red. The FBI released a dispatch saying they've heard an obscene amount of communication chatter in the last two hours indicating more attacks on soft targets are probable. They're setting up checkpoints around metropolitan areas nationwide and doubling security measures at border crossings, including the Mackinac, Ambassador, and Blue Water bridges. We're spread thin covering the visiting governors and the usual suspects in the region. You have something else to add?"

"I do. That car bomb killed Joseph Bradford, McCallum's former First Council. That makes the fourth member of his administration to be murdered this week. Ten minutes ago they tried to make a clean sweep of their hit list. This whole mess is centered on McCallum. We can use some help if you've got it."

"I wish I could, Dylan, but we can barely cover our responsibilities as it is. Besides, people aren't thinking right now. It'd be a hard sell convincing anyone that all the crap coming down is because somebody's going after a man eight years out of the White House. A lot more people died than those four men these past few days and the public, as well as the government, is nearing panic. We're just trying to get our arms around what's going on and trying to secure twenty two governors. You're making the right move going to the safe house, at least for now."

Intended or not, Dylan understood the subtext of the message. A former President of the United States just wasn't as important as half the country's sitting governors. For the moment chaos ruled and the nation's fear of widespread terrorist attacks shaped the psychological landscape. Novak had it right, in these anxious hours it would be impossible to get anyone to believe that an assassination plot targeted at

McCallum was the root of all the current trouble. Cooler heads needed to prevail.

They had to go it alone for a while.

"I understand," Dylan said. "We'll migrate north and check in when we get settled."

"The Grand Haven police are heading out to McCallum's estate," Novak said. "I'll let them know to bring more firepower. Hopefully they'll get lucky and nail those pricks that tried to take McCallum out."

"Hopefully," Dylan said. "I'll be in touch."

All eyes in the Towne Car fixed on him as he disconnected.

"On to the igloo," he said. "Federal intelligence agencies believe more terrorist attacks are on the way. They're locking down the country right now. Police units are converging on the estate to try and nab the assassins. With any luck this will all be over by morning."

Over by morning? Probably.

He just wasn't sure who would be left standing at sunrise.

- TWENTY-FOUR -

OWEN KEYES slammed the door of the 4x4 pick-up truck and trudged into the surrounding wetland. Mud and swamp water soaked his pant legs. Tierney, Dominic, and the others piled out of the cab and bed and moved quickly into the stench of the bog. The camouflage-painted 4x4 had taken them as far as it could from the county road and now sat buried up to the floorboards in mud.

The Circle had taken a hit. Bowman was dead. The submarine crew was captured. Griffin nursed a bullet in his shoulder. And Wilke's body lay in the bed of the pick-up. The endgame had just gotten a little more challenging.

Keyes checked over his shoulder. He thought about Wilke. He'd made sure they hadn't left him behind. It burned him up inside. He treated his dead better than President Warren McCallum had treated the living.

But that anger only tipped the iceberg. He'd failed to get the kingpin of his obsession. That damn Secret Service detail threw the whole OP askew. Someone in that group was sharp enough to see through even the submarine capture and realize that another element still prowled for McCallum.

Frustration built as he pondered.

Only one man on his executioner's list remained alive, but that man was the one he wanted most. He had to find where McCallum had been taken. Justice had to be served.

Tucked inside his shirt, the worn document of indictment burned hot against his skin. It seemed a lifetime ago that it landed in his hands. At first he hadn't believed what it said. After reading it through several times, however, the unthinkable took on a very grim authenticity.

McCallum drafted the executive order to assemble Yellow Jacket. Patterson, Ruby, and Taylor, his cabinet officials and close advisors, all agreed to the structure and dishonorable clauses of the anti-terrorist operation. First Council Bradford weighed in on the legal aspects of the covert campaign, advising the president how to execute it within the boundaries and through the loopholes of existing legislation. They all laid their gross negligence on the table. But President McCallum himself bore the brunt of the blame. He was chief architect of Yellow Jacket's heinous provision, and it was his signature that sent the soldiers into action.

The government had told Keyes that his father died in a helicopter crash during combat exercises in Qatar. Twenty-five years old back then, with six years invested in the navy, he mourned the loss of his father and rued the irony of him dying in an accident instead of on the field of battle. But when the truth finally surfaced, he decided that the accident would have been a much better fate than what had actually occurred. Michael Keyes, honored veteran of two wars, father to Owen Keyes, patriot and hero, died because a politician seven thousand miles away denied his existence.

The thought brought bile to his throat.

Cool and stagnant, the water soaking his foot brought him back to the now. He had another mile of sloshing through reeds and over deadwood before he reached the Lake Michigan shore. Not much further and they would be in the last leg of their march.

So far neither the police nor any other agency had picked up their trail. After the president had slipped away with his security team, Keyes and the others had hurried back to the pick-up stashed in the woods just off a primitive ORV trail and headed south on the nearest dirt road. They kept clear of developed areas, which in this part of Michigan was easy to do. Outside of Port Sheldon they veered off road and plowed through brush and thickets until reaching the wetland.

Keyes had monitored news radio along the way. He learned that the bombing in L.A. went off exactly as planned, and that frantic communication intercepts had convinced the FBI that a second 9/11 was unfolding. The seeds of pandemonium had been sown.

It appeared that Omar Abdullah was a man who kept his part of a bargain.

"Hear that?" Tierney whispered.

Keyes listened. "Lake surf. We're almost there."

They hiked to a thin line of trees, half of which were dead, and found themselves on a small bluff overlooking Lake Michigan. They climbed down the steep, jagged terrain overgrown with briars as quietly as they could. No need to be conspicuous, especially since hiking trails ran up and down the coast.

On shore, Keyes scanned the water. Despite pale moonlight he couldn't distinguish anything through the dark and distance.

Tierney and Dominic found the rock overhang where they had hidden the inflatable. They tore away the brush camouflage, and all six men carried the large rubber craft into the surf. Roth, Dominic, Six Pack, and Tierney took up oars and paddled.

Keyes lifted the two-way from his belt. "Mr. Rierdon, show yourself."

A spot of light flashed on and off northwest of their position. W-A-I-T-I-N-G.

"I've got you." He clipped the radio to his belt and settled in for the journey to the tugboat. He thought about missing his chance at McCallum. It incensed him. He didn't understand what could have tipped those agents to his presence at the estate. With every stroke of the oars, his anger compounded.

There had to be a way to locate McCallum and finish the job tonight. If he regrouped and waited days or weeks for another opportunity, the president would be too well protected. He had to move while the public sat paralyzed by fear of terrorism and the government spread itself thin covering every high-value target in the nation.

The raft bumped up against *Richard C.*

Keyes clamored aboard the tug and made his way to the pilothouse.

Rierdon turned from the navigation console. "How did you fare, Commander?"

Scowling, Keyes stormed past him and switched on the communication rack. He initiated a satellite uplink with the onboard phone. "Clear the deck."

Rierdon placed an unlit cigarette between his lips and nodded. "Aye, sir." He exited without another word.

Keyes dialed a number he'd never dialed before. The phone at the other end rang four times.

"Hello?"

"This is Owen Keyes. If you know what's good for you, you won't hang up."

"Christ, Keyes, I told you to never contact me directly!"

"Plans have changed. I need your assistance."

"How did you get this number?"

"I cover my bases. Now listen. McCallum survived my attempt. His security detail got him away. I need to know where they've taken him, and you're going to find out for me."

"Now wait just a minute. You don't talk to a United States senator like that."

"Spare me. You gave me the Yellow Jacket file, you started the ball rolling, and you are in shit up to your neck. Find McCallum for me or I'll expose you to every news syndicate from CNN to Al-Jazeera. Your face will be all over television by seven this morning. By noon your illustrious career will be finished."

A long stretch of silence played out. "You've gone too far. You've killed too many people. My God, you've taken down half the Midwest along with McCallum's cabinet."

"You knew what I was going to do. Don't play stupid now. Help me or you're cooked."

"Keyes, you bastard. I regret the day I came across that damn file. I wish I'd never put it in your hands."

"Revenge is a costly game. Didn't you know that?"

"This is costing too much. You had your shot at McCallum and missed. Call it a day and get the hell out of there."

Keyes clenched the receiver so tight he thought it would snap. "Not an option! McCallum is responsible for my father's death and every soldier that died in Iran. He will pay for that. It's my duty. I swore to defend this nation against enemies foreign and domestic, and by God he fits the bill."

"You're shedding a lot of innocent blood on your way to justice, Commander Keyes."

"Justice doesn't come cheap. Now are you going to help me or not?"

"How do you think I can find McCallum for you? I'm out in D.C., not in Michigan."

"You chair some heavyweight committees on the Hill. Use that influence to find out what the Secret Service has done with him."

Another long pause. "Give me an hour."

Bauer, MI

The Towne Car swerved off old 48th avenue and onto the long dirt drive leading to Linder's Airfield. The well-maintained grass runway and the proximity to the estate had attracted Dylan years ago. He preferred to move McCallum via the twin-engine Cessna owned and maintained by Karl Linder whenever possible. The private airstrip afforded him the luxury of not having to contend with security issues and crowds inherent to larger municipal and international airports.

Peter Douglas slowed the car as they approached the corrugated steel hanger. No out lights were burning, save for the single halogen shining down on the parking lot adjacent to the building. The runway ended just short of the driveway, and in passing Dylan noted the landing lights were off.

Peter Douglas noticed too. "Pretty dark. Looks like nobody home."

"Karl's here," Dylan said. "He told me he was at the airfield five minutes ago."

Rebecca studied the maintenance hanger and fuel shed positioned near the end of the central hanger. "The owner's name is Karl Linder? Sounds German."

"It is."

"My father was German," she said. "He was belligerent and drank a lot."

Dylan gave her a glance. "Sounds Irish to me."

McCallum grumbled. "Watch yourself. An old Irishman's at your elbow."

Dylan allowed himself a grin. "Karl once told me his father was a pilot in the Luftwaffe, and that he defected to England during the Blitz. After the war he came to America and built this airfield. Karl took over running the place after he died."

McCallum leaned sideways to get a better view. "Sixty years ago I doubt we'd be running to a German owned airfield for help."

A seam of light appeared on the central hanger's facing, a quarter of the distance down its length. Someone was pushing open one of the large hanger doors.

"Pete, pull inside right there. That's Karl."

Rebecca drew her Beretta. "How often do you use this airfield?"

"Fairly often. You think Keyes might know about it?"

"From what I've seen he doesn't miss a trick. I'd say it's fifty-fifty he's earmarked Linder's as an avenue of escape."

Dylan lowered his palm to the Glock. "Keyes couldn't have made it here before we did."

"Don't forget, he and Bowman were working separately. Who's to say there's not a third group covering contingencies?"

He cursed in a whisper and hit the button in his pocket. "Carney—Ringleader. We're not taking chances here. Follow us in and secure the interior."

Gillespie acknowledged.

Douglas steered the Towne Car into the hanger's bright, open bay.

Oil-stained and cracked, the concrete floor was bare. Overhead, steel trusses spanned the sixteen-foot ceiling. Karl stood near a blue air compressor tank in the far corner. He wore dingy gray overalls and sported a finely waxed handlebar mustache.

The Towne Car and the Durango rolled to a stop. In unison the car doors swung open and everyone jumped out. They fanned out across the floor, sweeping their weapons left and right.

Karl's eyes widened. He stepped backwards into the wall, bumping his head against a circuit breaker box. "Dylan, what is wrong?"

Keeping his pistol angled away from the old German, Dylan approached. "Are you alone?"

"Yes, yes, alone. What is wrong?"

He checked over his shoulder. "Gillespie, you and LaCroix get that door closed." He fixed on Karl again. "Has anyone out of the ordinary called or contacted you recently?"

"No." Karl shook his head, vibrating his mustache.

Seeing no guns, bombs or assassins, Dylan lowered his pistol. "Someone tried to assassinate President McCallum tonight. I need to get him north."

"Scheize, you said you were in hurry, not life-and-death emergency."

"I didn't want to worry you over the phone. I wanted to do that in person."

"Danke, Herr Commissar." Karl watched Rebecca help the McCallums out of the car. "How many are going?"

Dylan did a quick head count. "Seven."

"It will be crowded."

Karl turned to the electrical box behind him and opened the cover. He clicked on some breakers. In the dark bay adjacent, overhead fixtures hummed. Their filaments warmed slowly, so at first they cast only feeble light.

"Come." Karl started for the flickering bay.

Dylan kept with him.

In passing, Karl gave his usual nervous nod to McCallum. "Hello, Herr...Mr. President."

McCallum smiled briefly. "Thank you, Karl."

Gillespie and LaCroix closed the hanger door and moved to the trunk of the president's car. They unloaded the rifle and ammunition satchel that Dylan had stashed there.

The overhead lights finally blinked on and bathed the bay in brilliance. Under their gleam sat a twin-engine turbo prop Cessna 421. Pristine white with sharp red detailing, the streamlined aircraft waited with hatchway door open and steps down.

Karl smiled. "You are in luck. I have charter flight tomorrow morning, so I am fueled and ready."

Dylan turned to Douglas. "Pete, clear the plane."

Douglas nodded and climbed into the Cessna with weapon drawn.

Karl glanced at Rebecca again. Dylan realized he didn't know her.. "She's helping us out tonight. She's with the Bureau."

"I know," Karl said. "Agent Matthis. The Mallory girl."

Rebecca caught Dylan's eye with a raised eyebrow.

He smiled. "Your reputation precedes us."

Peter Douglas returned to the hatchway. "All clear."

"Everyone aboard."

The McCallums climbed the steps. Rebecca helped them up. Karl began a pre-flight walk about the aircraft.

Gillespie and LaCroix approached. Dylan noticed LaCroix's leg wound. "Paul, why didn't you tell me you were hurt?"

"You didn't ask."

"You're not coming with us. You need to get to a doctor."

"It's nothing a few bandages can't fix. I'm going."

"Damn it, Paul. If that leg is going to make you a liability, you're not doing me a favor by coming."

"I saw those guys at the estate. They're serious characters. You need all the help you can get."

Dylan found it hard to argue that point. He scrutinized the leg wound, trying to gauge its severity. He had to go on LaCroix's word. "You win. Have Gillespie help you dress that wound out of Karl's first-aid cabinet and get aboard. But it's for tonight only. Tomorrow morning you're off to a hospital." He took the ammunition satchel from him.

Gillespie handed Dylan the broken-down rifle case and helped LaCroix across the bay.

Rebecca came over. "The loyalty you get from them, it's impressive."

"It's not because of me." Dylan pointed a thumb toward the airplane. "It's McCallum. We respect who he is, what he did. It's that simple."

She eyed him carefully. "Don't discount yourself in that equation."

He smiled and moved toward the Cessna. "Last call for Linder Air flight 101."

He reached the steps just as Karl came around from the other side of the plane.

"Should I file flight plan?" the German asked.

Dylan stared at him. "Are you serious?"

Karl shrugged and climbed inside the airplane. Rebecca followed. Dylan waited for Gillespie and LaCroix to return before boarding.

The passenger cabin sat six. Four seats were centered in the fuselage. The McCallum's took the two facing forward. Rebecca and La-Croix took the two facing aft. Two more side-by-side seats were in the back of the plane, and Peter Douglas and Gillespie took those.

Dylan had to sit in the co-pilot's seat. He wormed his body behind the instrument panel to Karl's right and gave him a glance. "Shouldn't you be flying with a real co-pilot?"

"Yes." Karl continued his pre-flight checklist.

"Then let's get one of your guys in here."

"Nein. It is late, and you are in hurry to leave."

"I won't be much good to you if something goes wrong."

Karl laughed. "If it goes wrong enough, it will not matter who is sitting there."

Comforting thought.

Karl grabbed what looked like a garage door opener from his overall pocket and pressed a button on it. The sheet-metal door slid open. Smiling, he started the engines, let them come to temperature, and then rolled out of the hanger. He taxied over the gentle bumps in the grassy field toward the edge of the runway. The lights were on now. Dylan figured Karl had turned them on from the breaker box.

In position and satisfied all systems were ready, Karl applied power to the turboprops. The Cessna accelerated down the runway. Engine buzz filled the cockpit.

Not comfortable in small planes, Dylan grabbed his seat cushion and held his breath. After they had eaten up far more runway than he thought proper, Karl raised the nose. The shaking rattled Dylan's teeth. For a split second he imagined muzzle flashes in the trees beside the runway, and a fiery nose-over crash on take off. Fortunately the guns were in his head, and the Cessna lifted off the ground without a single bullet hole. They barely cleared the treetops beyond the airstrip.

"Wheels up."

Mother Earth fell away at an alarming speed, and Linder's Airfield's bright parking-lot light became a small, glowing speck. He didn't remember resuming the process, but Dylan realized he was breathing again.

Karl banked left, guiding the plane into its flight path to the U.P. He continued to climb to cruising altitude. The street lights of Grand Rapids sprawled below them. Miles of gridlock choked the expressways. Dylan imagined the FBI must have intercepted a whole lot of bad news to lock down the city so tight.

The thing that frightened him was that this same anxious scene was playing out in every major city in the country. And somewhere down in all that chaos stalked a man intent on killing Warren McCallum, the one person on Earth Dylan Reese had sworn to protect with his life.

TWENTY-FIVE

THE CESSNA took an hour and a half to reach Iron County Airport in Crystal Falls, the spot Karl and Dylan had agreed on as a good place to land. Other airports were closer to the safe house, but Dylan wanted to use a small, secluded airfield, one in which their landing might go unnoticed. Plus, Karl knew Iron County Airport and the people attending it well, and had been able to contact a friend to arrange ground transport for the president and his security detail.

Despite the airstrip's cracked asphalt and weeds, Karl brought the plane in for a remarkably smooth landing. He taxied off the runway and rolled to a stop near a single pair of headlights.

Dylan gave Karl a solid pat on his shoulder. "Thanks a million." Karl just smiled and nodded.

Squirming from the co-pilot's seat, Dylan moved into the crowded passenger cabin and checked on McCallum and the others. He singled out Gillespie. "Tommy, come with me."

The transport that Karl had secured was a Humvee owned by one of the private aviators living on the peninsula, Ed Bauer. Being a hunter, Bauer had painted his hummer with a camouflage pattern. He sat just short of the plane with motor running and headlights pointing south.

Dylan threw open the Cessna's hatchway door and folded the steps down. He drew his Glock, psyched himself, and stepped into the opening. He aimed at the driver's side windshield. "Mr. Bauer." He had to shout over the turbo props as they wound down. "Turn your cab light on and show me your hands."

The hummer's interior lit up and the driver lifted his hands to the ceiling.

Dylan rushed forward. Gillespie followed on his left. They reached the hummer and checked through the windows for any surprise passengers. There were none. Dylan pulled his badge from his pocket and flashed the five-pointed star. "I'm Special Agent Reese with the Secret Service." He opened the driver's door. "I apologize for the treatment, sir, but I can't afford to take chances." He extended an open hand. "Identification please."

Reaching carefully into his back pocket, Bauer, a thick man with a black beard, pulled out his wallet and handed it over. The passenger door flew open and Gillespie thrust his pistol into the cab. Bauer jumped and started to sweat.

Dylan tossed the wallet across to Gillespie. "Who is he, Tommy?"

Gillespie opened the wallet and scrutinized the driver's license. "Looks genuine." He scanned it again. "Hey, it's Eddie Bauer. That's funny."

Hands still up, Bauer stammered, "I'm not 'the' Eddie Bauer."

Gillespie gave the hummer and the driver's rustic clothing a double take. "You sure?"

Dylan motioned Bauer out of the vehicle. "I appreciate your co-operation, and I assure you we'll return your vehicle shortly."

Bauer stepped from the cab. "Return?"

Dylan lowered the Glock. "The government will reimburse you for any damage it may incur." He waved to the Cessna and the rest of the agents filed out. They hustled the McCallum's into the vehicle and piled in after them. Dylan took the wheel and Gillespie rode shotgun.

At half past midnight Dylan steered off airport grounds and headed east down Route 69 toward the safe house on the peninsula's southwestern coast. Population centers in the Upper Peninsula were few and far between, and most of Route 69 cut through long stretches of flat land with nothing but black pines and dark sky. He was amazed at how many more stars were visible without the light pollution he was accustomed to in the more densely populated Lower Peninsula. It made for quite a beautiful setting.

For a split second he wished he were driving through the night with only Rebecca in the car. The thought caught him off guard and in a bizarre way he felt guilty, as if she had read his mind at that instant. He glanced in the rear view mirror. She sat next to Kathryn McCallum, staring out the side window at the sky.

Dylan sensed an emotional shift among the passengers. McCallum had quieted since getting off the plane, seemed somber and reflective. The Old Man was thinking things through. Dylan couldn't fault him, a lot of bad things had happened in his life recently, and Keyes was determined to lay all the blame at his feet.

Traveling seventy over an empty road got them to the secluded safe house ten miles south of Escanaba in ninety minutes. The house bordered state forest property and sat just off the Lake Michigan shore. A massive A-frame with multiple dormers along the roof line and a wide covered porch stretching across the front, the 4,000 square foot log home looked more like a resort than a residence. Great panes of arched glass rose above the ornate front door. Its rustic façade did little to disguise the fact that the house reeked of opulence. It sat atop a steep ridge that ran right down to the lake. A hundred-yard band of aged spruce pines separated it from the water.

Rebecca saw enough of the safe house in the headlights to raise her eyebrows. "Where did the Secret Service get the funding to build this Tajmahal?"

"We apprehended a couple of counterfeiters," Dylan said. "They lived here."

He stopped the hummer on the circle drive near the front porch. The house was dark, and supposedly vacant. Gillespie and Douglas went inside to make sure no one was there, and in a few minutes called the others.

"It's musty in here," Douglas said, "I'll get the air going."

Rebecca walked the hardwood in the great foyer, craning her head to see the full two stories and the glass chandelier above. "I couldn't live in a place this big. It wouldn't feel right."

Gillespie walked by with the rifle case in hand. "I'd give it a shot."

"It's after two," Dylan said to the McCallums. "I think it would be best to get you to a safe room so you can get some sleep."

Kathryn agreed. The president nodded in deference to his wife. They followed Dylan down a hallway immediately off the foyer, passing some closed doors and descending a flight of stairs. At the bottom they found another hallway, this one shorter, which led to a single panel door.

The room was large, and a king-sized bed draped in a burgundy comforter was the centerpiece. Two chairs, a roll top desk, and a chest of drawers were all faux-colonial. There were no windows.

Dylan motioned them in. McCallum looked about the room as if appraising a new prison cell. He gestured to the walls. "You've put us in the basement. I'm libel to get claustrophobic."

"Hopefully this is short term."

Kathryn sat on the edge of the bed. Her husband sat beside her. She lifted the collar of her bath robe. "Will it be possible to get some clothes and other necessities tomorrow?"

"Absolutely. Make a list of what you need and I'll take care of it."

"How long?" she asked. "How long will we have to stay in this house?"

"I don't know. The world is out of balance right now. We need to apprehend the men who attacked us tonight before we can go back."

"It's because of me," McCallum said softly. "People are dying. People are scared, all because of what I did, because of Yellow Jacket, because I let those men die."

He looked tired and beaten.

"It's not your fault, sir. All this happening now, don't put it on your shoulders. Some psychopath sank those ships and pulled the trigger on Taylor, not you. And no matter how he tries to frame it, that blood is going to stay on him." Dylan paused. "Making the call on the Yellow Jacket team was a no-win proposition. Sometimes being the leader means having to make impossible decisions."

McCallum dropped his chin. "I put myself in this box, and I've put my wife and all of you in here with me."

Dylan stepped through the door into the hallway. "Being here is my decision. Don't believe otherwise." He gently closed the door and went back upstairs.

The lights were on in the great room and Dylan saw his reflection in the three towering glass panes on the southern wall. A television tuned to FOX News blared from open cabinet doors on a tall, pine entertainment stand. He crossed over the gigantic beige throw rug in the center of the floor, stepping around an overstuffed leather couch, and walked through the great room into the kitchen. Gillespie, La-Croix, and Rebecca had gathered around a granite-topped island and were watching news coverage of the L.A. bombing.

Dylan approached them. "Anything new?"

"Nothing on cable," Rebecca said. "I called Gerald, my partner in Detroit, and he told me they've been pulling their hair out trying to isolate credible threats from the communication traffic that's been spiking in the last four hours."

Dylan dialed the Secret Service office on his phone. Trevor Novak answered. "It's Reese. We made it to the safe house and are settling in. You still gnawing on that Swisher?"

"I'm about ready to light up," Novak said. "The FBI just apprehended two bona fide members of the Shiite Brigade three miles from the L.A. bombing site. They were fleeing the area armed with sub guns. Eyewitnesses identified them as having been near Bradford's office shortly before the blast. Some Intel people are expecting a string of coordinated nationwide terrorist attacks. Sound familiar?"

"Very. Any word from Grand Haven on nabbing the guys who tried to kill McCallum?"

"No. A SWAT team moved in but the grounds were empty. Grand Haven police received reports of a pickup truck driving reckless on back roads near Allendale but they haven't tracked it down yet." He went silent for three seconds. "How comfortable do you feel up there?"

Dylan took an account of his crew. "We're okay."

"Good, because I don't see this situation settling down for at least a day or two, and that's assuming there are no more attacks. With all that's going on, the governors are demanding to return to their home states. Since the FBI is bogged down investigating incoming intelligence, President Harrison has charged the Service with protecting the governors as they scatter to the four winds. Half of them won't fly because a number of threats specifically mentioned airlines. Some are driving out. Some are boarding trains. We're spread all over the map."

"Understood. We'll sit tight."

"It's not like we don't care, Dylan. Hell, you've got important people worried about you."

"What do you mean?"

"Senator Charles Burke himself called to make sure we were taking appropriate measures to protect the governors and President McCallum. Said the Anti-Terrorist Committee was holding an emergency session and he wanted all the pieces on the game board to get a handle on the situation. I sure would like to know myself."

Burke called? Maybe he had turned a new leaf. "Right. Thanks, Trevor." Dylan disconnected. "They didn't get anyone at the estate. And to add another dimension to this mess, two members of the Shiite Brigade were arrested in L.A. near the bomb site. Intel is still filtering through a stream of threats." He singled out Rebecca. "This could be bigger than we thought. We're on our own for a few days."

No one around the granite island said anything.

Peter Douglas stepped out of the bathroom just off the great room with a fresh bandage on his bullet graze. "What'd I miss?"

"Pete," Dylan said. "There's a key in a recessed section of that door molding behind you, the door to the basement. Feel around the top edge."

Douglas did as instructed.

"The key is for the gun locker concealed in the study closet. Break out the M-16s."

The drive to the safe house had knocked everybody down a few pegs. Gillespie, LaCroix, and Rebecca were starting to look as tired as Dylan felt. "You three pick out rooms and get some rest. Pete and I will be first watch. It's two-thirty now. We'll stand post until eight, and then we'll rotate. Paul, how's that leg?"

LaCroix rubbed a hand over bloodshot eyes. "I'm all right."

"Okay, you guys get going."

The weary trio bid farewell and fled the kitchen. LaCroix limped into a room on ground level. Rebecca and Gillespie climbed the staircase from the kitchen to a large loft overlooking the great room. Rebecca went left over the bridge to the room across the way. Gillespie went right, to the bedroom over the kitchen.

Douglas had gone to get the weapons.

Dylan watched Rebecca through the rungs of the banister until she disappeared behind the bearskin that hung in the center. He caught himself a little too late again. He turned his eyes to the television. Nothing new under the sun. He found the remote and clicked it off.

Douglas returned with two M-16s. Dylan took one and directed Pete to stand post on the sprawling deck out back. He dimmed the recessed lights in the great room to a faint glow, and then walked the long hallway to the foyer and stepped out onto the front porch. He found a weathered deck chair near the door and sat. Kicking his feet up on the rail, he rested the M-16 across his lap and watched the quarter moon descend in the west.

Cricket song pulsated in the woods and a foraging raccoon rustled through dried twigs near the house. Time slipped and Dylan listened, watched. Waited. He liked the Upper Peninsula, the peaceful respite of nature, the sounds of silence. The place almost had the power to calm his nerves. But not quite.

Ever since Novak told him the SWAT team came up empty, he'd been thinking about where the assassins might have gone. They were still out there, more than likely trying to figure out where their mark had disappeared to. The thought pecked at him like crows on a carcass. His imagination sent Sadeed's bullet spiraling toward his head again. His palms began to sweat and his heart rate quickened. He thought of Danny, and days they might never have together. He thought about Sarah, and how she had given up on him. Gunfire from the shootout at the estate rattled inside his head.

A metallic click sounded. It carried through the trees and overpowered the racket in his thoughts. He dropped his legs and came to his feet, swinging the M-16 down the length of the porch. The front door opened.

Rebecca stepped through the doorway.

He lowered the rifle. "You should be sleeping."

"It's not working out very well," she said. "Can't seem to get more than ten minutes at a time. Figured I might as well get out of bed and make sure you haven't dozed off." She walked toward him.

The woods were pre-dawn dark. To the east, the first hint of light began teasing the sky.

She leaned on the rail. "We made it to tomorrow."

He checked his watch. It was after five already. "Time flies when you're standing guard against bloodthirsty assassins."

She gave him a brief smile through the semi-darkness. "Have you called Sarah yet?"

"Uh...no. Not yet." The question threw him off. "Don't know if I'm going to. I'm not sure she wants to hear from me."

Rebecca faced him. "I'm sure she's heard about the attempt on McCallum by now. She'll want to hear from you that you're okay."

"How do you know that?"

"Despite my posturing, I'm still a woman."

"I never thought otherwise." He felt her gaze shift to a glare. "What's wrong?"

"Nothing." She looked into the trees. "I work hard to be a good agent, not so much a good woman."

"Who said you can't be both?"

"I do."

He smiled. "Now that's kind of silly." Her expression told him it wasn't silly to her at all. "Or not."

"Look, it's a different set of rules for me." She thought a few seconds. "At the estate last night, during the fire fight, were you scared?"

"Shitless. What's that got to do with anything?"

"I was scared too, but I can't say that out loud. It's more damning for a woman to admit that she has fear under fire. It's ammunition for every man who thinks we shouldn't be out here."

"Take it from me, everyone who comes under fire feels fear. If you don't you're either stupid or a fool. You're setting impossible standards for yourself. You did great out there, in the whole investigation. Take a little pride, Agent Matthis."

"Pride cometh before the fall."

"To everything there is a season."

She looked at him funny.

"It's from Ecclesiastes. McCallum said I need to read The Book more. I think he's right."

"He is."

"What made you want to join the FBI?"

"My father." The words came out stilted.

"Yeah, my dad encouraged me too. Did he want you to stand up for truth, justice, and the American way?"

"No, he abused me."

He stood blank, trying to figure out how to pull his question back.

She noted his stupor. "It was nothing sexual, just good old fashioned physical stuff."

Of all the condolences and bits of wisdom he could have offered, the best he could come out with was, "Sorry."

"Don't be, it's not your fault. It actually made me a stronger person." She smiled. "You know what they say. Whatever doesn't kill you…"

She had confided in him. He was certain television psychiatrists would call that a breakthrough of some kind. He wondered for a moment if he should return the gesture.

"When I said I was scared, I meant it." He set the rifle butt on the porch and pulled Sadeed's bullet out of his pocket. He held it in his open palm. "The day I almost bought it protecting McCallum, this is the slug that nearly put a hole in my skull." He studied it a few seconds. "Gillespie's right. Sometimes this damned thing controls my life. Not sure why I carry it around. It's a constant reminder of, well, of death, of what we face everyday, but I can't throw it away."

"Kind of like a cold piece of the grim reaper in your pocket."

"Kind of like that. I even have a recurring nightmare about it."

"Wow, a head full of issues. What happens in the dream?"

"The whole incident in the hotel hallway replays, like I'm there again, but in super slow motion. The bullet comes at my head, I can see it spinning, but I can't get out of the way. I guess it's driving home the fact that I'm powerless against fate."

"Stop the bullet," she said. It sounded like an order. "It's your dream, in your head. Tell the stupid thing to stop. Maybe the dream is trying to teach you that you can control your fate, you just haven't learned how to do it yet."

He smiled at her. He'd never come at it from that angle before.

"You might have something there. I'll give it a shot next time. Hey, I think you missed your calling as a shrink. Maybe I'll hire you to solve my other anxieties."

She smiled but didn't reply.

In the earliest light of day they stood and stared at one another for a long while.

She took a step closer. "What else are you afraid of?"

"Failing McCallum."

"Anything else?"

"Women with guns and law degrees."

She put a hand over his, over the bullet. Her touch went right through him and clouded his thoughts. He suddenly became aware of her scent, lilac. A breeze moved through her hair. He was gone. He leaned forward and their lips touched.

His phone chimed. Moment broken.

They parted and stared at one another. His phone rang again. She turned to the woods.

He put the phone to his ear. "Reese."

"You're keeping something from me, Agent Reese."

He didn't recognize the voice, but it carried authority.

He looked away from Rebecca. "Who is this?"

"If you knew what McCallum did, you wouldn't risk your life protecting him."

Dylan felt the bottom drop out of his stomach. "Keyes?"

The caller went silent.

Rebecca whirled about.

"You are standing in the way of justice, Reese. That man is a traitor to his countrymen."

"I know about Yellow Jacket. I know Michael Keyes was your father. You're not interested in justice. You want revenge."

"McCallum left them to die! He broke the first code of a soldier."

"Is that the same code that gives you the right to kill innocent civilians?"

"In war collateral damage is unavoidable."

"War? This isn't war; it's wholesale slaughter."

"Call it whatever you want," Keyes said. "Just keep in mind whose sin caused this hell."

"Your father knew the danger before he went in. He knew what could happen. Why don't you understand that?"

"Do your duty to country, Reese. Stand aside and let justice be served."

"I am doing my duty!" Dylan's raised voice chased a cluster of crows from the trees.

"You can't keep him from me forever. I will catch up to him someday."

"Don't bet on it."

Keyes measured out a dramatic pause. "If you had to choose, who would you protect, this traitor, or someone worth much, much more to you?"

"What are you talking about?"

"I'm looking for McCallum. You may be surprised at the places I search. I'm sure you have a parent, or wife, or even a child you're particularly fond of, Agent Reese. If you make this too difficult for me I may devise an alternate strategy."

"Try something like that and I'll be the one hunting you."

Keyes chuckled. "Food for thought. I'll be in touch."

"Go to hell!"

The line went dead. Dylan glared at the phone, thinking hard about throwing it into the woods.

Rebecca came forward. "In the Bureau they teach us to handle those types of phone conversations with a little more cool professionalism."

"I'm not in the Bureau."

"What did he say?"

"Nothing." He squeezed the phone tight. "Bottom line is he's still out there looking for McCallum. And I still have to stop him."

TWENTY-SIX

SOON AFTER DYLAN'S PHONE CALL, Rebecca had her cell out, dialing the Grand Rapids Bureau office. She thought she'd better check in with Jennings and let him know what had happened to her or at least leave a message for him. She and Dylan stood on the front porch on the edge of the wilderness, dialing the same building, but different floors, hundreds of miles away.

Jennings was actually in, which surprised her. Being a long way off from the nearest tower, she couldn't get a good cell connection, and her garbled conversation with him didn't last long. The only thing she really accomplished was to tell him that she'd been moving with McCallum's security detail since the assassination attempt and that she'd contact him latter.

She noticed Dylan faring a little better with his satellite phone. He reached his office and ripped someone up and down over Keyes getting hold of his name and number, and then demanded the Service assign some agents to watch Sarah's house. Now she knew what Keyes had said to get him angry. She felt a pang of guilt for getting so close to him when he still had issues in his personal life. The stress they were all under didn't help matters either.

There was no question she felt an attraction to him, a rarity to be sure. His sense of loyalty to McCallum registered with her. Perhaps that is what her subconscious longed for, a man capable of devotion to someone or something other than himself. Most men she met had nothing more than conquest or competition in mind. Just the same, the time wasn't right for that sort of pursuit, and she decided to take a step back.

Dylan pocketed his phone. "Okay, our stay here is open-ended." He paused. "What I mean is McCallum and his security detail are stuck here. You don't have a responsibility to protect him. No need for you to get sucked into this thing any further."

"Did Keyes threaten Sarah and Danny?"

He hesitated. "In a way, yes, but I got the office to put a few guys on her house. I doubt anything will come of it."

"Did anyone explain how he got your number?"

"No. That's the scary thing about this bastard, he's got connections."

She searched for the right approach. "Dylan, about what happened between us a little while ago. I'm not quite sure why it happened. I'm sorry."

"Don't be sorry. I'm not."

That wasn't a very big step back. "Now isn't a good time. Agreed?"

He paused before nodding.

"And as far as not having a responsibility to McCallum, you're right. But I do have a responsibility to apprehend Owen Keyes, and because he called you and made clear he hasn't given up, sticking around a little longer seems like a good idea. He just might find you."

"That's comforting. Thanks." He lifted the M-16 from the deck. "I figure we'll give the others an hour or so more to sleep."

The front door opened and Gillespie exited the house. Shirt and pants wrinkled, hair sticking up, he looked like a towering five-year-old waking from a nap. He scratched the side of his head. "I take it the night passed quietly."

"Pretty much." Dylan handed him the rifle. "Take a seat, I'll see if there's any coffee in this place."

Gillespie wiped his eyes and dropped into the deck chair.

Dylan and Rebecca went inside. They walked quietly down the hall and through the great room to the kitchen. "There weren't any new attacks last night," Dylan said. "There's some good news."

"Any word on the manhunt for Keyes?"

"Just that the police found the pickup truck they believe he used to flee the estate abandoned off road in a patch of wetlands."

She opened an overhead cupboard and searched for a pot, or grounds, or something having to do with coffee. "So they're not hot on his trail."

"Right. And if they're not hot on his trail, he's got all sorts of time to concentrate on finding us."

Behind the third cupboard door she found a white coffee maker and pulled it down. "What's the first thing on your agenda today?"

He opened a drawer. Just silverware. "Get in touch with the local police department; see if we can get help guarding the house. When Mrs. McCallum wakes up she'll make a list of things she needs, clothes and staples and stuff like that. It'd be a good idea if we all made lists.

None of us were planning on coming up here last night."

President McCallum appeared in the great room and headed for the kitchen. "Kathryn has already made her list," he said with gravel in his voice. He lifted a yellow sheet of notepad paper.

"Good morning, sir." Dylan opened another drawer. "We're just looking for some coffee."

McCallum pulled a stool out from the island and sat. He had dark circles under his eyes. "I've got one more thing to add to this list." He set the paper down and scribbled something at the bottom with a pen. "I didn't sleep a wink last night. My ticker's too tired to go very long without rest. Pick up some sleeping pills for me. They've got pretty effective over-the-counter varieties now."

"No problem." Dylan opened a third drawer. "Jackpot. Vacuum-pack pouches and a stack of filters. Even I can make a pot when it's this easy."

Rebecca sat next to the president. "How is Mrs. McCallum doing?"

He gave a weak smile. "Better than I am. That woman never ceases to amaze me. Sure she came through the fire of a couple of presidential campaigns, and eight years under the D.C. microscope, but nothing prepares one for something like this. I really hit a grand slam when I married her."

"I guess what they say is true. Behind every great man..." She patted his hand.

That garnered a genuine chuckle from him. "I'll be the first to agree with you."

Dylan cut open a packet of ground coffee and poured it into a filter. "I'll be heading out in a little bit so if there's anything else you need get it on that list now."

"How 'bout a trip to the past and a shot at redemption."

"You must not have heard him," Rebecca said. "He asked for things you need."

After fixing everyone with caffeine, Dylan and Rebecca drove off in the hummer to Escanaba. Remembering their moment at sunrise, she steered clear of personal conversation. They pulled in to town a little after seven and Dylan found a parking spot in front of an old department store. The façade looked recently renovated, with crisp red brick and freshly painted wood trim. She took the list of needful things from him. He headed to the police station to request the use of a deputy or two.

Upper Peninsula coast, five miles north of Cedar River

Keyes spat a stream of chaw on the forest floor near his feet. He made sure the 9mm was secure in his shoulder holster and then glanced at the canopy of leaves overhead. The trees effectively blocked the noonday sun and provided a cool repose for him and his men as they unpacked their gear from the inflatable and transformed themselves from soldiers into backpackers.

He considered his call to Agent Reese. It surprised him when Reese called him by name. There really was a crackerjack wise guy among them. At this point, though, it made little difference if they knew his name. The importance of the call lay in the effect he believed it created. At first it would put Reese on alert, but after some thought, he'd realize that the man on the line had no idea where to find McCallum.

Keyes appreciated the importance of every little detail to help him in his cause, especially now that he had to operate off the page. In reality, thanks to the senator, he did know where Reese had taken McCallum. He marveled that a politician had actually been useful to him. Smirking at his resourcefulness, he peered through the surrounding bark and branch to the water beyond.

Richard C. drifted half a mile off the coast.

The tugboat had taken fourteen hours to reach this shoreline.

They'd stuffed broken-down rifles, ammunition, fatigues, MP-5s, and NV scopes into their backpacks. Tierney and Dominic directed their men to conceal the inflatable beneath a blanket of dried leaves and undergrowth. Dressed now in khaki shorts, T-shirts, and hiking boots, the Circle came together near a rustic trail in the Escanaba River State Forest.

"1500 hours," Keyes said. "We've got ten miles ahead of us."

"How did you figure it out?" Griffin asked, adjusting his pack so that the straps did not lie over his shoulder wound. "How did you find where they took McCallum?"

"I've got friends in high places."

"How confident are you in this information?" Tierney asked.

"Confident enough to travel fourteen hours to get here."

Tierney fished a cigarette from a pack and set it between his lips. "You have the layout of this house?"

Keyes grabbed the cigarette and threw it on the ground. "Not a good habit for a healthy hiker to have. And no, all I have is its location. We'll have to be creative."

Roth worked his thumb underneath his pack strap and shifted his weight from one foot to the other. "The president is yours, Commander, but I want the damned Service agent who killed Wilke."

"Get in line," Tierney said. "If I see him first you're out of luck, Mr. Roth."

"And the prick who shot me," Griffin added. "I didn't get a look at him, but what the hell, they're all gonna be dead when we're finished."

Six Pack grew more excited as they talked. "I just want to leave my mark on this somehow." He laughed. "Never thought I'd get a chance to write a line of history."

Dominic sniffed the air, shifted pieces of bark around with his boot.

"You've been quiet since the estate," Keyes said. "Is anything wrong, Dom?"

Dominic lifted his chin. "No, sir. Just waiting to move out."

Keyes wasn't buying. "Still debating posses and lynch mobs?"

"No, Commander. I've got that figured out."

"And what did you figure?"

"When it gets right down to it there's not a dime's worth of difference between the two, so I guess it just doesn't matter."

Not quite what Keyes wanted to hear. He spat some chew then drew his pistol and held it loose at his side. "Let's cut the crap, Dom. You're either all the way in or all the way out. We're at the end of the game and I've got to know who's going to play with their heart."

Tierney and the others fell silent.

Six Pack stared at his mentor. "Dom?"

The big Italian stood there calm, eyes focused on Keyes. "You won't need that, Commander. In for a penny, in for a pound, and I threw in my penny a long time ago."

Six Pack slapped his shoulder. "You had me going."

"Did I?" A smile cracked Dominic's demeanor. "Don't worry, nubie. I wouldn't let you go writing history by yourself."

Keyes considered him a while longer. He holstered the 9mm. "Welcome back." He looked up the trail. "Now let's get moving. We've got some ground to cover if we're going to pay a visit to Warren McCallum tonight."

"I'm all over that," Roth said. "Time to square things with the Secret Service."

Keyes took point position and started up the narrow hiking trail that followed the contour of the coast. Griffin fell in line, with Six Pack, Roth, and Dominic following.

Tierney brought up the rear. He glanced ahead at Keyes, measured the distance, and drew a cigarette from his pack. He lit up. Dominic walked directly in front of him. He unconsciously lowered his hand to where the Desert Eagle would normally be. In keeping with their disguise, however, the mammoth handgun now traveled inside his backpack. He considered the big Italian and began to think that at least one of their number would not make it through the night.

At the safe house

Dylan heard his name spoken by a soothing voice, a female voice. His eyes were closed, and he felt sleep evaporating. The world assembled around him. The pillow felt soft, and he struggled to get his bearings. *Am I at the guest house? Home?* He didn't want to move.

"Dylan." The voice again. He opened his eyes.

Across the bed, Rebecca raised an eyebrow.

He recalled their kiss, and for a frantic instant tried to remember if they had slept together. He suddenly realized she wasn't in the bed at all, but kneeling beside it, fully clothed.

He was dressed too, for that matter.

She stood and lifted a crinkled sack of fast food. "It's nearly eight-thirty. You wanted us to wake you."

He sat up. He'd been sleeping five hours. "Ever hear of knocking?"

"I did. You didn't hear."

He reached for the bag and pulled it to him. "Is the world on fire?"

"No more than usual."

He peeled the foil skin off a hamburger and dropped his feet to the floor. "Did the doctor show up for LaCroix?"

"About two hours ago. He said the bullet had gone straight through his leg and that the wound was a good clean one." She walked to the edge of the bed. "I don't consider any wound good."

"Any wound that doesn't kill or maim you is a good one." He took a bite of the burger.

"What about psychological scarring?"

Not sure if she was referring to his bullet phobia or her father's abuse, he shelved the wise-ass comment on the tip of his tongue. He swallowed. "Different subject."

"The McCallums have already called it a night. They've retired to their, what does the president call it? Right, their burrow." She crossed her arms. "He's been quiet all afternoon, more on the depressed side."

Dylan lifted a soft drink cup from the nightstand. "He's got a maniacal naval officer after him. I'd be depressed too."

"I feel like your first lieutenant reporting on the troops. Are you coming out or not?"

He eyed her and took another bite of hamburger. "You've been hanging around those guys too long."

She turned to leave but spun back around. "You owe me five bucks for dinner."

He stood. "What a deal. And I didn't even have to cook it myself."

She smiled, with a sarcastic tilt if he read it right, and left the bedroom. He followed her into the great room. Gillespie and LaCroix were chitchatting at the island in the kitchen area. Through the wall-length windows to his right Peter Douglas was back on guard duty, pacing the deck with an M-16.

Dylan nodded to his men and walked down the hallway to the foyer. He peered out through one of the small window panes circling the front door. Halfway down the long drive he spotted the hood of a police car parked off to the side. He had requested assistance from the sheriff's office that morning, and Deputy Schiff was all they could provide.

A stream of evening sun came through the divided-light window high up over the door. The angle at which the light came through the mutton bars cast an image of a cross on the opposite wall. Rays through the chandelier fashioned a vibrant rainbow around it. Dylan considered the image, thought about an innocent man dying, about supreme sacrifice.

Strange. He ran his fingers across his palms. No sweat. No hot flash. No picture of Sadeed in his head. Something in that refracting light had chased away his fear.

Would darkness bring it back?

He walked from the foyer and shifted his thoughts.

What was the point of Keyes' call? Did he really think he could talk Dylan into turning his back on the president? He seemed too smart a man to believe he could do that. Did he hope Dylan would slip up and mention some clue as to where they were? That would be a desperate move. Did he hope to scare Dylan into leaving McCallum's side to protect Sarah and Danny? None of these possibilities seemed a valid reason for the conversation. Then what?

Maybe Keyes had a more subtle goal in mind. Maybe he meant to reassure Dylan that he was doing a good job, so good in fact that Keyes just didn't know where next to search for McCallum. Maybe that's exactly what he was supposed to take away from the call. If so, it could only mean one thing. Keyes might actually have some idea where to look, and he wanted his opponent to relax.

But how could he find out the location of the safe house? Probably the same way he had discovered Dylan's name and phone number. He was connected somehow. The safe house began to feel not so safe.

He walked into the great room and approached Rebecca, Gillespie, and LaCroix at the island. "If we had to move McCallum, where might we move him to? Any ideas?"

"What's wrong with here?" Gillespie said.

"Too many people know about this house."

"Service people know about it. What are you saying?"

"I think Owen Keyes might have someone on the inside feeding him information. It'd be best if we move to a location that only we know about."

"He's right," Rebecca said. "It's only a matter of time before he finds this place."

The loose atmosphere inside the house tightened. Dylan sensed it. Good. The guys needed to be alert, not relaxed. "Think it over. I want to talk about options tonight." He addressed Gillespie and LaCroix. "Rebecca said McCallum seemed depressed this afternoon. You guys notice that?"

"He wasn't spitting jokes," Gillespie said. "But a lot of crap has happened lately. The Old Man is just sick and tired."

LaCroix tapped his fingers on the island. "He did seem down. Enigma tried to lift him out of it but he didn't respond to her."

"I'm concerned," Dylan said. "We just bought him a damn bottle of sleeping pills!"

Rebecca's eyes opened wide.

Gillespie pushed back from the island. "Shit!"

Dylan raised his hands. "I'm only speculating. And remember,

Kathryn is down there with him. She'll watch out for him if he's in that state of mind."

"We should check on him," LaCroix said.

"Right, but I don't want him to know what we're thinking. So Paul, hobble down there and poke your head in their room, tell McCallum I've reassigned all you guys and that you'll be keeping watch outside their door."

"Okay, and then what?"

"Then pull up a chair outside their door. You are being reassigned. Keep an ear toward that room for any possible trouble."

LaCroix's face fell. "Great."

"Here you are, Paul."

Mrs. McCallum handed LaCroix a mug of coffee. She and the president sometimes liked an evening cup, and had just brewed some with the coffee maker Dylan purchased that morning. "Sorry you're stuck down here with us now."

LaCroix took the mug and smiled. "It's all part of the job." He glanced inside the room to where the president sat. "If you need anything at all, I'll be right out here."

"Thank you, Paul."

He stepped back and she closed the door.

She returned to her husband and sat in the wooden chair across from him. He looked tired. She lifted her coffee cup from the open roll top and rested it in her lap. "We're very fortunate to have these men protecting us."

"I know, Kate. I know." He stared at her a long while. "I've had a remarkable life. I can't imagine having lived it with anyone other than you."

She sipped her coffee and smiled. "We have some time left, you know. Despite what's happening now, I believe we have a few more seasons together."

"I love you, Kate." His eyes turned glassy. "More so now than when we first married. You know that don't you?"

"I love you too, dear, and I'm proud of you. You've done so much. You've made a difference. Don't ever forget that. Don't let this Keyes person take that from you."

He leaned forward and placed his hands on his knees. "Keyes. I've thought long and hard about him. I started out feeling completely responsible for his rampage, but not anymore. He bears that cross on his own shoulders. The good Lord is going to have a whale of a talk with him on Judgment Day." McCallum settled and softened his posture. "I wonder if I'll be standing there right next to him, trying to explain my actions."

"Don't put yourself in his category. He's a brutal murderer."

"And what am I?"

"You are a man who presided over turbulent times, who suffered through the tragedy of men dying while carrying out his orders. Every president since Washington has had to bear that burden."

"But they didn't turn their backs on their soldiers."

"Neither did you." Kathryn touched his hand. "I'm sure those men in Iran didn't hold you responsible."

"One of their sons is doing just that." He frowned and looked away. "And he's doing a terrible job of punishing me for it. He's killed or injured everyone around me but hasn't found the mark yet." He shook his head. "Those people on the ship with Patterson, the people who died in Joe Bradford's law office, they're innocent bystanders in this madness. And you, Kate, you're in danger just being with me. Same goes for Dylan and the detail, and Agent Matthis; they're all risking their lives because of me. I can't let it happen anymore."

She set her cup on the desk. Her eyelids felt heavy. "What do you mean?"

He looked deep into her eyes. "I won't let Keyes harm you on account of me."

She wiped a hand over sleepy eyes and fought back a wave of fatigue. "Please, Warren, don't do anything foolish."

"There's nothing foolish in protecting the people I love and respect."

She slumped forward but caught herself from falling. Exhaustion seemed to have come out of nowhere. She'd had two cups of coffee. *Why isn't the caffeine keeping me awake?*

"You're tired, Kate." He stood and helped her out of the chair. "Lie down and get some rest."

She heard a rattling sound come from his pocket as she put her head on the pillow. The sleeping pills. The bottle Dylan brought back from town. "Why?" She couldn't string the words together. "Why...are you...doing..."

He turned his chair so that it faced the bed and watched her drift off. "Because I love you more than my own life, and if that son of a bitch Keyes is going to take me, he's going to take me alone."

She closed her eyes and McCallum wept quietly. He wiped tears from his face and stared at the bedroom door, wondering how long he would have to wait for Paul LaCroix to succumb to the sleeping pills in his coffee.

TWENTY-SEVEN

THE SUN dropped behind the trees. At ten-thirty, darkness devoured the safe house. Rebecca walked through the great room listening to silence. With Douglas on guard outside, Dylan studying a map on the couch, Gillespie in the loft playing solitaire, and LaCroix downstairs, only the hum of the ceiling fan and the crinkling of the map made any noise.

She stood over Dylan's shoulder, noting the M-16 at his side and a can of high-octane soda pop sitting on the coffee table. "Don't you get headaches from drinking that stuff?"

He shrugged. "No, I get headaches from security leaks."

His map detailed the greater Midwest.

"Find a new home?" she said.

"I thought seeing a map might give me some ideas, but nothing yet."

"How about an FBI safe house?"

"I'd rather not. If Keyes has eyes in the Secret Service, it's not a stretch to assume he's got a line on you guys too."

"That's not a good thought."

"I know. I'm speculating but I've got to stay ahead of him."

She left him to continue his search and climbed the steps to the loft. Gillespie sat up there at a hardwood table, with rows of playing cards in front of him. The Remington .308 lay across the table, ammunition clip in place and night vision scope mounted.

She approached. "What's new in the loft, Tommy?"

He pondered the jack of diamonds. "I'm getting my ass kicked by the deck."

"You want an opponent?"

"Sure." He threw down the jack and began assembling the cards.

She lifted the rifle off the table.

"Take a seat, Red Dragon." He smirked. "What do you say to strip poker?"

Rifle in hand, she glared at him, giving the impression she might turn it his way. "Can you at least pretend I'm one of the guys?"

He leaned forward on his elbows. "Okay, two lesbians walk into a bar—"

She shot a hand up to silence him. "Enough." She propped the .308 against the rail beside the large bear skin. "What happened in youth that arrested your development?"

He smiled. "Usual stuff, I suppose, binge drinking, college football. What made you the happy public servant you are today?"

She sat across from him. "Shut up and deal."

Outside the safe house at the bottom of the slope near the water, Owen Keyes peered through the night vision scope on Roth's rifle. Aiming up the rise through a break in the pines, he tracked Peter Douglas from one end of the deck to the other. The image in the scope appeared in shades of green.

Douglas walked in towards the house. Keyes lost site of him. He tossed the weapon back to Roth.

Keeping their footsteps quiet, they moved several yards south and crouched behind a tall outcropping of rock. The rest of the group had assembled there. They were now dressed in dark fatigues, no longer carefree hikers.

In a whisper just loud enough to be heard above the wash of the lake, Keyes said to Tierney, "Time to move. Give me ten minutes to get in position up top. John, you, Dom, and Six Pack work your way up the slope from this point. We have dense tree cover on this side; it shouldn't be a problem to get close without detection. Roth and Griffin, perch yourselves in those trees we scouted. Go loud on my word."

The men nodded.

The men of the Circle gave their weapons one last check. They plugged ear jack cords into their radios and girded themselves for action. Roth and Griffin shouldered rifles and broke from the group, heading for their sniper nests.

Clenching an MP-5, Six Pack bounced on his heels.

Dominic sensed the kid was scared.

Six feet away, Tierney studied them both with a suspicious eye.

Keyes took an MP-5 into his hands and started up the long slope. He reached level ground a hundred yards south of the safe house and moved from tree to tree. Chirping crickets covered any rustle or snap his boots stirred from the ground. Keeping at a safe distance, he maneuvered behind the police car on the drive.

The deputy behind the wheel sat in the dark with the window open and sipped from a Styrofoam cup.

Keyes crept up. He recalled Agent Reese's remark about slaughtering innocent bystanders. The remark bothered him. He didn't think himself a cold blooded murderer, but rather a patriot.

He drew up alongside the police car and swung the butt of the MP-5 into the driver's window. A dull thunk and the deputy collapsed across the center console. Keyes wiped a splash of blood from his weapon. He moved toward the house. *Cold blooded my ass.*

High in a tree around back, Roth found a heavy branch to support his weight. He had climbed as far as he could and now sat nearly level with the deck at the rear of the house. He set his back against the trunk and seated himself in a comfortable position. Pulling the Armalite AR-18 rifle off his shoulder, he searched for a crease to steady the barrel. His line of fire ran straight through an opening in the pine branches and leaves, a hundred-yard shot from sniper to target.

Griffin was presumably positioned at a similar elevation in a tree thirty yards north.

Roth found a branch to support the rifle, but realized the pine cluster limited his field of vision. Only half of the deck was unobstructed. Not good, but he didn't have time to move now. When they had scouted the trees earlier, this one seemed the most promising in regards to line of sight. Now that he was there, he could see its shortfalls. Not to worry. He'd make it work.

The shadowy agent standing guard on the deck did not seem aware of the gathering forces around him. This just wasn't his day.

Enough light spilled out of the great windows in the rear of the house so that Roth didn't have to turn on his scope's night vision electronics. He sighted through the eyepiece. The agent was silhouetted nicely. Roth placed the crosshairs right over the man's head and laid his finger across the trigger guard. "Come on, Keyes. Give the word."

Tierney, Dominic, and Six Pack had climbed half the distance up the slope. Although the pines did offer cover, dried needles and loose soil made the trek precarious. Tierney led the trio. Dominic was second in line. The Italian found each step more difficult than the last, and not because of the terrain. He'd been going over and over the situation for days. This OP, it just wasn't what he thought it would be. When he signed on, Keyes had told him about Yellow Jacket, and the five men they were to target. At that time it seemed a just plan, but people other than those five had died, and he was repulsed. In the assault at the estate he hadn't fired a shot, refusing to be part of the carnage any longer. He didn't know McCallum personally, but had come to the conclusion that regardless the president's decision during Yellow Jacket, meting out justice did not rightfully belong in his hands.

Adding to his angst, Tierney's brutality, his way of embracing death, his icy hold on Roth and Wilke, appeared to be seducing Six Pack. The kid had his whole life ahead of him. He shouldn't waste it in John Tierney's shadow.

Dominic's foot slipped on a fallen branch and he slowed his pace.

Tierney's palm dropped to the Desert Eagle.

Dominic curled his fingers around the Browning. "This is a fucked up lynch mob, John."

Tierney stopped. "Don't make this mistake."

Dominic slid the Browning from its holster.

Tierney drew the Desert Eagle and pivoted about.

They stood ten yards apart, aiming at one another.

Six Pack stopped cold, three steps to Dominic's side.

"I spoke up for you," Tierney said. "I told Keyes you'd work out. Now look at you."

Dominic tightened his grip on the pistol. "The OP went to hell. I'm getting out." He nodded toward Six Pack. "The kid doesn't need this shit ruining his life. I'm taking him with me."

Tierney glanced left, smiled. "You really should have planned this better."

Dominic didn't understand, until he sensed movement beside him.

Six Pack came forward and aimed his MP-5 directly at his mentor's chest. "You can't make this decision for me."

The spirit drained from Dominic's body. The kid was making the worst mistake of his life.

"Drop the gun," Six Pack ordered.

Head low, Dominic let the Browning slip from his fingers.

Tierney lowered his pistol and glanced up the slope. "When Keyes gives the word to open fire, Mr. Martin, start with Dom."

Six Pack gave an uncertain nod.

Dominic burned in place. Why did the kid throw in with Tierney? It sickened him. It hurt him. *Damn kid doesn't know what he's doing.*

"Drop that MP from your shoulder, Dom." Six Pack took a step closer.

Dominic pulled the weapon down and let if fall. Standing this close, he could see Six Pack was as scared as he'd ever seen him. *I can't make this decision for him?*

The barrel of the kid's MP-5 dipped toward the ground.

Like hell.

Dominic sprang like a cobra and enveloped Six Pack in his arms, pinning the sub gun to his side. They crashed to the ground. The wind left the kid's chest in a whoosh and his MP-5 discharged a burst of ammunition. The quiet night shattered.

Six Pack wrapped tight in his iron arms, Dominic found a rock with his boot and kicked off. They rolled down the slope, bouncing over uneven ground, rocks and sticks bludgeoning their bodies.

Peter Douglas thought he'd heard voices, but the burst of gunfire from downslope left no question. Keyes was here. He leveled the M-16 over the hand rail. The night was too dark, he couldn't see anything. He retreated toward the house.

The next gunshot he heard came from dead ahead.

Roth sighted through the scope at Douglas. Keyes hadn't given the word but some idiot down there had fired. Surprise was gone. Douglas was moving backward. Nearly out of sight. That damned agent wasn't going to escape. Tracking his target, Roth slid his finger inside the trigger guard and fired.

Dylan jerked his head from the map at the sputter of gunfire. He checked outside and saw Douglas searching the darkness beyond the deck.

A sharp report sounded, breaking glass. The pop can on the coffee table exploded.

Dylan threw himself on the floor. He dragged the M-16 down with him.

Another blast echoed. Douglas took the hit low, in his abdomen, and fell in a seated position with his back against the sliding glass door. Dylan scrambled toward him across the floor.

Douglas lifted his M-16 and opened up, spraying the trees in a wide sweep.

From his perch Roth watched Douglas fall from view. He cursed. That agent should be dead, but the first shot had gotten away from him. Too quick. Through the large window panes people were moving about on the loft. He set the AR-18 to automatic and keyed his radio. "Griffin, cover the deck, they're out of my sight down there. I'm taking level two."

In the loft, Rebecca and Gillespie were on their feet. Down in the great room Dylan crawled across the floor. Douglas had been shot. "My rifle," Gillespie yelled. "Quick."

Rebecca took three steps and grabbed the weapon. The gunmetal felt cool on her hand. She spun around to toss it over but the railing beside her exploded. Wood splinters shot into the air. The side of her face felt afire, her arm too. Instinct dropped her to the floor.

The .308 fell from her grasp and clattered on the hardwood just beyond her fingertips. She reached for it. A burst of automatic fire pounded the floorboards near her hand. She withdrew and crawled backwards faster than she thought possible. Bullets chased her until she found shelter in the bedroom across the loft. She sat on the floor against the wall trying to catch her breath, wondering what had burnt the side of her face.

She felt around her cheek. A three-inch splinter of wood was sticking out of her skin. She braced herself and yanked it out. Burning pain brought tears to her eyes and a whimper from her throat. Another wooden shard had pierced her arm and she pulled that one from her flesh too.

Across the loft, Gillespie had upended the heavy table and dropped it behind the big bearskin. He hunkered down behind it and caught Rebecca's eye. "Are you alright?"

She really had to think about it. "Yeah," she shouted. "Damn rifle is in no-man's land."

"I can get it."

The weapon lay six feet from his makeshift barricade. He reached toward it, probing with his hand beyond the bearskin cloak. A blast of gunfire tore into the hide and pounded the tabletop. He pulled his digits back. "Okay, Red Dragon, I'm going to have to think about this."

"Great. Now we're in real trouble."

Dylan came to his feet just inside the kitchen, slamming against the wall near a plate full of light switches. He swept his hand down over them all and the house went dark. He secured the M-16 in his right hand and tried to push the sliding glass door open with his left. It didn't move. Douglas was leaning against it. His blood smeared the glass.

Dylan gave it a good shove and Douglas fell sideways. He stuck his M-16 through the opening and fired into the trees. In one motion he reached down, grabbed hold of Douglas' collar and pulled with all he had.

Douglas' shoes cleared the threshold and an answering volley struck the sliding door. Tempered glass exploded, showering them in small chunks of window. Dylan shouted and heaved Douglas into the kitchen. They crashed down onto the ceramic, out of the gunmen's sight.

The lights went out. Gillespie saw his chance. He leapt for his .308. His heart pounded through to his fingertips as he grabbed the weapon. He sensed the bullets coming and scurried back to his well-lacquered shelter. The rifle rounds never came. He breathed a sigh of relief. "They must be blind now."

Roth grunted at the dark safe house. He took his eye from the scope and switched on the night vision electronics. A nice bright quarter-moon shone above. That's all he would need. He put his eye back to the scope. The loft was now rendered in a nightmarish green shade. He adjusted the optics and intensity and smiled. He liked the color.

Dylan sat across from Douglas on the kitchen floor. The bullet looked to have gone through his partner's stomach. Pain twisted his face and drew sweat from his pores.

"I'll get you out of here. Hold on."

"I didn't hear them." Douglas grimaced. "Shit, I didn't hear them."

Dylan opened drawers until he found one filled with dish towels. He pulled out a few and pressed them against the wound. "Gotta stop the bleeding."

He remembered Deputy Schiff sitting out front and reached for the radio on his belt. "Deputy Schiff, we need assistance in here." He waited but no reply came. "Schiff, report." Nothing. His stomach knotted. Somebody must have taken him out. If so, that meant men were converging on the house from all sides.

A tremor rumbled through Dylan's chest. He heard Sadeed laughing. He keyed the radio again. "LaCroix, do you have McCallum secure?" Silence.

His hands were sweating. "Stay alert, Pete."

He took up his M-16 and maneuvered around the granite island. The great room had become a kill zone. The hallway was thirty feet away. It was his only route to McCallum. It might just as well have been a mile away. He reloaded the M-16 with a fresh clip from his pocket. It was his last. Preparing to sprint across the floor, he closed his eyes and drew in a breath. Sadeed's face smiled in the dark. He opened his eyes, shook it off.

Three—Two—One—Break.

He dashed into the great room. Bullets exploded along the wall behind him, shattering picture plates and pocking sheetrock. He thought for sure one sizzled past his head and he dived behind the couch.

Fear boiled in his belly, but anger curdled in there too. If he got pinned down here, if McCallum died because he couldn't make it to him...

He rose over the back of the couch and swung the M-16 toward the trees left of the house out back. He unleashed a sustained volley, disintegrating whatever was left of the large glass pane and lacing the position he figured the sniper had nested. He'd made a close guess. A muzzle flash lit up the leaves.

In the loft, Gillespie keyed in on that muzzle flash. It was farther north than he figured the shooter to be, but what the hell. He had a target now. He didn't even have to poke his head above his barricade. He could line up the shot from around the corner.

He switched on his starlight scope and fiddled with the adjustments. Dylan was plugging away downstairs with the M-16. Gillespie knew his partner had little chance of hitting his mark without a scope or night optics.

He rested the .308 on his raised knee and focused on the flashing barrel in the trees. It took a moment but he oriented himself to the green image in the scope and picked out the shooter amongst the branches. He squeezed he trigger. A single shot from the .308 rang in the loft.

The flashing in the trees stopped. "Got him!"

Dylan listened for incoming rounds. There were none. He'd run out of ammunition but sprang the clip from the M-16 jut to confirm it.

He tossed the rifle down and drew his Glock. The route to McCallum was clear.

Gillespie drew back behind his barricade.

Rebecca called from the bedroom, "Gimme a status report, Tommy."

"I got the guy gunning for Dylan."

"What about the guy taking shots at us?"

"Could have been the same guy."

Rebecca went deeper into the room and returned with a sturdy plastic hanger in hand. Wincing at the puncture in her arm, she slid the blazer off her shoulders and hooked it on the edge of the hanger. She stuck it through the doorway. Three seconds elapsed before a cluster of bullets tore it to shreds. She dropped the hanger. "Not the same guy."

"Okay, so there were two."

Gillespie considered her little test. It was dark in the loft but that guy out there had picked up on the movement pretty quick. And he was accurate in placing his shots. He had to be using night gear, perhaps goggles or a starlight scope like his. If that were the case…

Using the bearskin to conceal his movement, he pushed the table sideways. It made him nervous with only a furry hide between him and an angry sniper, but he had to chance it.

Old Ben had taken a few rounds through his pelt. Gillespie found a suitable tear and stuck the .308's barrel through up to the scope. "Rebecca, show him your blazer again."

Staying low, she recovered the hanger and put the tattered garment on display.

The sniper didn't take the bait.

"On to me, are you?" Gillespie scanned the trees through the scope, hoping to spot the green reflection from the sniper's night vision equipment, hoping to God to spot it before the sniper spotted his.

At the onset of gunfire, McCallum knew his plan to draw danger away from the others had failed. Distraught, he circled the room in a daze, fretting that the fire fight upstairs may be killing men trying to protect him. No more of this! It had to end now. He glanced once more at Kathryn sleeping on the bed, and then pushed open the bedroom door.

LaCroix sprawled unconscious in his chair in the hall.

McCallum stepped over his legs and started up the stairs.

Furious at his men, Keyes ran to the house. He picked a window left of the front door and peered inside. The room was dark and unoccupied. He smashed the glass with the stock of his MP-5. The gun battle out back covered the noise nicely. He reached in and unlocked the window, and then pushed it open and crawled through.

Off to his right a pair of closed French doors led to the darkened foyer. He clicked the MP-5 to short-burst mode, which would fire rounds in clusters of two or three with each trigger action. Moving to the doors, he turned the knob on the right and pushed.

Dylan ran down the hallway. He slowed his pace near the foyer. It wasn't wise to rush into a dark area, and the foyer ahead fit that description. A shadow moved against the tiny windows around the front door. LaCroix? Probably not. But he couldn't just shoot, he had to be sure. He moved quiet over a throw rug.

The overhead chandelier suddenly exploded with light and blinded him. His pupils recoiled. That thundering drumbeat he heard was the pulse in his head.

Across the floor McCallum stood with a hand on the light switch. A big man dressed in black from head to toe stood near the front door. Something told Dylan it was Keyes. He held a sub gun and fixed his dilated gaze on the president.

Dylan's feet rooted into the floor, and the hand holding the Glock froze at his side.

Keyes lifted the submachine gun.

Falling. The sensation seized Dylan. His chest heaved and he gulped in air. Harried thoughts collided. *Aim the Glock and shoot the bastard.* But the shot had to be perfect, lethal. He couldn't guarantee it. That wasn't good enough.

His subconscious made the decision. His feet uprooted and he felt his body hurling toward McCallum. Stop the bullet. Rebecca was right, he had to do it.

McCallum shouted for him to stop.

The MP-5 jumped in Keyes hand.

Like an echo chamber, gunfire reverberated.

He didn't see the slugs coming as he had with Sadeed. But they came. Three holes blew into his chest. He careened forward. Balance disappeared. Like a sack of stones he crashed down, his face cracking hard on the oak planks.

He laid motionless, blood spilling from his chest and breath came in difficult draws.

Gunfire.

Rebecca whirled her head about. "That was inside the house."

Gillespie didn't respond.

"Damn it, Tommy. Find that guy and shoot him. We've got to get down there."

"Keep your skirt on, sweetheart."

He parsed the green images in the scope, desperate to discern the shape of a rifle, or a head, amid the foliage. Sweeping slowly across the heavy branches of a large maple, his heart rose and choked off his air. A green dot, like a beacon, suddenly appeared, shining right at him.

That's it! That's it! Shoot!

He squeezed the trigger. The .308 barked, and he girded himself for the sniper's reprisal.

It didn't come. The green beacon was gone.

"We're clear," he shouted. "Move, move."

McCallum took a step toward Dylan. Keyes warned him back with a shout. McCallum stopped, although he didn't know why. He had wanted to be gunned down, but something kept him from that suicidal tendency. The reason suddenly dawned on him. He wanted to see Owen Keyes dead.

Keyes stared down at Dylan's body. "Another man dead because of you."

Face redder than fire, McCallum exploded. "Keyes, you rotten son of a bitch. How many more are you going to kill before you get to me?" He slapped his chest. "Do it! Take me out of your misery."

"You die when I say." Keyes nodded at Dylan. "Was that Reese?"

McCallum hesitated. "Yes."

"He knew what you did to my father. He knew and still sacrificed himself. Did that make you feel good, Mr. President? Maybe that's it. When they sacrifice, you feel like God."

"You're the only one here with a God complex."

"You betrayed those men in Iran, and you betrayed Reese. You're just a piece of propaganda packaged in a lie. All those men died for nothing."

"I betrayed nobody! Your father died defending his country. If you had half the sense you were born with you'd understand that."

Keyes eyes darkened. "There's a special place in hell for traitors. You and Judas, you're two of a kind."

McCallum stared down his accuser. "You're father was a good man. He'd be disgusted at what you've done. You could have been like him, Owen, but you let hate destroy you."

Lying still on the floor, Dylan was pleased to hear the reports of his death, because hearing them meant he was still alive. The ungodly pain in his chest and his labored breathing also helped to reaffirm his existence. His eyelids fluttered open and he spotted his pistol on the floor six inches from his outstretched hand. He tried to grab it but his arm lay there like a chunk of lead. His gasp for air left him wanting more. He guessed his lung had collapsed, but he couldn't quit on the Old Man. He tried for the gun again. Hand twitching, his arm slid forward.

A boot kicked the Glock away.

Keyes rolled him over with his foot and looked into his fading eyes. "I don't get you, Reese. You're dying for a traitor. Life's bleeding out of you and you're still trying to protect him."

"Duty," Dylan said, forcing his voice. He gasped for air. "What happened...to yours?"

Keyes' lip twitched. "You're a fool."

"Maybe." Dylan coughed. "But...Michael Keyes...would have done...the same thing."

Keyes huffed and glared a hole through McCallum. He raised the MP-5. "For all the blood on your hands."

McCallum showed his palms. "There's nothing here, Owen. Check your own."

Keyes snarled.

And then the bullets tore into him.

McCallum jumped with the gunfire, checked himself for blood. None. He turned.

Rebecca rushed into the foyer, firing rounds into Keyes' barrel chest.

He absorbed the slugs, staggered. Vengeful will kept him on his feet. She fired again, then again. He finally went down on his knees. The MP-5 slipped from his fingers.

She inched closer, ready to squeeze the trigger again.

He fell over like a pillar of iron and crashed to the floor, eyes facing Dylan.

Dylan stared back.

They connected in a dying instant, each man trying to understand the other.

Rebecca dropped to Dylan's side. His shirt glistened red with blood. His eyes looked skyward. "My God. Dylan, can you hear me?"

He gave a weak smile and focused on her face. "I stopped…the bullet."

John Tierney had reached level ground and approached the safe house. After Dominic had taken Six Pack downslope, he thought of going after them, but the ensuing gun battle changed his mind. Keyes would need help at the house. As he moved alongside the log wall, he noticed the AR-18s go silent. Roth and Griffin must have been taken out.

He rounded the corner of the house to the front. Grasping a sub gun tight, he neared the porch. He moved cautiously along the deck. Light spilled from the foyer windows. Through the deck rails he saw Keyes go down, heard the Beretta firing shot after shot. The scene incensed him, and he lifted the MP-5 to fire through the glass at the woman with the pistol.

A rifle report carried through the trees and his leg blew out from under him. He dropped to his left knee, keeping weight off the bleeding and burning right. He let the MP-5 fall into the tall grass and grabbed his thigh.

A voice called out before the gunshot faded. "Now how the hell did that happen?"

He followed the voice to the corner of the house, where the dark shape of a man stood aiming a rifle at him.

Gillespie peered through the starlight scope, watching the clear, green image of John Tierney consider his plight. "There's a hole in your leg instead of your head," Gillespie said. "I must have overcompensated for something. That makes me two for three tonight."

Tierney straightened his back and slid his hand closer to the Desert Eagle.

"Nobody's that fast," Gillespie warned. "But if you insist, I'll be batting a thousand."

Tierney stopped reaching for the pistol grip.

"You're the guy with the hand cannon. I had a feeling I'd be running into you again."

Tierney stared back at the dark figure. "Are you the man who killed Wilke at the estate?"

"Depends who Wilke is."

Anger swelling and leg throbbing, Tierney sized up Gillespie. He felt he could still move quick, maybe quick enough to clear the cross hairs and plug that agent. His fingers twitched.

"Open or closed?" Gillespie said.

Tierney didn't understand, but wasn't about to give him the pleasure of his asking.

"If I put a hole in your head," Gillespie explained, "you'll need a closed casket. I put a shot through your heart and your friends can still kiss you goodbye."

Tierney considered his bleak options.

"You're a stubborn man," Gillespie observed.

For the first time in his life John Tierney faced his mortality up close. The soldier in him screamed to fight, but his hand, with a mind of its own, moved clear of the pistol. He clasped his fingers atop his head and closed his eyes. Footsteps rushed toward him, and then a hand pushed him face down in the grass.

Gillespie deprived him of his coveted pistol.

With the cool ground against his cheek and the rifle barrel at the base of his skull, he did not fight when his arm was wrenched behind him. Lying there in the grass he began thinking ahead to his impending trial and incarceration. He had a lot of planning to do and figured he best get on with it. John Tierney could not stay locked up for long.

TWENTY-EIGHT

REBECCA took Dylan's satellite phone and called for help. She secured an EMT dispatch and alerted the State Police post in Escanaba to the incident at the safe house. Ambulances and paramedics arrived in short order. They went to work stabilizing Dylan and Douglas and moved them to the waiting transportation. Gillespie and Rebecca hurried along with the stretchers.

While being lifted into the ambulance, Dylan grabbed Gillespie's hand and slipped something into his palm.

Paramedics slammed the doors and the ambulance sped away. Gillespie watched it turn onto the main road. He lifted the object in his palm into the light of the flashers of a nearby EMS vehicle. It was Sadeed's bullet. Gillespie smiled. "My precious."

Two miles south of the safe house, Dominic tossed Six Pack onto the ground near the lake. The kid groaned when he hit, and complained about the bullet hole in his foot. Dominic ignored him.

Richard C. was anchored close to shore and bobbed in the swells. Rierdon had nearly made land in the small inflatable.

"You ruined everything." Anger dragged Six Pack's voice low. "Why did you let Keyes down? Why did you take me with you?"

Dominic whirled and threw a finger in his face. "I'm going to say this once, Tyler, and you listen close. I messed up when I joined Keyes. I made it worse by allowing him to bring you aboard. What we did was wrong. Don't let Keyes' talk about justice and duty blind you." He poked Six Pack in the chest. "Listen to your heart once in a while, not just your head. It'll tell you what's what. It took me too fucking long to figure that out, and I want you to benefit from my education. Don't waist your life being a mercenary, especially under deluded men like Keyes."

"It's my decision, Dom. Mine."

Dominic stood. "You're right about that. I won't be there next time to pull your ass out of the fire. You just think about this long and hard before you make your next move."

Rierdon pulled the inflatable to shore. He scanned the beach. "Where's the rest?"

Dominic met his eyes. "This is it."

"Keyes?"

"It's over. Police will be sweeping through here soon. We've got to get moving."

Dominic and Rierdon helped Six Pack into the raft, and then paddled out to *Richard C.* Rierdon fired up the engines and headed for open water. Dominic and Six Pack settled in the stern under the stars, letting the breeze wash over them. The kid did not look in his mentor's direction, nor did he speak a word to him. Dominic let him be, pleased for the moment just to have gotten him away from a very bad situation, not to mention himself.

They sailed through the darkness and he assessed his life. What direction should it take now? Keyes had gotten him off track, and he wondered if he could get back in line. He didn't know where to begin.

*   *   *

Dylan awoke in a hospital bed. Tubes and wires and things were sticking out of him. He thought back to Keyes' assault on the safe house. Details were sketchy in the last hour he could remember. He recalled nothing after being thrown into the ambulance. Despite the pain in his chest, he said a little prayer for being spared.

News of his resurrection spread. Before too long Rebecca and McCallum came to visit.

"I'm losing count," McCallum said. "How many times have you saved my life now?"

"I wish I could say every time feels like the first."

The president smiled. "Don't stay on your back too long. With you, Pete, and Paul out of action, Tommy's got some new agents on my detail and I think he's getting used to being head of security."

Dylan managed to return the smile. "Is Keyes dead?"

"Yes," Rebecca said, "and two of his men. Tommy captured a guy named Tierney. The State Police searched the area but didn't find anyone else."

"How is Kathryn doing?"

McCallum nodded. "A little shaken, but relieved that it's over."

"Is it? We know Keyes masterminded the plan, and we know why he did it. The question we haven't answered yet, the one that probably woke me up, is how did he find out about the particulars of Yellow

Jacket?"

Rebecca came to the bedside. "I found classified documents on him that laid out Operation Yellow Jacket, its purpose, its methods, and its designers. It names everyone involved, and bears President McCallum's signature."

Dylan tried to sit up, but a rush of pain persuaded him to stay down. "How did he get it?"

McCallum grumbled. "He didn't have security clearance to get anywhere near those files. Someone had to have given it to him."

"Probably the same person who tipped Keyes that we were at the safe house."

"And," Rebecca added, "the same person who gave him your cell number."

Dylan thought back on that first night in the safe house, his call to Trevor Novak. "When I reported to Novak that we had arrived at the Igloo, he mentioned that Senator Burke had been in touch with him, supposedly to be updated on security measures being implemented to protect the governors and President McCallum. That struck me as being odd. I mean, since when does Burke care about anyone besides himself, especially during a crisis."

Rebecca tilted her head. "Why would Burke have an ulterior motive for his call?"

"He dislikes me a great deal," McCallum said. "He thinks I stole the election from him. He never came to grips with that. After all these years it still festers under his skin."

"Does he have access to the Yellow Jacket files?" Rebecca asked.

"Burke chairs the Senate Armed Services Committee and the Anti-Terrorist Intelligence Committee," Dylan said. "He's got access all right."

McCallum chuckled with nervous undertones. "When he said goodbye back on Mackinac Island it did ring with finality. Perhaps he knew what was coming."

Rebecca considered their theory. "Do you two want the FBI to open an investigation into the matter?"

They both said "yes" at the same time.

* * *

Dylan lowered himself onto the couch in his apartment, carefully. Three weeks of healing and rehab had gone by, but he still had a long way to go. Back home now, he had spent most of his convalescence catching up on things he'd been missing, like being a father to Danny. To his dismay, but not surprise, Sarah remained out of reach.

He cracked a beer and thought about their time together. It seemed a lifetime ago. And now she had made her mind up about them, that there wouldn't be another try.

Someone knocked on the front door. He hobbled over to get it.

Rebecca stood on the other side. She wore a warm smile and a very sharp summer dress, white with the hemline just below the knees. Not quite her normal work attire.

He approved.

"Mind if I come in?"

He stepped aside and she strolled by. "What's the occasion?"

"It's been a few days since I've been by and I wanted to see how you're doing."

He closed the door and watched her walk to the couch. "I'm good." Not sure what else to say, he just gave a nervous smile.

"I'm actually taking a few days off from being a federal agent."

"Looks like you're doing a fine job." He gestured to the beer bottle in his hand. "Can I get you one?"

She eyed the bottle. "Sure."

Surprised, he went to the fridge and returned with an open bottle.

She took it from him. "There is one work-related issue I want to touch base with you on. Take a seat."

They sat on the couch and she swiped the television remote off the coffee table. She turned on a cable news channel. They watched a few moments before the anchor came back to the lead story of the day. A still shot of Senator Charles Burke filled half the screen, and the anchor reported, "In Washington today a senior senator on Capitol Hill was confronted by agents from the FBI and arrested. Bureau spokesmen say Charles Burke faces a litany of charges, including conspiracy to commit murder. Shocked congressional colleagues watched as the Michigan senator was led away in handcuffs."

Footage of Burke's arrest flashed onto the screen. Two agents ushered him through a throng of reporters and cameramen.

Dylan's jaw dropped. "How did you nail him?"

"He made it easy. Apparently he was doing some research work for the Anti-Terrorist Intelligence Committee a year and a half ago and uncovered the Yellow Jacket files. Document request archives list the file numbers of the documents he pulled. McCallum was able to identify the Yellow Jacket file number among them. He said he had ingrained that number in his head years ago. Also, that letter you gave me, the threat to McCallum? Burke licked the adhesive strip on the envelope. He left a trace DNA sample."

Dylan laughed. "Ah, see, that's why you need to use the peel-and-seal type."

She pulled her legs up under her. "I think we can say it's over."

He offered a toast with his beer bottle. "To justice served."

Their bottles clinked.

"Real justice," she added. "Not Keyes's distorted version of it." She regarded Dylan a moment. "It's amazing to think about, the stark contrasts in opinion that exist concerning Warren McCallum. The American public loves him, the Shiite Brigade, and Arabs in general, hate him. Owen Keyes thought him a betrayer, but Dylan Reese reveres the man. How can one man's traitor be another man's patriot?"

Dylan sipped his beer. "Guess you could say it's all in your perception."

"A whole lot of factors go into shaping our perceptions. It's a complex equation."

"Like I said, if you ever leave the Bureau, you've got a future in psychotherapy."

She smiled. "You could be my first client."

He glanced at her from the corner of his eye. "I'm not crazy about head doctors."

"Gillespie showed me the bullet you gave him. I got one phobia cured already."

"Beginners luck. And by the way, it took a near death experience to beat it. I don't think I can survive your therapy methods."

"Wait just a minute. You said you wanted me to help resolve your issues. You can't back out now"

He looked at the television screen. "Some issues are resolving themselves, or rather, are being resolved despite of me."

She sat silent a moment. "Sarah?"

He met her eyes. "The Owen Keyes conspiracy isn't the only thing that's over."

She let that sink in a few seconds. "I'm sorry," she said, "that I'm not sorry to hear that."

He stared at her a long while. "Have I thanked you for plugging Keyes and saving McCallum and my life?"

"Yes."

Another bit of silence.

"Have I thanked you for nailing Burke yet?"

"No."

"Thank you."

"Don't mention it."

He strummed his fingers on the couch back and glanced around the room. "Do you have plans for dinner tonight?"

"Yes."

His expression deflated.

"I'm going out with this guy in the Secret Service. A real charmer. He's sweet, sensitive, and dedicated. He shows real promise"

Dylan laughed. "At least I know it's not Gillespie."

She reached for his hand and laced their fingers together. "Let's go find a restaurant on the lake. I want to relax near the water for once. During the *Silversides* thing I'd get all wound up when I looked out there, wondering how many more people were going to die."

"I know what you mean." He gingerly rose from the couch, respectful of the bullet wounds in his chest. "You mind driving? Doctor told me pain meds, beer, and operating vehicles are not a good mix."

She smiled and stood. "No problem. Just don't plan on me cooking our food."

ACKNOWLEDGEMENTS

First and foremost, I thank Charlie Roesch, technical advisor, Great Lakes Naval Memorial and Museum board member, and one of USS *Silversides'* principal caretakers. His advice and support was invaluable to me as I took this story down the long road from rough manuscript to finished novel.

I also thank USNR veteran E. B. Caraway, Jr. and Bob Morin for sharing their submarine knowledge. Their review of the manuscript in its infancy allowed me to polish the brass, so to speak, and make the details ring true.

If after all this expert advice there still exits technical mistakes or lapses of authenticity in the story, the error is mine, and not the fault of Charley, E. B., or Bob.

On the home front I thank my wife, Melynda, for her patience and support throughout the arduous process of writing and re-writing *Descending from Duty*. She is the first to read my work, and therefore is the first to offer suggestions on improving it. Fortunately, I've learned to accept her suggestions. My stories seem to end up better when I do. Without her behind me this book would never have made it to press.

Julie L. Brown did a great job on the cover art, and I appreciate her contribution. Patricia Gragg did a remarkable job of editing me, and as with the technical details, if mistakes remain in the manuscript, they are all mine.

A special word of thanks to Erin Howarth of Wilderness Adventure Books for her assistance in the final stretch.

Of course there are the usual suspects, Brian Shureb, Jon Lillemoen, Tony Nielson and Andy Bugeia. They are my front line of readers. They typically stop the really bad stuff from getting through. I truly value their input and commentary, even when critical. Their support and candidness keep me going.

For more information on *Descending from Duty*, decorated fleet submarine USS *Silversides*, and other works by J. Ryan Fenzel, visit the author's website at www.jryanfenzel.com.

QUICK ORDER FORM

To order copies of DESCENDING FROM DUTY select one of the following options.

E-mail Orders:
Send an order request via e-mail to orders@ironcroft.com

Postal Orders:
Fill out this form and mail it to:

Ironcroft Publishing
DFD Dept.
PO Box 630
Hartland, MI 48353

Please send me ____copy (s) of DESCENDING FROM DUTY.

Name: _____

Address: _____

City: _____ State: _____ Zip: _____

e-mail address: _____

Sales Tax: Please add 6.00% for books shipped to Michigan addresses.

Shipping: U.S. customers $4.00 for first book and $2.00 for each additional copy. International customers please verify and include funds to cover current postal rates or your order may be delayed.

Payment: Send check or money order made out to Ironcroft Publishing in the amount of $12.95 for each copy ordered plus shipping and sales tax as stated above.

Ironcroft Publishing

www.ironcroft.com